Dear Little Bla

Thanks for pic [ ] e
of the great ne ning
romance novel ntastic
romantic read tnat we know you won't be able to put down!

Why don't you make your Little Black Dress experience
even better by logging on to

www.littleblackdressbooks.com

where you can:

- ♥ Enter our **monthly competitions** to win
  gorgeous prizes
- ♥ Get **hot-off-the-press** news about our latest titles
- ♥ Read **exclusive** preview chapters both from
  your **favourite** authors and from brilliant new
  writing talent
- ♥ Buy **up-and-coming** books online
- ♥ Sign up for an essential slice of romance via
  our **fortnightly email** newsletter

We love nothing more than to curl up and indulge in an
addictive romance, and so we're delighted to welcome you
into the Little Black Dress club!

With love from,

The *little black dress* team

Five interesting things about Sarah Monk:

1. I once met the Queen. Unfortunately it was when my husband and I were making our merry way arm in arm to the champagne tent at Ascot, mindless of the fact that she and her entourage were trying to do a procession. Although her minder stopped Terry from crashing through it with a muscular arm, when he stopped dead the momentum made me swing past and land flat on my back on the floor in front of her madge! Oh, the perils of too much champagne on a hot day . . .

2. I have a much adored Border Terrier dog named Freddie after Freddie Ljungberg. The husband (a Londoner and Gunner) thinks this is in honour of him being Arsenal number 8 for many years, but for me it's more commemorative of those amazing Calvin Kline ads . . .

3. When I'm not writing, I love to cook. My favourite kitchen invention is a recipe for a white chocolate and raspberry cheesecake, where one of the secret ingredients is vodka, and I harbour an unnatural and overwhelming desire to be a contestant on *Come Dine with Me*.

4. I've written quite a few books, but I actually started my writing career penning lots of short stories for the legend that is *Just Seventeen* magazine.

5. I almost became an Opera singer but I had to make a choice, and my love of writing saved the world's ears from being tortured by my voice. Although I'm afraid I still massacre the odd jazz number when drunkenness and opportunity collide!

A Romantic Getaway

Sarah Monk

little
black
dress

First published in 2008
by LITTLE BLACK DRESS
An imprint of HEADLINE PUBLISHING GROUP

A LITTLE BLACK DRESS paperback

1

ISBN 978 0 7553 4510 6

Typeset in Transit511BT by Avon DataSet Ltd,
Bidford-on-Avon, Warwickshire

Printed and bound in Great Britain by Clays Ltd, St Ives plc

Headline's policy is to use papers that are natural, renewable and
recyclable products and made from wood grown in sustainable forests.
The logging and manufacturing processes are expected to conform to the
environmental regulations of the country of origin.

HEADLINE PUBLISHING GROUP
An Hachette Livre UK Company
338 Euston Road
London NW1 3BH

www.littleblackdressbooks.com
www.headline.co.uk
www.hachettelivre.co.uk

For Terry, as everything always will be.
For my beautiful nieces, Naomi and Daniella.
For my boys, Ricky, Tony, Myles, Josh and Freddie.
And for James and Julia Junior yet to come . . .

Acknowledgements

Huge thanks to Amanda Preston at LBA, a true star, and to the lovely Claire and Leah and everyone at LBD. Thank you to Jane for her forgotten story about stolen trousers, to Dave, Diane and Jim, for anecdotes about life in Cornish hotels, and a belated thanks to Elaine for her insight (and for making sure I wasn't on the floor on my own), and to the gorgeous girls who have travelled the distance with me, you know who you are . . .

She could have been a girl in a shampoo advert. Sauntering down the street with that special bounce to her step, burnished golden-brown locks flowing in waves to her shoulders and gleaming in the sunlight. She was the kind of girl that actually made men turn to look, or dash up to her with flowers, or fall out of windows.

So why was it that Liesel Ellis was so bloody useless at relationships? No problem getting into them, but keeping them going longer than a couple of weeks . . . well, that was another matter altogether.

She didn't know she was gorgeous.

When Liesel looked in the mirror, she saw skin pale from too much time stuck in a building lit only by fluorescence and no windows, and dark shadows under her eyes from late nights working at her second job waitressing and bartending in a busy café bar near her anonymous insurance office just off Oxford Street. She didn't see the sweet mouth so quick to smile, the hazel eyes that turned almost gold when the sun shone on them.

Okay, so her hair was quite nice . . . when it wasn't scraped back into a ponytail to stop it from getting in other people's food.

But as for the rest of her . . .

She caught sight of herself in a white-goods shop window, her face reflected green and yellow and rather lizard-like in the concave curve of it, and stuck out her tongue.

She saw the knobbly knees, the awkward elbows that so often accidentally jabbed their way into conflict with passers-by and in particular restaurant clientele. She saw the way she glanced around nervously to make sure no one was watching or judging her, and then laughed at herself before someone else could.

When Liesel looked at her reflection, she didn't see what other people saw. To her, the Liesel that was looking back at her was still a gauche sixteen-year-old kid, the same kid who'd lost her parents in a car crash just a few days before what should have been a milestone birthday for such different reasons.

She saw the fear and the uncertainty of the future that tragedy in the past could inflict. Sure, ten years on there was more to her than a battle-scarred child. She and her sister Marilyn had worked hard at keeping themselves together mentally, and quite literally physically as well. Marilyn – nineteen, nearly twenty, their birthdays only three weeks and a star sign apart – had quit her university course and come rushing home to claim her only sister before the Social Services could.

It was funny: although the pain had, as they said, lessened by degrees as time passed, she still thought of her parents every single day. But ten years on, the sisters were stronger, closer, a little bit wiser and most definitely older, you couldn't escape that one, and oh my goodness – Liesel leaned in closer to her distorted reflection – was that a wrinkle?

Thank heavens, it was just that the glass was scratched.

She peered closer still. Mike, her boyfriend of exactly three weeks, had called and asked her out for a drink after work: something to look forward to after yet another otherwise dull and dismal day of data. It was a joy in itself to be going to a bar to get a drink rather than to serve them, but she wished she had time to go home and make herself look more presentable for him.

The verdict from the shop front wasn't too bad. Lipstick intact, mascara not too clumpy, fairly good hair day. She undid the top button of her boring work blouse to give the staid outfit a little more va-va-voom.

'Don't worry, you look gorgeous,' said a male voice behind her.

Liesel jumped backwards, caught out and hating it. She flicked a nervous smile at the rather handsome man in the suit who had thrown her the compliment, then, turning pink with embarrassment, turned and hurried on the hundred yards or so to her bus stop.

En route she earned herself three wolf whistles from the construction site she passed, a melodic horn salute from two men in a BMW convertible and a 'hey baby' from a double-taking dude who looked like Thierry Henry.

By the time the big London bus rumbled into view, they were both exactly the same colour.

Marilyn Hamilton, née Ellis, was contemplating her own name.

'Hamilton,' she said out loud. 'Marilyn bloody Hamilton.'

How she hated that name.

It hadn't always been that way. When Nick first asked her to marry him, she had been so excited, spending the next day at work scrawling her new name on the edge of old ledgers. Marilyn Hamilton. Mrs Marilyn Hamilton. Mrs Nicholas Hamilton. Nicholas and Marilyn Hamilton.

The connotations were endless, the joy, seemingly, even more so. To change her name to Hamilton had been like winning the lottery. Now she just felt like she'd lost the winning ticket.

It was strange how a divorced woman kept the name of the man she was no longer married to.

When she and Nick had split up, she had so longed to return to Ellis, Hamilton seeming to her now a mark of betrayal rather than a transfer of love, but in the end she had stayed Marilyn Hamilton for the sake of another man.

Alex.

Her son.

Alex was Alex Hamilton, and although he had often asked that he be allowed to become Ellis too, neither she nor the law would allow him to make this decision until he was eighteen and therefore old enough in both their eyes to do so with full understanding.

And so out of loyalty to him, she would also remain Hamilton. Not because she felt they needed to share the same surname – there were plenty of kids nowadays who knew perfectly well who their parents were without having this in common – but simply because he really wanted to change his name, and if he couldn't, then it wasn't fair if she did.

There were certain things you needed the support of your parents for when you were growing up, and Marilyn felt that this, no matter how unusual, was one of them.

Another one was confidence. Confidence that you were an okay person, that you were doing things right. Kids learned from the people closest to them. Liesel and Marilyn had only had each other. They had felt their way through life together, tentatively, and holding tightly to each other's hand for support.

Practical Marilyn and dreamy Liesel.

So different and yet so alike, bound together by a fierce loyalty and a courage they didn't even realise they had.

When their parents had died, Liesel, who had always been a happy, sunny child, seemed to go into overdrive, as though it were her job to keep the smiles going.

Marilyn's reaction had been to marry too young, at twenty-one to be precise. Trying to recreate the family they had lost. Alex had come along a year later. Which was one of the reasons why Nick had buggered off five years after that.

It was only after he cleared his wardrobe, emptied their joint bank account and disappeared that Marilyn found out he'd been having an affair for two years with his boss, the glamorous and much older Samantha. When she had been shipped to the Australian branch of his company, Nick had followed her like a puppy trotting after his mistress, tongue lolling, tail wagging, begging for treats.

They'd never heard from him again, at least not directly.

Kindly Stephen Kingston, the family solicitor, was instructed to pass on Nick's requests: the immediate sale of the house, and a quick divorce. And once these two were granted – the first because the size of the mortgage gave Marilyn a bigger sinking feeling than Captain Smith contemplating icebergs, the second because as far as she was concerned, unfaithful equalled 'end of' – it was as though Nick had never existed.

They had never heard from him again. Not even a phone call, or a birthday or Christmas card for Alex.

And that was why she hated the name Hamilton.

Marilyn and Alex had moved in with Liesel.

Liesel would never forget the day they turned up on her doorstep, comic-mad Alex in the Superman outfit his parents had just given him for his birthday. He was stoical beyond belief. He took Marilyn endless cups of tea, as if it were some kind of medicine that would stop Mummy looking so sad, and hugged both his mother and his aunt as if his cuddles were oxygen and they would stop breathing without them. And whilst Marilyn cried for

England, although never when she thought anyone else could see or hear her, Alex stayed determinedly cheerful and never shed a single tear.

But for some odd reason he never changed out of his Superman outfit again.

And then there were three.

It had been hard, but they'd done it together.

Team Alex, as Marilyn had so dreadfully Americanised it. Every time she said it, Liesel didn't know whether to hug her or hit her round the head with something soft but effective. But the euphemism had summed them up perfectly. Everything they did, they did for the vulnerable little boy in the outgrown Superman costume.

It was why Marilyn, who had been studying marine biology, now worked school hours doing book-keeping, and studied nights to become an accountant.

And it was why Liesel had stuck at a job she hated for almost six years, and worked in a bar four nights a week so she could save up for Christmas and birthdays and a week at a campsite in Margate every summer that she swore was as much for Marilyn's sanity as it was for Alex.

It was a tough life, but they worked hard to make it a good one, Liesel keeping the sunshine going and Marilyn holding together the reality. Which was why Marilyn had kept this afternoon's appointment with Stephen Kingston a secret from her sister and her son. As far as she was concerned, there was only one reason now for Stephen to get in touch, and that was that Nick had come to his senses and decided that he should resume contact with his son.

She had always thought that one day he might come back and stake his claim. Upset the apple-cart, as her mother would have phrased it. So when Stephen's secretary had called her the previous day asking for her to come and see him as soon as possible, Marilyn was immediately fearful that she was suddenly going to be up to her neck in Granny Smiths.

But it had been something very different.

Something very different indeed.

Marilyn needed a drink. For someone who drank about one glass of wine a month, this fact told a story on its own.

An hour later, Liesel left the gloomy, crowded bar. She looked up at the pale almost-summer sun sinking behind the grime-dulled neon London skyline and tried to decide whether to cry or not. She felt like she ought to, but really, if she was being honest, she didn't think she could be bothered.

She'd known something was up as soon as she saw Mike at the bar knocking back a shot and calling for another straight away, and the way when he saw her his eyes darted left and right as though trying to escape from the restraints of his skull.

They also hadn't been together long enough for the nervous cough and the collar-tugging to mean anything but doom, so she knew immediately that she wasn't in for a good night, but she was more than halfway through a glass of Pinot Grigio when he finally plucked up the courage to spit it out.

'It's not you, it's me,' had been the cliché to start, followed by 'I think you want more of a committed relationship than I'm ready for at the moment.'

Oh well, at least he hadn't been a total coward and dumped her by text like the last boyfriend. She had harboured high hopes for this one as well: he was funny and charming and good looking, and he had a good job too. She had even taken him home to meet Marilyn and Alex last week. Had that perhaps had something to do with it? It was funny how many men were put off by the fact that she shared a tiny two-bedroom flat with her sister and her nephew. Then again, you also got the odd one who was a touch too enthusiastic about the fact that she shared a room with her sister.

'Men!' Liesel huffed as she walked to the bus stop.

Needing to be loved, yet not feeling that she deserved love from anyone, she bounced from relationship to relationship like a honeybee from flower to flower in search of sustenance. And the only one thus far that had managed to be enduring was her relationship with her sister and her nephew.

They came as a unit. It was the way it was and the way it always would be. Even when Marilyn had married Nick, Liesel had still lived with them, although when she turned eighteen she announced that she had been a gooseberry for far too long, and insisted on moving out to the poky flat that was still their home to this day, Marilyn practically hanging on to her ankles in an effort to stop her from leaving.

In a way, Liesel felt that the breakdown of Marilyn and Nick's relationship had been accelerated by the sisters' closeness.

Maybe her own constant quest for a lasting, steady relationship was a reflection of the fact that in some way she felt it was her turn to provide the little family with some stability. Alex had no grandparents or uncles; he needed a male figure in his life. Since Nick, Marilyn had been staunchly single. Since Nick, Liesel had been almost permanently attached. No wonder Mike had made an early break for freedom.

'I am a serial monogamist,' she announced to herself as she got on the bus and flopped down on to a free seat.

The old lady sitting next to her looked up from her magazine and smiled quizzically.

'Well it's either that or I'm a total man-eater.' Liesel shrugged.

'Don't eat too many men, dear,' her neighbour croaked, offering up a bag of boiled sweets. 'They can give you terrible indigestion.'

And so here she was, single again.

But when she realised that she was humming 'Another One Bites the Dust' as she walked home from the bus stop, she knew that she was going to be okay.

She even took the three flights of stairs two at a time, up to the utterly dismal seventies-built flat that had been bursting at the seams even before Marilyn and Alex had moved in.

Liesel and Marilyn had a love/hate relationship with the flat. They thanked the Lord every day that they had a place to call home. They berated him every evening that it was this particular hovel. The grottiest flat in the history of a lifetime of grotty flat rentals.

They shared a dream of turning their week of freedom by the sea into a lifetime. Of permanently escaping the city that both nurtured and neutered them. No matter how much you disliked something, it was always scary to let go of familiarity, of a regular pay packet. The longer they stayed, the more they hated it; the longer they stayed, the harder they found it to leave.

They had often joked that they could pitch a tent on a beach somewhere and pretend to be gypsies. After all, a tent was about all they could afford. Their favourite evening viewing when one of them wasn't working or the other studying were the programmes about people who were quitting the city for a new life in the country. They both envied and admired anyone brave enough to take the plunge and leave behind everything they knew to start again somewhere else.

But Marilyn and Liesel had responsibilities . . . and what a lovely responsibility he was, Liesel thought, looking in on her nephew, who was sitting cross-legged on the floor of his room, killing zombies on the computer game his aunt and mother had bought with their Christmas bonuses.

Liesel couldn't have loved Alex more if he was actually her own.

The second bedroom, which was no more than a box room really, had just enough room for Alex's bunk bed, and a chest of drawers which was home to socks, pants, a TV and his PlayStation. Fortunately he didn't really need a wardrobe, due to the fact that he only ever wore Superman outfits. He had five, one for almost every day of the week, and two sets of Superman pyjamas.

Squeezing in behind him, Liesel sang her usual greeting of 'Hey, kiddo.'

Alex's response was always to drop whatever he was doing and flying-tackle her with a hug. This in return would elicit a kiss to his unruly golden mop.

'You had a good day?' was always the next question, to which Liesel would reply without fail, 'Yes,' even if she'd had the worst day in the history of being a woman in a man's world, at which point he would beam with satisfaction and return to whatever was today's chosen after-school activity.

Who needed men when she had the best boy in the world waiting at home for her?

Today's hug helped soothe away some of her regret over Mike. And a good old moan to good old Marilyn would erase the rest in no time.

Marilyn would normally be in the kitchen making supper, but today there were no delicious smells filling the small space they shared, no pots of pasta bubbling on the old gas stove. In fact Liesel found her sister in the sitting room, slumped on the sofa, which was definitely not one of their evening rituals, but she was too keen to pass on her own news to notice immediately.

'Mike dumped me today!' She threw herself on to one of the old floral sofas, the springs groaning in protest. ' "It's not you, it's me," ' she mimicked crossly. 'How many times have I heard that line before? What's wrong with me, Marilyn? Why can't I keep a man? Do you think I should relax my morals and, you know, "put out" a bit? Could that be it? My refusal to shag until I know their middle name and inside leg measurement? *It's not you, it's me*. What's that supposed to mean? Oh, and what a day at work as well. Moaning Martha came back from holiday today. I thought the break might mellow her, but she's now just a big fat whinge with sunburn. Oh Lord, I loathe my job. Actually make that jobs, plural. I dropped a plate of cheesy fries on a customer last night and Carlos bit my head off so hard I should just be a body walking round with a bleeding stump of a neck, you know, like one of those zombies on Alex's computer game . . .'

Liesel trailed off. By now Marilyn would normally have cut in with placatory comments, murmurs of support.

'Do you know, I think it's official. I hate my life.'

Usually such a melodramatic statement would have sparked a flurry of sympathy, followed by chiding not to be so stupid, but today Marilyn glanced up at her sister and said one word, and one word only.

'Good.'

Liesel narrowed her eyes and looked at her in surprise. Marilyn was normally bloody good at the sympathetic shoulder thing.

It was then that she noticed the bottle of cheap wine on the table, the kind they treated themselves to on happy days and hellish days, two pounds ninety five from the corner shop, and christened plug-hole cleaner, for the way that the dregs made the stainless-steel plug hole gleam better than any bleach ever could.

Liesel looked up from the wine to her sister, slumped on the squashy old sofa opposite.

'Did you just say good?' she enquired in disbelief.

Marilyn nodded, a touch too furiously. 'You said you hate your life, and I said good,' she confirmed.

It was only now that Liesel took a good look at her. Marilyn's big brown eyes were wide with what Liesel could only describe as shock. They weren't red, which meant she hadn't been crying, which was good, but it was obvious that something had happened.

'Marilyn? Are you okay?'

'Honestly? I don't know.'

'What is it?' Liesel was at her side in seconds, frowning in concern, her hands reaching out to take her sister's.

'I had to go and see Stephen today.'

'Stephen?' Liesel frowned, taking a moment to remember the solicitor Marilyn hadn't seen since her acrimonious divorce. 'But why . . . what . . .' she stuttered, immediately alert. 'What did he want? Why didn't you call me?'

'Because I was worried it was about *him*, that he was coming back for Alex . . .'

'Oh my God, that's not it, is it? Please tell me that's not it. He doesn't want to fight for custody now, does he, not after three years on the other side of the world with no word? Surely he can't do that?'

'It's not that. I mean, yes, it's about Alex, but it's not about his father . . . Well, I suppose it is about Nick in a way, but it's not directly about Nick, although I guess it must affect him . . .'

Liesel watched her sister in open-mouthed horror. Marilyn rambling, and Marilyn mentioning 'he who must not be named' twice in one sentence . . . Something was definitely up, something serious.

In a rare role reversal, Liesel summoned some inner calm for herself, and taking a firmer, less trembling grip of Marilyn's also trembling hands asked, 'Okay. So Alex is fine?'

Marilyn nodded.

'And you're fine?'

She nodded again.

'You don't look fine.'

'Well, I'm not really,' Marilyn said, and to Liesel's horror promptly began to cry, an occurrence so rare that Liesel immediately feared the worst.

'Please tell me Nick's not coming back from Australia with the mega-bitch-boss woman he so stupidly left you for, to try and take our boy away?'

Marilyn shook her head.

'Thank you, God. So what *has* happened?'

Marilyn swallowed noisily, and then to Liesel's utter surprise began to smile through her tears.

'We're getting out of here, Liesel, that's what's happened. We're finally bloody getting out of here.'

'**O**kay.' Marilyn exhaled slowly, 'Do you remember Alex's Great-Aunt Nancy?'

'The mad one who actually wore a too-real fur coat that had too-real mange, and a fascinator fashioned out of porcupine quills to your wedding? The one who sends Alex fifty pence sellotaped into a recycled card every Christmas and birthday. How on earth could I forgot her? Why?'

'Well, she's died.'

'Oh dear.' Liesel gulped, immediately feeling guilty for speaking ill of the dead, even though she hadn't known she was dead when she was speaking.

'And she's left everything she owns to Alex.'

'Oh, great. Maybe he'll be tempted out of his Superman outfit for the first time in five years and replace it with the fur coat and the fascinator,' Liesel quipped.

'There's a little bit more to it than that.'

'But I remember *him* saying that she was as poor as the proverbial church mouse. She was in a big old nursing home in Cornwall, wasn't she?'

'Well, yes, but *he* wasn't exactly renowned for the truth now, was he? Yes, she lived in Cornwall, but apparently it's not a nursing home, it's a hotel.'

'Okay . . .' Liesel said slowly, sensing more to come.

'And she didn't just live there . . .' Marilyn looked up at

her sister, and Liesel was relieved to see that the tears flooding from her eyes were accompanied by an amazed, rather dazed smile. 'She owned it.'

'She owned it,' Liesel repeated.

Marilyn nodded, and scrubbed a hand across her face to wipe away the tears.

'Which means . . .'

'Alex owns a hotel!' Liesel shrieked. 'Oh my Lord. That's unbelievable. How much is it worth?'

'Well, it depends if you take it as a business or a property.'

'Ballpark, Marilyn,' Liesel demanded impatiently. 'Just ballpark.'

'Well, apparently, property prices have sky-rocketed down there . . .'

'And?'

'And it's worth somewhere in the region of one and a half million pounds.' As she said the million part of the figure, Marilyn's taut smile finally cracked and she began to giggle: a manic, rather frightening laugh that turned into a rattling cough that she doused with another swig of plug-hole cleaner.

'Oh my God, my nephew's a millionaire,' Liesel gasped, taking Marilyn's glass from her hand and downing the rest of her drink. 'You can sell it and buy him a house, with a garden. Alex can have a garden, Marilyn, and he can go to a decent school, and we can buy him a new Superman outfit that actually fits him, and he can—'

'It's not quite as simple as that,' Marilyn interrupted, hiccuping through her laughter.

Liesel immediately drooped, the way a person who's used to disappointment can let the excitement escape as quickly as a punctured balloon.

'No,' she said flatly. 'Of course it isn't.'

'We can't sell it. Well, we can, but not yet.'

'What do you mean?'

Marilyn took a deep breath and nodded solemnly. She always did this when she was about to impart something important. But to Liesel's frustration she still didn't say anything, and took her sister's hands instead.

'Leez . . .' She paused.

'Spit it out, Maz!' Liesel pleaded in frustration.

Marilyn nodded.

'Leez,' she began again, but Liesel's face was enough to make her drop the long speech she had been planning all evening whilst waiting for her sister to come home, and cut to the chase. 'We have to run it for a season first.'

'We have to what?'

'Run the hotel. For the entire summer season.'

'Run a hotel! But we don't know how . . . I mean, how do you do that?'

'I don't know, but there's a clause in the will that says we have to. Well, that Alex and I have to, but you know what "we" is when it's us?'

'We equals three.' Liesel dutifully quoted Marilyn cheesy family saying number two. 'But can we?'

'We have to, or Alex forfeits any rights to it.'

Liesel's eyes popped wide with outrage.

'And it goes to *him*?'

Marilyn shook her head vehemently.

'No, no. He didn't even get a mention. She obviously thinks as much of him as we do.'

'So what happens?'

'It goes to Godrich.'

'Godrich?' Liesel frowned, her nose wrinkling.

Marilyn started to laugh again, the hysteria still evident.

'Godrich von Woofenhausen.' She nodded.

'Who on earth . . .?'

'He's a dog. We have to run the hotel for a season or

Alex doesn't get a penny and it all goes to her bloody dog.'

'Her dog! We always knew she was mad.'

'I know. How can a dog run a hotel?'

'It'll probably do a better job than we can.' Liesel joined in Marilyn's slightly hysterical laughter for a moment before they both glanced towards the corridor, conscious of Alex, and calmed themselves.

'So what do we do now?'

Marilyn bit her bottom lip for a second.

'Well, I *was* hoping you'd agree to come and run the hotel with me. I can't do it on my own, Liesel, and I have to do it for Alex. What future has he got here?'

Liesel nodded. 'This would set him up for life. And we don't have to stay there for ever. We run it, fulfil the stipulations of the will, and then we can sell it and buy a house wherever we want, put Alex into whatever school we want . . .'

'But it means changing everything, leaving everything. Would you give up everything you have here to go?'

'What, like the jobs I hate, the friends and family we don't have, our wonderfully poky flat with the fabulous view of Hackney Central from the bathroom window, mad Mary next door and her drunken idiot friends singing and rowing until daybreak every night, the traffic, the crime, the grime . . . I'd have to swap all of that to live by the sea? By the sea, Marilyn, where the fish live . . .'

'Well, when you put it like that . . .' Marilyn grinned again, and then began to frown. Her job of persuading Liesel almost done, her own doubts now had room to kick back in. 'But like you say, *can* we do it?'

'You've always told me we can do anything we put our minds to. What does Alex think?'

'I haven't told him yet. I was waiting for you to come home.'

'Then get him in here and let's tell him.'

'You mean you're definitely with me?' Marilyn suddenly looked hopeful again. 'You think we should go?'

'*With* you? I'm packing my bucket and spade and my bikini, hopping on my bike and getting there before you! First one to see the sea, remember . . .'

'Buys the ice cream! Yes!' Marilyn squeaked, grabbing Liesel's face between her hands and planting a big wet kiss on her forehead. 'God, I love you.'

'Bloody good job someone does!' Liesel said, pretending to pout.

Marilyn cocked her head to one side and smiled sympathetically.

'Oh yeah, Mike, sorry about that . . .'

'Well, I'm not. Go get Alex!'

Marilyn danced out to fetch her son, whilst Liesel sank back down on to the sofa and shook her head to see if it rattled or if the news had actually sunk in there. 'She could turn on a coin,' her mother used to say about a particular friend whose disposition seemed to change on a whim. It was funny how life had the same habit.

Nothing would ever be the same again. They were leaving London. The dream had finally become a reality. Not that the dream had ever included running a hotel, but hey, if that was what it took, they'd do it.

She would never have said no to Marilyn anyway, even if every single fibre of her being was screaming the word. Marilyn had said that she couldn't do it without her, and as far as Liesel was concerned, that meant she was going no matter what. And after all, the tiny, itchy bubble in the pit of her stomach was definitely one of excitement, of anticipation.

Alex came in, blinking and bug-eyed from his computer game, and they sat him down and explained everything as best and as honestly as they could. The only bit that really seemed to register was when they told him that Great-Aunt Nancy had passed away, at which point his eyes went very wide, and he asked, 'Did it hurt? When she died?'

Marilyn had bitten her bottom lip.

'I don't think so, Alex. She was very old, I think maybe she just went to sleep and didn't wake up.'

'Like Nigel?' Nigel had been Alex's pet hamster.

'I suppose. So, Alex, what do you think? How would you like to own a hotel?'

'A hotel?' Alex blinked at her.

'Yeah. Do you want to own your very own hotel?'

His eyes slid right as he thought about this unexpected question for a moment.

'Not really . . . but can I keep the dog?'

Time, which in daily drudge had seemed like the sloth-like slither of an ageing snail, had suddenly begun to free fall.

Marilyn in particular was truly beginning to regret the decision that four weeks was plenty of time for them to quit London and head down to the South West. Yes, it was probably enough time for them to give notice at their jobs, to notify Alex's school and find him another, to organise a hire van and pack up the little stuff from the tiny flat that they would be taking to Cornwall with them. But four weeks to close down one life and start another? That was a different thing.

It was the little things that seemed to take the time, the daft bits you forgot, like cancelling the milk delivery and taking meter readings. It didn't take long to say goodbye to everyone they knew. The three of them were such a tight unit, and they had so little spare time that friends had been few. Although they were surprised to find that there were a number of people they didn't think they knew particularly well all wanting an explanation, expressing regret and wishing them luck.

'I never knew we were so popular,' Marilyn observed to Alex when Mad Mary from next door, in a rare sober moment, had unexpectedly burst into tears at the news.

Liesel seemed to be relishing every moment of the move.

She literally danced home on the day that she handed in her notice at the office and the wine bar, and announced, 'I'd heard that quitting a job you hate is a really good feeling, but quitting two jobs I hate in one day, well, that must just be as close as I think I'll ever come to ecstasy.' Then she hugged her sister and, picking up a laughing, embarrassed Alex, tangoed him round the sitting room.

Overwhelmed with excitement but malnourished with detail, they had spent a Saturday morning together at an internet café instead of their usual jaunt to the park and Googled the hotel, but had come up with nothing, not even one hit: no news, no reviews, no photographs, nothing.

'Doesn't bode well for their current marketing strategies,' Marilyn had said with a small laugh and a smile that made it seem like she was joking, but Liesel knew her better.

'Don't worry, they'll soon have you there to sort them all out.'

'You're going to be a great hotel manager, Mum.' Alex had nodded his agreement. 'And Auntie Liesel's going to be the best assistant hotel manager,' he added loyally, repeating the roles they had discussed for themselves. Then he frowned, as though trying to work something out in his own merry little kind of logical way. 'If Mum's the manager, and Auntie Leez is the assistant manager, and you said we're all working there as a team, what does that make me? Am I the assistant assistant manager, or have I got to wait until I'm eighteen for that?'

Marilyn and Liesel looked at each other for a moment and smiled.

'You're the boss, kiddo,' Liesel said, hugging him. 'You're the boss.'

*

The final week passed in a flurry of last-minute packing.

'The sooner we leave, the sooner we get there,' was Marilyn's quote of the week as she bustled about, a blur of constant activity.

The hotel and the owner's accommodation was all fully furnished, so they didn't need to take anything except their own personal belongings. The furniture they had was easily parted with, a ratty old collection of charity-shop finds that had seen better days before finding its way into Liesel's little flat.

There had never been much in the way of family heirlooms.

Their parents had been happy-go-lucky types who didn't hold much store with material things. As children, they had moved house so many times, their mother had referred to them as a band of gypsies. They had even spent one entire summer travelling through Wales in a camper van, which had of course been a grand adventure, until the onset of a cold autumn had sent them scuttling to a rented cottage in the Mendips.

They had always rented. Never owned. Their father was a club singer who did a great Elvis impression and travelled to where the work was; their mother felt that being such was her full-time job, a philosophy that Marilyn would have loved to emulate with Alex, but of course found impossible.

In a way their childhood, whilst rootless, had been idyllic, but when their parents passed away the girls had found themselves without a home. They themselves had then moved from one 'rented hovel', as Marilyn called them, to another. Until Marilyn met Nick.

He was charming, good looking, and what was more, already owned his own house. Liesel always joked that she didn't know whether Marilyn had fallen more in love with his quirky four-storey town house in Islington than with the man himself.

Despite this joke, she knew that her sister had fallen head over heels, and it wasn't the loss of the house that had made her sob herself to sleep every night for a month, or burst into tears every time she heard the theme tune to *Neighbours*.

Liesel had tried as hard as she could to make her poky flat a home for her sister and her nephew, but if there was one thing they had learned along the way, it was that people and not possessions made a place a home.

On the final evening, despite super-efficient organisation, they still weren't finished.

Liesel was prevaricating over clothes in the bedroom and Marilyn was packing the last things to have been used in the kitchen.

In reality they were both taking a moment to say goodbye. As much as they longed to leave, there was still a poignancy to it that had both girls with a lump in their throat, although Marilyn didn't have much time for reflection, as sweet-toothed Alex soon came sauntering in, in search of his evening shot of sugar.

'Mum, have you packed the biscuit tin yet?'

'Of course not.' She indicated to where it was partially hidden behind a box on the table.

Alex grinned and, lifting the lid, peered inside intently before asking, 'Mum, what's a shithole?'

Marilyn stopped packing saucepans in a box and spun around to face Alex.

'Where on earth did you pick that up from?'

'Auntie Liesel was on the phone to Carlos the Horrible the other week, and she told him that she didn't want to work in his . . .' Alex's eyes slid left as he tried to remember the phrase that had intrigued him so much, word for word, 'rank, slime-infested shithole of a bar any more. What's a shithole?' he repeated. 'You always said I should ask you when I don't know a word.'

'Well . . .' Marilyn pondered, wondering how best to answer this one. 'Auntie Liesel didn't like where she worked very much.'

'So a shithole is a place that you don't like very much?'

'Well, I suppose so, yes, but there are much better words to use than that,' she added pointedly as Liesel, overhearing, emerged from the bedroom looking sheepish.

'Okay,' Alex said, nodding. 'Can I have a chocolate one, please?'

Marilyn nodded. 'Sure, but then I need you to pack away your computer games, okay? The sooner we leave, the sooner we get there.'

'Done it already.'

'This week's comics?'

'In a box by the door.'

'Toys all done?'

Alex nodded, digging into the biscuit tin and pulling out a digestive.

'Your room's empty?'

He nodded again.

'You're keen.'

'The sooner we leave, the sooner we get there,' he replied cheerily, biting into his biscuit.

Considering they were only taking personal belongings and no furniture, the hired van was remarkably full, box upon box stacked in the back.

'I never knew we had so much stuff!' Marilyn exclaimed, placing the last of the boxes in the back and locking the door.

'We didn't. I thought I'd do one last Londonite thing

and ram raid the local electrical shop,' Liesel joked. 'This lot is three flat-screen televisions, five stereo systems, and eighteen toasted sandwich makers.'

'I wish,' Marilyn laughed. 'We could flog them for petrol money.'

The three of them squeezed themselves into the long front seat. Marilyn, taking first turn to drive, turned on the engine, ground the van into first with an inexperienced thrust of the gearstick then turned to her family and grinned.

'I can't believe this is happening, guys.'

'Well, believe it, sis, 'cause we're just about to pull away.'

Marilyn nodded.

'Say goodbye to Hackney, Liesel.'

'Goodbye, Hackney,' Liesel answered dutifully.

'Say goodbye to Hackney, Alex.'

Alex leaned across his mother and waved out of the window.

'So long, shithole,' he announced happily.

Marilyn cocked an eyebrow and gunned Liesel down with her eyeballs.

The road was empty. Marilyn's eyes were closed. The glowing neon clock in the van's dashboard said that it was four thirty-five, and at this time of year, Liesel knew, it would only be another half an hour or so before the darkness lifted and the sun began to rise.

Despite the noisy throb of the engine, Alex was solidly asleep and had somehow managed to stretch himself out in slumber so that his head was on his mother's lap and his feet on Liesel's. Changing gear in the big white van was hard enough without having to move Alex's trainers every time she did so, but not having the heart to wake him, Liesel had managed it every time up till now, as she crunched into third gear and swallowed an expletive when the gearbox screamed in protest.

'Really sorry,' she muttered as Marilyn's, but fortunately not Alex's, eyes shot open in alarm.

'No worries, I wasn't asleep.'

'Not sleeping?'

'Can't.'

'Sorry, this thing's not that easy to drive.'

'I know, but it's not your gear changes.'

'You're nervous, aren't you?' asked Liesel, knowing her sister well.

Marilyn nodded. 'Why do you think we've had to stop at so many service stations?'

'Well, another hour or so and we should be there.'

'Really? Where are we?'

'Coming up to Jamaica Inn.'

'Ooh, Daphne du Maurier! Shall we stop and take a look?'

'It's the middle of the night.'

'It's nearly five in the morning. The sun'll be up soon. Come on, Liesel.'

'What about Sleeping Beauty? You know what he's like if he doesn't get his eight hours.'

'Mmm, more Super Grouch than Superman.'

'We'll come back. We're going to be here until the end of the summer at least.'

'You think we'll have time? We're going to have a hotel to run . . .' Marilyn paused and her mouth fell open in shock as if this phenomenal fact had only just sunk in. 'Bloody hell. We're going to run a hotel, Liesel.'

'I know.'

'Isn't that incredible?'

'I know. Well, we'll be our own bosses. Or at least technically Alex will be our boss, and I'd much rather work for him than Carlos the Horrible. I know we've got a lot to learn, and it will be hard work, but we'll make a bloody good go of it, won't we?'

Marilyn nodded. 'We certainly know how to put in the hours.'

'And we'll make time to do other stuff. There's so much to see and do down here. There's Truro, with its art galleries and restaurants – ooh, and it's got a cathedral too – and there's sailing at Falmouth, and there's a castle at St Mawes, and talking of castles, something Alex will absolutely love is Tintagel, King Arthur and all that stuff . . .' Starting off at a whisper because of her nephew, Liesel's voice began to rise with excitement. 'And did you know, there's a really good Sea Life Centre at Newquay which you'll love, along with the Tate Modern at St Ives, the Eden Project, not to mention the beaches.' Liesel's face lit up with excitement. 'We could even learn to surf, Marilyn!'

'You don't like swimming in the sea.'

'No, but I like the idea of being a beach babe. Strolling down the sand in my cut-offs and a bikini, with a board under my arm.'

Marilyn nodded. She could just picture Liesel, hair tinged blond by the sunshine, lithe figure tanned and toned and gleaming . . . and herself trotting along behind looking like a killer whale in a black wetsuit. Although she and Liesel looked very alike, with the same golden-brown hair and big hazel eyes, she had never had Liesel's capacity to eat what she wanted without gaining weight. Especially since she'd had Alex. She had always felt like they were two of a set of matryoshka dolls, with herself being the larger one on the outside. The larger one with not quite such exquisite bone structure, and ten extra pounds between knees and nipples. She pinched one of the inches that was lolling muffin-like over the top of her jeans waistband, and promised herself that once they'd settled in she'd go back on her diet.

'It's all been so fast . . .' Liesel was still enthusing. 'We haven't really had time to think about anything other than getting out of Hackney. Well . . .' She paused and gestured with one hand at the stark landscape of Bodmin Moor around them. 'Now we're out, and it's been a long journey . . . lots of time to think, to actually get excited . . .'

'Missing London already, then?' Marilyn laughed.

'Like my backside . . .' Liesel winked at her sister, an in-joke.

'It's all behind me.' They chorused the punch line together.

*

Finally, as daylight began to filter through the darkness, Liesel saw the sign for Piran Bay, and with a fresh burst of energy took the turning towards the coast, putting her foot down a little bit more. Not that it made any difference: she was sure the engine was going at its own pace regardless of how low to the floor she pushed the accelerator.

From straight and dual the road became narrow, and more curved and sinewy than a grass snake slithering through the trees that bent in overhead to meet and form a tunnel. After the dark beauty of Bodmin Moor, Liesel drank in the lush surroundings with awe and wonder, revelling in the dappled light that fell like cobwebs of lace across the windscreen, until she emerged from the trees and saw a sight that made her slow down and pull over. The gradual braking woke Marilyn, who jolted upright in disoriented concern and asked breathlessly, 'What is it? Are we here?'

'Not quite.'

'Do you want to swap again? Are you tired?'

'No. I'm fine.'

'Then why have we stopped?'

Liesel pointed out of the window. 'That's why we've stopped.'

Marilyn rubbed the sleep from her eyes and looked. They were parked just off the road in a lay-by, up on a cliff that soared almost a hundred feet above the water, the edge marked by thick, resilient tufts of grass and heather blowing in the breeze. Beyond them, stretching endlessly to meet the horizon, a barely distinguishable link of blue to blue, was the ocean. The rising sun sent fingers of light creeping like vines across the water, caressing the undulating surface like a lover, colours segueing together as night fused into day.

'Wow,' breathed Marilyn.

'Exactly.'

'It's so beautiful.'

Marilyn gently shook Alex, who stirred and yawned and slowly opened his eyes, blinking like a little mole emerging from the earth into the sunlight.

'Are we there yet?' were the first words that sprang from his lips.

'Almost,' Marilyn said soothingly. 'We thought you might like to see the sea first.'

'We're at the seaside?'

His mother nodded.

'Can we get an ice cream?'

Liesel and Marilyn looked at each other and smiled softly.

'First one to see the sea . . .' Marilyn began.

'. . . buys the ice cream,' Liesel finished.

Their dad had always used to say this to them every time they took a trip to the seaside. It had been his little trick, as they were always so excited to be the first to spot the rolling ocean. Instead of being in competition, they would instantly band together to make sure that neither was first, or confessed to being so at least.

And Dad always bought the ice cream.

Synchronised, they both wound down the windows and all three hung their heads out like dogs desperate for the scent of the big wide world, with all its interesting smells, to hit their nostrils.

'Taste that air.'

Alex took Liesel literally and stuck out his tongue.

'It tastes salty,' he said after a moment, and then added as a considered afterthought, 'and clean, like it's just had a bath.'

'No fog, smog or bus diesel?'

'Exactly.'

In the distance, a small town was sprawled along the coastline, houses hugging hillsides fringed by sandy beaches. A toy town, picture-postcard perfect.

'So pretty!' breathed Marilyn.

'Where's that?' Alex asked.

'Well, according to the signs,' Liesel replied with a smile, 'that's our new home.'

Fifteen minutes later, they were driving down into Piran.

'Right,' Marilyn murmured, scouring the solicitor's directions, 'there's a left turning past the post office, next to a large house called Windswept, into Carantoc Beach Road . . .' She waited until she felt the van turn left. 'Then follow the road down where it swings round to the right, four houses on the left, and then the next place we come to should be . . .'

She paused and looked up as Liesel slowed to a halt and let out an audible gasp.

'. . . Hotel Cornucopia.' Her mouth fell open like her sister's and her son's; Alex's nose was stuck to the window, his breath leaving circles on the glass. 'No, it can't be . . .' She looked at her directions again. 'We must have gone wrong somewhere. This can't be it . . .'

But the sign set in the stone wall in front of her could not be mistaken.

'Welcome to the Hotel Cornucopia,' breathed Liesel, and then she began to laugh like a madwoman.

Not quite able to believe that they were in the right place, Liesel had parked where she had stopped in the road and they had all tumbled out of the van to stand at the top of the drive leading to the hotel and stare down it in absolute open-mouthed awe.

The drive itself was heralded by two stone pillars, and flanked along its length by azaleas bursting with every shade of pink through purple to blue that you could imagine. Beyond them the tidal river ran to the sea, which sat in the distance half a mile or so away; the road ran parallel to this river up along the headland, where the houses ended and hinterland and dunes began.

The Cornucopia was perched on a four-acre plot of land between the road and the river, and was most certainly not the weatherboard-clad Victorian B&B they had all been expecting.

'It's a castle!' Alex breathed ecstatically. 'I'm going to live in a castle!'

'Oh my good Lord,' Liesel exlaimed, sinking at the knees a little in shock. Before them, magnificent, stood a miniature Cinderella's castle, complete with pitched roofs and a tower. A sand castle made of stone, a Gothic folly, a fantasy fairy-tale doll's house blown up to human size.

'It can't be the right place,' Marilyn repeated, all the time hoping against hope that it was.

'The sign says it is.' Liesel shrugged.

'Hotel Cor-nu-co-pia,' said Alex, tracing with his fingers the etched wood of the nameplate that graced one of the pillars to the side of the drive. He spelled the now familiar-sounding but unfamiliar-looking word phonetic-ally, the way Marilyn and Liesel had taught him to learn things he found difficult.

'Would you look at this place!'

'Steven Kingston didn't forewarn you?'

'Steven Kingston was as bald with his details as he is on his head. What's the time?'

'Almost six thirty.'

'Lorraine is going to meet us here at eight.'

'Lorraine? Ah yes, the mysterious Miss Veasey, employee of the month, who is set to enlighten us as to all things Cornucopia. Well, if she's not coming until eight, that gives us a couple of hours to have a bloody good nose round!' Liesel exclaimed gleefully.

'We're going in?' Marilyn asked nervously.

'You've got keys, haven't you?'

'Yes, but do you really think we should?'

'Why on earth not? What do you want us to do, wait in the van till someone comes and gives us permission to open our own front door?'

'Well, perhaps we *should* wait for this Lorraine person.'

'Why should we? There's no one here, is there?'

Marilyn shook her head.

'It's been closed since Nancy died.'

'And it's our home now. What do you think, Alex?'

'Is this really ours, Mum?'

Marilyn nodded.

'Then we can go in, can't we? Specially 'cause you've got a key and everything.'

Marilyn nodded again slowly. They were both right: why should she feel like she was trespassing when it was all in black and white and rubber-stamped by legal bods that this amazing place now belonged to Alex?

She fetched the thin envelope of information the solicitor had given her from the glove box of the van, and pulled from it the big old-fashioned key. Then the three of them hurried excitedly down the steep drive.

The door to the house was straight out of a storybook, arched and heavy, the wood bonded with thick metalwork. Marilyn inserted the key, pushed the door a few inches, hesitated, gathered her courage again, pushed a bit more . . . and was almost knocked to the floor as a huge grey dog barged clumsily past them and lolloped frantically to the bushes that lined the sloping driveway, where with what Liesel could have sworn was a sigh, it lifted a long leg against an azalea and enjoyed the most prolonged pee she had ever witnessed.

'That must be Godrich,' she observed, offering a staggering Marilyn a steadying hand.

'That's not a dog, it's an elephant with hair.'

'A woolly mammoth,' Alex offered helpfully.

'Whatever it is, I think it's making an escape,' Marilyn observed as the dog, having finally finished peeing, set off in a loping run up the sloping driveway.

'Well, we'd better stop it; we've sworn to nurture and nourish, remember, not let loose and lose ... Godrich!' Liesel called.

The dog paused in mid-gallop and looked around.

'Godrich, come here now.' She attempted to sound firm, and to her amazement, the dog did indeed turn around and trot back down to her. 'Sit,' she said.

The dog sat.

'Barbara Woodhouse, eat your heart out.' Liesel beamed. 'We've always said I have a way with animals.'

'Yes, but we've always meant of the male variety.'

'Godrich's a boy.' Alex bent down and helpfully peered underneath the dog just to make sure.

'I meant male *human*.' Marilyn laughed.

Liesel was still dog training.

'Lie down,' she said.

'Now you're pushing your luck,' Marilyn said, as the dog looked at her dolefully out of large grey wrinkled eyes without moving a muscle.

'Do you think he'd lie down for a Mars bar?' Liesel fished in her jacket pocket.

'Not sure, but I know someone else who would,' Marilyn said, as Alex pretended to beg at his aunt's feet.

Laughing, Liesel handed him the chocolate bar.

'Ta, Leez. Can I share it with Godrich?'

'Dogs shouldn't eat chocolate. It's not good for them.'

'Girls shouldn't eat cakes. It's not good for their arses,' Alex said matter-of-factly, unwrapping the Mars bar. 'Mum, what is an arse?'

'Your Auntie Liesel is,' Marilyn replied, pulling a face

at Liesel, 'for forgetting that you repeat whatever she says parrot fashion.'

'Really? 'S funny.' Alex bit into the chocolate and chewed thoughtfully. 'I thought it was another word for bum.'

The two women swapped looks, one accusing but amused despite itself, the other apologetic, again. Whilst they were looking at each other and not him, Alex broke the remains of the chocolate bar in two and surreptitiously fed half to a salivating Godrich.

'Ps and Qs duly minded,' Liesel assured her sister. 'Now, are you going to go through the door you've just opened, or are we going to stand here and stare through the gap?'

'Shall we go in?' Marilyn asked tentatively.

'You still feel like we shouldn't?'

Marilyn offered a wavering smile.

'Maybe we should ask Godrich,' Liesel teased her gently. 'After all, he's next in line to the throne. Godrich,' she said, turning to the huge shaggy animal, 'do you mind if we come in?'

As if in answer, the large dog pushed past them and went inside himself.

'He said yes!' Alex announced with a grin, and shot in after Godrich, closely followed by Liesel.

5

Hearing them inside, making exclamations, Marilyn followed tentatively, as if the ghost of Great-Aunt Nancy might suddenly jump out and tell them it was all a joke and ask them to leave immediately.

What she saw brought her to an abrupt halt.

The hallway was vast, cavernous and galleried, a carved wooden stairway the main feature, twice as wide as normal stairs and gleaming with polish. The floor was tiled, old-fashioned Victorian tiles, obviously the originals, their greens, burgundies and creams complementing the burgundy carpet that clung with the help of brass rods to the stairway.

The walls were dark panelled wood to head height and then a twist of green and red leaves on a background of cream above.

'Oh, wow! I'm sure the wallpaper's original William Morris,' Marilyn breathed, running her fingers over it in gentle reverence.

'Or Johnny Morris. Jungle mania,' Liesel quipped.

'Don't you think it's beautiful?'

'Sure, but it's very nineteenth century.'

'What did you expect in a house like this?'

To the right hand side of the vast atrium was a reception desk, long and imposing and made of the same polished dark wood as the heavy balustrade of the stairway. The only thing on the desk was a brass bell, which both Alex and Liesel in their running-around-in-circles excitement rang several times, the chime echoing throughout the house.

Behind reception, they could see a doorway through to a large open office, from which led another door marked 'Manager'.

'Let's explore!' Liesel exclaimed, grabbing her nephew's hand, and knowing that Marilyn would follow, they pelted off down a corridor.

Beyond the hallway and the offices, the ground floor revealed a formal sitting room and a huge dining room, both with several sets of French windows leading out on to a beautiful, if slightly crumbling, stone terrace; and a large, well-equipped kitchen with a small staff room and a narrow corridor of storerooms off it.

An arched inner hallway to the right of the stairs led to ladies' and gents' toilets and a further door, beyond which were two ground-floor guest rooms, both with French windows opening on to a walled garden.

Upstairs were two floors, the first with four beautifully sized but rather antiquated guest bedrooms, and the second with three more tucked quaintly under sloping ceilings.

One of the first-floor rooms, marked 'Honeymoon Suite', housed a four-poster of elephantine proportions, complete with heavy tapestry drapes and a mattress so thick you really needed a stepladder to climb aboard, unless of course you were Liesel and Alex, in which case you used a red velvet footstool as a springboard.

All the fixtures and fittings were good quality, clean and well cared for, but as old as the hills. It was like stepping back in time.

'This place is amazing!' Marilyn repeated in each room.

'This place is a museum,' Liesel countered.

'Well, if we don't have any luck running it as a hotel, maybe that's what we should open it as.'

Finally, to the left-hand side of the hall, hidden behind an intricate tapestry curtain that depicted a hunting scene of harts and hounds, they discovered the door to the tower. It was marked 'PRIVATE'.

'This must be us,' Liesel said with a nervous smile.

'Welcome to our new home. Who's carrying who over the threshold?' Marilyn joked.

'You take Godrich, I'll take Alex.' Liesel swept a laughing Alex up into a fireman's lift.

'Great, you get the cute kid, I get the thing that looks like it's just crawled out of a swamp and smells like it died whilst it was in there,' Marilyn grumbled, reluctantly calling the big shaggy hound to heel.

Through the heavy felt-backed door was another hallway with stairs turning backwards on themselves like folded paper, which led to a room on each floor.

The ground floor was home to a proper old-fashioned parlour, with Queen Anne-style chairs and lace doilies. It had a beautiful open fireplace that had Marilyn clapping her hands with delight. In front of the fireplace was a rug that looked like Godrich's twin brother skinned and flattened, and prominent on the wall above the mantelpiece was a painting of an elderly lady with corrugated grey hair and a frown that was so flinty it could spark up the coals in the grate on its own.

'Great-Aunt Nancy,' Marilyn announced in hushed, almost reverent tones. 'Your benefactor,' she explained to Alex.

'My benny what?' He frowned in puzzlement.

'Benefactor. It means someone who very kindly gives you something, usually something worth money that helps with your future.'

'Well, that's a picture for the porcelain.' Liesel nodded sagely.

This time both Alex and Marilyn looked confused.

'Perfect hanging position in the bathroom above the toilet,' she explained with a grin.

'Don't be so irreverent . . . er, I mean rude,' Marilyn amended before Alex could demand another English lesson.

'Well, it's not exactly . . .' Liesel searched for the right word that would describe it without offending, 'friendly looking.'

To her surprise, Marilyn nodded her agreement, albeit looking a little guilty.

'You could say that about the whole room, really. It's an edge-of-chair, pinkies-out-whilst-sipping-from-bone-china kind of place at the moment, isn't it?'

Mentally removing the old-fashioned furniture, Marilyn wondered if there was enough leeway in the hotel's repairs and renewals budget to buy some more sofas, and replace the chintzy wallpaper with something painted and more neutral.

'Do you think it's all like this?' Liesel asked with a frown.

'Shall we brave it and see?'

The first floor housed a large bathroom that was thankfully far more modern, apart from the old-fashioned claw-footed bath that sat in state in the middle of the room.

'Ooh, someone pass me a Cadbury's flake and some bubble bath,' Liesel drooled, dropping Alex into the bath.

There were three floors left. Like excited kids, they decided to start at the top and work their way down.

'Come on, nephew, let's go pick our bedrooms,' Liesel said, grabbing Alex's hand and thundering up the narrow stairs. 'I'm assuming that as there are three more floors, we get one each!'

Marilyn watched them indulgently. Honestly, sometimes it was like having two children, but despite the fact
that it could be wearing always having to be the
responsible one, she was grateful that Alex had Liesel to
have fun with.

'We're at the top,' her sister yelled down to her. 'Come
on, slow coach. It's amazing, you can see the sea from
here.'

'Yeah, come on, slow coach,' Alex echoed.

The room at the top was bigger than the others, as it
had no flight of stairs going up to take up floor space.
Because of this, it had its own en suite shower room. It
also had deep window seats that Alex threw himself into,
kneeling with his nose pressed against the window. The
furniture and the decor were pretty much the same as the
rest of the tower rooms: a queen-size bed, built-in
wardrobes, floral wallpaper, dried flowers, and small
paintings of more flowers and leafy landscapes. There was
also a dog basket and a full water bowl by the radiator.

'This must be Godrich's room,' Liesel joked, as the
hound folded its long legs into the basket and lay down,
nose poking and eyes blinking dolefully over the edge at
them.

'It must have been Great-Aunt Nancy's room,' Marilyn
amended, as she picked up a framed photograph from the
bedside table. It was a picture of Alex dressed as a shepherd
for the school nativity play the previous Christmas.

'How did she get that?' Liesel frowned, peering over
Marilyn's shoulder.

'I sent it to her in her Christmas card. I thought she
might like it.' Marilyn picked up the photograph and ran
a finger over the dusty glass. 'It's kind of sad, really.
She's . . . I mean she *was* Alex's only living relative on *his*
side. Alex was her family. The least we could have done
was visit.'

'Did she ever ask you to?'

'Well . . . no, she didn't.'

'There you go, then. You know what you're like, Marilyn, you never go anywhere without a formal invitation.'

'I know, but still . . .'

'Can I have this room, Mum?' Alex piped up, interrupting them.

'You want this one?' Marilyn looked at him in surprise. It was such an old lady's room, with its chintz and its floral wallpaper, she was surprised it appealed to him.

'Please? Can I?'

'You really want to be right up here on your own?' Marilyn crossed to the window, and gasped involuntarily as she too saw the stunning view of the tidal river, the rolling hillside opposite and the dunes and the sea in the distance.

She dragged her eyes away to see Alex nodding furiously.

'Liesel?' Marilyn queried.

Liesel shrugged. 'Every superhero has to have his lair. Batman had the bat cave, after all. Clark Kent had his phone box.'

'I'm not sleeping in a phone box.'

'No, you're sleeping in the best room in the whole hotel,' Marilyn said with a smile, pulling her son to her and dropping a kiss on his ruffled golden hair.

'You're forgetting the Honeymoon Suite,' Liesel reminded her.

'What's a four-poster compared to that view?' Marilyn sighed, turning back to it, 'Is that it, you like the view?'

Alex nodded, but it was noncommittal.

'He wants to share with Godrich,' explained Liesel, who understood already. 'And it doesn't look like Godrich's going to be budged.'

'Well if that's what you want, and you're sure you wouldn't prefer being in between me and Auntie Liesel?'

'An Alex sandwich?' Liesel grinned, but the boy shook his head.

'I like it here. If that's okay.'

'Of course it's okay.'

'Yay!' Alex yelled an exclamation of delight and staked his claim completely by hurling himself bodily face first on to the bed, and then promptly falling asleep, in that deliciously instant way that only kids could manage.

'Are you sure you're okay with Alex having that room?' Marilyn asked as they checked out the en suite, which fortunately, like the main bathroom, was one of the most modern things in the private living quarters.

'Hey, it's his hotel, I say it's only right he gets first pick. Besides, would you want to share with the hound of the basket cases?' Liesel indicated Godrich, who was pretending to snore.

Marilyn shook her head fiercely.

'Well, Alex seems pretty enamoured of the dog already.'

'Let's hope Godrich is as wild about him, eh?'

'Mmm. You don't suppose it bites, do you?'

'The dog or Lorraine?' Marilyn looked at her watch. 'She'll be here soon.'

'You're not nervous about meeting her, are you?'

'Kind of . . . well, yeah, I am. She's worked here for over ten years, and then suddenly we swan in and take over.'

'Hello . . .'

As if on cue, a rather nervous call quavered up the stairs, and Marilyn clutched Liesel's arm.

'Talk of the devil. She's early.'

'Good sign.'

'Hello?' This time it was even more shaky.

'She sounds as petrified as me.'

'Maybe she thinks we're burglars.'

Marilyn tried to laugh, couldn't, tried to think of a good excuse to send Liesel to meet Lorraine instead, couldn't, and shrugged helplessly.

'Well, I suppose I'd better go and say hello. Are you staying with Alex in case he wakes up and wonders where the hell he is?'

'He'll be fine for a minute. I'll come with you, help with the intros.'

Marilyn nodded gratefully. She always did what she had to do, but practical did not go hand in hand with gregarious. Liesel was the people person, the meeter and greeter.

'We still haven't sorted out which rooms we're having,' Marilyn said as a means to prevaricate.

'You should be near Alex, I'll go under you.'

'Sounds good to me.'

'Job done, then ... Now, let's go and meet Alex's employee, and remember, until he's eighteen, you're the boss.'

Lorraine Veasey was standing in the middle of the aircraft hangar of a hallway, wringing her hands and looking as dark and gloomy as the decor.

Fairly diminutive in height, she had long, straight black hair, parted in the middle, a round face as doughy as an uncooked pudding, and big silver-blue eyes that looked as fearful and startled as those of a wild animal caught out of cover. A black skirt, white shirt, thick tights and sensible shoes completed the look and the first impressions. At a guess, Marilyn would have put Lorraine at a similar age as herself, with the other woman perhaps a little bit younger, but she didn't know whether that was the smoothness of the pale skin, or the fact that Lorraine looked like a child standing lost and alone in the middle of the departure hall at Grand Central.

How could Marilyn be nervous when the girl was obviously terrified herself?

She summoned up her warmest smile and held out a hand in greeting.

'Hi, you must be Lorraine. I'm Marilyn Hamilton, Alex's mum, and this is my sister, Liesel Ellis.'

'I'm Lorraine ... L-L-Lorraine Veasey.' The handshake was as feeble as the smile she attempted to offer.

'Thank you so much for agreeing to come in early and show us the ropes. It's appreciated.'

'Well, I had to come in to start cleaning the rooms anyway,' the girl replied, her eyes flicking shyly from sister to sister.

Marilyn looked at Liesel in surprise: their grand tour earlier had shown them that the place was spotless.

'But you've done a great job already. The rooms are immaculate, we couldn't see anything that needed cleaning.'

To Marilyn's amazement, rather than looking happy at this, Lorraine's face seemed to crumple with disappointment, so to clear the atmosphere that descended with her frown, Liesel stepped in with some questions.

'Is the house very old? It's an amazing place. You've worked here a long time, haven't you? Do you know much about its history?'

'It was built by an eccentric Victorian earl, a distant cousin of Queen Victoria, for his mistress, Elizabeth. The house was built in 1898, and the tower was added five years later. Rumour has it that she cheated on him with another man, and so he deliberately requested of his architect that the tower be integrated into the main house by means of one door only, so that he could lock her in it when he was up in London with his wife.' Lorraine sounded as though she was giving a well-rehearsed guided tour.

'I don't know why he didn't just bin her.' Liesel shook her head. 'If someone cheated on me they'd be out of my house, not having a new bit of it built just for them.'

'She was apparently very beautiful.' Lorraine sighed wistfully when she said this. 'Men do strange things over beautiful women.'

'Well, it sounds more like a prison than a privilege to me,' Marilyn said, looking back at the tapestry covering the heavy door and shuddering a little.

'The house was a private home until 1946, when it became a hotel.' Lorraine continued the scripted lecture. 'The late Mrs Hamilton took over from the previous owner in 1970, running the hotel very successfully for almost forty years, until of course . . .' She stopped speaking and sighed. 'Until, of course,' she continued after a moment, 'she passed the hotel on to your son, her great-nephew, Alexander Hamilton.'

Liesel suppressed the urge to clap, thinking quite rightly that it wouldn't be taken in quite the spirit in which it was meant, as a bravo for this soliloquy.

'Who will hopefully run it successfully for at least the summer season or it gets passed on to Godrich,' Liesel blurted without thinking. 'Who I'm certain won't be able to run it very well at all, seeing as he's a dog . . .'

Marilyn glanced hastily at Lorraine, unsure how much she or any of the other staff members knew about the strange proviso in Nancy's will. She had every intention of telling them the entire truth and giving them the choice about staying on under such uncertain conditions, but from the total lack of surprise on Lorraine's face, it was obvious that she was aware of the situation. She didn't comment, however; she simply turned to Marilyn and asked, 'Do you want me to take you through everything in the office?'

Marilyn shook her head.

'Why don't we do this in the kitchen instead? I don't know about you, but I could do with a nice cup of tea.'

'And a bowl of Coco Pops?' came a voice from the tower doorway. Alex skidded across the floor in his socks and came to an abrupt grinning halt behind them, peering around his mother at Lorraine, half keen, half shy.

'Lorraine, this is my son, Alex. Alex, this is Lorraine, she works here.'

Alex beamed artlessly at Lorraine, and for the first time the woman actually managed a ghost of a smile.

'I'm afraid we don't have Coco Pops, but we have got cornflakes, or toast and marmalade?'

'Toast and marmalade and tea all round, then,' Liesel suggested. 'Come on, I'll be mother.'

The kitchen was on an industrial scale, and, like the rest of the house, absolutely spotless.

'I've tried to keep the place as Mrs Hamilton would have wanted it,' Lorraine said, automatically picking up a cloth and wiping imaginary dirt off a gleaming surface.

'So you've been in charge?' Marilyn asked.

'Well, I was the housekeeper, and then when Nancy passed away, she said in her will that I was to take over running the place until you turned up, so I suppose that kind of makes me acting manager at the moment, not that I expect you to keep me as that . . .'

'So who's running housekeeping at the moment?'

'Oh, no one, really. I still do that.'

'And reception?'

'I do that too.'

'And who's in charge of the restaurant?'

'That's me.'

'Night portering?'

'Well, we never had much call when Mrs Hamilton was in the tower, but since then . . . I suppose that would be . . . me.' The mouth was getting smaller and the eyes bigger with each answer.

'You've been doing it all?'

Lorraine nodded.

'So are there actually any other staff?'

'Oh, yes.' The small mouth spread into a broad beam. This was a question she could easily answer.

'Great.' Marilyn smiled her relief. 'And when will we get to meet them?'

'Eric, that's the chef, well, he should be here to meet you as well.'

Marilyn nodded, encouraging her to go on. 'And . . .'

'And he's late sometimes,' Lorraine offered hesitantly, as if she were responding to a question but wasn't quite sure she'd got the answer right.

'Okay, and who else is there?'

'Who else?' Lorraine's face flicked up the vacant sign again.

'Any more members of staff?'

'Oh, right, yes. Well, there's Kashia, but she's only part time. She does the waitressing at breakfast.'

'So who does the waitressing at dinner?'

'Oh, right, yes . . . Well, that'll be me too.'

'You must be absolutely exhausted,' Liesel sighed, resting her chin in her hands and blinking soulfully at Lorraine.

The dose of undisguised sympathy only served to make the girl seem more uncomfortable.

'Well, someone had to hold the fort. And we have been closed since the funeral, you know, out of respect and . . . and other stuff.'

'So when do you, I mean we, reopen?'

'Tomorrow.'

'Tomorrow?!'

Lorraine nodded. 'Mr and Mrs Heather arrive at three. They come every year. They always have the same room, number six. Ground floor, garden view, because Mrs Heather has an arthritic hip. Then Mr and Mrs Sedgewick are due at six; this is their first time here, but they were recommended to us by the two Miss Winstanleys, who stayed in room eight last August for a week, and are due back, same room, same week, this year. The Heathers and the Sedgewicks are both staying for five days. Then we have a Mr Lockheart arriving the following week. He's never stayed here before.'

'So there are nine letting rooms; only two are booked out this week, and then just one the following?'

Lorraine nodded again. 'Things have been a bit up in the air since Nancy passed away.'

'Of course they have.' Lorraine looked so guilty about this, Marilyn patted her hand reassuringly. 'It's only to be expected, and don't you worry, I'll take care of that kind of thing from now on. If you can just let me know how you drum up your business normally, where you advertise, that kind of thing . . . in fact, perhaps now would be a good time to go and take a look through the office . . .' Marilyn put down her empty tea cup and stood up purposefully.

Liesel held out her hand to Alex, who was sticky with marmalade.

'Come on, Mum's got her business head on. Shall we go and explore?'

He nodded. 'Can we take the dog?'

'Course we can. Is that okay, Maz, if we wander off?'

'It's a great idea.'

'Can we take Godrich?'

'Even better one.'

*

Outside, the sun was shining and the birds were singing. The two of them made their way out of the house and around the back to the garden. Here a wide stone terrace skirted the house, a low balustrade marking its edge. Beyond the terrace a lawn stepped in tiers to a tumble of rocks, which led down to a three-hundred-foot stretch of sand below, cut in two by what at the moment was a thin silver streak of stream.

Opposite, the land began to climb again to fields where sheep and cows grazed, wooded copses, pathways meandering their way through the canopies of green in the direction of the sea. To the right in the distance, about a half-mile walk, lay the beach and the sea itself beyond, azure in the glinting sunlight.

'So what do you think?'

'Wow,' said Alex, his eyes shining bright as the sunshine.

'Well put, young man. Well put.'

'Why's the sea so far away when the sand is only over there?' he asked, pointing to the end of the garden.

'I think this is a tidal river bed, which means the river comes in and out with the tide.'

'Which means that stream will turn into a river?'

Liesel nodded. 'The whole stretch of sand from bank to bank might fill with water.'

'Woah!' Alex breathed his appreciation. 'So that's definitely sand down there, not mud?'

Liesel nodded. 'Yep.'

Alex turned to his aunt, and his big brown eyes, so like his mother's, lit up with glee.

Two hours later, Marilyn escaped from the office, where Lorraine had given her a not-so-potted history of the workings of the Cornucopia, and went looking for her son and her sister. She found Liesel quite happily watching the world go by, buried up to her neck in the sand, as if it was the most natural thing in the world.

Suppressing a smile, Marilyn sat down beside her. Liesel grinned up at her in greeting.

'You and Lorraine done?'

'Yeah, for now. I told her to go home and get some rest and we'll see her again in the morning. Had to fight to get her out of the door, though; she was adamant she needed to bleach all the loos before tomorrow.'

'But everywhere's spotless.'

'Tell me about it. Do you know, I think she actually really likes cleaning.'

'You're kidding me. So how did it go with all the paperwork?'

'Paperwork? Hard work,' Marilyn stated bluntly, crossing her eyes. 'She's a strange girl.'

'Would you call her a girl?'

'Well, she can't be that much older than me.'

'Exactly.'

'Want some more sand in places only moisturiser should go?'

'No thank you, and did I tell you how youthful and girlish you look today?'

'Enjoy it whilst it lasts, because I shall probably be totally grey and haggard with wrinkles by the end of the summer.'

'Why? What's the verdict on the hotel?'

'It's going to be hard work, Liesel.'

'We both knew that already.'

'I know, but I didn't realise quite how much. It's like stepping back in time. The systems, if you can call them systems, are so antiquated it's untrue. I'm surprised they didn't have an abacus still lurking in that office.'

'What about guests? Have we actually got any beyond the ones Lorraine told us about?'

'Well, there's odds and sods of repeat bookings throughout the next four months, but not enough to keep the place going. And because we don't even have our own website, it's all word-of-mouth or passing trade.'

'And who passes by a no-through road?'

'Exactly. From what I can gather, apart from repeaters, the rest of the trade is made up of people who take a wrong turning trying to get to the beach.'

'You thinking of placing an ad?' Liesel nodded as best she could towards the *Yellow Pages* her sister was clutching.

'Oh no, that's for dinner. As the saying goes, an army marches on its stomach, and I don't know about yours, but it feels like a long time since that toast and marmalade. So what do you fancy, Chinese, Indian or pizza?'

'Better ask number one son.'

'Actually, that's a point, where is Alex?'

'I was beginning to wonder that myself . . .'

'I'd better go and check.'

'Good idea.'

Marilyn got to her feet.

'Er, Marilyn, there's just one other thing before you go,' Liesel called after her.

'What's that, Leez?'

'I think the tide is on its way in, and I'm kind of stuck between a rock and a hard place here. Would you just mind fetching a spade and digging me out?'

Nerves were overtaken by excitement. The first guests weren't arriving until after lunch. Liesel, unable to sleep, was up at five and walking the length of the tidal river bed to the beach, where the rolling tide was waiting to follow her back, swelling the banks of the river to magnificently buxom proportions and turning the Cornucopia into a moated castle.

Marvelling at the beauty of it, she was inspired to serve breakfast for Marilyn and Alex on the terrace, despite the fact that it wasn't the warmest of days. But somehow, sitting in the weak sunshine wrapped in warm jumpers, nibbling on cold toast and drinking rapidly cooling tea, with the water lapping at the edge of the garden down below them, seemed so sweet.

Their very first guests, the Heathers, arrived promptly at three, the given time to occupy their room. They were adorable, fell instantly in love with Alex, who they said reminded them of their own grandson, and were so overwhelmingly grateful for everything they were given that it was a pleasure to wait on them.

'Where are the other six?' Liesel whispered to Marilyn with a grin after helping the Heathers to their room with their cases.

'Sorry?'

'The dwarves. We've got Happy in duplicate. Honestly,

they're such a sweet couple. They're out of a fairy tale; nobody is that cute and that nice.'

'And that tiny.' Marilyn nodded her agreement. 'I must admit, you do keep expecting them to burst into song.'

The only slight glitch was when the elderly couple asked if afternoon tea could be served on the terrace instead of in the sitting room.

'Afternoon tea?' Liesel queried to Lorraine, who nodded.

'We always serve tea and cake at four for anyone who wants it, either in the sitting room or on the terrace: their choice, normally depends on the weather.' She nodded slowly as though imparting an almighty secret.

'Whether it's raining or not?'

'Absolutely.'

'Right, well, that's fine then.'

'Well, it would be . . .'

'But?'

'We haven't got any cakes. Eric usually makes them fresh every day after breakfast.'

'And Eric wasn't here for breakfast because it was just us, no guests.'

'Exactly. He'll be in at about five to prep for dinner, but that's too late for tea at four, isn't it . . .'

'Well, the only one around here who knows how to make a half-decent cake is Alex. He was taught at school, and now he knows the recipe off by heart,' Marilyn said hesitantly. 'For an eight-year-old boy with a sweet tooth, it was quite an easy skill to retain, and he makes a lovely Victoria sponge, but will that do?'

Lorraine nodded enthusiastically. 'Mr and Mrs Heather love a good Victoria sponge.'

Liesel found Alex in the garden, towing a reluctant Godrich around on his lead, one of Alex's spare Superman capes draped around the huge dog's bony withers.

'Hey, kiddo. Fancy doing a bit of baking?'

'Can Godrich help?'

'You know he's not allowed in the kitchen.'

Alex's head went to one side as he considered.

'No thanks. Think I'd rather play with Godrich.'

By the look of martyrdom on the dog's face, it was a sentiment he didn't share.

Liesel thought quickly.

'You can make a cake especially for Godrich if you want to . . .'

Liesel knew her nephew inside out. Five minutes later, a quickly rinsed Superman was in an apron and a chef's hat, his face covered in flour, and a relieved Godrich was burying the borrowed Superman cape under the azaleas in the garden.

Tea was duly served, only fifteen minutes later than advertised, the only one seemingly concerned by this minor delay being Lorraine, who between three fifty-five and four fifteen took hand-wringing to the level of an Olympic sport.

At five Lorraine hurried into the kitchen, where Marilyn was doing an impromptu stock check, her big bug eyes popping even further out of her head with worry. Eric had called in sick. It looked like Lorraine was ready to join him: her face was flushed, her hands were shaking, you could almost hear her heartbeat booming from her chest.

Marilyn looked up at her and smiled reassuringly.

'I think I can just about manage to cook dinner for eight people myself.'

'There are four in the dining room this evening.'

'And there are four of us in the kitchen as well.'

Marilyn could see her doing a head count: Liesel, Marilyn, Alex. She could almost see her wavering on

Godrich being the fourth mentioned, before she finally accepted the fact that Marilyn was including her for dinner as well.

Her astonishment was really rather sad.

'Please don't tell me you work through without having anything to eat?'

'Well, I just grab a quick cheese sandwich if I get a bit peckish.'

'If we're cooking a meal for everyone else, it seems silly not to make sure that there's enough for all of us as well.'

The reception bell rang and Lorraine almost hit the ceiling.

'The Sedgewicks!' she shrieked in panic, as if imparting the news that Attila the Hun and his hordes were rampaging into the hotel, and as she was in charge of reception on this first day, she bolted out as though she was being chased by something that wanted to eat her.

'Can you pop a couple of Valium in Lorraine's dinner?' Liesel joked as Marilyn put on an apron. 'Her nerves are so shot you'd think her last job was as a moving target on a firing range.'

'I know. It's like she expects to be shouted at for everything that goes wrong, whether it's her fault or not,' Marilyn agreed. 'Well, right now,' she looked at her watch, 'we have a dinner to make. What do you think, can we do it?'

'You always say we can do anything we put our minds to.'

'Yes, but as you well know, that's normally when I'm terrified that I can't.'

'A bit of reverse psychology works wonders.' Liesel grinned. 'Come on, let's see what we've got to work with before we start ringing the local takeaways.'

Further exploration of the kitchen had revealed an

enormous walk-in refrigerator, which Marilyn now approached with her practical head firmly back on.

'Right, what have we got in here then?' she said, opening the door and addressing the refrigerator itself.

Marilyn was a good plain home cook, as their grandmother used to say; she and Liesel were also very adept at making something out of not an awful lot, as are most people who have ever lived within a tight budget.

An hour later, a beautiful beef in beer casserole, jacket potatoes bursting with butter, and fresh vegetables were on offer for the main course. Liesel had prettied up a prawn cocktail, and Alex's feather-light sponge had been given a dose of cream and treacle and some dried dates and had adapted wonderfully into a sticky toffee pudding.

Lorraine had tried to help, but as Marilyn, Liesel and Alex had their own rhythm in a kitchen together, she had ended up taking a back seat, watching their resource-fulness in awe, buzzing around them and getting in the way, washing things before they'd finished with them, whisking away pans to plunge them in scorching water and scour them to within an inch of their metallic lives.

Liesel, the seasoned waitress, insisted on serving, Lorraine, hovering again, needing to help, impressed with her speed and efficiency and the number of plates she could carry with one hand.

The guests fed and watered and lingering over coffee and mints, the four of them sat down themselves to eat.

Looking desperately uncomfortable, even more so for the others' attempts to draw her into conversation to try and make her feel more at ease, Lorraine wolfed her food so quickly her heartburn must be atrocious and then scurried away, supposedly to check the linen cupboard one last time before Marilyn managed to catch her by the arm and gently frogmarch her out of the front door to send her home. It was almost as difficult to evict Alex from the kitchen to go and do more normal kid stuff like watching television.

'That was really good fun, Mum,' he said, as though cooking and washing dishes was a rare treat, far better than any television programme or computer game. 'Can I do it again tomorrow?'

'Perhaps.' Marilyn smiled, raising her eyebrows at Liesel as Alex finally disappeared through into their private quarters. 'I shall get arrested for child slave labour if I let him do any more!' She sighed.

'He enjoyed himself.'

'Yeah, he did, didn't he.' Marilyn stopped frowning and nodded her agreement.

'And we did good, didn't we?' Liesel persisted.

'We did, although I don't know if we'd manage it when the place is full. There are thirty covers in the dining room.'

'Covers?'

'It means we can cater for thirty people at full capacity.'

'Ooh, hark at you, you've got the hotel lingo already,' Liesel joked. 'The room looks bigger than that, though.'

'That's seated.'

'Oh, I see.'

'If we ever get a full hotel.' Cautious Marilyn had to add a rider.

'Of course we will.' Liesel put a reassuring arm around her sister's shoulders. 'This is going to be the best hotel in Piran Cove. In fact, now we're pretty much done in the catering department, I'm going to go and get the bar ready.'

'And I'm going to persuade my son that he should really start to get ready for bed.'

'Well, I know which job I'd rather have.'

*

Liesel had never known a bar so blissfully quiet. The Sedgwicks had drunk one après-dinner sherry apiece and gone to bed at nine, which left Liesel with just the Heathers, who, although livelier with their two brandies each and friendly chatter, were tired from their journey and retired shortly after. She shut the bar and went outside and stood on the terrace, leaning against the balustrade watching the moon shining on the water below and thanking the bright shining stars above her head for her quiet evening.

Marilyn joined her minutes later, having fought to put an overexcited Alex to bed, bribing him with hot chocolate, Cornish shortbread for both him and Godrich, and a video on his portable.

The two girls stood in companionable silence, both taking some time to catch their breath and actually look around at where they were, and send up a silent prayer of thanks for being there.

'So what did you think to our first proper day?' Marilyn finally asked.

'Heaven,' Liesel breathed, leaning even further forward to drink in the air heavy with oxygen and salt water, instead of bus fumes and pollution.

And Marilyn simply nodded.

The alarm went off at five the following morning.

Liesel fell out of bed, staggered groggily towards the door and promptly walked straight into the wardrobe.

Wasn't it horrible when you woke up and didn't know where you were? Half asleep, she was still following the path of the Hackney flat from bedroom to bathroom. Instead, she staggered to the window and pulled the curtains, letting the half-light of the new day flood in.

She already loved her room, despite the pink floral wallpaper that looked like a nylon nightdress run riot, and the red-patterned carpet that clashed with the wallpaper so violently it should really be wearing a hoodie and have 'LOVE' and 'HATE' tattooed on its knuckles.

She already had plans to check for hidden floorboards she could polish to a golden hue, and had decided to paint the walls a soft gold colour to match the sunshine that levered its way with tenacious fingers through the gaps in the dull brown curtains.

She couldn't see the sea from her room, she was too low down the tower, but she had a wonderful view of the river, and if she sat on the window ledge and leaned backwards as far as she dared, she could also see the beach and, when the tide came in, a tiny corner of the ocean.

This morning the tide *was* in, completely in, and the place was transformed again, the water snaking in a curve around the house so you could almost feel like you were on your own little island.

Liesel went in search of her sister. It was strange not to be sharing a room with Marilyn: lovely to be on her own and horrible not to have Marilyn there both at the same time.

Marilyn's room, on the floor above, was still in darkness. Liesel gently pushed the door open a fraction. This room was the twin of her own, another homage to bad-taste decor, but with all the potential of a fresh-faced student on a scholarship to a posh school.

Marilyn was sleeping like a dormouse, curled up and looking comfortable. She had worked so hard since they had arrived here two days ago, not only learning all she could from Lorraine, but making a valiant attempt at unpacking all their boxes too. She had even started to help Alex turn his bedroom into the room of an eight year old rather than a seventy-eight year old, spending the time running round with a black rubbish sack binning doilies and dried flowers.

Liesel didn't have the heart to wake her. She decided that if Eric hadn't turned up, she could surely manage to produce four fried breakfasts on her own. And she only had to cook them. Lorraine had assured them the previous evening that Kashia, the waitress, was very reliable – although that had been said with a sniff, which indicated other issues – and would definitely be in this morning to serve.

Switching her sister's alarm clock to eight thirty, she closed the bedroom door quietly and slipped up the stairs to check on Alex. She wouldn't have been surprised to see Godrich on the bed and Alex in the dog basket, such was the current dynamic of their fledgling relationship.

It wasn't quite as bad as that. They were both on the bed, both with mouths wide open, fast asleep, breathing heavily. Godrich was taking up two thirds of the big double bed, legs twitching frantically as he dreamed of some canine activity, kicking Alex in the back with every imagined leap and bound.

Liesel smiled. It was good to see Alex sleeping so soundly despite the disturbance. He was due to start at the local school the following week, and she could guarantee that he wouldn't be sleeping so peacefully then, such were his nerves about his first day and how his new classmates would take to him. And the fact that his new school had a strict uniform policy and he knew that this would be the point where his mother would have to try and peel him out of his beloved cape and blue tights.

Alex never said very much, but Liesel knew him inside out, and she knew that the closer the day came, the more he would retreat into himself, getting anxious and withdrawn, hiding behind his cape, and the more often he would be creeping into either her or Marilyn's bed in the small hours of the morning.

Ignoring the big bath, which was calling her like a siren to a sailor, Liesel showered quickly, pulled on some clothes and trotted downstairs, reassured by the noise of clinking cutlery as she entered the hall that Kashia had turned up as promised.

There was indeed a woman setting up two of the tables in the dining room. The total opposite to short, dumpy, lank-brown-haired Lorraine, she was tall and blonde and statuesque and she could have been really rather glamorous if her eyes weren't quite so suspicious and the full mouth wasn't turned down quite so much at the corners.

'Hi, you must be Kashia,' Liesel called happily, bouncing into the room with a grin and her hand held out in greeting.

The woman actually stepped away from her, startled

more by Liesel's level of enthusiasm than by her sudden appearance.

'You are Kashia, aren't you? You're not some mad burglar who breaks in to steal all our stuff but has a strange compulsion to organise place settings before they go?' Liesel, uncomfortable, resorted to her usual defence of humour, and was rewarded with a smile, a tight, not totally comprehending smile, but a smile none the less.

'Yes. I is Kashia Fabritziovich.'

'I'm Liesel.'

'Ah, the miss. Yes.'

'Please, just Liesel is fine.'

'That is German name, no? You are German?'

'No, but my mum was rather fanatical about *The Sound of Music*.'

Kashia's rather startling grey eyes crossed in confusion.

'I was named after a character in a film.'

'Ah, okay.' She said it without any particular interest, and turned back to laying her tables.

'Can I help you with anything?'

'I no need help to serve four peoples.'

'That's true. Um, well, do you know if Eric has made it in?'

'He is in kitchen.'

'Great, lovely, I'll go and see if he needs a hand, then.' But Kashia had already turned away and was once more apparently completely engrossed in polishing spoons. 'Nice to meet you,' Liesel threw after her anyway.

So Kashia was going to be a tough nut to crack, but Liesel liked a challenge. She believed that even the surliest person was basically good underneath, and that people who weren't as sunny as she was were masking deep-rooted problems, and if someone had problems . . . well, Marilyn had always taught her that you worked through your problems with the help of those who loved you.

Maybe Kashia didn't have anyone to love. Liesel wondered idly as she trotted through to the kitchen what Piran Cove and Piran Bay were like for single men: not that she wanted one for herself – there had been too many disappointments men-wise recently to want a repeat performance so soon – but if Kashia were alone, and her fingers *had* been ringless, Leisel wouldn't be averse to a bit of matchmaking.

Maybe the elusive Eric was single. Then again, she seemed to recall Lorraine mentioning that he was rather a lot older than they were.

A tall, thin man was standing at the table, large mixing bowl in the crook of his arm, vigorously whisking. He looked so frail that Liesel thought the vibration of this action might crack him rather than the eggs.

He had a long, thin face to match the long, thin body, grey eyes behind thick glasses, and grey hair that stood upright and tufted like the synthetic hair on a toy Troll. His eyes were bloodshot and crossing with tiredness, their flaws magnified by the lenses. Liesel could see the road map of broken blood vessels criss-crossing the opaque yellow surface. But they were kind eyes, tired from more than just weariness, but overwhelmingly kind.

'You still don't look well,' she murmured sympathetic-ally.

The man looked up and blinked at her in surprise.

'Sorry.' She held out a hand. 'I'm Liesel. You must be Eric.'

He nodded and held out his own hand, which Liesel took and found to be warm and shaking like a leaf in a breeze.

'Are you feeling better today? I was just thinking you still look poorly. Would you like a cup of tea?'

He nodded gratefully. 'That'd be great, miss, if you don't mind.'

'Liesel, please, and are you sure you should be here?'

'Oh yeah. I'm right sorry about last night, miss . . .' He faltered as Liesel laughed and mouthed her name at him again. 'Er, I mean Miss Liesel.'

'Well you can't help being ill. I know the last thing I feel like doing when I'm poorly is cooking. Besides, it'd be terrible if you passed something on to Mr and Mrs Heather; they don't look strong enough to stand up to a mild gust of wind, let alone a dose of horrible germs.'

Eric managed a small laugh.

'Trust me, it's not catching.'

Liesel frowned. 'Still, are you sure you should be here?'

He nodded.

'Great. Well, I'll make us that tea, and then I'll put my pinny on and you can tell me what you need me to do to help.'

Liesel made three cups and took one through to Kashia, who looked thoroughly surprised and took it reluctantly, as though Liesel were passing her a goblet of frothing poison rather than a hot mug of English Breakfast.

'Definite issues,' Liesel muttered to herself as she headed back to the kitchen. Eric, however, was another matter altogether. After an initial shyness, she found that he was funny and friendly, and after an hour of her own chatter to put him at ease, she had him talking away as if they were old friends, telling tales of his youth and passing on snippets of information about himself. Liesel had so far found out that he had trained as a chef in the forces, he lived alone a little further up the coast in Newquay, he had a grown-up son who was abroad, and he was a widower. He didn't say much about this, and Liesel knew not to press on the subject of lost loved ones. If a person wanted to talk, then they would do so without prompting.

He was also a quick and skilful chef, and seemed to have a natural flair for presentation. And despite Lorraine's tales of a poor attendance record, Liesel could see exactly why Great-Aunt Nancy had kept him on. Everything he touched turned to culinary gold. His bacon and sausages were cooked to perfection; a simple grilled tomato was made cordon bleu with the help of some herbs, a scattering of parmesan, and what Liesel had quickly christened 'the Eric Touch'. He made the lightest, fluffiest, butteriest scrambled eggs she had ever tasted, and poached them to perfection as well, something that impressed Liesel beyond comprehension, as every time she tried this herself, she produced something resembling a greyish-yellow bullet.

By the time Marilyn came down, yawning, stretching and looking thoroughly guilty but flushed with the pleasure that comes with an unexpected lie-in, not only had the Heathers and the Sedgewicks been fed and watered and had departed together for a trip to St Ives, but Liesel was stuffed to the gills with enough breakfast for two people, having been unable to resist trying everything, and was trying to burn off the calories by vigorously helping Eric to clear up the kitchen.

'Morning. Oh, Liesel, be a love and make me one of those,' Marilyn pleaded, eyeing Liesel's third mug of steaming tea jealously.

'Have this one. I've already had two.'

'Ta, sis.' She took the mug and smiled apologetically. 'You've been up for ages and I've been snoring like a warthog. I can't believe you let me sleep in. I feel so guilty.'

'Well don't. You deserve a lie in every so often and we've managed quite nicely between us, haven't we, Eric.'

'That we have, Miss Liesel.' He nodded happily.

'Eric, this is my sister Marilyn. Marilyn, Eric, the fabulous chef.'

Eric, looking embarrassed at the compliment, wiped his hands on his apron and they shook.

He looked so frail, Marilyn's motherly instincts immediately kicked in as well.

'It's lovely to meet you, Eric, but if you don't mind me saying, you don't look well. Are you sure you should be in?'

Eric glanced at Liesel.

'We're already done that one, Maz. And we've already done breakfast too, which means that Eric can go home now anyway, can't he?'

Eric looked dubiously at Marilyn.

'I've still got the cakes to do, Mrs Hamilton.'

'Marilyn, please. And don't worry about the cakes. Alex has asked if he can do them again today, as he enjoyed it so much yesterday. If that's okay with you, of course.'

'If the young man's keen, Miss Marilyn. Although I'd be happy to stay and make them with him. I've got some lovely recipes that would be nice to share with someone who likes to cook.'

'I think Alex would like that too.' Marilyn smiled, deciding that she liked this tall, sallow-faced man already.

'What would I like, Mum?' Alex bounded into the kitchen after his mother, wearing his newest Superman outfit, the bright red cape, not yet faded by the sun or the washing machine, flowing behind as he ran. Despite looking bright and invincible, as soon as he saw Eric he skidded behind Marilyn.

'This is Eric, Alex. He does the cooking here.'

'You're a cook!' Alex breathed ecstatically, as if his mum had just told him Eric wore skin-tight cartoon-coloured Lycra and could fly.

'And you're a superhero!' Eric exclaimed, bending his willowy frame to meet Alex at eye level, 'Between us we're going to make some fantastic cakes!'

'So what do you think?' Marilyn asked in an aside as Eric showed Alex how to tie on a proper chef's apron.

'I'm really impressed. Do you know, he was in the Navy, a chef on a battleship, and he once cooked dinner for two hundred people in a force ten gale. He's lovely too, a real sweetheart. A truly nice man. And I bet he was a bit of a looker in his day as well.'

'You think?' Marilyn didn't look convinced.

'Yeah, something about the eyes, a bit of a sparkle despite the fact they're so bloodshot.'

'So you're enamoured already?'

'Absolutely. In fact I think I might have him as my new boyfriend.'

'Well, I knew you'd find a new one quickly, but this beats even my expectations.'

Liesel stuck her tongue out at her sister.

'I'm not looking for another man . . . I'm not!' she added indignantly as Marilyn raised her eyebrows. 'Not for myself, anyway. I think Kashia might need one.'

'You've met Kashia?'

Liesel nodded.

'What did she seem like?'

'Prickly,' Liesel said. 'Very attractive. A bit Sharon Stone-ish, although more voluptuous, less skinny clothes-horse, and her face isn't quite so elfin either, maybe more like Scarlett Johansson, but no, she's far too old . . .'

'Old?'

'Early forties maybe, but still very glam, more Scarlett Johansson's fit mother . . .'

'Not at all like Sharon Stone then, really?' Marilyn's mouth quirked into a smile.

'Maybe not.' Liesel laughed.

'So do you think we're going to have problems with them?'

'Well, Lorraine's not exactly *normal*, is she, and Kashia looks more likely to stab you than shake your hand; they both seem pretty uptight in different ways. Maybe what they need is a bloody good—'

'Liesel!' Marilyn shrieked before her sister could say exactly what Marilyn knew she was going to say. 'Not everything equates to sex, or the opposite sex.'

'It always seems to as far as I'm concerned.' Liesel was joking, but Marilyn's answer still surprised her.

'Well, I suppose it's not your fault you're irresistible.' Marilyn shrugged and then started to laugh as Liesel spluttered so hard she spat out a large piece of half-chewed toast. 'Nice.' She swooped with the dustpan and brush. 'Not so irresistible when spitting half-chewed food all over the place.'

'I'm not irresistible at all!' Liesel screeched as if her sister had just insulted her.

'If you're not irresistible, why do you think you've had so many men? You're like a cute little puppy, all big eyes and glossy hair and enthusiasm. Everyone wants to pet a puppy.'

'Then the puppy grows up and gets booted out on the side of a motorway.' Liesel, animal-lover, shuddered at her own analogy.

'That's not what I meant.'

'So what you mean is that men go for my looks, and then when they find out my personality's rubbish they bugger off?'

'That's not what I meant at all either!' Marilyn shrieked in indignation. 'What I meant is that you're a beautiful girl who is always going to get a lot of attention. Now, not many people will admit it for fear of being seen as shallow, but looks are the very first thing people judge on. The kind of man you've been "pulling", for want of a better word, is the kind of man who looks at you and goes, "wow, she's gorgeous", and then can't cope with the fact that you're looking for a proper long-term relationship and don't just want to be someone's arm candy.'

Liesel was silent for a moment, obviously digesting this, and then she looked kind of sorrowfully at her sister, all eyes and trembling lips, like the puppy had just been told off for something, and asked, 'How many boyfriends have I had?'

'Is this is a trick question?'

'No, I'm being serious.' Liesel smacked her sister good-naturedly on the arm. 'How many?'

'You expect me to remember them all?' Marilyn quipped, but Liesel's face fell again.

'That's exactly my point. There are too many to remember.'

'I was only kidding. Proper boyfriends, you've only had two. That's not that many.'

'Maybe, but look at all the in-betweenies: the one-offs, the dinner dates, the two-weekers, the lasts-a-month-until-they-realise-I'm-not-going-to-sleep-with-them-just-because-they-paid-for-dinner-this-time-instead-of-going-Dutch. There have been too many men in my life, and not enough *men* in my life. If you know what I mean.'

'I think so,' Marilyn replied uncertainly. 'Too many of the *wrong* men?'

'Exactly. Which means I'm a really poor judge when it comes to the unfairer sex.'

'I wouldn't say you're a bad judge, you're just a bit too . . . well . . . open. You prefer to see the good in people rather than the bad, and it doesn't help that you're so nice too. If a man asks you out, you haven't got the heart to say no in case you hurt his feelings, and so you end up going out with an awful lot of men who just don't suit you.'

'Maybe you're right. Maybe I should take a bit of a break from romance, full stop. I've never really had any time on my own, and we're going to be so busy anyway, this would probably be a good time to do it . . .' Liesel trailed off as she realised that Marilyn was looking at her, arms crossed, disbelieving smile on her face. 'I mean it, Maz.'

'I'm sure you do.'

'No more men. Not for a while, at least. I'm going to have some "me" time.'

Marilyn nodded, but it was one of those nods and one of those faces that quite clearly indicated a slightly patronising disbelief.

'You don't believe me, do you?'

'I believe you, but it's . . . well, don't you think it's kind of melodramatic: Liesel Ellis Vows No More Men!' Marilyn boomed in a movie-trailer voice.

'You don't think I can do it?' Liesel cried indignantly.

'You can do anything you set your mind to.' It was the old Marilyn maxim off pat.

'Just not this?'

'Not everything in life has to be about all or nothing, you know. You should be looking for balance, or at least for a man who doesn't just want to be with you for what you look like. You want someone a bit deeper than that. So no, I don't think it's a very good idea to take a vow of chastity; I think you should just be a bit more careful about who you agree to go on a date with in the future.'

Marilyn managed to make herself stop talking and remind herself that although she was the closest thing Liesel had to a mother, her mother she was not, and sometimes she had to curb the desire to lecture and guide in the same way as she did with Alex. After all, Liesel was an adult, entitled to her own opinions, entitled to make her own mistakes . . . Oh hell, who was she kidding? She'd no more see her kid sister go through any form of pain that she could possibly have stopped or eased than she would her eight-year-old son, and so she let her mouth motor on.

'I mean, all this Men are from Kathmandu and women are from Lakeside stuff, well, it has its moments, but the truth is, a decent person is a decent person and an arsehole is an arsehole, be they male, female, hermaphrodite or Martian, but what I'm trying to say is that you – being as shiningly gorgeous as any Sharon Stone or Scarlett Johansson, just in your own Liesel Ellis way – you, Liesel, gorgeous Liesel, my own little lonely goatherd, you need to be more careful than us mere mortals, that's all . . . that's all I'm trying to say.'

She stopped, and looked at her sister, who was looking at her with an open mouth.

'You did follow that, didn't you?' Marilyn had to ask.

Liesel nodded. 'You just told me that I need to be more careful with men because I'm gorgeous. You really think I'm gorgeous?' Liesel, not good with genuine compliments, pouted and fluttered her eyelashes at her sister.

'You got the looks, I got the brains,' Marilyn joked.

'Hey!'

'You look just like Mum when she was your age,' she added appeasingly.

'You really think so?' Liesel started to beam again.

'You know so too; you remember me showing you that picture of us all at Snowdon . . .'

And that was it, they were off, the kitchen vacated, work forgotten and the dog-eared box of family photographs fetched from where it had been placed reverently in the sideboard in the private sitting room.

Soon the floor and the hideous rug that covered it were swimming in a sea of old photographs. Then Alex's baby pictures came out, at which point Alex came in with cakes to be tried and tested, Eric following with a tray of tea. Eric was asked to stay and Lorraine was forcibly divorced from her duster and polish to join them, and the whole thing became quite a jolly little party, even to the point where Liesel put a hand on Marilyn's arm and said to her quietly, 'Look at Lorraine.'

And Marilyn looked over to see that Lorraine was actually smiling.

It was Liesel's turn on reception the following morning. But it was a different Liesel to the one who had flitted around the Hotel Cornucopia the previous day like a bohemian butterfly in her ripped jeans and multicoloured silk top from the Monsoon sale. She had lain awake the previous night thinking of her conversation with Marilyn.

People judged on first appearances. She wanted people to look beyond what they saw when they first set eyes on her. Aside from this, there was something else she had found out that had made her feel like a total idiot.

Kashia had grown up in poverty in an unstable country. She had four other jobs beside the one at the Cornucopia and sent the majority of her wages home to help her family.

Eric, who had won these confidences over the years with kindness and an unspoken promise of silence on the subject, had seen something in Liesel that had made him share them with her. Truth be known, he would have told Nancy Hamilton if he thought it would have helped any. Now Liesel, having insinuated even in semi-jest that Kashia's barbed-wire attitude was down to lack of sex, felt smaller than the smallest, most inconsequential thing on the planet.

Contrite was not an adequate word; humbled would be better.

'Don't judge a book by its cover,' Eric had said when confessing what he knew. An old adage, but so true.

When she looked in the mirror this morning, Liesel didn't see gorgeous, but she did see stupid. And so today, a different Liesel sat behind reception. No make-up, hair pulled back into a ponytail that was a touch severe, staid clothes in the form of black trousers, low heels and plain white shirt; she even toyed with the idea of borrowing a pair of the glasses Marilyn wore when she pored over her accounts, but they made her vision and her head go alarmingly fuzzy.

Still, the whole effect was very 'efficient secretary' and not so much 'unsuspecting sex bomb', which was an image that Liesel found rather worrying.

Lorraine, staggering past under the weight of clean linen just delivered, didn't notice the new look, but Kashia, cleaning silverware, did a double-take.

'What do you think? I decided yesterday's jeans and T-shirt didn't quite give out the right image for the hotel.'

'Is very Lorraine,' Kashia replied with what Liesel was certain was a little sneer, but was almost equally as certain wasn't a sneer actually at *her*.

'I'll take that as a compliment,' Liesel grinned, knowing full well it wasn't how it was meant. 'You look rather wonderful yourself today, you know.'

Kashia's eyes narrowed as her suspicious mind tried to ascertain whether Liesel was being sincere or whether she was making fun of her and Kashia should exact revenge by cutting Liesel's insanely glossy hair off whilst she slept, but the girl's smile looked genuine, and Kashia had come across enough duplicitous people to be pretty certain she knew when someone was telling the truth.

'Okay. Thank you,' she replied rather grudgingly after some moments.

Eric, bless him, didn't even notice that Liesel had

dramatically changed her style; to him she was simply Liesel, lovely girl, new friend, whether she be wearing hipster jeans and funky T-shirt, or kitted out like Miss Moneypenny.

Marilyn, however, was visibly taken aback.

'So what have you come dressed as?' she quipped.

'Respectable me.'

'Okay.'

'Receptionist me,' Liesel persisted. 'I don't want people to notice the outside . . .'

'Well you'd only achieve that if you were invisible,' Marilyn replied drily.

'Clothes maketh the man.'

'Yes, and I need to maketh the beds. I'll see you later.'

'Not if I'm invisible you won't,' Liesel quipped back.

She may have looked efficient, but there was still little for her to do on reception.

The Heathers and the Sedgewicks had been a gentle introduction to the life of hotel management. The day following their departure the hotel was empty, and according to the reservations book, an antiquated thing that looked like it belonged in a museum, it would remain that way until the day that Mr Lockheart was due to arrive. After that, the bookings were scarily sporadic. How could a hotel no one knew existed attract any new customers?

Marilyn got out her calculator and somehow squeezed them a marketing budget out of nowhere, placing an advert on Teletext and in the Sunday papers.

She and Liesel then scoured the rooms for chintz, removing lace doilies, toilet-roll covers, anything knitted or crocheted, plastic flowers, and eiderdowns that were a touch too pink and shiny, stuffing everything gleefully into big black bin bags.

The transformation was amazing, taking the rooms from boarding-house kitsch to an old-world elegance that even had a dubious Lorraine clapping her hands in appreciation. Although the appreciation soon turned to abject fear when the next of Marilyn's acquisitions arrived the following morning: a computer to replace the reservations book and finally get them on the Wonderful World Wide Web for all to see.

'We're going computerised!' Lorraine exclaimed in horror. Then, as the screen burst into life with a welcoming fanfare, came the terrified whimper, 'It looks very complicated.'

'Oh, it is, terribly,' Liesel replied, nodding knowledge-ably.

Lorraine looked devastated until Liesel showed she was only joking by winking at her, and almost got a smile in return.

Despite the lack of guests, it was amazing how busy they could be with other things, such as making sure that they conformed to the strict fire, health and safety, and food hygiene regulations, as well as maintenance, gardening, linen, supplies, and constant cleaning – thank heavens for Lorraine, the human equivalent of a Dyson.

Although they had been amazed by Lorraine's vast array of hats within the hotel, Marilyn and Liesel soon found they had taken on the same butterfly persona themselves, flitting from job to job depending on what was needed at any given time.

Hence, despite the fact that they had decided that Marilyn would be general manager, looking after the finances, making sure the hotel was as full as possible, advertising, and guest relations; Liesel would take charge of the bar and reception and the restaurant would be juggled between the three of them; and Lorraine would retain her original position as head housekeeper/chief chambermaid, along with her new and cherished role of assistant manager, they all seemed to run around doing all sorts of jobs. Even Alex was keen to pitch in, seduced by the idea of baking an endless supply of cake with his new friend Eric in the kitchen.

The two of them, the only males in the place apart from Godrich, had formed a quick and instant bond despite the fifty years between them. They both loved to cook, and a pleasure as a separate enterprise became a joy as a joint one. Added to that, Eric had an endless supply of bad jokes, and the laughter that emanated from the kitchen was often to be heard floating through the hotel like little bubbles of sunshine.

Alex hadn't as yet professed to miss anything about his previous life in London, not even his friends, and was already taking on the golden glow that most of the Cornish folk seemed to have to their skin all year round.

In fact, despite the rush and the worry, they were all settling in really well. The tower already felt more like home after just a few days than the flat had done after several years. And as for the hotel, well, it was bloody hard work, even empty, but it was all so new and exciting, rather like how it started out in a relationship when you knew nothing about each other and everything was about discovery.

All they needed now was some guests.

And then, as a result of one of her adverts, Marilyn took a booking for a party of eight to arrive in two days' time. To celebrate this breakthrough, she decided that everyone deserved a treat, and when they all turned up for work the following morning, believing that she'd called them in to ready the hotel for the newcomers, she produced two picnic baskets and a pile of blankets and led them all down to the beach for a brunch of ham-and-egg sandwiches and hot cross buns, accompanied by two bottles of Buck's Fizz. She proceeded to pop and pour with much aplomb, and made a little speech about how much she appreciated how hard everyone had been working to get the hotel up and running again, which had their tiny staff as high as troops being rallied for war.

Liesel was so proud of her sister. She seemed to have settled right in, taking over the role of captain of their little ship so easily and naturally that it just seemed right to everyone else as well.

Even Lorraine and Kashia, who Liesel had observed so far to be distinctly wary of each other, had warmed to their new owners as quickly as their new owners were warming to life out of the city.

Lorraine in particular had developed a rather slavish devotion to Marilyn.

This morning, they were locked away in the manager's office, trawling their way through accounts and paperwork. Liesel didn't envy Marilyn the job. Lorraine's face on the way in had been like that of a prisoner being taken to the gallows.

Liesel was manning reception, but at the same time trying to fix the meat slicer, which seemed to jam every other day.

To anyone else, the sight of a slip of a girl wielding a huge monkey wrench might seem incongruous, but the role of handyman had had to fall to someone in their household, and seeing as Marilyn had always taken care of their accounts and paperwork, Liesel had felt it only fair that she should do her share and be the one to change plugs and fuses and fix things when they broke. She was therefore the very proud owner of a rather impressive tool set, including a large wrench that had fixed an awful lot of household problems you wouldn't expect a wrench to fix.

Marilyn often joked that Liesel should open up her own handyman business and call it Bash It and Hope, but despite the fact that her methods were pretty haphazard, they had worked okay for them so far.

They didn't seem to be doing the trick on the meat slicer, though. The blooming thing kept getting stuck. Maybe what it needed wasn't BHB (Big Hammer Bashing) but some TLC (Tender Lubricating Care). Liesel put down the wrench and reached for the WD40 instead.

Meat slicer fixed, she took two more bookings for the following week, and then, miracle of miracles in their quiet corner of the world, a party of six people – an elderly couple with their son and daughter-in-law and daughter and son-in-law (at last, guests under fifty!) – phoned on spec to see if there were any rooms available for the next two nights.

With Mr Lockheart due to arrive that morning as well, they were nearly half full.

Liesel, despite being sworn off men, was secretly hoping for a tall, dark, handsome stranger, though a short, cute, blond one would do as well, someone to look at from a distance and very gently flirt with if the occasion called.

Although she hadn't yet given up on her resolution to be more unavailable, she had softened it a little to allow herself some mild flirting at arm's length.

'Things are looking up, Alex,' she grinned as Alex, fresh from television-watching in the tower, skidded in his socks, cape flying, across the hallway to his favourite spot behind the desk.

'Looking up at what, Auntie Leez?'

'Just looking up, honey. It's a saying; it means that things are getting better, more interesting . . .' Liesel glanced up as a tall, dark stranger entered reception. 'Much more interesting,' she murmured, pulling the pen she was chewing out of her mouth and pinning a smile on her lips instead.

'Hello.' The stranger smiled, and Liesel added 'handsome' to complete the cliché.

'Hello. You must be Mr Lockheart.'

'Oh, I must, must I?'

Liesel frowned. 'You're not Mr Lockheart?'

The man leant on the reception desk, cocked a Roger Moore eyebrow at her and winked.

'I can be if you really want me to.'

Liesel was suddenly rather too aware of the grime on her face and in her hair.

'Especially if you're Mrs Hamilton.'

'I'm not Mrs Hamilton . . .'

The smile slipped.

'I'm her sister.'

The smile immediately perked back into place again, but it was too late for observant Liesel, whose first impression had gone from squeeze to sleaze in the same split second.

The smile wasn't real; the smile wanted something.

'You're here to try and sell us something, aren't you,' she said bluntly, convinced now that the smart suit and practised charming smile were those of a salesman.

But the man just laughed easily.

'Actually, you couldn't be further from the truth. I'm here to try and buy something.'

'Buy something?' She blinked in confusion as she sifted through her memory cells, trying to pull up something that she could possibly have of value to sell.

The man held out a hand.

'My name is Sean Sutton.'

He said it like Liesel should know it. She could see him waiting for the recognition and acknowledgement. She remained pointedly blank.

'Of the Sutton Group?' He looked disappointed she hadn't heard of him.

'Sorry.' Liesel shrugged, and then, not a naturally mean person, added, 'But we are new to Cornwall . . .' to try and soften the obvious blow of his anonymity.

'Well, is Mrs Hamilton free?' The confident stranger took a step backwards and looked less sure of himself.

'She's tied up in meetings all morning,' Liesel lied, certain that the last thing Marilyn needed after a morning of accounting was an unscheduled meeting. Unfortunately, Marilyn chose that particular moment to emerge from the office, and Sean Sutton transferred his attentions as quickly and easily as he had lost his smile.

'Ah, you must be Mrs Hamilton. I'm Sean Sutton.'

Liesel was surprised to see Marilyn nod in both greeting and recognition and come over to the man, hand outstretched. He took it. They shook. He held it for a fraction of a second too long afterwards.

'I was wondering if there was somewhere we could talk? In private . . .'

To Liesel's surprise, Marilyn nodded again, and lifting the hatch that gave access into the reception and office areas, gestured him through.

'Sure, come into our world.'

Liesel's frowning gaze followed as her sister led the newcomer into the manager's office. She had left the door open, but Lorraine had chosen that moment to hoover the hall stairs, and so Liesel couldn't hear a thing that was being said.

After five minutes of straining to listen and hearing nothing, she got bored, remembered she hadn't eaten all morning and went into the kitchen to make sandwiches and tea for everyone. She also made a cup of tea for the mysterious Sean Sutton, a not-so-subtle excuse to go into the office and try and catch what was going on, but as she re-emerged from the kitchen, they were already in the vast hall saying their goodbyes,

Sean Sutton once again holding Marilyn's hand for far too long.

He looked over at Liesel, transferring the ingratiating smile to her.

'It was so lovely to meet you both. I'm sure our paths will be crossing again very soon. Very soon indeed,' he added, winking at her, and then he sauntered out.

Liesel took offence at the cocksure wink.

'Creep.' She wrinkled her nose and put her tongue out after his departing back.

'Liesel,' Marilyn warned. 'You need to be nice to him.'

Liesel raised her eyebrows in question.

'Why? I don't even know who the man is.'

'Yes, he found that quite amusing, actually.'

'I bet . . . not.'

'He's Newquay's very own version of Richard Branson.'

'In his own mind or that of the population?'

Marilyn frowned. 'This isn't like you. You don't normally take an instant dislike to people.'

Liesel frowned as well. 'I don't, do I?'

'Maybe it's an adverse reaction to a ferocious instant attraction.' Marilyn winked at her as well.

'Have you been watching fifties movies again in bed?'

'Well, it's the closest I get to a love life.'

'So how did you know who he was?'

'Wait there.'

Marilyn fetched a newspaper from the office and spread it out in front of her sister. Liesel was confronted with a flattering head shot of the man in question, and a headline that shouted 'Local Developer Wins Award – Piran Bay's answer to Richard Branson wins prestigious design award for redevelopment of industrial eyesore'.

'So he gets headlines in the local rag; that's not exactly huge kudos, when the front page is dedicated entirely to a

Girl Guide from Port Gaverne who's just knitted thirty miniature hats for abandoned penguins.'

Marilyn laughed, but shook her finger in reprimand anyway.

'Like I said, you need to be nice.'

'Why?'

'Well, he's just offered to buy the hotel, for starters.'

'Seriously?' Liesel blinked in surprise.

Marilyn nodded. 'A pretty good offer, actually.'

'What did you say?'

'I explained that we weren't in a position to sell the hotel until the end of the season, but that I'd certainly bear it in mind if we make it that far.'

'Of course we will.'

'You think?'

'It's been a doddle so far.'

'Stood behind a desk waiting to book in our one new arrival today? You should come into that office and take a look at the accounts.' Marilyn flicked her eyes from the newspaper to her sister. 'Nancy worked hard her whole life, and had finally got to the point where she didn't need to fill the hotel. Looking at the books, they were keeping themselves under the VAT limit, and under a certain tax level too, hence no advertising, just her sporadic repeaters. We're too small for the coach companies, we're too far off the beaten track for pick-ups; apart from Nancy's repeaters, nobody really knows that the Cornucopia exists.'

'Seriously, are things really that bad?'

'Not bad. But they could be so much better. Nancy had an insurance policy that has made the bank account a little bit healthier, but the actual trading figures are terrible.'

'But we've got enough money to survive the season?'

'We should have, yes. Assuming you and I aren't that bothered about actually taking much in the way of wages.

But it's the end of the season I'm more concerned about. The value of a business is calculated a little differently to a house. The better this place runs, the more it's valued at, and the more we get for Alex when we sell. If we can raise our turnover, it would make a substantial difference. Despite the fact that he wants to develop the hotel into residential apartments, Sean Sutton is offering us the value of the property as a business at the moment. We could make it worth substantially more than that.'

'Well, I'm in . . . and by the way, the new booking system works.'

Marilyn smiled hopefully. 'You mean . . .'

'We've finally taken some bookings,' Liesel announced triumphantly.

'Oh, thank the Lord!' Marilyn was so pleased she clapped her hands like a little girl, and then, as a car pulled up outside, she peered out of the window and announced, 'Ooh, and it looks like Mr Lockheart has just arrived.'

'Tall, dark and handsome?' Liesel asked hopefully.

'Short, bald and ageing,' Marilyn replied.

'Thank heavens for that,' Liesel grinned.

Eric was off sick again.

The dinner menu said that the guests tonight had a choice of soup or pâté, which Eric had fortunately already made, followed by beef Wellington or herb-crusted salmon, which he obviously hadn't. Even Marilyn was daunted.

'Do you think they'd notice if we substituted the beef Wellington with a lasagne and the herb-crusted salmon with cod in breadcrumbs?' she joked weakly, poring over her trusty Nigella.

Liesel shrugged sympathetically.

'Eric could have waited until tomorrow to throw a sickie; once the Lathams and the Stones have checked out tomorrow morning, we're empty again. We should rename this place the *Mary Celeste*. It's been open for years; you'd think they'd have more people who know about it, wouldn't you?'

'We're working on that one; things will get better, I'm sure. Now, we'd better feed the guests we do have or they won't recommend us to their friends, so back to this bloody meal . . .' She wrenched open the store cupboard door. 'We're out of flour.' Her face fell even further.

'Don't panic, there's bound to be some in Eric's back store.'

Whilst Liesel trotted off to the outbuildings where

Eric kept his bulk items, Marilyn began blitzing bread-crumbs, parsley and dill for the herb crust. By the time Liesel stuck her head around the door, fifteen long minutes later, both Marilyn and the salmon were crusted, but she was still feeling pretty damn pleased with herself.

'Come into the hall, sis,' Liesel said, apparently reluctant to come fully into the kitchen.

Marilyn held out her sticky hands and made a 'can't you see I'm too busy for games?' face.

'Come on, I've got something to show you.'

'I take it it's not a bag of self-raising?'

Liesel grinned and shook her head.

'If you want to show it to me, why are you lurking in the doorway?'

'Because I can't come into the kitchen.'

'Why on earth not?'

'Well, you'll find out if you come into the hall,' she replied infuriatingly, and retreated backwards through the swing door.

Marilyn sighed, but washed her hands none the less and followed her sister out into the hall for the big reveal.

Liesel was cradling something that Marilyn couldn't quite make out, but from the gentle way she was holding that something, it was obvious it wasn't the bag of flour she'd gone out to fetch.

Marilyn leaned in closer, to see a pair of huge brown eyes blinking back at her.

'A kitten!'

'I found her outside by the bins.'

'Poor thing, look at the state of her.'

'She's only a baby.'

'And so skinny,' Marilyn cooed, gently taking the little cat from her sister. 'It's like lifting air.'

'I know. You take her into the sitting room, I'll fetch her something to eat.'

Dinner dilemma temporarily forgotten, the two girls focused on feeding the kitten rather than their guests.

'I suppose we'd better call the RSPCA,' Marilyn said reluctantly, as the little cat hungrily hoovered up a plate of pilchards, and then, her belly protruding like she'd just swallowed a tennis ball, looked for a soft, warm bed in the form of Marilyn's lap.

'I think we should keep her.'

Marilyn looked up at her sister hopefully.

'But you don't like cats.'

'It's not that I don't like cats, I just prefer dogs. But you love cats.'

'I know . . . I've always wanted one, but the apartment was hardly pet friendly. Should we really have her in the hotel either?'

'Why not? We have a totally unhygienic dog roaming loose.'

'I know, but at least Godrich knows that he's not allowed in the kitchen or the dining room. It's hard to instil the same kind of boundaries in a cat.'

'But she's got nowhere else to go.' Liesel pretended to pout. 'She's homeless, friendless, she's going to end up as a sad, sorry stray in the local home . . . Look at those eyes, it's like she's talking to you: please keep me, Marilyn, please keep me . . .'

The cat had curled up happily under Marilyn's ample boobs and was purring like a tractor engine.

'Suckered,' Marilyn sighed, but she was grinning broadly, the palm of her hand gently working the soft hairs on the back of the cat's head.

'So what are we going to call her?'

'You think we have a say in this?'

'Okay, what's Alex going to call her?'

'Something totally inappropriate, no doubt. Do you know, he asked me what a todger was yesterday.'

'And what did you tell him?'

Marilyn laughed guiltily. 'I'm afraid I lied and told him it was the name for an old toad.'

Liesel hiccuped with laughter. 'And you're normally so honest with him.'

'I know, but I didn't have the energy to try and explain what vernacular meant.'

'Well, I suppose it would seem logical to an eight-year-old: toad, codger, put them together, todger. Perfect sense.' Liesel winked as Marilyn crossed her eyes and groaned.

The telephone on the reception desk began to ring.

'Saved by the bell!' Liesel quipped, sprinting to answer it.

Ten minutes later, eyes bright with excitement, she was back in with Marilyn, who was still stroking the sleeping kitten.

'We have a full hotel for the weekend!'

'You're kidding!'

'No way. That was a lady called Mrs Greenwood. They've been let down by the Piran Heights, who've apparently been closed by the fire department for having the wrong-shaped smoke detectors or something. It's an eightieth birthday party, sixtieth wedding anniversary this weekend, and they're having a big family reunion. Some of them are coming from far-flung parts of the country and they need somewhere to stay, and they want to know if we can accommodate them instead.'

'Of course we can, we're completely empty!'

'But there's one more thing: tomorrow night there's a party for about sixty people.'

'Oh, lovely.' Marilyn beamed, blissful in her ignorance. 'Where are they having that?'

'Here.' Liesel smiled hopefully at her sister.

Marilyn just about managed to stop herself from hurtling upright so fast she would have sent the kitten flying through the French windows.

'Right, okay,' she said, firmly pushing her dislodged capable hat back on her head. 'We can organise a party in a day, no problem.' She spoke with more conviction than she felt.

'And they want food.'

'For sixty! We only have room for thirty to sit down in the restaurant.'

'I explained that, but they said they're desperate and they'd be happy with a buffet.'

'You still have to sit to eat a buffet. Or perch somewhere, at least.'

'We could put out more tables and chairs on the terrace. The forecast for the weekend is sunshine all the way.'

'Do we have more tables and chairs?'

'There's a load of garden furniture in one of the outhouses. It'll probably need a good scrub-down.'

The magic word 'scrub' conjured up the cleaning genie.

'You want something washing down?' Lorraine asked hopefully.

'What would we do without her?' Liesel laughed, as two minutes later Lorraine headed off with a bucket of soapy water and a new sponge.

'Close?' suggested Marilyn.

'Oh, and there was one other thing. Can we do a cake?'

They both looked at each other.

'Alex!'

A full hotel.

Lorraine wasn't the only one with palpitations.

Thankfully, Eric turned in for work the next morning,

not so bright, but very early, and so full of apologies that they could have asked him to cater for six thousand and he would have bent over backwards to do it.

Alex, once more drafted into the role of assistant chef, was in his element.

'He loves it, doesn't he?' Liesel commented with a smile as Eric showed him the rudiments of a vol-au-vent.

'I think he enjoys spending time with Eric as much as he likes the cooking side of things.'

'Male company.' Liesel winked, 'We all need a bit of it now and then.'

'Unless of course you're sworn off it for the summer.'

'Well, that's better than living in purdah until I'm forty.'

'Purdah can be a very nice place, you know.'

'Sure, but the neighbours are a bit boring.'

Along with the tables and chairs for the terrace, they found coloured lanterns, which they strung around the house and along the balustrade and placed in the centre of the tables.

'Too much?' Marilyn asked when they had finished.

Liesel shook her head. 'It's a party, it looks gorgeous. Just wait till the lights go down and the lanterns are on. It will look so romantic.' She nodded happily. 'For the anniversary.'

'Can you imagine being married that long?' Marilyn mused.

'No way.'

'It would have been my tenth anniversary next year.'

Liesel looked at her sister in surprise. It wasn't often Marilyn mentioned her marriage.

'Really that long?' She feigned ignorance as an encouragement to talk. A blunt 'I know' would have ended the conversation, and she knew that Marilyn talking about Nick meant that she must have been thinking about him for a long time.

Marilyn sighed her affirmation but said nothing else, so Liesel passed her another lantern, and whilst she tied it to a branch of the old cedar tree in the garden asked her, 'Is it hard being here? You know. It being so connected to him.'

'Being here is all about Alex, nothing else,' came the measured reply.

'I know, but Lorraine told me that Nancy said Nick used to come here a lot when he was younger.'

'I know.'

'She told you the same?'

'No, I found some old photographs in Alex's room.'

'You didn't say.'

'Nothing to say really. I asked Alex if he wanted them. He said he didn't, so I put them in a box in the loft, just in case he changes his mind some time in the future.' Marilyn finished tying and turned to face her sister. 'And because I know you're going to ask, no, it didn't upset me, it was just weird.' She shrugged, and then added, 'Some relationships are meant to be and some aren't.'

Liesel, recognising the close in conversation, turned it back to the evening's festivities.

'Well, to be with someone for sixty years is just amazing. No wonder they want to celebrate. Do you think they have a special song?'

Marilyn's mouth fell open in horror.

'Song!' she repeated as though Liesel had just sworn.

'What?'

'Music!' she shrieked. 'You can't have a party without music.'

'I didn't even think about that.' Liesel's shoulders sank. 'What are we going to do?'

'I don't know!' Now Marilyn looked panicked.

'Well, we've got to think of something or it'll be you and me on Alex's karaoke machine singing "It's Raining

Men" and "I Will Survive" over and over again all
night . . .'

Fortunately, Eric knew someone. A phone call later
and they had a DJ on his way.

Eric's friend Disco Dave arrived at three to set up his
equipment. About seventy-two and dressed like the love
child of Elvis Presley and Liberace, he smelt of gin,
peppermints and pipe tobacco and had the broadest
Cornish accent the girls had ever heard. It was pretty
difficult to understand a word he was saying, but by the
time he had assembled his disco booth in the bar with its
festoons of multicoloured tube lighting that flashed in
time to the beat of the music, the hotel was beginning to
look pretty special.

Alex came out just in time to help with the balloons,
until Marilyn found him inhaling helium and singing Bee
Gees songs with Disco Dave, and sent him back into the
kitchen to help Eric instead.

A minibus carrying ten of the guests arrived at five.
They were in remarkably high spirits considering they
had driven down all the way from Blackpool, and made
short work of about thirty of Alex and Eric's scones with
cream and jam, then piled to their rooms to get ready for
the party.

The sound of half a dozen hairdryers running
simultaneously was Liesel's cue to open the bar.

'When women are drying their hair, men are sitting on
the bed pulling on their socks,' she announced. 'Which
means that in about five minutes they'll be heading for the
bar to get in a few quick ones whilst the make-up is going
on. Actually, make that ten minutes: at their age, these
guys will need that long just to bend over to get their
socks on.'

Sure enough, ten minutes later there was a collective

stampede. Despite the fact that they were all on the elderly side, they were a merry bunch out to have a good time.

Mr and Mrs Golightly and their friends the Emersons were the ringleaders. They bought cocktails all round for everyone in the bar, including Liesel, who had to politely decline several times before they gave up asking, and then cajoled Disco Dave into starting up early by feeding him several vodka martinis, stirred not shaken, none of which, unfortunately, he politely declined.

When the other guests began to arrive, those already *in situ* were already conga-ing around the house to the delightful strains of 'Agadoo'.

'It's going to be a fun evening!' Marilyn sighed, rolling her eyes in amusement.

'Always better than a dull one.' Liesel grinned happily.

By eight thirty, they had a hotel full of partying people. The music was loud, the conversation, trying to be heard above the music, louder still, punctuated with raucous laughter, rude jokes and snatches of song. The happy couple, who didn't look a day over seventy, had bought champagne all round, and drunk people were falling on the food like ravenous, but appreciative, vultures.

Kashia had been asked to come in for the evening to help out. She and Lorraine were in charge of the buffet, keeping it topped up until the food ran out or the guests exploded, collecting plates and cutlery. Marilyn, Eric and Alex were in the kitchen, keeping the supply as endless as possible, Alex wallowing in a new-found joy regarding vol-au-vents and what could go in the little pastry cases other than prawns or mushrooms.

Liesel was serving drinks and being chatted up by the nineteen-year-old grandson of the couple whose anniversary it was. Seemingly the only person in the building under forty, and reluctant to join the old fogeys, he had found huge solace in the fact that the barmaid reminded him a little of his fantasy poster girl, Kelly Brook, though 'Luscious Liesel' as he had only dared to name her in his head, had a cuter nose.

As the sun went down, everyone gravitated outside. The terrace looked like something out of a fairy tale, the multicoloured lights swinging gently in the light breeze and reflecting across the water.

Disco Dave had had far too many martinis and was playing Christmas songs, but no one seemed to mind; in fact, it somehow added to the festive atmosphere.

At ten, as instructed by the Greenwoods, Eric brought out the layered cake that Alex had made the previous evening. Expertly iced that day by Eric, it had turned from a very tasty but rather wonky leaning tower of sponge into a three-tier fantasy of white icing and multicoloured sugar roses.

'That guy is just amazing,' Marilyn sighed, noticing as Eric lit the candles that he had a tear in his eye. 'He takes such pride in his work.' And then, as the happy couple blew out the candles to raucous cheers from gathered friends and relatives, 'It's going really well, isn't it? Then again it should be, considering we've been working on this almost nonstop for the last twenty-four hours.' As if to prove a point, she yawned widely.

'You holding up okay?'

Marilyn nodded. 'Brings new meaning to the phrase "exhausted but happy".'

'I'd still rather use it in relation to sex,' Liesel grinned.

'What's sex?' Marilyn sighed.

'You know that thing you had to do to conceive your son? Talking of whom, where is he?' Liesel said, stepping into the hall and looking around for her nephew.

'At ten thirty at night?' Marilyn looked at her watch and raised her eyebrows. 'In bed, of course.'

'You think?'

'That's where I sent him over an hour ago.'

Liesel indicated the buffet table in the dining room with an incline of her head.

Marilyn squinted, seeing nothing out of order until she looked from the tabletop, where her eyes were naturally drawn, to the table bottom. A pair of feet and a plumed tail were sticking out from underneath the white linen cloth. The plumed tail was wagging, the feet tapping in time to 'Let It Snow'.

Marilyn lifted the tablecloth.

Her son's peachy skin and the dog's hairy face were both covered in crumbs sweet and savoury and the ominous dark stain of chocolate cake.

Godrich thumped his tail weakly.

Alex's guilty smile was just as feeble.

Such was his awareness of his own behaviour, it only needed one word.

'Bed!' thundered Marilyn, and they both shot off across the hall and through the tower door.

The last guest went to bed just before midnight.

Eric had been working like a Trojan and was looking a little peaky, so Marilyn had insisted that he go home. Before he left, however, *he* had insisted on making a quick casserole for the girls and had left dinner plated up in the oven for when they finished, so, dining room finally cleared, they headed into the kitchen to eat.

Kashia had finished with the dishwasher, and collecting three large plates of stew from the oven, unexpectedly served Liesel and Marilyn and then sat down with her own food.

Liesel threw a surprised 'thanks' to Kashia and then noticed that Lorraine was still plateless.

'You sit, I'll fetch,' she said cheerfully, putting her hand on Lorraine's shoulder and steering her to a chair before she could make her excuses and bolt for home. It was still easier to get Alex to go to bed than it was to get Lorraine to sit down and eat with them. Liesel was convinced that if she could get her comfortable enough to do this, then it would be some miracle breakthrough, a major crack in the protective shell the girl had enamelled around herself.

But the oven was bare.

'Kashia, were there four plates in here?'

'I no see,' Kashia said without looking up. 'Is hot, I carry three, cannot carry four, so I no look for other plate.'

'Well, there's nothing in here.'

'I'm not really hungry anyway.' Lorraine was already pushing back her chair.

'Don't be daft.' Marilyn handed Lorraine her own plate, and Liesel automatically fetched another and shared her food with Marilyn.

'That's not enough for you both.' Lorraine's eyes widened in horror, and she pushed the plate back towards Marilyn.

Marilyn immediately pushed it back again.

'I've had five vol-au-vents this evening. Alex made me try every flavour, even the jelly and custard ones. I'll be lucky if I can get this much down.'

Lorraine looked pleadingly at Liesel.

'I had eight.' Liesel grinned at her. 'I particularly enjoyed the ice cream and hot tinned pineapple ones. Yum.'

With no excuse or get-out, Lorraine had no option but to eat, but despite the fact that Eric's food was, as always, delicious, it looked as though she was struggling to get it down.

Kashia ate as though there were ravenous dogs waiting to steal her food from her, then pushed back her chair and announced, 'I must to leave now,' before grabbing her coat and stampeding out of the building.

As soon as she had gone, Liesel, who hated conflict, decided to grab the bullshit by the horns and try and sort out what was going on.

'Have you two had a falling-out?' she enquired as nonchalantly as possible. Marilyn raised her eyebrows at her sister. Asking Lorraine that was like asking Napoleon if he fancied invading a country tomorrow.

'I don't know what you mean,' Lorraine said, her lips barely moving as she spoke.

'Come on, Lol, it's no secret you two aren't exactly the best of friends on a good day, but tonight . . .' She left it open and deliberately continued to look at Lorraine until the girl was forced to answer.

'It was just a silly misunderstanding, that's all.'

'About what?'

'Trousers,' Lorraine muttered.

'Trousers?' Liesel repeated, eyes crossing in surprise.

'She got ketchup on them at breakfast. When she changed to go home she forgot them. I knew she couldn't work in dirty clothes tonight, so I popped them in the washing machine because I was doing the duvet cover from room four and they were both the same colour, and Kashia hasn't got a washing machine where she lives so I knew it would mean an extra trip to the launderette when she always does her washing on Tuesday nights. I hung them up in the courtyard along with the duvet cover to dry and when I went to fetch them in they were gone. I've looked everywhere but I can't find them, and so now she thinks I've stolen her trousers.'

'She thinks you've stolen her trousers?' Liesel repeated incredulously. Kashia was at least a foot taller then Lorraine. 'What would you steal her trousers for? To use as a hammock?'

'I wouldn't steal anything,' Lorraine replied earnestly, totally missing the joke.

'We know you wouldn't.' Marilyn patted Lorraine's back consolingly. 'Don't worry, we'll have a word with Kashia and see if we can't get things sorted out.'

Marilyn checked that Alex was once more safely in bed, and then the sisters, both at the stage where they'd gone too far to sleep, sat out on the terrace with the lights twinkling and a glass of wine each.

'What is it with those two?' Liesel yawned and stretched out her legs to rest her tired feet on the stone balustrade.

'They just don't get on.' Marilyn shrugged.

'They don't even try.'

'Not everyone is nice to each other, Leez.'

'But they have to spend so much time together, you'd think they'd make the effort.'

'Maybe they think that friendship should be effortless, and if you have to try, then it's not meant to be.'

'Anything worth having is worth working for.' Liesel quoted one of Marilyn's favourite sayings back at her.

'Do you still believe that?'

'Having had it drummed into me since I was sixteen and complaining about studying for my exams, you think I'd just forget it?'

'I just thought that maybe after slogging your guts out in this place for the past few weeks you might have changed your mind. You've worked so hard, Leez, I'm really grateful.'

'I'm enjoying it. And I'm grateful too.'

'What, that I've dragged you down to the sticks to work you like a donkey?'

'No, that you've got me out of dirty, smoky old London to one of the most beautiful places I've ever seen, and away from two jobs that I hated to doing something that I'm actually having fun with.'

They looked at each other for a moment.

'Should we hug now, do you think.'

'Oh, definitely.'

Marilyn wrapped her arms around her sister and hugged her warmly, breathing in the familiar scent of her hair, which, as always, smelt of flowers. No matter what Liesel did, her hair always smelt of flowers. She could roll around in a cow pat and come up smelling of forget-me-nots.

'Are you really enjoying it?'

Liesel nodded. 'Absolutely. You?'

'Knackered but happy. Talking of which, we have another early start tomorrow, so bed when we've finished our wine, okay?'

'Yes, Mum.'

Liesel was dreaming.

She was riding a white horse along the beach, galloping through the surf as it broke on the sand, and then the horse turned into the break of the surf and she was in the sea, the salt water covering her face, smothering her, no air to breathe . . .

'Auntie Leez, Auntie Leez, wake up, wake up!'

Liesel shot bolt upright in alarm, spitting out the edge of the duvet, which she had somehow managed to get in her mouth, to find Alex jumping agitatedly on the side of her bed.

'What is it, what is it?' she gasped in panic, convinced from the stricken look on his face and the panicked note in his voice that the hotel was on fire at the very least.

'It's Godrich.'

'Oh no,' Liesel groaned. 'What's that stupid dog done now?'

Forcing her eyes open, she looked at the alarm clock on her bedside table. It was ten to four; she'd had exactly two hours and twenty minutes' sleep, and she was due to get up again at six.

'I woke up and he was gone, so I went to look for him and someone had left the tower door open and he's gone in the dining room and got stuck in the big dresser where Kashia keeps all her stuff and he can't get out!'

'He's what?' Liesel wasn't quite sure if she was still dreaming. What Alex was saying really didn't make much sense.

'He's stuck!' Alex repeated, and taking her hand he tugged her from the bed and towed her down the narrow stairs and through into the hotel dining room.

The dog had somehow pushed his head through the ornate fretwork of the door. The old worm-eaten wood was fragile enough to allow him in, but resolutely refused to budge to let him pull out, and Godrich was whining, unhappy and uncomfortable. Liesel didn't know whether to laugh or panic.

'What on earth was he doing?'

'I think he wanted that,' Alex replied, pointing to a plate of congealed food pushed to the back of the cupboard.

'So that's where Lorraine's dinner went to. Why on earth would someone put it in there . . . and *oh my word,*' Liesel exclaimed, pulling back as a foul smell assaulted her nostrils, 'why has it gone off so quickly?'

'I don't think the smell is Lorraine's dinner. I think it's Godrich. I think he's been sick,' Alex replied, wrinkling his nose.

'Inside the cupboard?'

The boy nodded.

'Where's the key?'

'Kashia has it.'

'Great.'

The dog began to whine.

'Can we cut him out?' Alex pleaded.

'We could try, but I'd worry about cutting *him*, he's jammed in so tightly. I think I'm going to have to call the vet.'

'But it's four o'clock in the morning.'

'Don't I know it,' Liesel replied, yawning pointedly,

and then smiled reassuringly at Alex's distraught face. 'Don't you worry, they'll have an emergency number. Someone will come out, especially when I tell them he's sick too. Tell you what, I'll get the phone and you grab the *Yellow Pages*.'

Whilst they were gone, Godrich's whine turned into a howl.

At this rate he'd wake the entire hotel, Liesel thought. They hurried back to the dining room, Liesel punching in the vet's number as Alex called it out from the book.

'Hi, do you do home visits? I've got a sick stuck dog . . .'

Liesel covered the receiver and mouthed at Alex, 'What is he?'

'He's a dog, silly,' Alex replied

'I meant what kind of dog?'

Alex shrugged. 'A big one?' he offered.

'A big one,' Liesel repeated into the phone. 'A big *loud* one,' she added as Godrich began to howl again. 'I'm sorry, but we're really not sure. The only thing we're positive about is that he's sick . . . What's that? You want us to bring him in?'

She looked over at Godrich, his head wedged firmly in the fretwork of the huge dresser.

'Well I suppose I could, if I can find a saw . . .' she suggested hesitantly, and then smiled in relief. 'You'll send someone straight out? Oh, that's wonderful, thank you.'

Despite the pressure on his voice box, Godrich managed to let out the loudest, most mournful of howls.

'Hello?' called a tremulous voice. It was Marilyn, in her dressing gown and slippers, looking dark-eyed and tired. 'What on earth's going on? The halls are alive with the sound of Godrich.'

'Even at this hour you can still manage it, can't you.'

Marilyn grinned. 'I'm your sister, it's my job.'

'Well, I'm afraid it's also your job to help look after Godrich.'

'What's wrong with him?'

'He's stuck, and he's been sick,' Liesel said bluntly, stepping back to reveal Godrich's predicament to her sister.

Marilyn shook her head in wonderment.

'I won't even ask how or why.'

Godrich howled again, and more footsteps filled the corridor.

It was a contingent from the party: Mr and Mrs Emerson, Mrs Emerson resplendent in her curlers, closely followed by Mr and Mrs Golightly, still tipsy from the way they wobbled slightly as they walked.

'Everything okay, dears?'

Liesel didn't have to explain again; they took in the situation at a glance.

'We've got a large pot of Vaseline in the room,' offered Mr Golightly.

Fortunately, only Liesel and Marilyn noticed the saucer eyes and sharp-elbowed nudge from Mrs Golightly. Alex was in the window seat, looking out, anxiously.

'Vet's here!' he yelled, flying off to let him in.

Thank goodness, sighed Liesel, who hadn't relished the idea of getting elbow-deep in Mr and Mrs Golightly's Vaseline and then having to anoint Godrich with it as well. She stopped stroking the shaking dog and turned around, still on her knees, to see Marilyn with her mouth hanging open, Mrs Emerson hurriedly whipping out her curlers, and even the portly Mrs Golightly rearranging the neckline of her dressing gown to reveal a touch more ample cleavage, which didn't go unnoticed by Mr Golightly, whose own reaction was to puff out his chest, take his wife by the hand, and lead her back towards their bedroom.

Liesel tried to steal a glance sideways to see what all the fuss was about, but Mrs Emerson was firmly in the way. Then Godrich howled again mournfully, and she hurriedly stepped aside to let the vet through.

Liesel couldn't see his face; she could just see a fit body. Liesel liked a fit body as much as any girl, but she knew that for Marilyn to be gobsmacked he must be a bit more than just fit.

His Barbour jacket was discarded on the floor next to the dresser to reveal a broad chest covered by a soft brown cashmere jumper, with a shirt underneath, both pushed up at the sleeves to show strong tanned forearms; dark chocolate jeans encased firm thighs, and Caterpillar boots appeared alongside Liesel's bare feet as he kneeled down beside her and was finally revealed in full. Well, in profile anyway.

He had dark hair that fell in a silken flop of fringe across his face as he bent to reassure the animal, and beyond that Liesel could see a straight nose, firm mouth, long eyelashes, and such good skin a girl could get jealous.

In fact, he was devastatingly good looking, beautiful almost.

And he was so *not* her type.

Liesel always went for the same thing: a cheeky smile and the gift of the gab. She liked wonky mouths, noses that were crooked or slightly too big, beautiful imperfections. She did not go for gorgeous.

'This is Godrich,' she said, stroking the dog's shaking withers.

'I know. Godrich and I are old friends.'

'Why doesn't that surprise me?'

Careful hands and a small hacksaw released Godrich with surprising speed. The vet gently checked the dog's eyes and his stomach, then sat back on his haunches.

'No harm done, by the looks of things, although I'm afraid the same can't be said about your dresser.'

'So he's okay?' Liesel said, smiling encouragingly at Alex.

'He's fine. Aren't you, Godrich? What I can tell you, however, which obviously hasn't been passed on to you, is that he has an ongoing reflux problem, which basically means he struggles to digest his food, and when he gets stressed or nervous—'

'He pukes.' Alex put it bluntly.

The vet nodded. 'Nancy had him on a special diet.'

'You knew Nancy?'

'Well, seeing as Godrich gets the veterinary equivalent of frequent flyer miles for his trips to the surgery, I got to know her quite well.'

'What was she like?'

'Smart. But a total sucker when it came to this animal. Apart from the reflux, he's pretty healthy, but he's learnt that being ill means getting special attention.'

'He's a canine hypochondriac?' Liesel suggested.

'Exactly,' he said, straightening up. 'See what I mean?' he added as the recently released Godrich rolled his eyes, staggered sideways and slumped diva-like on to the floor, opening one eye after a couple of seconds to see why no one had immediately rushed to his attention.

'I must admit, we have been struggling with him a little.'

'Well, animal emotions are obviously not quite as complex as human ones, but they're not as simplistic as some people think.'

'So you're saying he's . . .'

'Weird.' The vet nodded, with a slight smile at Marilyn. 'Nancy Hamilton used to baby him. I think if he's treated more like the dog he is than the child substitute Nancy made him, he might straighten out a little.'

Marilyn nodded her agreement.

'Thank you so much, Mr . . . er . . .'

'Tom Spencer.' He held out a hand. 'We'll probably be seeing quite a lot of each other, I'm afraid.'

'I'm Marilyn, this is my son Alex, and this is my sister . . .'

He shook Marilyn's hand, then Alex's, and then turned to Liesel, who held out her own hand . . . and kind of lost it halfway there, as only now she was looking directly at him did she notice his eyes.

They were almond-shaped, and the colour of them seemed to flit light and liquid between gold and green.

If there was just one thing where Liesel was a sucker for gorgeous, it was eyes, and oh my Lord, were his eyes beautiful.

'Hi, I'm Lee . . . Lee . . . Lee . . .' she stuttered, mesmerised.

Only Marilyn trying to muffle her laughter brought her back to her senses.

'Liesel.' She spat it out like a sneeze.

'Bless you,' Marilyn mouthed from behind him.

Tom Spencer smiled, and heaven help her, he had a lopsided smile, one that turned up at one corner just a bit more than the other.

'I take it your mother liked *The Sound of Music*?'

'I . . . er . . . I . . .' She began to stutter again, told herself firmly to 'Pull yourself together, woman!' and managed thankfully to focus on the too-perfect features and progress to regular speech. 'How did you guess? I mean, I know it's pretty obvious, but not always so instantly.'

'My mother was the same.'

'Tom Cruise?' Marilyn suggested.

He shook his head. 'No, I'm afraid as a teenager she was madly in love with Tom Jones.'

'Well, it's not unusual,' she quipped back with a wink at her sister.

Tom rolled his eyes in exactly the same way that Liesel did when she got the *Sound of Music* puns.

'I get it all the time too,' Liesel sympathised. 'You wouldn't believe how many jokes there are about *The Sound of Music*.'

'I know what you mean. My worst one, being a vet is "What's New, Pussycat".'

'Well, every time you tend to a goat, think of Liesel,' Marilyn said.

' "Lonely Goatherd"?' He nodded, and grinned again, and this time Liesel noticed that he had a slightly crooked eye tooth. Oh Lord, another imperfection.

Just then his beeper went off.

'Sorry. That's me again. Got to run, I'm afraid.'

He suddenly looked so tired that Liesel had to fight an overwhelming urge to offer to lend him her bed for a quick refresher

'Up all night, eh?' she said, and then blushed furiously at the connotations, and then blushed some more because she was blushing and that was a dead giveaway that she was embarrassingly aware of the unintentional double entendre.

But then Mrs Emerson put a hand on Tom Spencer's arm and asked, 'I don't suppose you could take a look at my chest before you shoot off?'

'He's a vet, love, not a doctor,' her husband interjected, shaking his head in mirth.

'I know that, but I still wouldn't mind him looking at my chest,' she chortled.

Liesel could have happily hugged her. It always made a person feel better when someone else made a bigger idiot of themselves than you.

*

'I want to be a vet when I grow up,' Alex announced as he watched Tom Spencer drive off in his big black Range Rover.

'And Liesel wants to *do* a vet when she grows up,' Marilyn replied, winking at Liesel.

'What do you mean, Mum?'

'Nothing, my angel,' Marilyn grinned, slinging an arm round his shoulders and kissing his ruffled hair. 'Come on, let's get you and Godrich back to bed, eh?'

'You mean that Auntie Leez fancies Tom the vet, don't you?' Liesel heard Alex ask as his mother shepherded him off.

'No, she doesn't!' Liesel protested a touch too loudly.

'When someone's eyes almost pop out of their head like on a Tom and Jerry cartoon, does that mean they fancy someone?'

'Quite often, yes,' Marilyn replied, grinning back over her shoulder at Liesel.

'Either that or they're being throttled by their sister,' Liesel threw back at her.

'In that case, I think Mrs Emerson fancied Tom the vet.'

'Oh yes, definitely.'

'And the kitten fancies mice.'

'No, when the kitten's eyes bulge it's because she wants to eat the mice.'

'Does that mean Auntie Leez wants to eat Tom?' Alex joked.

'Actually, Alex, I think she could eat him all up, yes.'

The jokes continued over an early Saturday morning breakfast of bacon sandwiches. Albeit extremely bad jokes.

'Do you fancy *tom* . . . ato ketchup on your sarnie, Liesel?' was the worst thing Marilyn managed.

'There are more pressing issues than the fact that I *might* have found the vet last night *slightly* attractive.' Liesel, who had been trying hard to ignore the comments, finally bit back.

'You mean trouser pressing issues.' Marilyn was obviously in a jovial mood.

'That's the one.' Liesel managed to smile this time.

'We need to have a chat with them. They can't carry on like this.'

'I agree.'

'So you take Kashia and I'll talk to Lorraine.'

'Great. You get the pussycat and I'll try and pull the thorn out of the lion's paw.'

'Well, you're always saying that people are your thing . . . but if you don't think you can handle Kashia . . .'

'I didn't say that.'

'So you'll talk to her?'

'Sure.'

'Before we serve breakfast?'

'Before we serve breakfast.' Liesel nodded an affirmation.

'Good.' Marilyn pushed one of Alex's freshly laundered capes across the table towards her. 'You'd better take one of these with you just in case you need to make a quick exit.'

Liesel cornered Kashia in the dining room as she was setting out the cereals.

'I hide dinner as Lorraine have stolen my trousers,' Kashia announced, her heavily accented voice spitting out the name with murderous venom.

'We spoke to Lorraine about this last night and she didn't steal your trousers, Kashia.'

'She did, she take the trousers and she no give them back to me.'

'Why on earth would Lorraine steal your trousers?'

'She no like me. She is mean to me.'

'So because you think she stole your trousers, you hid her dinner in the dresser?'

Kashia nodded triumphantly. 'She steal my trousers, I hide her dinner. Tatty titty.'

'She means tit for tat,' piped up a voice from behind the door.

'Thank you, Alex.'

'I've been teaching her English,' he added proudly, coming into view.

'Talking of English, I think your mum said something about some homework?' Liesel said pointedly.

'He is good boy,' Kashia said, watching him wave back at her as he left the room. 'He is my friend now.'

'I wish you and Lorraine could be friends.'

Kashia's response was a derisive snort.

'Why can't you just get on with each other?'

'We too different peoples.'

'Different can be good. Different can complement.'

'She is mad with the cleaning, how you say obsession, she drive me to crazy, always with the dust cloth and the polish, and always so busy with things she must do that are done already. You know how many times she clean the same thing over and over. Always is never good enough. She is same with me, things I do, always is never good enough. She drive me to crazy, by being a crazy. Is not fair.'

'Okay, I agree, she can be a little overzealous sometimes.'

'What you say this word zealous?'

'A bit too keen. She likes things done right, which is good, but she works *much* too hard to make sure that things are done properly.'

Kashia nodded. 'Is true. You is right. She try to still be like it was with first Mrs Hamilton, but that is wrong thing to be. I no ever speak bad of gone peoples, but is good first Mrs Hamilton no here any more. She is hard lady. Your Mrs Hamilton much better lady. Much fair. She say I do good job. She no say I must to work harder all the time when I already is trying to work very hard anyways.'

'We know you work hard, Kashia,' Liesel said sincerely. 'We're really happy with your work.'

For a moment Kashia once again looked wary, but then Liesel saw a vulnerability break through the mask, and Kashia looked so fragile it made her want to cry.

'You thinks I is good?'

'Yes, we thinks . . . I mean we do think you are good. In fact we think you're brilliant and there's no way we could do without you. You've been so good we were going to ask you to come and do dinners as well.'

'You have enough need of me?'

Liesel nodded furiously. It wasn't exactly a lie. She had discussed the possibility with Marilyn. It might mean money would be a bit tighter, but they'd find a way.

'What do you think? Would you like that?'

'I have job in evenings but I no like it. The man who own bar is not nice man. He is evil man. He is Satan.'

'How about it then? Are you going to phone Satan and tell him you quit?'

'You mean it? You have me here evenings?'

Liesel nodded. 'But no more goading Lorraine, okay?'

'How you mean, goating?'

'Goading,' Liesel repeated, emphasising the 'd'. 'It means this.' And holding out a finger, she gently poked Kashia repeatedly in the ribs until she actually started to laugh.

'Oh, I see how is,' Kashia said, stepping away and recovering her composure. 'To goating is to be very annoying.'

'That's the one.' Liesel grinned.

'Okays then. If you keep promise to stop Lorraine goating me about my works, I will promise to stop goating her.'

Liesel nodded her agreement, and then held out a hand to shake for good measure.

'Deal,' she said.

'Deals,' repeated Kashia, taking it and shaking, and then to Liesel's amazement, Kashia hugged her.

Breakfast was almost as busy as dinner. Eric had called in sick again, so Liesel was in charge of the bacon and sausages, whilst Marilyn tried to replicate Eric's famous scrambled eggs, Lorraine brewed the tea and coffee and stirred the beans and tomatoes, and Kashia, good mood ruined by Eric's absence, muttering in Polish throughout, charred her way sullenly through two loaves of bread, before battering them rather them buttering them, viciously stabbing the Cornish Gold butter and wielding the knife like Sweeney Todd with a back order for pies.

Liesel glanced sideways at Kashia, decided that she was too busy with the toast to eavesdrop, and lowered her voice.

'You know what we discussed about Kashia waiting on at night so you or I are freed up to spend more time with Alex . . .'

'Yes, and we agreed that although it would be good, we couldn't afford to . . .' Marilyn trailed off as she realised Liesel had her 'Father forgive me for what I have done' face on. 'And so you've gone ahead and asked her anyway.'

'Sorry, Maz, it just seemed like the right thing to do at the time. She's so insecure. I think the trouble between her and Lorraine could be solved by her feeling more involved here . . . and if we're honest, it would make a difference to us too. I know the money side of things isn't exactly great . . .'

Marilyn silenced her sister by holding up her whisk.

'We'll work it out.'

'Oh, I knew you'd say that.' Liesel beamed.

'To be honest, with Eric and his regular sickies, we need the help even more,' Marilyn added.

'I hope he's okay.'

'He just seemed to go downhill last night. When he arrived he was fine, going great guns in fact, right up until the happy couple came in to say cheers, and then he just faded like a flower with no water. Talking of which, do you think Godrich's still looking a little peaky?'

Liesel frowned in confusion at the sudden change of subject. Godrich looked perfectly fine to her.

'You think he looks ill?'

'Well . . .' Marilyn smacked her lips together and blew, like a mechanic appraising a car engine, 'that wouldn't be for me to say, would it; we'd need the opinion of an expert . . . like the vet.'

'Oh Marilyn, don't start.'

'Why not? He was cute and you know it.'

'So not my type.'

'Good. It's about time you had a bit of variety, considering your type is usually a total waste of space.'

Liesel was about to argue the point, but then, realising that Marilyn was right actually, laughed instead.

'Maybe. But put your spoon away, Marilyn. I have no intention of getting involved with anyone whilst we're here.'

'I know, I know, your new vow of chastity or celibacy or whatever it was you'd decided on.'

'Both,' Liesel said firmly, and then, after a few moments, added almost too nonchalantly, 'And someone that good looking couldn't possibly be single anyway.'

'There wasn't a ring on *that* finger.'

'You noticed that?'

'Me and every other woman in the room apart from you.'

'All the other women were pensioners.'

'And they still looked. Now that tells you something.'

'Okay, so there was something about him.'

'Something about him?' Marilyn repeated. 'Liesel, he was bloody gorgeous. If I was a few years younger I could get my teeth sunk in myself.'

'A few years younger! You're probably the same age.'

'Exactly. Which means he's too young for me. Never go out with someone the same age as yourself.'

'Why on earth not?'

'Because men tend to age better and you don't want your other half to look younger than you.'

'Or prettier?'

'He's not prettier than you. You're beautiful.'

'You're biased.'

'Maybe, but I'm still right. You two would make a lovely couple.'

'Marilyn, how can you say that? We don't even know the guy.'

'I'm just being shallow for once and going on looks.'

'He was gorgeous, wasn't he?'

'Finally she listens.'

'But I'm still not going to make an idiot of myself by carting Godrich in to see him again when he's quite clearly not sick.'

Wasn't it strange how sometimes when you adamantly declared something to be true, fate decided to step in and call you a liar? Despite Liesel's proclamation that Godrich was now in the prime of health, the same day brought more drama as Alex's familiar wail once more came floating through the hotel.

'Auntie Leez! Auntie Leez!'

Liesel came running from the downstairs ladies' loo, where a stubbornly dripping tap needed a good bashing with her wrench.

'What is it, Alex? What is it?' she panted breathlessly, suddenly experiencing a not totally pleasant stab of déjà vu.

'Godrich's been sick again.'

'Have you been giving him Mars bars?'

'No, I didn't, I promise. I don't think he's well for real this time.'

'Where is he?'

'In the sitting room. He's really poorly, Auntie Leez, honest . . .'

Lorraine was already there with a mop and bucket and the disinfectant.

'Dog's ill.' Even she was convinced, and there was no sign of the usual bad acting that came with Godrich playing up for attention: the eyeball-rolling and the fake groaning; in fact, he looked pretty limp and lifeless and his usually shifting eyes were a little sunken.

'We'd better get him to the vet,' Liesel said quickly. 'Go call your mum to come home from the wholesaler now, tell her we need the car.'

But when she tried to lift Godrich, he groaned in pain.

'I'm going to have to ask them to come out . . .' Liesel called Alex back. 'Don't worry, they'll send someone out to fix him.'

She pulled her mobile from her back pocket and hurriedly punched in the number.

'Hi, it's Liesel Ellis from the Cornucopia. I'm afraid Godrich's not very well again. I'd bring him in but he's refusing to move, and every time I try to pick him up he cries out in pain . . . No, I know he's a bigger showman than David Blaine, but this time I truly think he's sick. In fact I'm quite worried. You'll get someone out to us? Oh, thank you so much.' She gave a thumbs-up to Alex, who was starting to look tearful.

Twenty minutes and a touch too much vomit later, and a silver Volvo estate pulled into the driveway. Liesel and Lorraine were watching from the hallway.

'It can't be the vet, it's not his car,' said Liesel.

'Well, we're not expecting any new guests to check in.'

'No, but it could be someone coming on spec.'

'I don't think so, they're wearing wellies.'

They watched as the newcomer got out of the car. He was short and dark and was wearing round John Lennon glasses to go with an almost Beatles-style pudding-bowl haircut. He had a sweet, friendly face set in a smile that was rather shy.

'That's definitely the vet,' Lorraine said, looking at the big doctor-style bag he was carrying and what appeared to be the standard-issue Barbour he was wearing.

'Just not the vet I was hoping for . . .' Liesel muttered

to herself, surprised by her own admission and the disappointment she felt.

'Hi, you called for a vet?'

Well, that settled it. It was the vet. It just wasn't *the* vet.

He held out a hand. 'Adrian Lee.'

Of course. Spencer, Childs and Lee.

It was a three-in-one chance of getting the delectable Spencer, and this time her luck was out. This was the Lee branch of the outfit.

Liesel tried to hide her thumping disappointment. After all, the man was here because the dog was sick, not because she was lovesick . . . Oops, that one had slipped into her thoughts like Godrich sliding into the pantry. Was she lovesick? No. She couldn't be. She didn't even know the man. He wasn't her type. And what was more, she was in a period of self-imposed purdah; she had promised herself a break from the rigours of romance. Her first instincts had been right: she had sworn off men for the summer, and that was how things should stay.

'Focus, Liesel,' she muttered under her breath, and forcing a thankful smile, she greeted Adrian Lee and took him through to the sitting room, where Godrich was collapsed on the rug with his head on Alex's lap. Both boy and dog were looking woeful, despite the fact that Marilyn had just come back from the cash-and-carry and was doing her best to reassure Alex that Godrich would be fine.

Adrian Lee knelt down next to them and smiled gently at Alex.

'Is he your dog?'

Alex nodded. 'My great-auntie left him to me. I'm supposed to take care of him.'

'Well, don't you worry, we'll make him all better for you. He's been sick, right?'

'Four times.' Alex nodded, and pointed at Lorraine. 'Lorraine cleaned it up every time.'

'Good for Lorraine.' Adrian Lee smiled appreciatively at her, and Lorraine still on hand with mop and bucket and industrial-size bottle of disinfectant, blushed furiously.

Liesel looked at her in surprise. She hadn't even known that pale-skinned Lorraine *could* blush.

'Let's take a look at him, shall we? I have to say, he does look rather sorry for himself . . .'

He gently felt Godrich's stomach, and the dog promptly lifted his head and threw up on his wellies.

'Oh Lord, I'm so sorry!' Marilyn blurted, as if she had done it herself.

'Well, it's better out than in, as my mother used to say, and at least I know what's wrong with him now.'

Adrian Lee stepped back, gingerly took his wellies off, and inspected the damage, nodding thoughtfully.

'He's eaten something he shouldn't have.'

'Like what?'

'Well, unless I'm very much mistaken,' he pointed to the mess, 'that is a part-digested chocolate bar wrapper. Chocolate is really bad for dogs, especially when it's still wrapped in paper and foil.'

'Is he going to be okay?' Alex sniffed guiltily.

'I would think so. I'm just going to give him a quick injection, to help his poor tummy settle a touch, and if you can make sure he has access to plenty of water, please, young man . . . Plenty of water, but no more chocolate, okay?'

Alex nodded, his elfin face serious but etched with his obvious relief.

Lorraine, who'd hastily scuttled away with the vet's wellies as soon as he'd taken them off, now returned with them cleaner than they had been when he had first arrived. After shoving them towards Liesel, who chose to ignore her, she finally gave in and handed them shyly back to Adrian Lee herself.

'Wow, spotless, thank you.'

Lorraine smiled, the goofiest little smile Liesel had ever seen on her normally terrified or tense face; and then she turned and ran.

'He's starting to look better already,' Marilyn said not long after the young vet had left them. Godrich's eyes had lost the glassy, glazed look that had worried them so much.

But since the dog had been pronounced out of danger, Liesel had been thinking about Lorraine.

'Did you see that?'

'What?'

'Lorraine was . . . well, for want of a better word, mooning.'

'Mooning?' Marilyn immediately had terrible visions of Lorraine waving her bare bottom at the young vet.

'You know, all eyes and longing.'

'Oh, I see. Relief. You think she liked him?'

'Oh yes, I think so.'

'What is it with the vets in this town and the people in this hotel? All we need now is for Childs to turn up and steal Kashia's heart and we have a full set.'

'Or yours.'

'Right.' Marilyn snorted with derision, 'And knowing my luck, Childs will be seventy-two with a limp and halitosis.'

'And you'll still fall for him, knowing you and your soft spot for lame ducks.'

'I don't think so. I already have the only man I want in my life.'

'You can't live solely for Alex.'

'Why not?'

'Because it wouldn't be fair on him to be the only focus

for your heart. That's a weighty responsibility for a kid. I can just imagine him as a teenager, saddled with one of those sad, clinging mothers who hate every single girlfriend they ever have and throw a wobbly if they don't phone home every day . . . that's if you ever let him leave home. You'll probably blackmail him into living with you until he's in his forties.'

Marilyn was laughing.

'Well, sometimes overdramatisation is the only way to make you see sense.' Liesel excused the picture she had painted all too vividly.

'Maybe I'll think about dating again when he's eighteen.'

'Oh, only another ten years then. My summer of chastity will seem like ten minutes in comparison.'

'It probably will be ten minutes in total . . .' Marilyn teased her.

'I told you I'm going to stick to it, and I mean it.'

'Sure you do. I know for a fact that you were hoping it would be a different vet that turned up today.'

Liesel thought about denial, but Marilyn knew her too well. It would really be a total waste of breath to say she hadn't been hoping to see Tom Spencer again.

'Enough about me. Just because I'm denying myself a love life doesn't mean I can't help someone else get one of their own.'

'What do you mean?'

'Watch this.' Liesel went to the doorway and called out to Lorraine, who was busy polishing the carved stair rail.

'What did you think to the vet, Lorraine?'

'Vet?' Lorraine tried to look puzzled, like she didn't know what Liesel was talking about, as if the man had barely registered with her.

'Yes, the vet,' Liesel persisted gently. 'What did you think to him?'

'Who?' Lorraine asked. She wasn't a very good liar; the pursed frog lips and wide darting eyes gave the game away.

'You know bloody well who I mean, Lorraine Veasey . . .'

'He seemed like a very nice man,' squeaked Lorraine before burying her face in a duster and escaping upstairs to the first floor, taking the steps two at a time in her haste to hide behind the noise and anonymity of the hoover.

'There you go. Smitten. Just like I said.'

'I think you might be right.' Marilyn seemed surprised.

'We all get the love bug at some point in our lives.'

'Sure, but I really thought Lorraine was far too clean for any kind of bugs to dare to go there.'

The following day, Sunday morning, the guests had been fed and watered and Liesel had a cunning plan; she just needed a little assistance.

Superman was heading outside, towing Godrich on his lead. He had a bucket and spade slung over his shoulder and was wearing a hat from which hung corks on lengths of string.

'Alex? What are you doing?'

'I'm going to the beach on a dig.'

'And what have you done to your hat?'

'Eric says if I keep digging I should get through to Australia by tea, and I need to blend in with the natives.'

'Oh, right, okay.' Liesel nodded, nonplussed but smiling. 'I don't suppose the dig could wait a while?'

'Well, the tide is on the turn.' Alex, repeating one of Eric's favourite sayings, nodded sagely.

'Sure it is, honey, but I could really do with your help with something.'

'Okay. What's up?'

'Lorraine. I think she's in love.'

'Ugh!' Alex pulled a face and shook his head. 'What is it with girls and love? Haven't they got anything better to do?'

'What, like digging through to Australia?' Liesel teased him.

Alex grinned back.

'Okay, then. What do you want me to do?'

'Well, you can guess who it is that she likes, can't you?' He shook his head.

'Have you ever seen a cleaner pair of wellies . . .' Liesel prompted.

'Oh yeah, the vet with the glasses. He liked her too.'

'Do you think so? I'm glad you said that, 'cause I really think he does, and I was worried I might have imagined it.'

'Nah. He likes her, you can tell.'

'Great. How?' asked Liesel, chuffed that someone else shared the same conviction.

' 'Cause he looked at her just like you looked at Mr Spencer,' Alex said resolutely. 'And Mum says you've got him something chronic, which she said means that you really like him . . . Auntie Leez, why have you gone bright red?'

Liesel suddenly looked like Lorraine under her own interrogation, all pursed lips and denial bursting to the surface.

'Yes . . . um . . . well . . . Lorraine and Adrian Lee . . . I thought if we could get Adrian back here somehow . . .'

'You mean like if Godrich was sick again?' Alex frowned.

'Yeah, but only *pretend* sick.'

'You mean we have to tell lies?'

'Well, yes, I suppose, but it's for a good cause.'

'Okay.' Alex shrugged trustingly, 'I can make him roll over now. Watch . . . Bathtime, Godrich,' he called.

Godrich immediately flopped heavily to the floor, paws twitching, eyeballs rolling, and began to whine.

'Well done, Alex!'

'Do you think he looks ill?'

'A bit more fake anguish wouldn't hurt. Try waving his worming tablets in front of him, he hates those.'

The worming tablets produced some more convincing whines and a bit of asthmatic breathing.

'Honestly, that dog deserves an Oscar. We should change his name to Gielgud instead of Godrich. What do you think, Alex?'

'I think it's time to call the vet!' Alex grinned, and then he frowned. 'Will we get into trouble for pretending it's an emergency?'

'Well, it is kind of an emergency. Godrich might not be sick, but Lorraine certainly is.'

'Yeah!' Alex said, pulling a face. 'She's LOVEsick.'

Half an hour later, Alex, who was on sentry duty in his bedroom, hurtled into the sitting room shouting, 'He's nearly here! His car's just turned into our road.'

'And we got Mr Lee, right?'

'Of course we did.'

'Of course?'

Alex put his hand to his ear as though it were the telephone, screwed up his face and pretended to sob into the imaginary receiver. 'Please can you send Mr Lee back? He's the only one that can save my dog . . .'

'I never knew my nephew was so devious.'

'It's for a good cause,' Alex parroted.

'Great, now go get Lorraine whilst I threaten Godrich with a good wash. Tell her there's an imminent stain situation and we urgently need her help. Hurry.'

Two minutes later, Lorraine appeared looking worried.

'Alex said you wanted me.'

'Godrich's not well again. We might need your expertise with a mop and bucket.'

The door swung open and Marilyn, closely followed by Alex, ushered a nervous-looking Adrian into the room. If Marilyn hadn't been blocking the door, Lorraine would have bolted. As it was, she had nowhere to go, and so instead she froze, unfortunately with a bit of a gormless expression on her face.

'Mr Lee's come to see Godrich.' Marilyn looked puzzled.

'He's had a relapse,' Liesel said hurriedly.

'What seems to be wrong with him today?'

'We're really not sure. Similar symptoms to yesterday, except this time he hasn't been sick.'

Adrian Lee crouched down next to the dog, who, not too keen on vets, started to look genuinely worried.

'He doesn't look too bad to me. Have you been making sure he drinks plenty of water?'

Liesel waved the loofah and Godrich let out a mournful howl and started shaking.

'Mmmm.' Adrian bent closer. 'Perhaps he's still a little dehydrated from yesterday.'

Gentle hands checked stomach, eyes and ears, and then he sat back on his haunches and shook his head.

'I can understand why you're concerned, but I think perhaps he's just feeling a little sorry for himself after yesterday.'

'So we've called you out for no reason?' Liesel turned up the acting a notch, as Marilyn was watching her with accusing eyes. 'I'm so sorry.'

'Well, it's far better to be safe than sorry, and besides . . .' and to Liesel's utter delight, he turned to Lorraine, 'I'm really glad I've had a chance to see you again.'

'You are?' Lorraine's eyes almost popped out of her head with surprise.

'Yes, I wanted to say thank you for my wellies. They've never been so clean. In fact, I don't think any mud would dare to stick to them again, they're that spick and span.'

'It was a pleasure,' Lorraine replied shyly.

Liesel didn't know whether to frown or grin. A pleasure? Cleaning dog sick off a pair of brogues? Boy, Lorraine had it bad. And she had been right about Adrian too. They were standing there smiling at each other, like three year olds on their first day of playschool sending eyeball signals to buddy up. There was definitely something mutual going on, but they were both as bad as each other: standing and smiling was about as far as they would get without another helping hand.

'We've got a . . . um . . . a . . .' Liesel cast her eyes about the room for inspiration. There was an advert on the soundless television for a supermarket; some television celebrity was promoting bottles of wine, buy one, get one half price. 'A wine tasting,' she blurted. 'Yes, that's it, we've got a wine tasting here next Saturday.'

'Wine tasting?' Marilyn mouthed, eyes wide with concern.

'Perhaps you'd like to come?' Liesel persevered, sending frantic signals to her sister not to cock it up by denying the existence of the wine tasting.

He didn't even hesitate.

'Will you be there?'

Lorraine looked in confusion at Liesel, who prompted her by nodding furiously.

Lorraine nodded too.

'I'd love to come. That would be really nice, thank you.'

His beeper went off.

'Got to go,' he said, reading it quickly. 'Emergency at Clancy's farm . . . but I'll definitely see you Saturday.'

'Eight o'clock,' Liesel said, swiftly calculating dinner end times.

'Bring some friends,' Marilyn called after him, trying hard not to laugh. 'Anyone else at the practice who likes a nice glass of wine, perhaps. As long as their name begins with T and ends in om . . .' she added when certain he was out of earshot.

As soon as Lorraine had left the room as well, she turned to her sister.

'Honestly, Liesel, what are you like! I'm out for an hour and you rope Alex and poor old Godrich into this . . . this . . . farce! And a wine tasting of all things!'

'I was thinking on my feet.'

'Next time can you please use your brain instead?'

'I was helping Lorraine find love.'

'And what makes you think she can't find it for herself?'

Liesel's pointed look was enough of an answer.

'Okay, okay, point taken. But what on earth do we do now?'

'Well, I don't know about you,' Liesel smiled, trying to catch Marilyn in her enthusiasm, 'but I've got a wine tasting to organise.'

The first thing was a phone call to the local brewery who supplied the beer and liquor for the bar and restaurant. After a friendly chat, not only did Liesel have a mixed case of wines arriving on Saturday afternoon, she also had four boxes of free glasses, a ten per cent discount on their usual prices, and a keen rep offering to act as sommelier for the evening.

'I've still got it,' she boasted as she got off the phone.

'Yeah, it's just a shame you've decided not to use it.' Marilyn winked at her. 'Now you can work that same magic on rustling us up some guests other than the one person you've actually invited.'

'Oh my God! You're right. What do I do now?'

'Do what you're good at,' Marilyn teased her. 'Make something out of nothing.'

Where could she get enough people to hold a wine tasting? How many people did you need? They had some guests in next weekend. She was sure they could be tempted by a free glass of Chablis and some nibbles, but who else? She thought for a moment. Invites, she needed invites. Ten minutes on CorelDraw on the new computer and she had something presentable. Now she just had to find someone to give them to. Perhaps it was about time she got to know the neighbours.

Whether taking Godrich would be an in with the neighbours or an instant out she wasn't sure, but he had been such a star, he deserved a nice walk. She also felt rather guilty for making the poor dog think it was bathtime again when he'd only been subjected to his weekly wash yesterday. She strapped on his collar and lead, and walked him out of the hotel grounds and up towards the headland.

The Cornucopia was one of only two hotels in Piran Cove. The rest of the properties were an assortment of holiday homes, shuttered, postboxes cluttered with junk mail, and some nice permanent residences. She started with the houses she knew were occupied.

By the time she'd knocked on every door, she had seven definites, two maybes, and a 'sod off and leave me alone' from a rather grumpy sergeant major type who'd answered the door wearing a lady's floral bathrobe.

So with herself and Marilyn, Lorraine, Kashia and Eric roped in too, and the four guests they had booked, there would be between fifteen and twenty people. Not many, but it was a decent enough number, and it would have to do, because she had reached the end of the road, literally. All that stretched beyond her was the rugged end of the headland with its coarse grass and heathers, a shafting promontory between the two bays.

The only thing she could do now would be to go back to the hotel, get the car and drive off the headland and into Piran itself, or perhaps she could walk around to Piran Bay.

The other side of the headland was apparently home to a beautiful stretch of beach. Godrich might as well get a good walk out of it, and she'd heard there were a couple of larger hotels there too; maybe she could drum up a few more volunteers for the vino evening.

So instead of turning back, Liesel followed the path as it swung around the seaward point of the headland, and turned away from Piran Cove into Piran Bay, climbing upwards over the brow of the hill. As she reached the peak and saw the view of the other side stretched out before her, her mouth fell open in absolute awe.

A mile and a half at most between them, and yet it was like landing in another resort entirely. It was like being shipwrecked on a desert island only to discover two months of desperate survival later that there was a six-star Sandals resort just around the corner from the beach where you'd built your hovel out of palm leaves.

What lay before her, stretched out in panoramic glory from her vantage point at the top of the hill, was two miles of golden sand covered in surfers sprinting for the water in their wetsuits like swarms of black ants, and emmets, as the locals called visitors. The houses here were fewer but grander; there were several posh apartment blocks, a raft of B&Bs, and four large hotels, and all, from the lowliest guesthouse to the grand and prominent Piran Bay Hotel, were proudly displaying signs stating 'No Vacancies'.

She thought of Marilyn with her charts and her forecasts and her website and her advertising budget, and all they really needed was a sign saying 'Hotel Cornucopia this way, vacancies, honest.'

'Bloody hell!' she yelled aloud.

'Quite a view, isn't it?' said a voice from behind her.

Liesel turned round in embarrassment to see a man, perhaps in his late fifties, in walking boots and windcheater, standing watching her. Despite her outburst, or perhaps because of it, he was smiling broadly, and he looked so friendly, she couldn't help but smile back.

'Amazing. I can quite honestly say I've never seen anything like it.'

'Your first time in Piran?'

Liesel shook her head. 'Would you believe, I live here.'

'The other end of town?'

She bit her lip in embarrassment.

'The other side of the headland, actually, in the cove.'

'And this is your first venture over to the dark side we call the bay? You obviously haven't been here long.'

'A few weeks,' she admitted, shamefaced.

'Weeks!' he repeated in disbelief.

'In my totally lame defence, we've been too busy since we moved in.'

'Well, welcome to Piran Bay. I'm Jimmy . . and I can't think of any houses in the cove that have sold recently, so . . .' he narrowed his eyes, 'that must mean that you are either Miss Ellis or Mrs Hamilton.'

Liesel must have looked surprised, because he beamed with delight and, putting an arm around her shoulders, gave her a friendly squeeze.

'I'm Miss Ellis.' She frowned. 'I mean Liesel.'

'Don't worry, my darling, everyone knows everyone else's news around here. You think you hear the crash of the waves beating against the cliffs in the night, but it's actually the jungle drums spreading gossip. Your business is never your own in Cornwall. Now, I hear that your business is actually your nephew's. Tell me, is that true, has mad old Nancy left the hotel to an eight-year-old boy?'

Liesel nodded. 'The Cornucopia belongs to my nephew Alex . . . well, at least it does if we can keep it running for the season. You'll never guess who it goes to if we can't . . .' She indicated Godrich.

'You're kidding me?'

He had such a kind face and easy manner that as they walked down into Piran Bay together, Liesel found herself telling this stranger the entire story, right up to this morning and Lorraine's crush on the vet – whom he knew and said was 'a sweet if slightly backward-in-coming-forward kind of boy' – and the wine tasting.

'You're doing the right thing giving them a helping hand, and a wine tasting, that would be fabulous, we'll definitely be there. We both adore a good bottle of wine, or a bad one come to that . . . In fact, why don't we start now? Come in and have a drink and meet the other half.'

'Come in?'

Jimmy pointed to the nearby Piran Bay Hotel, a magnificent balconied creation that looked like it belonged in some sunshine-soaked bay in the Mediterranean.

'*Chez nous*,' he said with obvious pride.

'You own this?'

He nodded and fluttered his eyelashes coyly to temper the fact that he was showing off a little.

'What about this guy?' Liesel indicated Godrich.

Jimmy pointed to a sign in the reception window that read 'All Welcome'.

'That just about sums us up, luvvie. Bring him in. More the merrier.'

Utterly different to the Cornucopia, which felt like a grand house, the Piran Bay was a true hotel in every sense of the word. For starters, it had a reception with three desks and four receptionists, and one hundred and four bedrooms, and there were signs for things like 'Gymnasium' and 'Spa' and 'Conference Suite'.

It also had two restaurants, and a funky café bar done out in contemporary blues and beige, where jazz was playing in the background and a dapper little man in a pink diamond motif golf jumper was sitting at a table in the wide picture window overlooking the sea, drinking a gin and tonic.

'Liesel, my lovely, this is my partner David. David, meet Liesel. She and her family are the new owners of the Cornucopia.'

'Well, it belongs to my nephew actually.'

'And you're helping him run it?' David stood and extended a friendly smile and a hand.

'Well, considering he's only eight at the moment . . .'

'Nancy left the Cornucopia to an eight year old? To be honest, that doesn't surprise me, knowing Nancy.'

'Did you know her well?' Liesel was curious to find out about Alex's elusive great-aunt.

'As well as anybody could know Nancy. We used to call her the Hermit Crab. Which is pretty self-explanatory really.'

'Reclusive and crabby,' Jimmy added just in case.

'Well, you're a pleasant surprise.' David offered Liesel a chair and signalled for the waiter. 'To be honest, we always thought that Nasty Nick would get the lot. A bottle of the Chablis, please, Caleb, and three *large* glasses.'

'You know Nick as well?' Liesel asked, wide-eyed. Honestly, today was full of revelations.

'Knew. Haven't seen him since he was a kid. He used to come down every year in the summer and terrorise the neighbourhood. Little sod he was.'

'Well, he's a big sod now.' She laughed.

'Why doesn't that surprise me? What happened to him?'

'He met and married my sister, left her for another woman, moved to Australia and has ignored his own son for the past three years.'

The two men exchanged a look of disgust.

'That's terrible,' Dave murmured.

Jimmy nodded. 'How could someone do that?'

'I always knew he was a bad lot.'

The wine arrived, and as Jimmy poured, David leaned in confidentially to Liesel and said, 'Our little dog Wendy hated him, and she was a good judge of character was our Wendy. I remember she bit him once, really hard on the ankle, drew blood as well. He didn't half kick up a fuss, but it was his own fault, he was teasing her so badly.'

'Oh yes,' Jimmy added, pursing his lips in disgust. 'I remember that well. The thing was, he could be very charming, but there was such a cruel streak in him. Did you see that, Liesel? Well, of course you have if he's not seen hide nor hair of his own son for three years. How terrible is that?'

'It's awful, isn't it.' Liesel nodded, thinking how wonderful it was to have someone to bitch with. No matter what Marilyn's feelings were on the matter, she would rarely be drawn into a conversation about Nick, because as far as she was concerned, and quite rightly, the only person who could be hurt by harsh words was Alex. But here, there were no little ears listening in, and two people who obviously had the same rather low opinion of Nick that Liesel held herself. To let loose all the feelings that had been pent up over the years to two pairs of extremely sympathetic ears, and over what could only be described as a rather heavenly bottle of wine, was absolute bliss. Jimmy and David had stories galore of how Nick and his friends used to steal from their stockroom, how he was caught putting firecrackers through old Mrs Nettleton's letter box . . . a whole catalogue of misdemeanours to accompany the first bottle and ease them on a flow of conversation into the second.

'I bet he was absolutely steaming when he found out that Nancy had excluded him from her will,' Jimmy was saying to Liesel as he refilled her glass for the umpteenth time. 'I bet he was expecting to get the lot, seeing as Nancy had no children of her own. I would have loved to have seen his spiteful little face when he found out it was going to you guys instead. How wonderful! At last Nancy did something good with her life.

'Anyway, how about we have something solid to soak up this rather lovely Chablis. It must be way past lunch.'

'It's two thirty,' David told him, looking at his watch. 'Shall we ask Chef to rustle us up something nice? What do you think, Liesel? Oh, I do love your name, it makes me want to burst into song . . . what shall we feed a nice girl like our Liesel . . .' he warbled to the tune of 'How Do You Solve a Problem Like Maria'.

'I'd love to stay, but I really should make a move,' Liesel said, extremely reluctantly.

'Oh, must you?'

'I've been skiving for far too long already. I'm supposed to be rounding up people for Saturday night.'

'If you must go, we'll get one of our chaps to drive you back,' David said, hugging her.

'And don't you worry about your wine tasting. We'll make sure there are enough people there for the vet not to get suspicious that he's being set up,' added Jimmy.

Alex had been watching out of the front door for the return of Liesel and Godrich.

'Auntie Liesel's just fallen out of a limo!' he called to his mother, who was sitting on reception doing paperwork.

'She's done what?' Marilyn put down her stock lists and joined her son at the open door to see her sister almost water-ski down the steep drive. Godrich, glad to be home despite the water and the dog treats the animal-loving David and Jimmy had kept him supplied with, acted as motorboat, Liesel towed behind him.

She practically fell in through the front door and into Marilyn's arms.

'I've been organising the wine tasting,' she sang happily.

'What, by practising drinking?'

'Do I reek of it?' Liesel thrust a hand to her mouth.

Marilyn nodded. 'Afraid so, but even if you didn't, the fact that you slid down the entire driveway on your arse was a bit of a giveaway.'

It was one of those times when you didn't realise how much you'd drunk until you tried to stand up and ended up legs splayed like Bambi on ice.

'Do you want a glass of water?' Marilyn asked in concern.

'If another glass of nice cold white wine isn't on offer.' Liesel grinned, staggering past her and flopping down on the hall floor, where she lay staring up at the whaleboned ceiling.

'How come the nicest men I meet are gay?' she asked as Marilyn hauled her up and, sending Alex to the kitchen for water, manoeuvred her through to the tower.

'Because gay men want nothing from you but friendship,' Marilyn replied.

'So we can blame sex for the demise of most relationships, then?'

'Probably,' Marilyn puffed as she pushed Liesel up the stairs towards her bedroom. 'Sex and housework.'

'Sex and *housework*?'

'Well, have you ever met a straight man who actually *wants* to help with the housework?'

'You're stereotyping, Maz,' slurred Liesel.

Marilyn shook with laughter as she helped Liesel into her room.

'How can I be doing something you can't even say at the moment?' she asked.

But Liesel had fallen face down on her bed, and promptly began to snore.

M onday morning, and a dreadfully hungover Liesel and a worried Marilyn were in the hallway with Alex.

'Alex? Oh come on, please, we talked all this through last night,' Marilyn pleaded.

Kashia was crossing the hallway carrying a full milk jug for the cereal table.

'There is problem?'

'The school has a uniform.' Marilyn inclined her head towards her son. No further explanation was needed. Alex was standing resolutely in his Superman outfit, arms folded firmly across his chest. Marilyn was holding grey trousers and white shirt, Liesel tie and blazer.

'Ah, I see.' Kashia carefully set down the milk jug on a side table and then, going over to Alex, crouched down in front of him so that their eyes were on a level.

'You are Superman, no?' she said quietly to him.

Alex nodded, eyes heavy with unspilt tears.

'That mean you Clark Kent also?'

He had to think for a minute about that one, but eventually nodded again.

'Well, Clark Kent, he wear his Superman shiny tights under his work suit, no? So nobody can see who he is, but he still wear it, okay?'

Marilyn and Liesel exchanged confused glances, but

after another few moments' deep thought, Alex looked at Kashia and nodded again, more determinedly this time, a big snorty sniff snorkling up most of the unshed tears. Then he calmly took the uniform from his aunt and mother and began to put it on.

Over his Superman outfit.

Then he smiled. A broad beam.

Kashia returned the smile, and went back to her milk jug.

The following day, Kashia came in with a tub of hair gel.

'For Superman slick hair,' she told Alex. 'To help with disguise.'

The day after, she bought in a Superman pen and a notebook.

'Superman is top reporter, no? You listen good in English, maybe some day you be one too.'

By the Friday, Alex had even decided that he could survive without his cape for the duration of the school day, much to Marilyn's delight.

'He doesn't go in looking like the Hunchback of Notre Dame's mini-me any more,' she told Liesel cheerfully. 'It's all thanks to Kashia.'

By Saturday night Liesel had had enough RSVPs to be able to relax and believe that the wine tasting could actually be enjoyable.

Despite the fact that it was a balmy summer's evening, she insisted on lighting the fire, as she felt that the crackling flames went with the ambience she was trying to create.

'Sophistication, that's what a wine tasting is all about,' she told Marilyn, as she vigorously polished the new wine glasses the nice but absurdly young rep from the brewery had brought them, along with the wine and himself as sommelier. Having arrived far too early, he was currently playing computer games with Alex in his bedroom.

'We can do sophisticated. We can do anything we put our minds to, remember. And we need more nibbles,' Liesel said, stealing a gherkin from a table by the window that Eric had set with titbits. 'We've got a lovely big Stilton I could chop into pieces and put out with some biscuits.'

'Yes, but do you know how much that lovely big Stilton cost us?'

'It'll be worth it. Stilton's salty, it'll make people drink more.'

'Do we want people to drink more?'

'Of course we do. You taste for free.' Liesel indicated the bottles on the table. 'But if you want a full glass you pay.'

'Ah, so this is an exercise in good business and not just a party to hook up our beloved but backward assistant manager with a vet who'll stick his hand up a cow's backside but hasn't got the guts to ask a girl out?'

'This evening brings benefits to not only our Lorraine, but also our budget.'

'Clever girl.'

'Trust me, by the end of the evening, they'll be engaged.'

With the invites stating a start time of eight, they gently hurried the four guests they had in through an early dinner with a promise of free drinks after, and then reconvened in reception at seven thirty.

Liesel had swapped the black trousers for a little black dress she had bought for three pounds on eBay. She looked sickeningly good in it, and Marilyn wondered if perchance she was secretly hoping that there might be more than one vet on the guest list this evening.

However, when Adrian Lee arrived promptly at eight, although he wasn't alone, the person with him was not Tom Spencer, but the third part of the trilogy, Jonathan Childs.

Childs wasn't the predicted seventy year old with a limp; he was in his fifties and rather dashing in an iron-haired-newsreader-in-a-sports-jacket kind of way, but his appearance, though most welcome, made the absence of the third vet seem even more noticeable in some way.

'I wonder why he didn't come. Adrian obviously spread the news: that girl over there is one of the receptionists at the vets' surgery,' said Liesel.

'Are you disappointed?' Marilyn asked.

'This wasn't about me, it was about Lorraine . . .'

'I know, but it would have been nice to kill two birds with one stone, eh?'

'We might still.' Liesel indicated Jonathan Childs. 'He's very attractive for an older man.'

'And married with three children and five grandchildren, apparently.'

'Damn, I'll just have to continue my hopeless lust for his absent partner, then, won't I?'

'Ah, so you're admitting you're in lust.'

'Have I ever denied that? But just because I fancy the leather pants off Bono doesn't mean I'm going to fly out to Dublin and try and get him into my lace ones. No, this evening is about trying to sort out Lorraine's love life, not mine.'

Kashia was covering for Liesel on the bar; Lorraine, happier hiding behind a serving dish, was circulating with nibbles.

'Well, it's a shame she's spent most of it avoiding him, then, isn't it?' Marilyn observed as Lorraine once again edged round the room in a half-moon motion, totally cutting off the part where Adrian Lee was standing.

Liesel beckoned her over.

'I think Adrian looks hungry, don't you?' She gently placed a hand in the small of Lorraine's back and gave her a little push in his direction. Lorraine seemed to gather far too much momentum far too quickly, did a fly-past, and literally threw a cheese puff at him before fleeing to the kitchen to hide behind Eric.

Liesel looked at her watch and sighed.

'He's been here nearly an hour already and she hasn't even said hello. He's going to leave soon; if she doesn't get her act together, this evening will have been a total waste of time.'

'You keep him occupied, I'll see if I can lure her out of the kitchen,' Marilyn suggested.

'If I spend any more time chatting to him, he'll think it's me that's interested in him and then things will get really complicated. Why doesn't she just grab the bull by the horns and talk to the guy?'

'We don't know for a fact if Adrian Lee is single.'

'Oh yes we do.'

'We do?'

'Yep. I've spent the past half an hour talking to the man. I think I know everything from his inside leg measurement to his worst childhood nightmare. And I also know that he really likes her.'

'You know this for a fact?'

Liesel nodded.

'You asked him, didn't you?'

She nodded again.

'Outright?'

'Just about.'

'As subtle as a Wag in a fur coat at a PETA party.'

'I'm only playing Cupid.'

'Cupid in a tank.'

'They're both shy, they need help, and subtle just

wasn't working. At least my heart's in the right place.'

'Your heart is currently in Tom Spencer's boxer shorts, which means your mind is clouded by hormones. You're denying yourself the chance of love for some stupid pact you've made with no one but yourself, so you're overcompensating by trying to matchmake for Lorraine.'

'What are you saying?'

'Exactly what you've been saying to Lorraine. You like him, Liesel. Why not see if there's more to it?'

'I don't even know the guy.'

'That's easily rectified, isn't it?'

There was a stand-off of eyeballs for a few moments, before Liesel gave in, flinging her arms in the air and saying, 'Okay, okay, I promise I'll throw myself at Tom Spencer the next time I see him, if you keep Adrian here long enough for me to get Lorraine out of the kitchen and actually talking to him.'

'Deal.' Marilyn held out her hand and they shook. 'Although I'm not asking you to throw yourself at anyone, I'm just asking you to be open to something.'

'Don't do as I do, do as I say?'

'Exactly. I'm your older sister, It's my job to be didactic where you're concerned. Now go and get Lorraine out of the kitchen.'

'Yes, sir!' Liesel saluted her sister.

Lorraine had gone so shy with longing she was practically putting herself on a shelf in the pantry when Liesel found her. Technically Lorraine was working tonight. Liesel could order her out and knew that she would go, but that wasn't her style. Instead she sat down next to her on a big sack of flour and took Lorraine's cold hand in hers for a moment, squeezing it reassuringly before letting go.

'You know tonight was a set-up, don't you?' she asked, deciding that honesty was probably the best approach.

Lorraine nodded, her bottom lip beginning to tremble.

'Have I done the wrong thing? Are you not very keen on the idea of getting fixed up with someone?'

Still she was silent.

'I'm really sorry. I shouldn't have done this . . .' Liesel was suddenly full of remorse, but then Lorraine finally spoke.

'Don't be sorry. I'm the one who should say sorry. You've gone to so much effort . . . just for me. Nobody's ever . . .' Her voice cracked and Liesel saw her take a hold of herself and start again. 'Nobody has ever cared about me enough to do something like this. I'm just so . . . just so . . .'

'It's all a bit overwhelming?'

'Yes.'

'But you do like Adrian?'

'Yes.'

'And would you like to be in a relationship?'

Lorraine nodded slowly. 'I love the idea of having someone. I've always been on my own. I'm not saying I've never been kissed, but well . . . I've never had a romance. A relationship. A boyfriend.' She almost whispered the last word. 'It's scary. Why would anyone want me. Now if I were only like you . . .'

'Like me!' Liesel exclaimed in surprise. 'You don't want to be like me. Every single guy I've been out with has dumped me. Every single one, without fail. And we're not talking count on both hands here, we're talking double figures. I'm useless at relationships, Lol, absolutely bloody useless. I pick the worst men in the world to go out with, whereas you . . . well, let me just say, seeing as you've been ignoring the poor sod, I've had to talk to Adrian rather a lot this evening, and trust me, he's as nice as they come. You've picked a good one there, Lorraine . . . and as for nobody wanting you, well *he* wants you.'

'You really think so?' The hope in her eyes was almost shattering.

'I know so, and you like him, don't you? This isn't just me being an old romantic?'

Lorraine smiled, the sweetest smile Liesel had ever seen grace the usually worried face.

'He's lovely,' she murmured.

'Then I'll make a deal with you. We'll be brave together, okay: you do this tonight, you make your leap of faith, and I'll help you through it, and then you can help me find myself a good one too? What do you say?' She held out a hand.

Lorraine hesitated for a fraction of a second, and then the soft, slightly worried smile turned into a firm, resolute line and she nodded and took it.

'Okay,' she said, exhaling heavily.

'Great. So are you going to come out of the pantry and into the party?'

Lorraine nodded.

'And no more serving, okay? You're mingling.'

She nodded again, this time not quite so resolutely.

'With me. Not on your own. I'll be right by your side the whole time.'

'Okay.'

'Now let's go get you some romance.'

Liesel played gooseberry for the first twenty minutes, but then Jimmy and David arrived, and Lorraine now seemed so comfortable in Adrian's company that Liesel felt it safe to leave her to greet her two new friends.

As promised, they had brought other people, a jolly party of ten, who were all like them, friendly and fun and effusive with their compliments.

'Fantastic evening . . . love your sister, what a sweetheart . . . you should make this a regular event . . .

delicious wine . . . the place looks great . . . the food's fantastic . . . look at the view.'

They seemed to know everyone there, including the two couples who were guests at the hotel, and soon had everyone mingling. Then Jimmy suggested putting on some music for dancing, and as the flowing wine was beginning to warm through any icy reserves, they soon managed to turn the evening into a real party.

Jimmy even took on Liesel's mantel as Cupid, joining the group where Adrian and Lorraine were *in situ* and doing some rather magical stirring of his own that resulted finally in Adrian actually asking Lorraine on a date.

'They're having a veterinarians' dinner-dance next week, and he's asked me if I'll go as his partner,' Lorraine sang, literally dancing up to Liesel.

'You are a star!' Liesel congratulated Jimmy, having witnessed the ease with which he had manoeuvred the conversation to enable this miracle to happen.

'I'm also Fred Astaire reincarnated.' He held out his arms. 'Fancy a foxtrot?'

'I'll try, but I have about as much rhythm as a broken metronome.'

Fortunately the rhythm changed to something a little easier to follow, and Jimmy managed to lead Liesel through a slow waltz before the tempo upped again.

'See you've found your feet,' he praised her as they segued smoothly into a rumba. 'Have you noticed that your pair of fledgling lovebirds have just slipped out into the moonlight?'

'Really?' Liesel breathed in delight, craning to see through the dancing, laughing throng out on to the terrace, 'Do you know, this evening is turning out to be so much better than I anticipated.'

But then, as the music stepped up a pace once again, Mrs Milner, one of the guests, who'd been hitting the

South African pinotage with a touch too much enthusiasm, cha-cha-cha'd backwards into the trestle table full of now almost empty wine bottles. The shuddering table sighed thankfully at the excuse to finally give up the ghost and promptly collapsed. Liesel leapt forward to push young Sonny the sommelier out of the way, and disappeared herself under the ensuing avalanche of bottles, glasses, linen and flowers.

For a moment the room fell worryingly silent, and then Marilyn was throwing herself into the pile of debris, closely followed by Eric and Kashia.

'Liesel, are you okay!'

Liesel sat up, shook crisps from her hair and, holding her left wrist in her right hand, held out her hand towards her sister. There, embedded in her thumb, was a shard of glass the size of a fifty-pence piece.

'Is there a doctor in the house?' Liesel joked weakly, her face as white as the tablecloth she sat shrouded in.

As Marilyn suppressed a scream, and Kashia didn't, a calm voice tempered the threatened chaos.

'No, but will a vet do?'

Unfortunately Liesel had to keep her eyes closed as Tom deftly removed the piece of glass with a pair of tweezers. She was so bloody pleased to see him, the butterflies in her stomach were worse than the dull throbbing pain in her thumb, and all she really wanted to do was look at him, take a really good long look and try and work out why it was she felt this way.

They were in the bathroom in the tower, just the two of them.

There were no doctors in the house, and of the three vets, two of them were drunk, one on wine, one on love. Seeing as he had only just arrived, Tom was the only one sober enough to remove the glass without doing more damage.

'There we are,' he said as with the utmost concentration he pulled the large shard free and dropped it into the sink, covering the cut it had left with an antiseptic-soaked cotton ball.

'Sorry,' he added as Liesel flinched at the sting. 'It could do with a stitch. Do you trust me to do it, or would you rather go down to Casualty?'

'I'd rather you did it, but I have to warn you, I'm not very good with needles.'

'Then close your eyes again.'

Liesel dutifully closed her eyes, wishing that she had the bottle to keep them open and look into his. She was still trying to work out what colour they were.

'Now I'm going to numb it with an anaesthetic spray, but it might still sting a little when I start to sew. You only need a couple of stitches in there, though, which is lucky, just two at the most, which won't take me long at all . . .'

And then he stopped speaking and stepped back, and it was only then that Liesel realised he had actually stitched her thumb whilst he was talking, without her even feeling a thing.

'Wow. You're good at that, aren't you?' she said, deciding that his eyes were a rich golden colour.

'Lots of practice. Give me a few more years and I might even be able to run you up a pair of curtains.'

'Did you ever think about being a doctor?' she asked, looking at his smiling mouth and wondering if he might perhaps be persuaded to kiss her thumb better.

'Never crossed my mind, to be honest. I love animals.'

'So do I,' Liesel answered genuinely. 'It must take longer to train to be a vet – you know, all the different bodies. At least with humans we're all the same shape . . . well nearly . . . we all have bits in the same place . . . well, there are the obvious differences between genders, but I'm pretty sure you know what I mean . . .'

He stopped bandaging and smiled at her, a smile that silenced her more effectively than any words could have done.

Actually, his eyes were green.

He finished his bandaging in peace, whilst Liesel held her breath so hard she started to feel dizzy. Maybe if she passed out he'd give her the kiss of life. Now there was a thought. Oh Lord, she really must stop with all the innuendo. He was just helping her out; kissing her better, or the kiss of life, or quite simply the kiss that was a prelude to mind-blowing sex, well, none of the above were on the agenda.

'There, job done,' he said, tying the loose ends of the gauze and stepping back.

'Thank you.'

'Just keep an eye on it, and if it starts to go red or get hot and itchy, go and see your doctor, okay?'

'Okay.'

'Well, it looks like your party is just about over.'

She nodded her agreement. 'It's hard to keep on tasting wine when most of it's soaked into the carpet.'

'You do know that Adrian doesn't usually drink wine?'

'He must like Lorraine a lot, then.'

'He's been talking about her constantly since last weekend.'

'Really?' Liesel asked in delight.

'Asked me to drop by tonight if I could, to give him a bit of moral support, but it didn't look like he needed me. When I arrived, they were outside, staring at the moon.'

'Talking?' Liesel asked. 'Kissing?' The tone turned hopeful.

'No, just staring, actually. I almost expected them both to start howling any second,' he joked, then looked at his watch. 'Well, I'd better get back to the surgery, I suppose: still on call.'

'Thanks for fixing me up.'

'Any time.' And then, as he snapped shut the bag that he usually used to treat his four-legged patients, he looked at her sideways and said, 'And thanks for fixing Adrian up too . . .'

'Me?' Liesel feigned innocence. 'You think I had something to do with that?'

'Well, let's just say a little bird told me as much.'

'Oh, you talk to the animals as well as treat them?' she laughed.

'Yeah, a regular Doctor Dolittle, me. No, I mean it, he's a nice guy and he deserves a break. It was sweet of you to give him that.'

'You don't think I was out of order for meddling?'

'No, because your heart's in the right place.'

'You can tell that just from bandaging my thumb?' she asked, all innocent.

He started to laugh.

'Good night, Liesel.'

'Good night, Tom.'

'So long, farewell, auf wiedersen, adieu, and all that.'

'I think you'd better leave before I start singing "What's New, Pussycat?".'

'Probably should, yeah.'

13

They had never seen Lorraine so happy. Not only did she have a date with Adrian on Saturday night, she also had a stain the size of a small country to remove from the dining-room carpet. She was in heaven. She even managed to sit down and join them for breakfast.

There was obviously something on Marilyn's mind, however: she had been giving Liesel pointed looks ever since she had handed her a cup of tea.

Finally she spoke.

'So when are you going to keep your promise, then?'

Liesel stopped munching on her toast and blinked blankly at her sister.

'What are you on about?'

'The handsome vet. You promised Lorraine if she took the plunge you'd follow her off the high board.'

'And if I see him again under more normal circumstances then I will be diving in there, I can assure you.'

'Why wait? You could go and get him to take another look at your thumb.'

'I can hardly call the vets' and ask for an appointment for myself!'

'Godrich?'

'He's not sick and they know it.'

'Okay, so Godrich may be better, but he's not the only animal in the house.'

'You mean the kitten?'

Marilyn nodded. 'We really should get her checked out, you know, make sure she's not chipped. There may well be someone out there scouring the streets for her . . .'

'The state she was in? She's definitely a stray.'

'Still, we'd better take her to the vets' just in case. And she does need her jabs. It would be neglect if we didn't get those done.'

'You think so?'

'I know so. It would be cruel not to . . .'

'And you want me to take her?'

'Well, it would be doing me a huge favour if you could. I've got a meeting with the Tourist Information people today about some advertising.'

'If you really need me to . . .'

'Go on then,' urged Marilyn with a smile. 'Pick up the phone and make an appointment. After all,' she added, bursting into song, 'when the dog bites, when the cat stinks, when you're feeling sad, you simply remember your favourite vet, and then you won't feel so bad . . .'

It was a legitimate visit, so why did she feel like such an idiot, sitting in the waiting room surrounded by owners and animals. The kitten, now christened Mitten, short for Mum's kitten, by Alex, sat on a cushion in a basket like an Easter egg being delivered by the Easter Bunny. It was like people could see inside Liesel's head and knew exactly why she was there. She was fishing, man fishing, and she was so ashamed. The daft thing was she might not even get Tom Spencer; she might get sweet and lovely Adrian or even the dapper Mr Child's.

'Mitten Hamilton to room three, please,' the receptionist called out.

Liesel had to stop herself from laughing. It was really rather endearing the way they called the pets' name; so far it had sounded like a convention at the Playboy mansion, what with Boots McKenzie, Bunny Ryder, Pinky Jackson and Fluffy Hoolahan going in before her.

Room 3. Well, three was her lucky number. 'Here goes nothing,' she told Mitten, walking down the disinfected corridor.

She carefully pushed open the door to see a head bent over an examination table, hair conker-shiny under the fluorescent lighting. Tom looked up and smiled.

'Good morning.'

He had a touch of Joaquin Phoenix in *Gladiator* to him, she decided as she smiled back. It was in the curve of the mouth and the fine cheekbones. She didn't know if this was a good or a bad thing. Whilst everyone she knew had been drooling over Russell Crowe, she'd developed a rather enormous crush on the baddie of the movie, and if she was comparing Tom favourably to him, then how on earth could she keep trying to deny that she found him extremely attractive? Which was very good and very, very bad at the same time. It was lovely to really like someone, a nice feeling, but when Liesel found someone extremely attractive, her brain went into a strange kind of meltdown; in fact, it felt like it grew little legs and ran off to hide in a corner, where it refused to communicate with the rest of her body, leaving it to lumber along like a bus without a driver, particularly her mouth, which got exceptionally stupidly loquacious without any form of cranial government.

'Godrich sends his love,' was the first moronic thing to come out of her mouth.

His own mouth quirked into that bloody smile again, which made her instantly think how nice it would be to kiss it, which made her even worse.

'How's the thumb?'

Liesel held up the expertly bandaged digit.

'Throbbing,' she said, then blushed and bit her lip. 'Thank you for strapping me up so nicely.'

Oh my God, I can't say a thing right! Liesel cringed deep inside, whilst trying to keep her face looking normal. It wasn't easy. She probably looked like she was busting for the loo or something. Fortunately, even though she had her stupid head on, he had his work head on.

'So what can we do for you today?'

Liesel held up the basket, and Mitten chose the right moment to put her paws on the edge and mew endearingly, her huge eyes like headlights.

To her relief, Tom immediately smiled.

'I didn't know you had a cat.'

'We didn't until recently.'

'So where did she come from?'

'Found her by the bins. I think she was a stray.'

'Was?'

'Part of the family now.'

'Lucky her.' He smiled, and Liesel felt her stomach begin to churn like the washing machine she had spent the morning trying to fix. 'And good for you. I wish more people would offer strays a good home. How is Godrich, by the way?'

'Well, his tummy seems to be tons better now he's back on the right kind of food, but he seems to hate us for it. If he even smells chocolate on your breath or your fingers he gives you such a look of utter dejected deprivation, you'd expect WSPA to parachute in to rescue him.'

'You'll just have to keep reminding yourselves that chocolate's poisonous to dogs and you're not doing him any favours by letting him have it, no matter how much he thinks he loves it.'

'That's such a bum deal, isn't it? To be absolutely passionate about something that's really bad for you.'

'What does he think to this little thing, then?'

'Haughtily aloof at the moment, which I suppose is better than wanting to eat her.'

'So you need her vaccinated?'

'Please, and check her for chips just to make sure she's not someone's lost pet. I know how upset we'd be to lose her now, so I can sympathise if someone else has . . . but if she comes up clean, can you chip her for us, please?'

'Of course.'

As Liesel spoke, he had lifted the kitten out of the basket and was examining her very gently. Mitten was purring so loudly she sounded like the ticking of a diesel engine.

Lucky Mitten, Liesel sighed to herself.

'You obviously have a way with your hands . . . I mean, er . . . with animals, a way with animals, which is probably a good thing considering you're a vet, or in fact it could be why you became a vet, because you have . . . er . . . a . . . way. With. Animals . . .' She stumbled to a halt when she realised he was looking at her, one side of his mouth quirked into a semi-smile.

This was nothing like the easy banter they had shared in the bathroom last night, when shock and wine had eased the obviously one-sided sexual tension.

The best thing to do would be to say nothing, and so she went from talking nineteen to the dozen to absolute silence, a volte-face she thought in itself would make her appear even odder, but there was nothing else for it.

It didn't help that when it came time for Mitten to have her shots, Liesel's needle phobia once more reared its ugly head, and she had to be sat down with a glass of water, a fact for which she apologised a touch too profusely.

By the time Mitten had been examined, wormed, injected and chipped, Liesel was as anxious to get out of there as the poor little cat had become.

She slumped back in the driver's seat of the car, closed her eyes and sighed heavily. Mitten had seen the vet; now Liesel needed to see a doctor. The kind that sorted out your mental problems.

'How did it go?' Marilyn asked the minute she got back.

'Well, it should have been me getting treatment instead of the kitten.'

'What on earth for?'

'Verbal diarrhoea.'

'How can you solve a problem like diarrhoea?' Marilyn shook her head in sympathy.

Liesel nodded sorrowfully.

'And seeing him again made me realise he's just so *fanciable*, Marilyn. He's gorgeous, and how can someone like me even think that someone like that could ever be interested?'

'How can you hold a moonbeam in your hand?' Marilyn nodded, patting Liesel's hand comfortingly.

Liesel finally twigged, and wrinkled her nose in umbrage.

'You cow, I'm pouring my heart out to you here and you're taking the piss.'

'I'm your sister, it's my job to keep you grounded. Come on.' Marilyn prodded her with a finger in the rib cage. 'Laugh, you know you want to.'

'No, I don't,' Liesel replied as grouchily as possible whilst trying to keep the corners of her mouth on a downward slant, 'And I'm back to being celibate too.'

'You are?'

She nodded determinedly. 'There are more things to life than men.'

'Oh, absolutely.'

'Like this place. We've got a lot of work to do. Where's my wrench?'

'You going to go fix something?'

'No, I'm going to use it to bash some sense into myself.'

The following morning Liesel went downstairs to help Eric with breakfast, only to find Kashia furiously frying bacon and sausages, stabbing at them hard with a fork as if the poor pig that provided them deserved to die twice and she was happy to do the honours.

'Kashia what are you doing?'

'Eric called, he sick again.' Kashia rolled her eyeballs. 'So I start on pig things for the breakfasts or we no be ready for time to start.'

Marilyn bustled through the swing door, whistling.

'No Eric?' she asked seeing Kashia viciously prodding a sausage, which promptly exploded in protest all over the hob.

'Called in sick again.' Liesel sighed. 'This isn't good; the poor man, he's been ill too many times. I'm really worried about him. In fact, I'm going to go and see him. Can you manage breakfast without me?'

'Of course we can.'

Liesel had only been to Eric's home once before, when she had given him a lift home from work another time he had professed to feeling 'a little peaky'. He lived in a block of what were loosely termed studio apartments, but which was in fact a Victorian house where the owner let out rooms. The front door to the building was open, and so she went up to the first floor and tentatively knocked on his door.

'Hi, Eric, it's Liesel. I brought you some stuff.'

She knocked again, and after a few seconds, Eric answered the door in his dressing gown, eyes bloodshot and shadowed.

Liesel held out the flask and the bag she was carrying.

'Soup and sandwiches,' she offered.

The room itself was tiny, considering it was sitting room, kitchen and bedroom all in one, but it was incredibly neat and clean, although cluttered to the extreme as all of the walls and every single surface were covered with photographs.

Most of them were shots of a dark-haired woman with a thin face and a sweet smile; the rest Liesel surmised were of Eric's son in various stages from boy to man. The newest addition, taking pride of place on his bedside table, was a group shot of everyone from the Cornucopia taken during the picnic on the beach.

Unsure of what kind of reception she would garner, Liesel was pleased that Eric seemed delighted to see her. And if she'd had any doubts that this latest sickie was for real, she determined straight away that he also looked absolutely dreadful.

But he *was* hiding something.

He had what Liesel soon recognised as the male air of guilt, something any woman who has ever been lied to by a man will instantly know without description. She'd seen it before in Nick, in buckets to be honest, and it had made her hypersensitive to it, like a pig sniffing out truffles that no one else can scent.

It took her two cups of chicken soup and a conversation about the hotel and Alex and menus before she spotted the almost empty whisky bottle that had been hurriedly stuffed behind a cushion on the old sofa and it all slotted into place.

Maybe it hadn't just been guilt that she could smell.

She knew he didn't drink at work. She'd never seen him do it, never smelt it on him or detected any signs of inebriation; she even fetched things from his bag and his pockets at his request, and he had never seemed to try and hide things from her.

And so she steered the conversation very gently to

the woman in the photographs that dominated the room.

It was his wife, as she had supposed; her name was Jean, and she had died suddenly in an accident twenty years ago, when their son, Ed, was fifteen.

'The same age as me when my mum and dad died,' Liesel murmured.

Eric sighed and his eyes filled with tears.

'Is this you?' Liesel held up a photograph of a young man in uniform.

'When I was in the Navy.'

'I always knew you were a handsome devil, Eric.'

He managed a smile.

'I was a cocky sod an' all, didn't believe in love at first sight, not me. Then along came Jean. I knew I loved her the moment I met her. She smiled at me and that was it. I was a goner.'

'Ah, that's lovely.'

'Made me want to run a bloody mile, to be frank. I was terrified. Knew I was caught, you see. Been enjoying my bachelor days and knew that was it. Over. Finished. One-man woman for the rest of my days.' He paused and turned his face away from her, and she knew that he was crying and he didn't want her to see him. She turned to the sideboard and pretended to look at more pictures until he had composed himself.

'Still hurts so much after all this time,' he finally said, his voice catching.

'I understand completely.'

'Aye, and that you do, young Liesel. Which makes me feel even more ashamed that sometimes I just . . .' He stopped and pointed to the whisky bottle. 'Not all the time I'm not like that; just sometimes it's the only thing that seems to take the pain away. You think after all this time I'd have learnt to cope, eh?'

Liesel shook her head. 'There's no time limit on something like this.'

'You lost your mum and your dad and you seem to manage,' he said, shamefaced.

'I've had Marilyn and Alex. Without them I think I would have ended up in a very different place.'

'You think?'

Liesel nodded sincerely. 'I know so. I wouldn't have coped without them. I had some really bad times myself.'

'Ah, well as it happens, I haven't been coping so good myself neither.'

As if Liesel's confession had been what he needed to open up completely, he went on to tell her about the pools of black depression that he drowned in every so often. He relied upon the whisky to bring an oblivion that to him was still awful but better than the bleak reality that kept coming back to punch him afresh in the face as if it had only just happened. And finally came the confession of the guilt he had carried with him ever since.

'It was my fault, you see. I should have been with her but I was offered overtime. She didn't like to drive on her own at night . . .'

He'd held it together as best as he could for the sake of their son, but when Ed had decided to go travelling, it had been as though there was nothing that could stop him from sliding every so often into what he called 'self-indulgence'.

And when all of this came tumbling out like an avalanche, he looked even guiltier and said quietly, 'I'm right sorry it's been affecting my work at the hotel, Miss Liesel. I'll have my notice for you by the morning.'

'You'll do no such thing!' Liesel retorted.

'It's only right. Any other place would have given me my marching orders by now.'

But Liesel ignored him and simply held out a hand.

'Come on,' she said.

He looked at her questioningly.

'You're coming to stay with us. I'm not leaving you here on your own.'

'But I've just offered my resignation.'

'I know, and I've refused to accept it.' Then, softening, she bent to her knees beside his stooped figure and said gently, 'You don't have to be on your own, Eric. Not any more. You've got us now. Come on, help me pack. You're coming home with me.'

'I can't.'

'You can. If you want to . . .' She held out a hand. 'Come on. Let's go home.'

Marilyn looked up from reception and took in the situation at a glance.

'I've brought Eric home,' Liesel stated simply.

Marilyn didn't even question; she simply nodded at Liesel, and smiled at Eric before steering him to the sofa and asking Lorraine to go and fetch a spare duvet. Once she had installed him on the sofa with tea and biscuits and an old movie on the television, she took Liesel into the kitchen, where she listened in silence as her sister explained about the cause of Eric's frequent bouts of sick leave, sighing heavily at the drinking but even more so when Liesel went on to describe his home.

'He's so alone. No wonder he gets so depressed. I can't take him back there, Marilyn.' Her eyes were pleading, the same look as when she had wanted to keep the kitten, but this was slightly different. Eric was no kitten. He was a full-grown man, sixty years and counting.

'He's a proud man, Liesel, he won't accept what he thinks is charity.'

'I know, and I wouldn't dream of offending him by offering him that, but we could *rent* him a room here. I know that what he'd be paying would be nowhere near what we'd get normally, but as we know so well, some things in life are much more important than money, and we're hardly bursting at the seams with guests, are we? And if we do, miracle of miracles, get to the point where we need all the rooms, he can stay in my room if you don't mind me coming in with you.'

'It'll be like old times,' Marilyn laughed.

'So that's a yes?'

She nodded. 'Of course it is.'

'Oh, you're the best sister in the world,' Liesel cried, hugging her hard.

'As long as that's what Eric wants. We can't railroad him into staying here if he doesn't want to.'

'Oh, he'll want to,' Liesel replied a touch too quickly.

Marilyn stepped back, folded her arms and narrowed her eyes.

'You already asked him, didn't you?'

Liesel bit her bottom lip and offered a smile. 'I may have hinted at it in the car on the way back here . . .' but to her relief Marilyn just shook her head and laughed.

'What are you like?'

'Sorry . . . I know I shouldn't have without asking first, but I knew you wouldn't say no.'

'Well, can you keep up being a devious moo for a few more minutes?'

'It's not normally in my nature, but seeing as you asked . . . Why?'

'I want you to steal Eric's mobile phone.'

'What on earth for?'

'His son needs to know.'

'And it's our place to tell him?'

'Probably not, no. But someone's got to. Eric can't keep hiding how he is from everyone. He needs help, and he needs the family he's got left. If it were me, would you want to know?'

'Of course I would.'

'And what would you do if someone called and said I needed you?'

'I'd come running.'

'There you go, then.'

Liesel still didn't look convinced, so Marilyn stopped Lorraine, who was tottering past under an oversized load of linen.

'What's Eric's son like, Lorraine?' she asked, automatically beginning to unload Lorraine by taking half of the linen from her.

'I've only met him once, but he seemed okay.'

Marilyn nodded a confirmation. From Lorraine, 'okay' was a big compliment.

'Well then, that's settled, I'm going to call him. He needs to know his dad's not coping very well. Leez?'

'Maz?'

'Please?'

Liesel sighed. 'Okay, I'll get the phone.'

Fortunately when Liesel went back in the sitting room, Eric was asleep. He looked so vulnerable, wiped out, washed out. Whereas most people looked younger in sleep, he looked older, more careworn, his face fallen into a frown. As she quietly searched in the pockets of the jacket slung over the back of the sofa, Liesel felt like a thief, a betrayer of confidence. It had been so important to Eric to keep that veneer of control. If his son knew nothing about his periods of depression, it was because that was how Eric had wanted it; he hadn't wanted to burden him. He had told Liesel how it had always been his son's dream to travel, how he had worked his way around the world, how proud he was of him for this, and how he would hate to do anything to jeopardise this big adventure. But this altruism had meant that Eric was left all alone.

Liesel couldn't imagine being completely on her own; she had always had Marilyn. She had never believed in the saying 'you can choose your friends, but you can't choose your family'. Not in the literal sense of it anyway. If she could choose her family despite what had happened, she'd still choose the one she had. Friends had seemed to come and go in their lives . . . until now.

She knew that even though they had only known each other for a short time, Eric would do anything for them. He had been a good friend to them since they had arrived, and now it was their turn. Maz, as always, was doing the right thing. Liesel reached inside his jacket pocket and, taking out the old-fashioned mobile, tiptoed carefully out of the room and back to the kitchen.

'Well done.' Marilyn was whispering despite the fact that they were on the other side of the house. She took the phone from Liesel and turned it on. Eric's call list was dismally bare.

'Have you ever known anyone with only five phone numbers on their mobile?' she sighed. 'Poor bloke, most of the incoming calls are from us. Here we are, Ed.' She punched the number into her own phone.

'Hi, is that Ed?'

She wandered outside as she spoke. Liesel, sensing a need for privacy, didn't follow, but when Marilyn finally came back into the kitchen, she was anxious for answers.

'He's coming down.'

'Just like that?'

'Just like that. I hardly needed to say anything at all, just who we were and that we were concerned about Eric. He sounded really worried. Said it was a long story and if we didn't mind could he come here to see him. He wanted to book a room. I told him not to be so daft, he could stay as our guest.'

'More waifs and strays.' Liesel smiled.

'You don't mind, do you?'

Liesel hugged her sister.

'Of course I don't. I'd have minded if you hadn't offered.'

Two days later, very early in the morning, a battered old van pulled up at the end of the drive, just as Marilyn and Liesel were bringing in the milk delivery. The door swung open with a protesting squeak of rusting hinges, and a man stepped out, a slight cockney-accented voice proclaiming, 'Cheers, mate. Much appreciated,' before the van drove on its way.

Caterpillar boots, ripped jeans, short brown hair dusted with premature flecks of grey, slightly spiky and in need of a cut, a five o'clock shadow, and strong arms over one of which was slung an enormous rucksack were the first things that Marilyn noticed.

Looking about himself, gathering his bearings, he saw the two girls watching and smiled hesitantly.

'Marilyn?' he called, walking towards them.

'Ed?'

'That's right.' He reached them and held out a hand.

Up close, Marilyn could see that his nose was slightly bent, as though it had been broken, and his eyes were the light bright blue of the morning sky above them. His tanned face creased into a warm smile as they shook.

'This is my sister Liesel.'

'Good to meet you at last. Thanks for calling me.'

'Thanks for coming.'

'If I'd known sooner . . .'

Marilyn stopped him.

'You'd have been here, I know you would. Well, you're here now. You'd better come in.'

He nodded his thanks, and then, as the girls struggled to lift the two milk crates between them, offered, 'Here, let me take those,' and picked them both up at once, still with rucksack *in situ*, and carried them through into the hotel.

'Where do you want them?'

'Kitchen, please. Through here,' said Marilyn, leading the way.

He put the milk crates down on the shiny stainless-steel surface of the worktop and looked about himself.

'Dad's domaine.' He nodded slowly. 'He always talks about you guys when I call him. Said how lovely you are. How things have been so much better since you've been here. But then he obviously only ever tells me the good and not the bad.'

'He's been trying to protect you.'

Ed laughed wryly.

'Do I look like I need protecting? Silly old sod,' he said, his voice soaked with affection and emotion. 'He loves it here. Thanks for giving him a little bit of stability; a lot of people would have given up on him by now for taking so much time off. He'd be lost without this place, without you guys.'

'It's not totally altruistic. He's a great chef, the best. We'd be lost without him too.'

'Where is he?'

'We made him have a lie-in, much to his disgust, but despite his protestations he's actually gone back to sleep. Why don't I show you to your room, you can freshen up a bit and then come and have some breakfast with us.'

'That would be great, cheers, and thanks for letting me stay here. Are you sure it's okay?'

Marilyn nodded maniacally.

'It's fine, honestly. It'll be really good for Eric to have you here.'

'I can't wait to see his face,' Liesel beamed.

'You didn't tell him I was coming?'

'We thought the surprise would be nice for him. Come on, I'll take you up and then we can serve your dad with a bit of bacon and a nice cup of tea.'

Eric bellowed with joy when he saw his son, then he went bright red, and then he cried. Then he hugged everyone and started apologising until he had to be begged to stop. After breakfast, the two men set off up the tidal river to the beach for a heart-to-heart that lasted all day.

Eric came back smiling.

Marilyn was the only one who noticed that Ed's jollity was a touch more forced.

As Eric, seemingly renewed, rolled up his sleeves and hit the kitchen to prepare dinner, Marilyn went in search of Ed. An already besotted Alex had taken him into the garden half an hour ago to show him Godrich's tricks, but Alex had just volunteered for pudding duty in the kitchen, so Ed was on his own somewhere. Marilyn found him sitting at a table on the terrace in the sunshine, nursing a glass of beer.

'Seems a bit hypocritical, doesn't it?'

In answer, Marilyn held up her own glass of wine and then sat down next to him.

He was quiet for a moment, long enough for Marilyn to study his face, bathed in the low evening sunshine. It was a well-used face, lined more than his years would merit, she assumed some from anguish, and some from laughter. The eyes were steady and held a certain wisdom and at this moment a certain sadness. After a while, he began to speak again.

'When Mum died, we each dealt with it in our way. Dad threw himself into his work and the occasional bottle neck, and I took off. I regret that now. They say that parents should look after their kids, but you know sometimes it gets to the point where it has to work the other way around. So what do I do now?' he asked nobody in particular, and then snorted with derision at his own question. 'That isn't even in doubt really. It's my turn to take care of him, and so I stay in Piran and make sure he gets this sorted out once and for all. Get him thinking of the good times. Once I can get it into that stubborn head that Mum would hate to see him this unhappy after all this time . . . Yeah, that's the way to get him over it. Get him focused on the future. Mum would hate to see him drinking his sorrows away. She'd hate the fact that we didn't stick together, either.' He finally turned to face Marilyn. 'I didn't leave because of Dad, you know, but I did leave in spite of him.'

It was clear he adored Eric and was furious with himself for having been so easily convinced that all was fine back home when it so clearly wasn't.

'He's proud of you, you know. Of what you've achieved.'

'And what exactly have I achieved? What have I got to show for ten years of travel? A passport full of stamps from foreign countries, and even those will be gone soon. My passport's up for renewal in September. I've done nothing, Marilyn.'

'Surely that depends on what you use as a measure. Think of all the amazing places you've been to, you've experienced. You know, if Alex gets to eighteen and decides he wants to sell this place and use the money to sod off round the world, then he'll be going with my blessing.'

'So you're staying until he's eighteen?' Ed smiled

gently at her. 'That's a touch longer than just the summer season.'

'It is, isn't it? Do you think that was a Freudian slip?'

'Maybe. It is beautiful here. I can understand why you might decide you want to stay.'

'Even though you were happy to leave?'

'I was happy to leave, yes, but do you know something, I think I'm equally as happy to be back.'

'Well, if you're going to stay on in Piran, then you're welcome to stay here, you know.'

'That's really kind of you, Marilyn, but you don't have room for me.'

'We're not exactly fighting off the bookings. We've got three empty rooms tonight.'

'Sure, but that's today. In the hotel business you can be empty one day and full the next; it's the way it goes.'

'You know hotels?'

'I've done a bit. When you're working your way around the world, a hotel or a bar is always a good bet for a job.'

'Okay, how about a compromise? We do have the room without affecting the business if you're prepared to slum it a bit.'

'I've been travelling in Asia for the past three months; a mat on the floor is four star to me.'

'What about a redundant storeroom? It's clean and dry, and if you're prepared to clear out the stuff that's somehow accumulated in there, then it's yours. I even think there's a spare bed in there somewhere under all the junk.'

'Sounds good to me. But what do you think Dad will say?'

'He'll be totally chuffed. As long as you're sure it's what you want. He won't want you to stay here just because of him, I can tell you that much. And before you say anything, it doesn't matter how old you are, you don't want to be a burden to your kids. Trust me, I'm speaking from experience here, seeing as my own son has been dressed as Superman since his dad left.'

'He can't look after his mum, but maybe Superman can?'

'You hit the nail on the head.'

'He seems like a good kid, he'll turn it around.'

'He needs . . .' Marilyn stopped herself. She had been going to say 'a father', but for some reason she was suddenly uncomfortable voicing the word. 'More male company,' she finally stuttered. 'It's been great that he's had Eric around; it was hard for him stuck in a tiny flat with just us two girls as role models.'

'I bet you've been great.'

'Sure, we've taught him how to cook, how to iron, how to sew . . .'

'Now you're doing yourself down. I bet you wield a mean power drill.'

'Well, I can change fuses, house plugs and spark plugs.' Marilyn smiled. 'And Liesel does a hell of a lot with a wrench, I can tell you. There are quite a few things that are beyond us, though. The bloody balustrade needs repointing; that's a job that's beyond even Liesel's wrench, unless of course we decide the safest thing is to knock it down instead of shoring it back up. Then again, if we did that, we'd have people flying off the terrace in the dark, which probably wouldn't be the best thing in the world . . .'

'At least you'd have Superman here to save them.' Ed smiled at her.

He had a nice smile, Marilyn noted, genuine and easy.

'Look, I've had an idea. Why don't you let me do it? The balustrade, I mean . . .'

'We can't afford to pay someone to do it at the moment.'

'I don't want you to pay me.'

'I can't let you do it for free.'

'Well, in a way I wouldn't be. You're paying Dad a full wage for doing half a job. You can't afford to carry him, so think of it as a job share.' He was coaxing her, his eyes pleading.

'You mean, you do the work and your father gets the money?'

'In a way, yes. You know that this job is Dad's lifeline, this place is the only home he's really got.'

Marilyn nodded.

'What do you say?'

'If you're working for us unpaid, how are you going to support yourself?'

'I'll get another job, I'll work nights or something. Get a bar job. There are plenty of places in town that need people.'

Marilyn shook her head.

'Please don't say no, Marilyn . . .'

'I'm not saying no.'

'You're not?'

'I'm saying that I have a better idea.'

Marilyn stood up and held out her hands.

'Come on.'

'What are you up to?' He narrowed his eyes and smiled at her.

'You'll find out in a minute.'

'Liesel? Liesel!'

'IMINERE!' came a muffled reply.

'Kitchen.' Marilyn grinned at Ed and, still holding on to his hand as if he were Alex, tugged him in after her.

Liesel was nowhere to be seen.

'Leez?'

'Over there.'

Ed pointed to the oven. An overalled Liesel was on her knees with her head inside it.

'Crikey, things aren't that bad, are they?' Marilyn chortled.

'Ha bloody ha.' Liesel scowled as she emerged back into the room. 'If only I could get the bloody thing on, then maybe I could gently gas myself to the other side!'

'It's not working?'

Liesel waved her beloved wrench at them.

'No matter how much I bang and batter.'

'Well, bang and batter no more, sister dearest. I'd like you to meet our new handyman!' Marilyn had to hold herself back from saying 'ta-da', and doing game-show-host hands.

She looked from Ed to Liesel and back again. Neither had said a word. She couldn't work out who looked the more surprised, and waited anxiously for the surprise to turn to the pleasure she hoped would follow.

After three breath-holding seconds, she was relieved to see them both begin to beam.

'Well, thank the Lord!' Liesel grinned, hauling herself up from the floor. 'Welcome to the madhouse.' She hugged them both and handed Ed the wrench. 'In that case, I'm going to go and have a nice long bubble bath.' She winked and walked out of the room.

'Are you sure about this?' Ed asked, weighing the wrench from hand to hand.

'It makes perfect sense. You need a job. We need some help.'

'Sure, but Dad said you're not exactly raking in the customers at the moment.'

Marilyn sighed an acknowledgement.

'That's true. We could be doing better, but we're doing okay, and there's enough money in the bank from Nancy's insurance to keep us going over the bad patches.' What she didn't add was that neither she nor Liesel took any sort of wage at the moment. Since taking Kashia on full time, Liesel had as promised insisted on just having enough 'pocket money' to buy the barest of essentials. Since her advertising had brought in less than fifty per cent of the people that Marilyn had hoped for, she too had refused to take any money other than for Alex. This wasn't as bad as it sounded, as the hotel provided most of what they needed: food, bed and board, even shampoo and shower gel. Taking on Ed would mean they were stretched even further, but in truth they needed him. The maintenance on the Cornucopia was a legitimate full-time job. There was always something that needed to be done, from the nonslip flooring in the kitchen right up to the guttering on the roof.

'We need you, Ed,' she reassured him.

This point was proved over the next couple of days. In just forty-eight hours, Ed repointed the balustrade, trimmed back the overgrown garden, fixed the oven – much to Liesel's delight – and stripped the floral wallpaper from Alex's room, ready for it to be repainted Superman-tights blue. In fact, he made himself so invaluable that Marilyn was beginning to wonder how they had ever managed without him. On top of that, he was as nice, decent, and honest as his father. Everyone loved him straight away, even Kashia, while Alex was instantly smitten. For a man who admitted he wasn't used to kids, Ed had a way with him that made them instant friends. He even managed to persuade Alex to ditch the zombie-killing after school one night and go fishing with him.

They arrived back just after dark. Their laughter could be heard coming from the car as they drove down the driveway.

'Did you catch anything?' Marilyn asked Alex as he

tugged Ed through the doorway clutching his hand.

'No . . .' he piped happily and looked at Ed for his cue.

'But you should have seen the one that got away,' Ed prompted him.

'Oh yeah, but you should have seen the one that got away,' Alex repeated.

He ran back to Ed's side, and they both held out their arms to full stretch.

'It was THIS big,' they chorused before convulsing into laughter.

'Well, for someone who didn't catch any fish, you sure do smell of it.' Marilyn grinned, pretending to hold her nose. 'Why don't you both go and get showered and changed and we'll start on dinner, okay?'

'Great. Ed got you a present.'

'We bought you this from the harbour.' Ed held open a blue-striped carrier bag, which Marilyn peered into a touch cautiously, to see several pounds of gleaming fish. 'Thought we could all have them for dinner tonight. Dad could put them on as a special for the restaurant as well, there's plenty.'

'That's . . . er . . . great, Ed, thank you.'

'Come on, Ed.' Alex tugged him through the tower door. 'I want to show you that computer game.'

'Showers!' Marilyn called after them.

As the heavy door swung shut behind them, Liesel held out her arms at full stretch and winked at Marilyn.

'It was THIS big!' she repeated, eyes wide with laughter. 'Do you think Ed was talking about the size of the fish or the size of his—'

'Liesel!' Marilyn blushed furiously. 'You shouldn't talk about Ed like that.'

15

It was the night of the Veterinary Association Annual Dinner Dance, and Lorraine's first proper date with Adrian. Keen to join in the preparation, the sisters had persuaded her to bring her things and stay the night at the hotel, bunking in with Liesel. Adrian was due to pick her up at seven, and so at five thirty she was ushered from the kitchen, where Eric was making dinner and Ed was fixing the 'rumbler', the big, noisy machine that peeled potatoes for them, to go get ready in the tower.

It wasn't very long before she was back.

She had obviously showered, but other than changing into a simple, but not in an understated, chic way, rather dated black satin prom dress, and letting her hair loose, instead of in its usual ponytail, she looked pretty much like the Lorraine who had entered the tower less than half an hour ago.

She was even wearing the same sensible low-heeled pumps that had accompanied the black-skirt-white-shirt combo she had worn for work that day.

Liesel and Marilyn exchanged looks, wanting to say something but not wanting to hurt feelings.

Kashia had no such reservations.

'You go out with new man like that? You cannot go out with vet Adrian Lee looking like you are patient of him.'

'What do you mean?' Lorraine blinked in concern.

'Come, you look.'

Kashia took her by the shoulders and steered her to the huge gilt-framed mirror hanging on the wall.

'See, you have no make-up.'

'I never wear make-up.'

'Sure, is okay for the work, but when you go out, sometimes is okay to help the face, is good. You have the white skin, you need some colour to the lips, to the cheeks, to the eyes. And the clothes, they look like you wear them to serve the dinner, and your hair,' she fluffed Lorraine's lank locks in despair, 'well, I sad to say that Godrich, he have better hairstyle.'

'So it's all no good?' Lorraine asked, looking like she was going to burst into tears.

Despite Marilyn's warning look, Kashia shook her head a touch too vigorously, and Lorraine's face fell even further.

'We've got a whole sackful of make-up between us.' Liesel stepped in hurriedly, agreeing with Kashia in her summation but not in the way she was presenting it. 'We can soon slap a bit of lipstick on you. And I have a dress that would probably look great on you too.'

'You don't like my dress?'

'It's a great dress,' Liesel said reassuringly. 'For the 1980s,' she whispered in an aside to her sister. 'But I think you'd look lovely in something a bit brighter than black . . . I've got a beautiful amethyst silk hanging in my wardrobe, I picked it up from Cancer Research in Kensington, brand-new Coast and only twelve pounds, always been a little bit loose on me,' she added as she caught Lorraine checking our her svelte figure with wide eyes. 'Should fit you perfectly.'

'And we have the same size feet.' Marilyn took Lorraine's hand. 'So I'm sure we can find a pair of pretty shoes to match. Oh, and you smell wonderful,' she added, desperate to give the poor girl a compliment of some kind.

'Liesel said I could borrow the Chanel you gave her for your birthday last year,' Lorraine said so forlornly that even Kashia softened.

'You no look so sad, we fix. You pretty girl, is easy.'

'I'm pretty?' Lorraine repeated it like Kashia had just told her she was a man.

'You is pretty, yes. You have face like shining moon with eyes of midnight sky she sit in.'

Lorraine's eyes of midnight sky almost popped out in surprise, not just at the poetic compliment, but at its source.

Kashia turned to Liesel.

'You have hair curlers, please? I hairdresser in Poland.'

They all stopped and looked at her in surprise.

'You were?'

She nodded. 'Sure. I good too. I give Lorraine hair like film star . . .'

Ed, on his way to fix a dripping tap in Alex's en suite bathroom, found Alex, Godrich and Mitten sitting in a row outside Liesel and Marilyn's bathroom.

'What's going on in there?'

'They're pimping Lorraine.'

'He means primping!' Marilyn yelled from the other side of the door.

Ed rolled his eyeballs in amusement and, leaning in to Alex, whispered. 'You were right with the first word. You know that programme on television where they take a car that's basically a really good runner but it's been a bit neglected, and make it look all smart and flashy?'

Alex nodded.

'That's what they're doing to Lorraine. Come on, kiddo.' He held out a hand. 'Let's go do man stuff.'

'Like what?'

'Fix the tap in your bathroom.'

Alex didn't look impressed, so Ed thought for a moment.

'Want to go bake another cake?'

Forty minutes later, brownies in the oven sending torturous wafts of melting chocolate throughout the hotel, Ed and Alex heard the soft thunk of the heavy door from the tower closing, and the clatter of heeled feet and the chatter of excited female voices in the hallway.

'Are they done?' Alex was sitting on the floor in front of the oven.

'The brownies or the girls?'

'Mum's out of the bathroom?' Alex scrambled to his feet. Having made Ed laugh with his too literal translation of the pimping analogy, with his visions of Lorraine emerging from the bathroom reupholstered in blood-red leather and sprayed a fetching cosmos black with go-faster stripes, Alex's interest was more with the makeover than the bakeover. Especially when Ed had explained that when women spent a really long time in the bathroom, they weren't usually lounging on the loo reading comics. Skittering into the hallway, his socked feet sliding on the polished floor, he skidded to a halt in front of Lorraine; who was being paraded like the float queen at a carnival, and exclaimed, 'Wow!'

'They're you go, Lorraine, your first compliment of the evening.' Marilyn laughed at Alex's slack jaw.

'And another man to ask an opinion of.' Liesel grinned at Ed. 'What do you think?'

It wasn't one of those movie makeovers, where they went in looking like a man in drag and came out like Elizabeth Taylor. She still looked like Lorraine, only it was Lorraine with her hair curled very prettily so that it hung in silky waves, and some lipstick on, in a nice dress. And it made a huge difference.

'You look great,' Ed said, the sincerity in his voice bringing tears instantly to a rather emotional Lorraine's eyes.

'You no cry!' Kashia warned her sternly. 'Liesel make you eyes like sexy cat and it all wash off if you cry!'

'You need a large glass of wine to help you relax and get you in the mood,' announced Marilyn, who was at least three times as excited at the prospect of the evening's date than the woman who was actually going on it.

Liesel rolled her eyes and shook her head.

'Lorraine has a small sherry on special occasions. A large glass of wine and she won't be relaxed, she'll be comatose.'

'Okay then, a small sherry, seeing as this is a special occasion.'

They had only been in the bar a few minutes when the sound of a car pulling up outside almost sent Lorraine running back into the bathroom.

'He's here!' trumpeted Alex, just in case anyone hadn't noticed.

'Are you ready?' Liesel asked.

Lorraine fought the urge to go fold linen, and knocked back her sherry.

Marilyn and Liesel were on the sofa, under a duvet. The old grandmother clock in the corner showed that it was just gone twelve, and they were both wilting, eyelids fluttering with the weight of denied sleep.

'I feel like I'm waiting up for my kid to come home.' Marilyn yawned.

'If you're like this now with Lorraine, can you imagine what you're going to be like when Alex has his first date?'

'Oh, I know, but despite her age, she's still like a kid. She's so unworldly, which makes her really vulnerable.'

'Relax, Adrian's one of the good guys.'

'You think I'm daft, don't you?'

Liesel shook her head and, reaching out, squeezed her sister's hand. 'No. I think it's lovely that you care so much, actually.'

'And I'm not the only one up after midnight, am I.' Marilyn winked back.

Outside in his car, Adrian Lee gripped the steering wheel and tried to pluck up the courage to kiss Lorraine good night. It had been a good evening, good enough for the shy, retiring Adrian to even dare to think that if he kissed her, she wouldn't slap him round the face, storm off and then refuse to take his calls ever again.

Adrian hadn't noticed the makeover. This was not because he wasn't an observant chap who didn't notice things like haircuts, or new dresses; it was because he was well and truly smitten and he thought she was gorgeous already. To him she looked like Aphrodite whether she had lipstick on or not, whether she was dressed in her cleaning overalls or the latest Versace.

But of course Lorraine didn't know this.

What Lorraine knew was that he had liked her enough to ask her out, but now that he had spent the last five hours in her company he might have changed his mind.

Oh, the perils of low self-esteem.

'Well, thank you for a lovely evening.'

She was ready to bolt. She had gathered up her handbag, and was almost reaching for the door handle. It was now or never. Could he? Dare he?

'Lorraine?' It came out kind of squeaky, but at least it came out.

Her hand stopped in mid-hover and she turned to him

in question, and then he saw it, his own insecurities echoed in her face. He started to laugh, and for a moment she looked mortified, but then he saw her lips begin to twitch, and she joined in, and that was when he found the courage he needed to reach out and cup that sweet face in his hands and kiss her oh so gently on the lips.

'It's a farce really, isn't it?' he told her when, smiling, he pulled away, his hands still on her face. 'This set of rules we feel we're supposed to abide by. People like us. Well, we just don't do it, do we . . . all this dating etiquette, it doesn't work for people like us.'

She liked that phrase, 'people like us'.

'I never thought I'd meet anyone else like me.'

He nodded. 'Me neither. Lorraine, I'm afraid I'm not the most romantic man in the world. I wouldn't really know what to do, to be honest, but if you think you could be happy with a man like me, who could offer you friendship and honesty instead of hearts and flowers, then perhaps we could give *us* a try? Be together . . .'

He might be declaring himself unromantic, but to Lorraine it was the most romantic thing she had ever heard.

She began to nod furiously.

'We've been talking all evening, but this is the first time I actually feel like we've been talking. Does that sound stupid?'

'No. I know exactly what you mean.' He let go of her face to take her hands. 'I'll call you tomorrow,' he told her.

And they both knew that, quite simply, he would.

Lorraine floated into the hotel, ballet-danced into the sitting room, pirouetted round Liesel and Marilyn, managing to hug them both as she spun

'So how did it go?' Liesel asked rather unnecessarily.

'I've got a boyfriend,' Lorraine sang at them.

They made a space between them and patted for her to sit down.

'We want to know everything, tell us everything.'

And so she did, literally and, Liesel could have sworn, almost word for word, right through from when he picked her up at the hotel to when he kissed her goodbye, and as she spoke of the kiss she couldn't help but jump to her feet and begin to dance around the room again. It was rather an odd spectacle, a bit like Queen Victoria suddenly coming across all giddy and girlish.

And then she remembered the only bit of the evening that had made it less than perfect, and she flopped from her toes to the flats of her size six feet, the sparkle continuing to spin about the room for a second on its own before bumping into the French doors and sparking itself out like a match being pinched between thumb and forefinger.

'Oh . . .' her face fell, 'and Tom's got a girlfriend.'

Well, it surely didn't come as that much of a surprise that the gorgeous Tom Spencer wasn't single. They had speculated as much already themselves. He's bound to have a girlfriend, they had said, and they'd been right. A girlfriend he had. More so in fact, because the girlfriend was more than just a girlfriend, she was a fully fledged fiancée. She had a ring (large and flawless) and a wedding dress on order and a date that was still O something.

Lorraine even had photographs. Had taken her digital camera to capture the evening.

Her name was Caroline. She was gorgeous, of course, all glossy dark hair and thoroughbred features. Smiled a lot too, very white teeth. If Liesel could find fault in any way, and boy did she try, it was perhaps that her top lip was a little thin, but it was pushing it to say that. And the dress she was wearing, well, the dress was beautiful, classy, obviously very expensive, all chic and shimmer and short to show off long toned legs.

And Tom in the photographs, well, he looked good in a DJ, but the thing that stuck most with Liesel was that he had his arm about Caroline's waist and was smiling broadly.

Liesel swallowed her disappointment and tried to find nice things to say about the girl in the picture, like how shiny her hair was and how neat her figure, but Marilyn and Lorraine were looking at her like someone had just told her she had failed an important exam, and they were waiting for the reaction.

They were smiling at her too much; she could feel the sympathy coming off them in waves, like strong perfume, sweet but slightly nauseating.

Suck it up and put on a smile, Liesel Ellis, she told herself. After all, you've only met the man a couple of times; you have no claims or rights

'Cute couple,' she said as steadily as she could. 'Now, tell me again, how many times did Adrian kiss you?'

'Twice,' Lorraine declared. 'And he said my hair looked gorgeous.'

'Your hair did look gorgeous.'

'Mmm.' Lorraine nodded thoughtfully. 'I've never had gorgeous hair before. Kashia is clever, isn't she?'

The following evening, when Kashia went to lay the table for dinner, she found a small box of her favourite, hard-to-source Polish chocolates waiting next to her freshly laundered and perfectly pressed work trousers. The note on top of them read simply, 'Thank you. Love, Lorraine.'

16

One of the things about living by the sea is the salt. Believe it or not, it doesn't just stay in the water, it gets everywhere: hair tangles with it, cars corrode more quickly, skin tastes of it, and then there are windows . . . What with the salt and the spray and occasional high winds, oh, and sea gulls of course, they were constantly in need of cleaning. It was a long and laborious job to get them sparkling again, as there were so many of them and so many things intent on dirtying them, and so they had split the whole thing into shifts.

Ed was cleaning the outside, Marilyn holding his ladder; Lorraine was on top-floor inside duty, Kashia on the second floor; Eric was in the kitchens and storerooms and Liesel was cleaning the rest of the bottom floor whilst keeping an eye on reception.

It was thus that Tom Spencer managed to pull up in his Range Rover and walk through the hall and into the sitting room, where Liesel was busy scrubbing the glass doors, without anyone noticing. When he said hello, she jumped so hard she almost fell off the chair she was using to reach the top bits.

'Oh Lord, I'm so sorry,' he said in alarm, rushing to grab an elbow to steady her. 'I didn't mean to startle you.'

Liesel, still rocking a little, turned to face him, forgetting for a moment to step down from the chair, so stunned was she to just see him there. And then she noticed that in the hand that wasn't still holding her, he was gently cupping the cutest little terrier puppy, a ball of soft fluff the colour of demerara sugar.

'Awwwwww.' Not high on eloquence, but it was still probably the most coherent thing she'd said to him to date.

'Gorgeous, isn't she?' he said, helping Liesel step down and offering her the dog to cuddle. 'Actually, she's the reason I'm here. Well, that and I wanted to check on you, your thumb, see how my handiwork was holding up.'

'It's good, thank you . . .' Liesel said, thumb insignificant as the puppy began to lick her face. 'What's her name?'

'She doesn't actually have one. She and her two brothers were dumped on the surgery doorstep three days ago. I think she's about twelve weeks old. We've checked them out and they're all fine and so I've been trying to find homes for them for the last couple of days. She's the last one of the litter, but I'd say she's the pick. I wanted to show her to you before I offered her to anyone else . . . You took in the little cat, so I figured maybe . . .'

'I might be a sucker for another stray?' Liesel said crouching down and placing the puppy on the floor to play.

'Okay, maybe just a little bit, but I also thought you might like her . . . and that it might be good for Godrich to have another dog in the place too. You know, to teach him how to be . . . well, more of a *dog*, I suppose.'

'She's certainly adorable,' Liesel cooed, stroking the cashmere-soft belly that was presented to her, 'but I don't know what Marilyn would say to having another animal in the hotel . . . especially one who isn't house-trained yet . . .' She cringed as the puppy squatted and happily peed on the rug.

'Oh no, I'm so sorry!'

'Don't worry, we all hate that rug. Besides, I happen to be perfectly equipped.' Liesel picked up the bucket and cloth she had been using to clean the windows.

'In that case, let me.'

Tom took the cloth from her and, bending over, began to mop.

Boy, he had a nice arse, Liesel decided from her vantage point behind him.

'You don't want this, do you, I'm so sorry . . .'

'Oh, I want it all right,' Liesel growled, still contemplating that perfect backside, and then realised that he had turned to look up at her. 'Er . . . I mean, yes I do, I do want her, I mean, who wouldn't, she's gorgeous . . .' Liesel you idiot, you're panting more than the dog. 'It's just that a hotel's not really the best place . . . and it's not just down to me . . . though she is adorable.'

'Your sister?' She knew he meant did she need to speak to Marilyn, but her nerves were still functioning better than her brain.

'She's kind of cute too,' she joked, badly.

'Flattery will get you everywhere.' Marilyn was leaning in through the doorway, shirt sleeves rolled up, hair crowned with flicks of soap suds from standing below a vigorously cleaning Ed. 'So who's this, then?'

'Marilyn, you remember Tom.'

'Of course I remember Tom.' Marilyn nodded a friendly hello and rolled her eyeballs in amusement. 'I meant the small thing currently chewing on the curtains.'

'It's a puppy.'

'I can see that, but what exactly is the puppy doing here?'

'Um, well, she needs a home, and Mr Spen . . . cer, I mean Tom thought that I might like him . . . I mean her.'

Marilyn raised her eyebrows. Liesel wasn't sure if she

was imagining things, but it honestly looked like she was trying very hard not to laugh.

'So *Mr Spencer*, I mean Tom, brought you a puppy, eh?'

'Yes, but Liesel was just explaining that perhaps a hotel isn't the best place for her, so maybe I should try and find her a home elsewhere.'

'I don't know about that. We seem to be filling up more with permanent residents nowadays than we do the temporary ones. And there's always room for a little one . . .'

Liesel strained to detect sarcasm in the last sentence but actually couldn't find any.

'You're being serious? We can keep her?'

Marilyn nodded. 'I don't see why not, as long as we can train her to behave around the guests.'

'What, just like Godrich does?'

'Point taken.'

'I can help you with that side of things,' Tom offered. 'I used to run a class until I got my partnership. No time any more, but I still know the rudiments.'

'What, like training her not to pee on the carpet?' Liesel asked as the puppy squatted on the rug again.

Embarrassed, Tom rushed to mop up, but Marilyn beat him to it, gingerly picking up the rug and stuffing it into a black bin bag she pulled from her pocket.

'I've been looking for an excuse to do that since we moved in; now I can get a nice new one. Well, there you go, it's all settled. We were just going to take a break and have a nice cold shandy from the bar. Do you two, sorry, I mean *three*, fancy joining us?'

They took their drinks out on to the terrace, and whilst Tom was chatting happily with Ed, Liesel sat down next to her sister.

'Thank you. For letting me keep her . . .'

'The man you've fallen head over heels for has just brought you the most adorable puppy. Who am I to say you couldn't keep her.'

'I haven't fallen—' Liesel began to object a touch too loudly.

Marilyn held up a hand.

'Don't even try to deny it,' she whispered, 'or I'll tell him to take the puppy away.'

Liesel hurriedly lifted the dog on to her lap, where the tiny animal began to chew daintily on the hem of her T-shirt.

'And unless I'm very much mistaken, the feeling could quite possibly be reciprocated.'

'You think he likes me?'

'Well, put it this way, how many times has he met you, and he suddenly turns up here with her.'

'She needed a home.'

'And you think he'd struggle to find her one? Look how cute she is. And you said she was the last of the litter; well, girls usually go before boys, Liesel.'

'But he has a girlfriend . . . sorry, fiancée.'

Marilyn sighed sympathetically.

'I know, and in those circumstances he seems far too decent a guy to make a move on you. Doesn't mean he doesn't like you, though. Anyway, what are you going to call her?' She looked at the puppy.

'You mean I get to pick and not Alex?'

'I think he'd understand on this occasion . . . as long as you don't call her Tom Junior after her *daddy*.'

Liesel stuck out her tongue but didn't bite.

'I can't really, seeing as she's a girl.'

'It could be short for Tomasina.'

'Tommie's not bad.' Liesel nodded, putting the puppy on the floor and then getting down on her knees next to her as the puppy rolled on her back for a tickle.

'You know, most men give girls they like perfume or jewellery,' Marilyn mused.

'Or silk underwear.' Liesel smiled back broadly, as the puppy wandered off towards Tom and Ed. She was obviously far more delighted with her than she would have been by even the most covetable Agent Provocateur.

'You could call her Pants. Alex would love that. It's a pun,' Marilyn added as Liesel frowned at her. 'Underwear, pants, a dog pants?'

'Or Knickers.' Liesel grinned, joining in the theme. 'I can just imagine it if I lose her in the park: 'Knickers, Knickers, where are you? I want my Knickers, has anyone seen my Knickers!'

'Trust you to take it too far.' Her sister laughed and shook her head. 'What about Ruby?'

Liesel suddenly smiled.

'Oh, I think I like that . . . It suits her too. Ruby . . .' Liesel called gently, waggling her fingers. 'Ruby, Ruby . . .'

And the puppy who loved to be tickled and who already loved the melodious sound of Liesel's adoring voice, trotted back to her new mistress and rolled over to present a soft round belly.

Tom left soon afterwards, but not before he had asked Liesel to come to his car with him. There he opened the cavernous boot and lifted out a dog basket inside which were two bowls, one for food, one for water, a lead that matched the tiny collar Ruby was already wearing, and a big bag of dog food.

'I didn't think it was fair to put the burden on you to buy these things for her, but I also didn't want to be too presumptuous and bring them in with me,' he explained.

'Thank you so much.'

'No. It's me that should be thanking you.'

'That's not true. I really can't imagine you having trouble finding someone to take her. Be honest now . . .'

He hung his head but he was still smiling.

'Okay, the truth is I'm rather smitten with her, but I can't have her myself because of other commitments, and you seemed like the kind of person that would give her the home I'd want for her.'

'But you barely know me.'

'I've seen enough.'

He reached out and picked up Liesel's hand and studied her thumb.

'Looking good.'

'Done by a pro, you see.'

'You're the only non-animal I've ever sutured.'

'Then I'm privileged.'

'Some people wouldn't look at it like that!' He grinned at her, and Liesel suddenly found herself just for a fraction of a second hating all things called Caroline. And then she told herself to be rational, not pathological, and managed to smile back, a normal smile, the kind you'd give a friend.

'And I meant what I said about training,' he reminded her, giving Ruby a last pat before getting in his car. 'The sooner we start with her, the better, really. Does Tuesday night suit? Say around seven?'

'That would be great,' Liesel called after him as he drove away, and couldn't help herself from adding under her breath, 'You bring the stern commands, and I'll provide the submission . . . Oh stop it, you moron!' she chastised herself as she went back to her window washing. 'He's engaged. He's engaged, he's engaged, he's engaged, he's engaged, he's engaged . . .' Who knows, if she repeated it often enough, it might just sink in.

17

Liesel was on reception, updating Hotel Perfect, the system Marilyn had installed along with the new computer to replace the outdated books that had logged all previous guests.

Little Ruby was curled up on her lap, sleeping as she always did flat on her back with all four legs in the air, which made it blooming difficult to type, but there was no way Liesel was going to dislodge the new love of her life when she was sleeping so sweetly and so peacefully.

Godrich was a dead weight on her feet. He had consumed a vast supper of leftover chicken kindly provided by Eric, and she could feel his stomach grumbling in complaint as it tried to digest this overload on her toes.

Reception was empty and quiet, apart from the bubbling laughter floating from the bar. The latest batch of guests were being entertained by Ed, who was telling some really long anecdote about Cornish potatoes that had had them all in stitches for the last ten minutes, even Marilyn the workaholic, perched on a bar stool, enthralled.

Liesel looked up at the sound of yet another blast of hysterics and cursed herself for being in such a black mood.

She didn't really need to be working; she could have been in there with them, sharing Marilyn's bottle of dry white and joining in the fun, but truth was, work was the only thing she had found in the past two hours that had taken her mind off the fact that it was nine o'clock, getting dark, and it looked like Tom had stood her up. Well, not her, Ruby; after all, he wasn't coming to see her, was he, he was coming to see Ruby. Not that he'd come to see anybody at all so far.

She punched in another address a touch too vigorously, and then cursed as the new computer took umbrage at the rough treatment and froze up on her.

'Oh bloody bugger bum bum bum!' she growled in abject frustration, and her spine becoming weak with disappointment, she collapsed in a heap on the keyboard, much to Ruby's consternation.

'Having a bad day?'

It had to be then, didn't it. When she looked up, Tom was leaning on reception looking down at her, a smile that was a mixture of amusement and concern flitting across his lips.

Ruby made a small whimper of complaint from under Liesel's bosom, and as Liesel sat bolt upright in embarrassment, the puppy stood on her hind legs and began to lick her vigorously on the chin before jumping up on to the long stretch of wood that was the reception desk and transferring the same affections to Tom.

'Looks like she's settled in okay.' He smiled and gently lowered the puppy to the floor before she could slide off of Lorraine's vigorously polished surface. 'I'm sorry I'm so late, but I was caught up at a stud farm near Cubert, a mare with colic. I was going to call you from the car to see if it was still okay to come over, but my battery's gone and I couldn't find my car charger anywhere.'

Liesel gulped hard, and just about managed to refrain from smacking herself around the face a few times to try and regain her senses, as she realised with a lurch of the stomach that not only was he here, but he was dressed courtesy of the BBC's drama department. He was wearing boots and breeches, muddy ones, and he smelt of horses, that lovely peppery, fresh, earthy smell. It made her shiver with delight. Mr Darcy eat your cold, aloof heart out. The only period drama she'd ever experienced up until today was when she was scarily late one month having just been dumped by Seth, the most long-term boyfriend she'd ever had. Sexy Seth. He had been the most gorgeous man she had ever dared to date.

But he had never looked this good.

Tom even had a streak of mud on his face and straw in his hair, and the Barbour was splattered with green and brown bits of heaven knows what, but he looked and smelt wholesome and healthy and roll-in-the-hay kind of wonderful.

'I don't find him in the least attractive,' Liesel told herself sternly.

'Liar,' she chorused back.

'Are you still okay to do this?' Tom was frowning. She obviously didn't look okay; that coupled with the fact she hadn't said a word since he'd arrived, not even hello.

'If you're sure you are,' she managed to say and pushed a smile out.

He looked tired. Purple shadowed bruises under each eye, eyes that today looked for a moment like a dark ocean.

'I chose to come and live by the sea because I love it so much and I hardly ever get the chance to spend time on the beach, so yes, to be honest, I'm looking forward to it.'

'Even in the dark?'

'It only looks dark from in here. Come outside.' He held out a hand, and for a mad moment Liesel was about to offer hers back, but realised just in time that he was asking for Ruby's new collar, which she had just taken from under the reception desk.

She handed it to him and he bent and gently secured it around the little dog's neck, all the time quietly talking to her to reassure her.

'She normally acts like I'm trying to strangle her when I put that on her.' Liesel laughed.

'Well, I've had plenty of practice: you're new to the game. And trust me, with dogs, most things to them are a game.'

'Practice on your own dogs?'

He shook his head. 'At the surgery.'

Liesel kicked off her pumps and pulled on her boots and then fetched Marilyn's big coat from the office.

'You really can't take one home yourself, then?'

'A puppy?'

'Uhuh.'

'Afraid not.'

'A vet with no pets?'

'I know.'

'The hours you work?'

He nodded.

'That's a shame,' she said solemnly.

He nodded again, because she was right.

'Maybe someday.'

'You'd like one?'

'I'd like six.' He grinned, turning to scratch Godrich's ragged head. The big dog had decided he was coming too, and loped after Tom and Ruby as they went outside.

Just behind them, Liesel marvelled once again at the sight of a man in boots and breeches. What was it about such attire that had a girl's heart skipping along like a kangaroo on speed? Maybe it was the way they moulded his legs and arse as affectionately and flatteringly as lipstick on a luscious mouth, or perhaps it was the promise of a whip as an accompaniment. Whatever it was, when he offered her his hand to help her through the steep bank of gorse that marked the end of the manicured lawn and the start of the brief stretch of coastal hinterland between them and the beach, she had to take a steadying breath before she took it.

Fortunately the two dogs were a welcome distraction, Liesel laughing loud as they bounded excitedly down the rock steps and on to the beach, racing each other to the edge of the tidal river, which was half out, where Godrich put on the brakes, dipping in his paws and wincing about the temperature like a little old lady on a cold day.

Ruby had simply run and belly-flopped joyously into the water, and was paddling around in large circles like she had been swimming all her short life and this wasn't the first ever time. Seeing his new friend braving the water and not dying instantly, in fact apparently enjoying herself immensely, Godrich took a deep breath and took the plunge himself.

Two front paws went into the water, and when it didn't attack, the back paws followed.

'See, she's made him braver.' Tom nodded his approval.

'She's made him lots of things. He loves Ruby.'

Love was probably an understatement. Godrich adored the puppy with a sweet, brotherly kind of passion. Wherever Ruby went, Godrich would never be too far behind, with poor devoted Alex bringing up the rear. He had taken to copying her too, a second adolescence, which in some ways had been very good for him, as Tom had been keen to point out when first persuading Liesel to give the puppy a home.

It was like she was showing him how a dog should really be.

And now, as Tom tried to teach the puppy to sit, stay, and walk to heel, Godrich was learning too.

Liesel watched them, hands in pockets.

He was so patient with them. They did as they were asked, and they got a treat, be it a small piece of chicken or some affection. In an hour or so he had Ruby sitting on command, lying down, and walking to heel, and almost always coming when she was called, depending on what else was around to delight and distract the inquisitive little animal.

Liesel had never owned a pet before. She had always wanted one, but never had one. It amazed her how she had fallen so heavily in love with Ruby in such a short space of time. Couldn't imagine life without her, even.

'She's so clever,' she said proudly, as Ruby ignored a passing sea gull to return to Tom's side. 'I can't believe how much you've managed to teach them.'

'Well, Godrich already knew how to do most of the manoeuvres.'

'Yeah, but he hardly ever did any of them until now.'

'He's not stupid, he just prefers to do his own thing.'

'You can't blame him for that really. Aren't most people the same?'

'But he's not people, he's a dog.'

'Shhhh,' Liesel joked, putting her finger to her lips. 'Don't remind him; he gets upset.'

'He still thinks he's human?'

'Definitely, but there has been a huge change in him since Ruby's been with us. Just as an example, he used to approach his food dish with such an air of caution, as if it was the food that was going to eat him and not the other way round. Every time you fed him it was like you were trying to poison him. Now because Ruby just gets stuck in, so does he. Do you know, he's even started sleeping like her? It's most disconcerting. Whereas she looks amazingly cute upside down with her legs in the air, Godrich looks decidedly odd, like a dead donkey in the middle of a field.'

And what Liesel didn't add was that as Ruby slept in her room, she would often be woken in the middle of the night by a large black nose pushing open her door, or awake with a start to see his corpse-like figure upside down on the end of her bed, sleeping so soundly you could use one of his four huge paws as a hatstand and he wouldn't flinch.

The strangest part, however, was the fact that despite his supposed disdain for Alex's rather zealous affections, he would never come down before Alex fell asleep, and would always disappear by morning, returning to Alex's room and his own basket or Alex's bed before Alex woke up, which Liesel thought was decidedly odd, considering the dog still spent most of his time trying to avoid the boy during the day.

'You were right about her being good for him,' she finished, finding a bag of sherbert lemons in her pocket and offering Tom one. 'Sometimes you need something or someone new to take you out of your box and make you focus on new feelings. It's so easy to get bogged down in stale emotions simply because they're familiar and familiar can feel comfortable and comfortable can feel like it fits, but that's just because it's loose and not because it actually suits your skin. It's like the feel of a good pair of jeans, as opposed to a perfect pair of jeans. Do you know what I mean?'

She glanced sideways at Tom and bit her bottom lip in embarrassment.

He wasn't quite looking at her with his mouth open in horror, but she thought the emotions registering on his face must be pretty close.

'I'm really sorry, I waffle sometimes . . . Marilyn will tell you. Just wind me up, open my mouth and watch me go. I come out with more rubbish sometimes than an overused waste-disposal unit.'

'Don't put yourself down. That was quite profound.'

'Profoundly stupid, yeah.'

'I didn't say that.'

'Maybe, but you looked like you were thinking it.'

'You just made me realise something, that's all.'

Yeah, like I'm a total and utter moron, Liesel thought, calling the dogs back and watching in affectionate despair as Godrich galumphed off in the opposite direction.

Ruby, however, trotted back immediately.

'Good girl! She's already more obedient than Godrich!' Liesel exclaimed.

Her embarrassment lost in delight, she scooped up the little dog and covered the smiling, hairy little face with kisses. Ruby, infected by Liesel's excitement, galloped off and rolled in sand until she was completely coated and you could have picked her up and rubbed down furniture with her, before galloping back and hurling herself into Liesel's arms for another cuddle.

She just laughed joyously as the animal covered her in sand.

Tom smiled as he watched them both. Liesel was so natural and unaffected. In a way she had the same kind of appeal as the puppy, he thought, unaware of the fact that he was echoing Marilyn. Just full of the joys of spring, to use an apt analogy.

He had been so preoccupied, he hadn't really noticed that now it was truly dark and the only light being shed was from the moon and the houses that lined the river bank, so when he looked at his watch he was surprised to see that it was nearly ten thirty.

'Have you seen the time?'

Liesel shook her head. She didn't wear a watch. A habit she really needed to redress, as it usually made her late for things.

'I suppose I'd better go.'

'Work tomorrow?'

He nodded.

'Not on nights, then?'

'Not this week. Not officially, anyway.'

'Have you got far to drive?'

'A little way. I live further up the coast in Port Isaac. It's about forty minutes away.'

'Have you eaten?' she asked as they started back over the rocks and into the garden.

'Not yet.'

'Fancy a plate of Eric's chicken chasseur? It's the bomb.'

'Sounds good, but I should really get back.'

'In that case I can get it "to go": a few minutes in the microwave when you get home and it will be fantastic, I promise.'

'If you're sure it's no trouble, that sounds great.'

'It's the least we can do after all you've done, for Ruby, for my thumb . . .'

'Payment in kind?' he joked.

'Succour instead of sex.' Liesel nodded without thinking, then smothered her mouth with her hand. 'I'll get that food,' she muttered, and flushing with embarrassment, she sprinted into the hotel, returning minutes later with a Tupperware dish filled to the brim with casserole still warm from the oven

'Thanks. Looks great.'

'Tastes great.'

'Same time next week?'

'It's a date,' Liesel replied, before really thinking through her choice of words. He didn't seem to notice, though, and she was still too flustered over the payment-in-kind comments to worry too much about this last slip.

'See you next week, then.'

'Yeah, just hold out your hand for a second.'

She wondered what he was about to do as he reached out and turned it palm up, but then he pulled a penknife from his pocket and quickly, deftly snipped out the two stitches.

'There you go.' He smiled, releasing her hand. 'Job done.'

She watched him leave, holding on to the little dog to make sure she didn't give chase, waving Ruby's paw after the departing car until she realised what she was doing and stopped in embarrassment.

'Nice walk?' Marilyn's voice behind her made her turn away.

'Dog training,' Liesel corrected her.

'Nice dog training, then?'

'Well, it would have been if I hadn't made a total idiot of myself with "Liesel's loquacious views on life".'

'I'm sure he doesn't think you're an idiot. What did you say to him?'

'Oh, just my usual prattle; emphasis on the "prat".'

'It's a good job you're sworn off men, then, isn't it?'

'But it wouldn't matter if I wasn't, because he thinks I'm an idiot anyway.'

'And he's engaged.' Marilyn repeated Liesel's usual mantra.

'And he's engaged.' Liesel nodded.

'And you're just friends,' Marilyn said, trying to keep a straight face.

'And we're just friends,' Liesel repeated seriously.

Ruby didn't have to wait until the same time next week for her next visit. He was back two days later, just as Liesel was opening up the bar for the few guests they had.

'I had a spare couple of hours, thought I'd give Ruby another session. Is this a bad time?' he asked, looking from sister to sister.

Liesel opened her mouth to explain that she had to work, but Marilyn cut in before she could speak.

'Not at all. We're really quiet tonight. Liesel's pretty much surplus to requirements for an hour or two . . . or three,' she added with a mischievous grin.

'Great. It's just that I'm not sure I can make it next week, and I had a free evening so I thought I'd come and see you . . . see Ruby . . . carry on with her training.'

'Go,' Marilyn urged as Liesel hesitated. 'We can manage fine here for a while.'

Ed was passing with the toolbox Liesel had bequeathed, fresh from fixing a catch on a door in the gents' loos.

'I'm all done. I can give you a hand behind the bar if you want.'

'There you go then.' Marilyn grinned. 'All sorted. Off you go.' And then, as Liesel hesitated, she gently pushed her towards the door.

Ed watched Marilyn watching her sister and Tom as they walked down the garden.

'What was all that about then?'

'Oh, just Liesel gone all shy because she has a stonking great crush on Tom Spencer.'

'Mmm, Dad mentioned something about that.'

'Did he tell you that Tom's engaged?'

'Yep, and he also said that hasn't stopped him coming round here on a rather regular basis. I'm surprised you're encouraging them, though. Seeing as he isn't free.'

Marilyn frowned as she thought for a moment.

'Actually, come to think of it, so am I. Go and tell her she's got to work after all.'

Ed laughed. It was a nice sound. It made Marilyn smile just to hear it.

'Between you and me,' she confided, 'I think it might be more than just a crush. I think she might be a little bit in love with him.'

'Well, that makes all the difference, doesn't it?'

'You think?'

'There's the old sayings, aren't there: "all's fair in love and war", "people who are sensible about love are incapable of it", "it doesn't matter if he's got a girlfriend, as long as she's not *your* friend" – you can probably guess I just made that one up to make you feel better about encouraging your sister to go off with a married man.'

'He's not married. Yet.' Marilyn laughed.

'And whilst the "yet" implies there may be a reprieve, it also says that at the same time there's every possibility of it still happening.'

'Which means I shouldn't really encourage her to waste her affection on someone who may not be free to reciprocate.'

' "Talk not of wasted affection, affection never was wasted," ' Ed replied. 'Another quote, Longfellow this time. Do you know, I've always wondered if he was . . .'

Marilyn, catching on immediately, started to giggle.

'You're the first person I've said that to who knew immediately what I meant.' He smiled at her.

Marilyn smiled back.

'You ever been in love, Ed?' she asked.

'Not yet.'

'Not yet?'

'I still hold out hope of it happening.'

'That's a rare commodity these days.'

'What is?'

'Hope.'

'I didn't have you down as a cynic, Mrs Hamilton.'

'Oh, please don't call me that,' Marilyn groaned.

'What, a cynic?'

'No, Mrs Hamilton.'

'Ah, I see. Hating your married name. That explains the cynicism. I take it you were in love . . . once.'

'Once upon a time,' Marilyn replied. 'But seeing as you're into proverbs, "once bitten, twice shy" . . .'

'I don't like that one.' He frowned. 'It smacks too much of giving in.'

'So you're more of a "if at first you don't succeed, try, try again"?'

'I suppose so, but I heard a much nicer one when I was in China last year . . .' He went behind the bar and poured Marilyn a glass of the wine he knew she liked. 'I don't know why, but it's just stuck with me, maybe because it's also about hope . . . "keep a green tree in your heart, and perhaps a singing bird will come . . ." '

They went to the beach this time, walking down past the rapidly dwindling river being sucked into the ocean as the tide turned and went out. The aim was to keep Ruby with them as they walked; Tom explained that the trick was to make sure that she found them far more interesting than anything else they could possibly encounter whilst out.

'You have to keep her attention focused on you, be it treats, or kind words, or fuss, or . . .' he reached into his jacket pocket and pulled out a ball, 'one of these.'

Liesel nodded, rapt with attention.

'You have to make sure that out of the whole world around her, you are the only thing she has eyes for . . . that being with you is what she likes best above everything else . . .' He threw the ball and yelled, 'Fetch!' and for a moment it was a toss-up who would give chase first, Ruby or Liesel.

An hour later, walking back to the hotel, Ruby was still sporadic in her desire to walk at heel, but Liesel had been a constant throughout the whole session.

'So what do you think to Cornwall?' Tom asked her.

'To be honest, I haven't seen an awful lot of it. We have

plans, but there always seem to be other things to do, and none of them ever seem to come off.'

'Such as?'

'I'm desperate to go to the Tate in St Ives . . . well, it doesn't even have to be the Tate. I've heard that there's a lovely artists' trail in St Agnes, and some great galleries in Truro . . .'

'You like art?'

Liesel nodded enthusiastically. 'Love it.'

'Do you paint or draw yourself?'

'Oh no,' she immediately replied, with charming honesty. 'Neither, I'm afraid. I'm like one of those people who are desperate to be the next Tom Jones but sound more like a tom cat when they actually open their mouths. Ooh, sorry, no dig intended: what I mean is that I think you can truly love art without being good at it yourself. Despite having as much talent with a paintbrush as Ruby with one tied to her tail, I studied art history at school and adored every second of it. I even thought about being an art historian for a while, but that would have meant A levels and university, and I couldn't . . .' She trailed off.

'You couldn't?' he prompted her.

'I couldn't stay at school,' she answered reluctantly. 'I needed to leave and get a job.'

'What happened?' he asked gently, aware from her face and the tone of her voice that there was a story of some significance behind the brief sentence.

'Real life kicked in.' Liesel dismissed the subject with four simple words that she had used on many occasions. They, and her obvious desire to curtail the conversation, had saved her a lot of explaining over the years.

It wasn't that she really minded telling people what had happened. What she didn't like was the sympathy this revelation garnered; it grated, embarrassed her almost. People feeling sorry for her was not what she wanted; she wanted them to treat her as they would any other person, but whenever you told someone that you were an orphan, albeit you were a woman in her twenties and not some poor abandoned child, their attitude automatically changed.

So yes, her parents were gone, but there were so many other people in the world in the same predicament and worse, and look at her, she was an adult now, and in the end, parents could only take you so far; at some point you had to realise it was your turn to take responsibility. Life was ultimately what you made of it for yourself.

He was looking at her, waiting for an explanation, not totally expecting one, but willing to listen if she was prepared to tell him. No wonder he was so good with animals; he had a quiet, calm patience, soothing almost, healing, that just brought trust. She knew that she could just tell him and that would be it; he would absorb the information, reflect, but not affect.

'My mum and dad died in a car accident when I was fifteen,' she said steadily.

He nodded slowly, the only betrayal of emotion the fact that he immediately caught the edge of his bottom lip between his teeth.

'That must have been terrible.'

'It was.'

And that was it.

He held her gaze for a moment as though marking his respect, and then, when Liesel offered nothing further, steered the conversation back to the initial subject.

'My friend's wife is an artist.'

'Really?'

The 'really' was bright, her relief at the reversion of the subject palpable.

'What does she do?'

'Landscapes, portraits, houses, animals, whatever

appeals to her sense of beauty,' he replied. 'She's very good. She has a few paintings in an exhibition at a gallery in Truro on Friday night. I've promised that I'll be there, and I have a plus one . . . Would you like to come?'

'Seriously?'

He nodded.

Her smile was like a spotlight.

'That would be fantastic, if I can get the night off.'

'Do you think that will be a problem?'

She shook her head vigorously, despite the fact that she truly didn't know. They had been so busy this last week, which was wonderful – 'the busier the better' was Marilyn's new 'catchphrase *de la semaine*' – but it meant that it had been all hands on deck.

'I wouldn't have thought so. I'll speak to Marilyn.'

'Sure,' he said, fishing in his pocket and pulling out a pen and a small square of card. 'Why don't you call me and let me know. Here.' He handed her a business card on the back of which he had written a number. 'That's my mobile.'

'Okay, thanks, I will.'

'Let's hope you can make it. I'll see you Friday maybe. If not, I'll try and squeeze in some more time with Ruby at the weekend.'

'That would be good too.'

'See you soon, then . . .'

Marilyn had handed the bar over to Ed and was in the sitting room, recumbent on the sofa, eating pork scratchings and watching the evening's episode of *Coronation Street* that she had set the old video player to record.

Despite the fact that it was essentially summer, and the weather was mild, Marilyn had taken to lighting the fire because it made the room seem really homely, and Marilyn liked homely.

Godrich was stretched out on the rug in front of the fire, as he loved it as much as Marilyn did. He had a terrible habit of lying far too close and singeing himself until he smelt disgusting, and Marilyn had to slowly and surreptitiously pull the rug with him on it a bit away as he wouldn't move.

When Liesel asked if it would be at all possible for her to have Friday evening off, Marilyn smiled up at her in confusion and reminded her, 'You don't have to ask my permission.'

'But I thought I worked for you.'

'With me,' Marilyn corrected her. 'We're a team, and teams pull for each other.'

'So that means Friday's okay?'

'Of course it is.'

'You don't need me?'

Marilyn knew her sister too well to reply 'no'.

'We always need you, but we can just about survive without you if we must. Ed can do the bar . . .'

'And everything else?' Liesel asked anxiously, suddenly feeling guilty at the prospect of an evening off when her sister had been working nonstop.

'Can be managed between me and the rest of the team.'

'So I should go?'

'Of course you should. You've been dying for weeks to indulge the culture vulture that perches permanently on your shoulder.'

Liesel grew a full-blown smile and kissed Marilyn on the forehead, before dancing from the room humming, 'I'm Just a Girl Who Can't Say No'.

'She's smiling too much,' Marilyn said to Godrich as the door closed behind her sister, and she heard the sound of the Cadbury's Flake bath being filled in the room above.

Godrich yawned widely and, stretching long toes, rolled on to his other side to crisp up his untoasted flank.

'I wish she wasn't smiling too much,' Marilyn continued, tossing him a pork scratching just slightly out of reach in an effort to make him move before he started to smoke. 'There's nothing worse than really liking someone who can't like you back.'

18

He picked her up from the hotel on Friday night at six thirty.

Not sure what one wore to an art exhibition, Liesel had thumbed through back issues of the *Cornish Guardian* that they kept in the guests' drawing room, and taken inspiration from photographs of recent events publicised in the 'What's On' section. She had copied the outfit of a woman who looked relaxed and happy to be there, and perfectly comfortable to be having her photograph taken by the local newshound. She had noticed, mainly through her years of bar work, that people who didn't feel they were dressed right for an occasion always looked uncomfortable.

Liesel's look for tonight consisted of her favourite jeans, black in case the dress code was no denim, tucked into high-heeled boots, with a pretty soft yellow peasant-style blouse she had borrowed from Marilyn, a thick silver bangle that had belonged to her mother, and her hair dried with a bit of bohemian tousle to it.

A slick of pale gloss to the full lips, a sprinkling of blusher on the apples of her cheeks, and mascara was all the make-up she ever wore, but the effect of the transformation this minimal amount of war paint made was amazing. And as she heard his car pull up and stepped out of the dark doorway into the warm glow of the early evening sunshine, it was as though a ray of low-lying sun had suddenly broken across the front of the house.

Tom had always seen her straight from work. The new 'secretary Liesel', with her hair pulled back and no make-up on, plain white shirt or head to toe in nondescript black. Hell, the first time he had seen her she had even been in a pair of stripy pyjamas and a dressing gown big enough to fit an elephant. Apart from that, it had always been old trainers or wellies, and a voluminous jacket if the wind was up added for their beach training sessions.

And now . . . Well, the first thought that hit him as he got out to open her door for her was 'God, she's pretty.' Had he not noticed this before? If truth be known he must have done, but this was the first time it had truly registered. He had been so wrapped up in just her, who she was, not how she looked. He liked her, pure and simple. He liked her freshness and her humour and in a way the refreshing naivety of her; she was simple, but not in a simpleton way, not stupid, just so open, so willing to see the good in everything. In this day and age it was easy to be cynical. Her openness was almost childlike in its trust, its humour, its hopefulness. But now he looked at her and saw her for who she was . . . and how she was.

She was Gisele Bündchen in miniature – no, not her, a beauty too tall and haughty to compare to the freshness of Liesel. She was Judy Garland grown up a little, an American with the face of an English rose. Judy Garland had been one of his mother's favourites, alongside Tom Jones of course. She loved music, his mother. A seemingly unemotional, stiff-upper-lip type, the only time he had ever caught her crying was when he found her in the drawing room with *Madam Butterfly* on full volume.

Liesel was as beautiful as the music.

*

For her part, Liesel looked at Tom and had to remind herself that he really wasn't her type. It wasn't her fault he was wearing her favourite type of jeans on a man, moleskin-soft Ted Bakers in navy blue that made his thighs look as though they were clad in shorn velvet and oh so tempting to caress with the palm of her hand. These cruel teasers were teamed with a long-sleeved collared top from Hugo Boss, three buttons, the top two undone, the shot silver grey of the silken fabric making his unusual eyes look tungsten instead of the green they had been the last time she had seen him.

As he got out of the big Range Rover and went round to greet her and open the door for her like the gentleman she already knew he was, they both stopped and, to put it bluntly, stared.

For a long time.

It was like being slapped with the court order after you had sat staring at the unopened red bills for months. You knew it was coming, but boy, had you done all you could to deny it. And with this sudden realisation, the ease of their new friendship turned uncomfortable.

To kill the silence as they drove, he turned up the stereo, which had been humming away quietly to itself, and without thinking Liesel began to sing along.

'I love this song,' she murmured, slightly shamefaced, when she realised he was watching her out of the corner of his eye.

'So do I,' he answered, and began to sing it himself until she joined in again.

His friends were Sally and Toby. They met up outside an art gallery in the delightfully named Lemon Quay in Truro.

Sally was plump and jolly and very pretty, with big amber eyes and a mop of unruly golden curls. She had the most infectious laugh Liesel had ever heard, making you want to make her laugh just to hear it, like the chuckle of a baby, so delicious you couldn't help but smile when you heard it.

Toby was similar to his wife, portly, perky, passionate, a cockney born, although Cornish bred. His nickname, Toby Jug, was very apt.

'Round and glazed and usually full of ale,' he told Liesel with a laugh like a drain sucking suds from a sink.

Toby and Tom had been friends since they were terrified new boys together at a strict boys' school, sharing adjacent desks in the form room of one Mr Herbert, long, lean and mean and nicknamed Herbert the Horrible, and insisting they would remain so until they shared adjacent bath chairs in a local nursing home.

The three of them had known each other long enough to form the kind of bond where conversation was a shorthand others had to take a moment to translate, but they were down-to-earth and friendly and made Liesel, who had suddenly gone shy, feel comfortable within minutes.

Sally had taken it upon herself to be an unofficial guide, and was showing her around the gallery whilst filling her in on the history of their friendship.

'We all went to school together. Well, at least the boys went to school together from prep up, and then their sixth form went co-ed and that's when I arrived.'

'Yep, sashayed into the form room like she owned the place,' Toby cut in from behind. 'I looked over at her, nudged Tom and said, "Here comes trouble," and I was right.'

'You actually said, "Here comes trouble and I want to get into it",' Tom reminded him with a wink.

'I have to confess that to be true,' Toby said, trying and failing dismally to look ashamed of himself. But Sally, who had heard the story many times before, simply smiled and turned to Liesel and chose a subject she knew would make her feel instantly at ease.

'I hear that Tom gave you one of the puppies. We were so tempted to take one of her brothers – they were gorgeous – but we're not at home enough to look after a dog properly. What did you call her?'

'Ruby,' Liesel replied.

'Sweet. And he's been training her for you too?'

'Yeah, he's been great, he's been a good friend to us.'

She reiterated the word 'friend' as if she felt the need to remind herself, and reassure Sally, that that was all he was. A friend. After all, he had a fiancée, a fiancée whom this woman must have known for many years. And 'fiancée' was a far more important word beginning with F in a man's life than 'friend'.

Sally watched how Liesel grew embarrassed at the turn in the conversation, and smiled softly. She had liked this girl instantly. Sally didn't like people with hidden agendas. Liesel was sweet and friendly and very open, and far too honest to be able to hide the fact that she had a stonking great crush on Tom. Then again, it wasn't unusual. Lots of people had them; why, Sally had even had one herself when she was sixteen and her decisions on the fanciability of men were based on who looked most like whichever film or pop star she was fantasising about at the time. It hadn't lasted long, though. Toby was the man for her, always had been, but there were plenty of other girls who weren't as fortunate as her.

The vets' surgery was always full of women clutching the healthiest-looking animals you could ever see simply so they had a chance to watch Tom Spencer run his hands over Tiddles or Rover and fantasise that it was their turn on the examination table.

What she really wanted to know was how Tom felt about this girl.

He and Caroline had seemed so distant lately; was this new friendship a symptom, or perhaps a cause . . .

'Tom tells me you're an art lover?'

Liesel nodded enthusiastically.

'How many pieces are you showing today?'

'Three.'

'Can I see them?'

Tom watched Sally take Liesel's arm and lead her off to look at a set of five sculptures that as far as he could make out were a pile of old spare parts from several defunct washing machines, whence much laughter and whispered conversation ensued.

'They seem to be getting on really well.' Toby appeared at his side with two more glasses of the free champagne that was being dispensed in the hope of lubricating the passage of wallets from pockets. 'She's a lovely girl.'

'She's a friend.'

'Of course she is.'

'I know what you're implying, Tobe; just because you're not actually saying it doesn't mean I don't know what you're thinking.'

'She obviously likes you very much.'

'She does?' The surprise and pleasure were obvious to both friends.

Toby's mouth twitched into a smile.

'I mean, I like her too,' Tom amended a touch too hurriedly.

His friend put a warm, fat-fingered hand on his arm, and knitted his usually jocular features into something more serious.

'Just be careful, okay?'

'Why be careful?'

'Because something's obviously happening between

you, and you're not the two-timing duplicitous love rat
your looks give you licence to be ... Well, hello, my
love ...' There was no time for further conversation as the
two women returned and Toby segued easily into a
completely separate conversation. 'I was just telling Tom
that Dante has informed me he's sold all your paintings
except for that God-awful one of your mother in the buff
which I have told him he can burn on the bonfires of hell
as far as I'm concerned ... Dante's Inferno, get it, get it?
I suggest we go on to Betsy's to celebrate. What do you
think, my darling?'

'About dinner or about turning my mother's likeness –
and by the way, Liesel dear, she is not naked, she is
wearing a bathing costume – or about turning my
mother's likeness,' she repeated, pretending to be
haughty, 'into French toast?'

'Dinner, of course. Your mother's made of asbestos,
they'd never get her going, which is something your father
often complained about, so no wonder you're an only
child ...'

'Sounds wonderful. Dinner, not my parents'
nonexistent sex life ...'

Tom looked at Liesel who was thoroughly enjoying the
banter, smiling broadly. It was funny, Caroline always
found it rather annoying.

'Why is it that no one ever likes to think of their parents
in flagrante?' Sally turned to Tom. 'You are coming for
dinner with us, aren't you? It is your favourite restaurant,
Tom,' she added temptingly as he appeared to hesitate.

Tom looked at Liesel and raised an eyebrow in
question.

'What do you think? Do you have to get back?'

She shook her head. 'Nope. I have the whole evening
off, so if you want to go ... or if you guys want a catch-up,
I can always hop in a taxi back ...' she began, suddenly

uncertain that the invite was inclusive, but Sally immediately cut her short in horror.

'Of course you're not getting a taxi home, you're coming to the restaurant with us. I want to hear all about your new life in Cornwall . . .' and taking Liesel's arm, she tucked it through her own again and began to walk towards the door. 'I know the Cornucopia quite well, you know, my aunt and Nancy were great friends when they were young. She took me there for tea once, and I spent all afternoon hanging from the top window of the tower pretending to be a princess . . .'

Betsy's was a tiny bolthole in a quaint Truro back street, that served up steak that melted under the knife, followed by Cornish clotted cream ice cream that made Liesel decide that after a lifetime of thinking she wasn't that keen on ice cream, she had just been eating the wrong kind.

The conversation flowed as easily as the bottles of red wine Toby ordered at regular intervals, and Tom refused at regular intervals.

'I have to drive,' he kept repeating.

'Stay at ours, stay at ours,' Toby kept urging as Tom had to repeatedly put his hand over his glass to stop him from refilling it.

'I have to get Liesel home.'

'I meant both of you. It's twin beds in the guest room,' he leaned over and confided rather loudly to Liesel, 'on account of the in-laws, who only sleep together on a leap year, i.e., father-in-law leaps, mother-in-law's too fat to jump out of the way.'

Sally dug him indignantly in the ribs, and he began to choke on his wine for long enough for Sally to interject with, 'He's only kidding. We have two spare rooms.'

'That's really kind of you, but I should get back. I don't mind getting a taxi, though.'

'Are you kidding? Do you know how much a cab is from here to Piran?'

'Well, Marilyn will come and get me if I call.'

'Nobody needs to come and get you, you can stay at ours.' Toby had recovered his voice.

Tom held up a hand to silence the dissent.

'Thanks for the offer, but not tonight, Josephine. Liesel, nobody is coming to get you; I offered to be your chauffeur for the evening and I'm not exactly doing a good job if I quit halfway through. Besides, I need a clear head for the morning anyway. I've got to go to the Courtland stud in the morning.'

'You're going to the Courtland?' Liesel asked, her mouth dropping in awe.

'You know of them?'

'Are you serious? They're one of the best breeders in the country. How amazing is that? I know the vet who looks after the Courtland horses . . .'

'I didn't know you liked horses.'

'I love horses. It's always been an ambition of mine to learn to ride.'

'Then you should come with me . . .'

'What on earth was that, then?' Toby asked as, having waved Tom's Range Rover out of sight, he and Sally headed to the kitchen for the coffee he was hankering after.

'I don't know what you mean,' Sally trilled in a voice that said she knew exactly what he meant.

'Once they got talking about horses, didn't you just feel like a total gooseberry? Like we were eavesdropping on a date?'

'They're just friends,' Sally said with a slight raising of her eyebrow and a wry smile. She flicked on the kettle and pulled two mugs out for coffee.

'Sure, and I'm Mel Gibson.'

'Oooh, will you be, just for tonight?'

'What, the old Toby Jug isn't enough for you any more?'

'Tell you what, you be Mel Gibson for me and I'll be Demi Moore for you.'

Toby grinned broadly. 'Come 'ere and gimme more, Demi Moore!' he growled lasciviously in a terrible Australian accent, grabbing his wife and kissing her thoroughly until the kettle hissing to a crescendo made her pull away from him, laughing.

'Maybe they are just friends,' Toby mused, his thoughts returning to the evening. 'It's inevitable they're going to get on, they're two of a kind. Both genuine, sweet people. Both don't realise how stunning they are,' he added. 'She was beautiful, wasn't she?'

'Amazing profile,' Sally agreed, pouring water into mugs. 'I'd love to draw her if she'd let me . . . her and Tom . . .'

She was quiet for a moment whilst she fetched milk and then sugared her husband's cup. Then she said, almost too nonchalantly, 'You know, they'd have absolutely gorgeous children . . .'

'Oh, you've got them married off already, have you!' was Toby's reaction.

'Absolutely.' Sally nodded, kissing the tip of her husband's nose before handing him a mug. 'She's a lovely girl. I think they'd be very good together. And it's so obvious they have feelings for each other.'

'Actually, I agree, but aren't you forgetting one minor detail?' He raised his eyebrows at her in question.

'If you mean Caroline, then no, I haven't forgotten about her.'

'But you think Tom should? I thought she was supposed to be your friend.'

'*Tom's* my friend,' Sally stressed. 'I want him to be happy, and I haven't seen him that way for some time.'

'Until tonight?' Toby asked, suddenly understanding.

'Until tonight,' Sally agreed.

'So what do we do?'

'Don't be silly,' she chided him affectionately. '*We* don't do anything.'

'Ah, I see, we leave them to work it out for themselves.'

'Exactly.'

'And what if he doesn't work it out?'

'He'll do what he always does,' Sally said sagely.

'Which is?'

'The right thing.'

The conversation that had started in the restaurant continued all the way back to Piran. It was nice to meet someone who was so genuinely interested in his work. Caroline hated to hear about it. It bored her rigid, to be honest. Whereas Liesel . . . well, the conversation had flowed, so much so that the journey back to Port Isaac from Piran seemed interminably long and quiet. As did home when he reached it. Silent.

He lived in a beautiful house, a three-storey mews cottage with an amazing sea view, immaculately modernised by the master craftsman of the local developers who had so lovingly restored it.

But when you really looked at it closely, it seemed so empty.

A fridge with very little in it.

Neat, clean and tidy thanks to his meticulous daily, Mrs Lovesage.

Furniture that had been bought on the net as he didn't have time to shop any other way, delivered whilst he was out and arranged once again by the indispensable Mrs Lovesage.

He had vowed to sort it out himself at a later date but it had never happened. So there it all was, still just the way Mrs Lovesage had thought it suited.

There was definitely no dog. Which as Liesel had said was a shame. But if there had been a dog, it would have been practically living here on its own.

All he did here was eat, sleep, shower, shave.

And all he did besides that was work.

He had friends, good friends, but he had watched the majority of them over the more recent years meet, mate, marry, multiply, whilst ribbing him good-naturedly about being married to his job.

Even when Caroline had been living in St Ives he had never seemed to have much time to meet up with her. Maybe that was why she had found it so easy to take the job in London. How could she miss him more in a different county when she so saw so little of him as it was?

They had discussed calling it a day when Caroline got the job in London, but decided that they could do the distance thing. That they had been together long enough to make it worth the work.

He did miss her, when he had time to think about it. In fact, the only truly personal touch in the house was a photograph of Caroline that was about five years old, placed on a side table by the sofa. But it was only on the table because *she* had put it there.

He picked it up and looked at it. It was in a powder-blue wooden frame that she had chosen carefully, she said, to match his seaside-inspired decor, but he thought it was actually more to match her eyes, and offset the pale-pink roses and Cornish cream complexion and the shiny dark brown hair.

She was a beautiful girl.

Even more so when she smiled.

She had truly smiled at him then. He couldn't

remember the last time she had looked at him like that. For a long time she had been physically distant, and he had grown so used to it that he hadn't noticed that for the last year that distance had become increasingly emotional as well.

He suddenly felt the urge to call her. They hadn't spoken since the weekend she came down to go to the dinner dance with him. Not even one text message. Was that terrible? It was well past midnight, but she had never been an early-to-bed kind of girl, so he picked up the phone and dialled. But the only reply he got was the stilted automated tone of a non-personalised answer machine urging him to leave a message.

He didn't leave a message. Instead, he sat down and tried to remember the sound of her voice and the true image of her face. He closed his eyes. And instantly saw a beautiful smiling face. The only problem was, it wasn't Caroline's.

'Oh shit.' Said out loud seemed to put it quite succinctly.

His eyes shot open in alarm. He wasn't that kind of guy. He was the kind of man who always tried to do the right thing. And the right thing was definitely not sitting here feeling guilty because he had suddenly realised he found someone other than the woman he was engaged to incredibly attractive.

He was woken by the phone ringing at two in the morning. He thought it must be a work emergency but it wasn't, it was Caroline. She sounded slightly drunk. Caroline didn't normally drink. She didn't normally call at two in the morning either; he hadn't expected a ringback until tomorrow at the earliest.

'It's me.' Her voice sounded odd.

'Hi, me. You okay?'

'Sure, good. You?'

'Yeah. Where were you?'

'Out with some friends, no one you know,' she added before he could ask. 'Some people from work.'

'You've had a good night?

'A couple of glasses of wine.' She sounded defensive.

He hadn't asked what she'd been drinking but they both knew that was what he'd meant.

'A couple?'

'Maybe three. We were celebrating a big deal. What are you anyway, the alcohol police?'

'No big deal, Car. It's just unusual for you, that's all.'

'Yeah, well maybe you don't . . .' She trailed off.

But he knew what she had been about to say: maybe he didn't know what was usual for her any more. Well maybe he didn't: they had barely seen each other since she left.

'Yeah, you're probably right.' He sighed.

There was a silence that for the first time between them felt uncomfortable.

'Are we drifting apart?'

It was an in-joke.

A joke to get back in.

She liked to sail. He hated it. He loved the sea, but to look at, not to be on. Loved to watch it shift restlessly, relentlessly, to turn in and out on itself, not in and out on his stomach. He'd stand on the shore and wave her off, happily walk the beach and the headland whilst she navigated deeper waters.

She joked that they drifted apart but she always came home.

It had felt a bit like that when she had left for London, except she hadn't come home much lately.

'I'll come down,' she suddenly offered.

'You will?'

'Don't sound so keen.'

'I'm surprised, that's all.'

There was a long silence, and then she said quietly, 'I haven't made much of an effort recently, have I?'

'It shouldn't be an effort, Car.'

'That's not what I meant,' she said quickly, defensive again. Then, after a moment, her voice softened. 'How about it? Say next weekend? You're not on call then, are you?'

'No.'

'Great. We can walk a few beaches, go out for dinner, get a little drunk, then lie in with the papers. In fact I might even see if I can get Friday off, make it a long one. What do you think?'

Walk a few beaches? She was trying. Caroline didn't walk beaches. He leant back on the pillow and closed his eyes. This time Caroline's face came to mind the first time he tried.

'That would be good,' he replied. And he meant it.

Due to see Liesel again the following Tuesday evening, he had phoned and made some excuse, which was part truth, about how busy he was, and then found himself going there anyway.

She was ridiculously pleased to see him. Didn't question his appearance, just assumed he had freed up some time after all, and called the dogs to tell them how lucky they were. She really wore her heart on her sleeve. It was one of the things he liked about her: there was no second guessing. And now he knew she had feelings for him, knew it from the way she blushed and stammered sometimes when she spoke to him, the way she was so aware of what she said to him and how it could be misconstrued, and he couldn't for the life of him think how he hadn't noticed it before.

If he was honest with himself, he liked it.

But if he was going to be honest with her, then he couldn't encourage it.

Toby's warning flashed into his mind: 'something's obviously happening between you'. And as he looked at Liesel's sweet smiling face it suddenly dawned on him how right his friend had been.

He shouldn't have come. He could fake an emergency, some incident at work; she wouldn't question it, he knew that, she'd just accept it as par for the course with his job. Not like Caroline. Caroline hated the hours he worked, wished he was a banker or something.

I shouldn't compare them, he told himself for the umpteenth time, and immediately felt even guiltier for being there. He should go; a work emergency was a good idea.

But then Ruby, who had been to fetch her collar, came running, leather hanging from her mouth, tail wagging furiously, as delighted to spend time with him as Liesel obviously had been, and he was trapped, not by their pleasure in his company, but by his own in theirs.

'She's grown,' he said, scooping the little dog up into his arms.

'She's put on a pound and a half since you last saw her,' Liesel said proudly, 'and you'll be pleased to hear that Godrich has lost the same amount through abstinence from the dreaded Mars bars.'

'That's great news. Come on, let's take these dogs out.'

The tide was in and the guests were out, and so they went into the garden.

'We're going to teach her to sit and stay,' he announced, pulling the usual bag of treats from his pocket.

'I thought we'd already done that.'

'Sure, but this time we're going to walk away and she still has to stay until she's called to come.'

'Okay.'

As soon as Liesel began to walk away, the puppy came pelting after her, vaulted into her arms and covered her chin in kisses. Liesel, despite the obvious failure of the task, laughed in delight.

Tom watched her with a smile on his own face.

She caught him, looked embarrassed. 'What?' she demanded, suddenly convinced she had something between her teeth.

'You're always smiling, did you know that?'

Liesel shrugged. 'That's not good, is it?'

'It isn't?'

'Nope. 'Cause it means I'm going to be really wrinkly when I'm older.' She laughed, burying her face in the puppy's neck and breathing in the scent of soft clean fur and mown grass.

Watching her, Tom got the feeling Liesel wouldn't care about things like wrinkles. For such a beautiful girl, unusually, vanity didn't seem to be one of her traits. Caroline was always immaculately groomed; she would spend hours in front of the mirror with an assortment of lotions and potions and little pots that promised miracles.

Liesel's voice brought him out of his musings.

'There's a lot to smile about at the moment.' She was obviously pondering his comment.

'There is?'

She nodded furiously.

'It's so great here. I was excited about coming, but apprehensive too, you know. New things can be scary, can't they, but I love the hotel, I love the people, I love the way the air tastes, I love to be able to hear the soft sound of the sea from my bedroom, I love Ruby and I even love Godrich, and I love the way that Alex is blossoming . . .'

'Is there anything you don't like?'

'About Cornwall?'

'Doesn't have to be Cornwall.'

'Good, because there's nothing I don't like about Cornwall yet.'

'Anything at all really, then?'

She thought for a long time before replying.

'Well, I don't like to be cold. Especially a cold wind. You know the kind that gets in your ears. If Marilyn didn't tease me unmercifully every time I put them on, I'd be the kind of girl that had ear muffs clamped to her head from October through to March.'

'And that's it?'

Again a long pause.

'I'm not keen on spinach . . . well, that's not true, I like spinach, but I really can't stand it when it's cooked so that it ends up all wet and soggy.'

He was laughing again.

'You like laughing at me, don't you?'

'I like the fact that you make me laugh. You ask a girl what she doesn't like and all you get back is cold ears and soggy spinach. You're amazing, Liesel Ellis.'

'Is that amazing as in those American shows, you know like the Amazing world of Deep South Roadside Museums or something, where the amazing is just a euphemism for weird?'

And of course he started to laugh even harder until they both fell silent and shared a look. And for some reason she suddenly lost the smile.

'I don't like cruelty,' she said quietly.

It hadn't been what she meant at all, but it suddenly made him think: was spending time with her cruel? And then his pager bleeped, and despite the fact that it was just his mother reminding him of a family meal, he used it as an excuse to leave.

'I have to go.' Not wanting to lie, he offered no further explanation, but she simply found her smile again, and nodded, and thanked him for the time spent with Ruby.

19

Caroline had visited as promised and they'd had a good weekend together. Uncomfortable at first, but they had known each other too long for that to last. She was all talk of London and her job and the people she worked with, her flat where she'd just had her bedroom redecorated, her new boss whom everyone had been terrified of before they met him, this new bar she had found, a fantastic new restaurant. They talked about things, and not feelings.

Finally, too honest to keep it to himself, he had told her about Liesel in an offhand, made-a-new-friend kind of way, and she had made some comment about his penchant for waifs and strays and how she was surprised he didn't have a house full of stray animals, but oh no, he couldn't possibly because he was always at work.

It was a spiteful little dig and they both knew it. And then they'd argued, of course, but not about Liesel; it was the usual argument they had. She'd come home more if he was home more, but what was the point if he was always out working? He loved his job more than he loved her.

Yes, he loved his job, but maybe he was always out working because there was nothing to come home to, and she was the one who'd chosen to move three hundred miles for her job.

It had ended as their arguments often did, with a sulky

silence from her, conciliation from him because he hated an atmosphere, and then sex, because it was the only thing that truly broke the tension, and because she had got drunk and started crying and told him that she loved him and hated the fact that they were drifting apart, and clung to him.

When she woke up the next morning, hungover, contrite, loving, she had been more like the Caroline he remembered. And then, very casually, over breakfast, with no introduction into the subject at all, she had looked at him sideways and said, 'So is this Lisa pretty?'

She had taken him by surprise and his gut reaction was to answer honestly.

'Her name's Liesel, and yes, she's very pretty.'

'We're just friends,' he added after a loaded silence. Which in its own context was the truth; after all, anything beyond friendship had just happened in his head, and not between them.

'I don't know if I like you having very pretty friends,' she had replied, and then quickly changed the subject to something she had been reading in the paper.

After their evening out, Marilyn had followed a similar if slightly less subtle line of questioning, but 'we're just friends' had become Liesel's new mantra. Marilyn hazarded a guess that if she asked now, her sister would deny ever having confessed that she found him attractive. 'We're just friends', however, to Marilyn didn't quite cut it. She might not know Tom Spencer all that well, but she knew her sister, and in Liesel's head at least there was a lot more going on than that.

He was here now, with Liesel and Ruby in the garden. Admittedly, it had been a while since he had last come to see them; almost two weeks, to be precise. Two weeks in which Liesel had taken phone- and window-watching to a new art, getting more and more morose as time went on and yet still issuing denials.

When he had turned up tonight, it was as if someone had suddenly switched her inner light back on.

Alex had asked his mother, 'Where's Auntie Leez?' and when she had said that she was out with Tom, his reply had been, 'Is he her boyfriend?' Marilyn had automatically said no, but then immediately felt like she was lying.

They could deny it until they were blue in the face, but anyone could see, anyone but them that was, that they *were* having a relationship. Okay, so maybe there was no touching or kissing or any of the other physical things that people in a relationship together did, and okay, some people could look at it and say that in that case surely what they had was a friendship, but a friendship didn't have all the other things that were going on between them, like longing glances and lingering looks and widening pupils. That was what gave them away, Marilyn suddenly realised as she pondered: it was their eyes, it was all in the eyes.

The bottom line was, the only ones they were kidding were themselves. Deception, particularly deceiving yourself, normally only led to one thing. The one thing Marilyn had always pledged to save her sister from if possible. She'd already had enough heartbreak in her life. They both had. Maybe they should rename the hotel. Marilyn started singing their dad's favourite, 'Heartbreak Hotel', softly to herself.

It had been almost ten days since he had last been to see Ruby. Liesel felt that in a way the break had done her good, given her a chance to reflect on the situation as it really was. Just this little fantasy playing in her head. She had therefore determined that they *could* just be friends. And friends were honest with each other, weren't they? So once they had got the hellos out of the way and were on their own in the garden, she rugby-tackled him with a little bit of it.

'You've been avoiding me.'

He was bending to pat Ruby and looked up at her in surprise.

'No I haven't.'

'Please don't lie. I can't stand liars, and I really enjoy liking you.'

Tom smiled. Damn it, even when he was feeling like shit, she always managed to make him smile.

'So what is it?' she demanded, crossing her arms to suit her defiant stance, but still not managing to mask that underlying vulnerability that drew him to her. The best thing, as she had quite rightly pointed out, would be to be as truthful as possible.

'I'm in a relationship . . .' he started.

'I know that.'

'Which means that . . .'

'Which means that we can't be friends?' she prompted him.

'To be honest . . .' He hesitated.

'No lies, remember,' she urged him.

'No lies, right . . .' He took a deep breath and took her at her word. 'To be honest, Liesel, I find you far too attractive to just be friends with you.'

'Ah, I see,' Liesel mused, mentally kicking herself for being so stupidly pleased about this piece of information. 'So you're worried about temptation? Well, you don't have to worry. You're not my type.'

'I thought you said you don't like liars.'

'I'm not lying. You're not my type.'

'Then why is there so obviously something happening here?'

He had her there.

'Um . . . because I suppose a girl shouldn't label her type so restrictively.'

'So the honest answer is I'm not your *usual* type?'

Liesel nodded slowly. 'Okay, you have me on that one, but you don't need to worry, I'm sworn off men whilst we're running the hotel.'

'Why?'

'I'm fed up with men and I'm not really free at the moment to have a proper relationship, what with everything going on.'

'Me too.'

'You're fed up with men?' she teased him.

'I think you know I meant the latter.'

'There you go then. Neither of us has the time, or the . . .' She paused. She had been about to say 'desire' and realised that was totally the wrong word, because it was pretty obvious the desire was there in bucket and spades full. 'Or the inclination,' she added a bit weakly. 'And what's more, I don't chase men who are happily settled in a relationship either. And I don't think I could change my morals as easily as I can change my taste in men. So you see, it's perfectly safe for us to . . .'

'Just be friends,' he finished for her.

'Friends,' Liesel reiterated, nodding, and she held out her hand, and he smiled, took it and they shook.

And then didn't let go.

And still didn't let go.

And then somehow they just collided.

Bodies, and then lips, in a hungry, urgent kiss that lasted searing seconds, before they exploded as quickly and far more awkwardly apart, looking every which way except at each other.

'Oh God, I'm sorry . . .'

'I'm *so* sorry . . .'

'I don't know what I was thinking . . .'

'I don't know how I could have . . .'

Then Tom fled in one direction, and Liesel staggered backwards until her butt came to rest against the balcony, where she stayed in a state of semi-coma until Godrich came galloping across the garden and jumped up at her, his great paws landing squarely in her chest and sending her toppling backwards into the azaleas below.

Ten minutes later and she was still there, legs in the air, propped against the stone of the balustrade, sweet-smelling azaleas bruised and crushed beneath her, intact azaleas framing her prostrate body, staring up at the stars above her, brilliant in a clear black sky.

She had just kissed, nay snogged – and she hated that word, but it had been so beyond just a kiss it needed another name – anyway, she had just snogged a practically married man. Bad Liesel. Bad, bad Liesel.

But it had been good. Oh so good, good Liesel. And she had said she would never go for a *happily* settled man, and for him to have kissed her like that . . . well, you don't, do you; if you're happy with someone you just don't kiss someone else, especially not like *that*.

If you're happy with someone, you stay true.

So now she knew that he found her 'too attractive', and he wasn't totally happy in his relationship. She also knew that she was still lying upside down in an azalea bush because she felt she deserved to be there. What if his girlfriend, sorry, fiancée, was as sweet and loyal and loving as Marilyn had been with Nick.

Oh Lord! Liesel was Nick's *Samantha*!

She couldn't be Samantha. She couldn't do that to another woman.

But she had to confess she had fallen for Tom Spencer, quite literally, actually.

So where did that leave her? Apart from upside down in a bush.

She had to talk to someone.

She dragged herself up out of the bruised azaleas and went in search of her sister.

Marilyn was in the kitchen helping Ed load the huge dishwasher. Alex stood on a stool stirring up a mixing bowl of ingredients for his favourite Victoria sponge. The radio was on and they were all singing along, camp and laughing, to 'I Should Be So Lucky'.

How bloody apt, Liesel thought. I should be so lucky. I should be so lucky if a man like Tom Spencer, who has just confessed to finding me far too attractive to just be friends, could be single as well. One look at Liesel's face, and Marilyn was ushering her across the hallway and into their private sitting room.

'What?' she demanded. 'What!'

Liesel couldn't stop the huge grin that had been threatening ever since Tom's confession from finding its rightful home on her face. Despite the fact that at this precise moment in time, a grin just didn't feel right. It felt kind of obscene, actually.

'He finds me far too attractive to just be friends with me.' It felt even better to say it out loud.

Marilyn immediately sat down to digest this information.

'Really?'

'Uhuh.' Liesel nodded.

'Oh dear.'

'I know.' Liesel sat down next to her sister.

'But also oh wow. But then again, oh dear.'

'I knew you'd understand.'

'So what do you do now?'

'I was hoping you might be able to tell me that one.'

'Is he still here?'

Liesel shook her head.

'We kissed and then he ran. He looked so guilty. I can't be another Samantha, Marilyn.'

'You could never be like her. She didn't care who she hurt, whereas you . . .' Marilyn smiled softly at her sister, 'you wouldn't wish heartache on your worst enemy. If you had any, that is . . .'

'I couldn't put someone else through what you had to go through.'

'I know that, Leez. But sometimes people in relationships fall for other people because they're not happy any more. It's a sad fact of life, but it's still a fact. You know, I used to be adamant that Nick leaving me for someone else was all down to him being too damn selfish, but then I took a long, hard, honest look at things and realised that if he was truly happy with me, then he would never have gone.'

'But you did everything you could to make him happy.'

'Mostly, yes. But to be fair, Leez, I wasn't the absolute saint you make me out to be. I was a pain in the arse sometimes too, you know.'

'Like how?'

'Well, I'm afraid I used to nag rather a lot.'

'Yeah but you had stuff to nag about. He was never around, Maz; you coped with Alex on your own most of the time.'

'Not on my own,' Marilyn replied, putting a warm hand on her sister's arm.

'Um, that's another thing. I always feel like it was partly my fault. Maybe if you hadn't been stuck with me, you could have had the space to be a proper family.'

'If there's one thing I need you to understand and always remember, it's this . . .' She took Liesel's hand. 'As far as I'm concerned, a family without you in it will never be a proper family, for me or for Alex. And to be honest, after you moved out, things got worse. I resented Nick even more for not being there. When I had you to keep me company it didn't seem so bad if he stayed at the office until nearly midnight. Yes, I hated him working long hours, but I didn't complain about the lifestyle that came with the fact that he earned good money. A relationship is a two-way street, to use a well-worn cliché. Basically what I'm trying to say is that even if you think you were truly and royally dumped on, you can never consider yourself to be completely blameless. It would be a very high horse you were riding if you did.'

Liesel blinked at her sister, amazed and, to be perfectly honest, impressed.

'So in short, I no longer blame him for leaving me. I just wish he hadn't abandoned Alex the way he did. That's something I'm still really struggling with. Something I can't give him an excuse for.'

Liesel nodded vehemently in agreement.

'Some women complain about weekend dads. You know, pick the kids up Saturday morning, take them bowling and for a McDonald's, stuff them full of sweets, send them home hyperactive, buy them birthday cards and presents, spoil them rotten at Christmas: Superdad, who flies in, winds them up to bursting point then buggers off again, leaving you to cope with the comedown, but oh, what I'd give for a dad who did that for Alex.'

For a moment she looked so sad, but then Alex burst into the room, animated and loud with excitement.

'Mum, Ed said he'll take me bowling at the week-end, if you say it's okay. Can I go, please, Mum, can I, can I?'

Marilyn looked at her son, looked at Liesel, and laughed at the irony of it.

'Of course it's okay.'

You wouldn't have thought the smile could get any bigger but it did.

'Yay! Thank you.' He flung his arms around her briefly before scampering out of the room, throwing back over his shoulder, 'Eric's coming too. We're going to have a lads' night out.'

Marilyn watched him hurtle from the room yelling for Ed with a slightly wistful look on her face.

'It's doing him good, being one of the guys,' Liesel said gently.

'I know. I miss my hugs, though. Did you see how long that one lasted?'

'Oh, all of half a second.'

'Have you noticed?'

'That he's hanging back from the hugs and kisses since Ed and Eric joined the household?'

'He's growing up.' Marilyn nodded, and then swallowed a sob that was a mixture of sadness and pride.

'Well I'm still good for them,' Liesel offered, holding out her arms for a quick hug.

'So what are you going to do about the best-looking vet in Kernow, then?'

'Well, I know what I'd *like* to do . . .'

'Liesel, get your mind out of the gutter.'

'Trust me, sister dearest, that's the last place my mind is at the moment.'

'Okay, so get it out of Tom Spencer's bed, then.'

'I'll get my mind out if you can help think of a way to get my body in,' Liesel joked. And then, as Marilyn sighed, concerned, she added, 'Don't worry. There's nothing I can do. He's engaged to someone else and I don't think I'll be seeing very much of him from this point on, to be honest.'

'Why on earth not? He just kissed you, Liesel.'

'Just a hunch,' Liesel said, thinking of how horrified he

had looked afterwards. 'Anyway, we kissed *each other*, and trust me, it wasn't a premeditated thing either.'

'Then what was it?'

'A moment of pure unadulterated lust,' Liesel replied matter-of-factly.

'Well, that tells you something.'

'Sure, but you didn't see how fast he ran away afterwards. That tells me a lot more . . . that and the fact we'd already had the "I'm practically a married man" chat. You know, I really think the best thing I can do is try and pretend he doesn't exist.'

'Oh yeah, that's the adult approach to dealing with something, pretend you don't have a something to deal with. What if Tom doesn't quite see it that way?'

'Uh-uh!' Liesel chided her. 'Don't mention that name. From this moment on he doesn't exist, remember.'

Marilyn looked at the fake smile on Liesel's face and realised that her sister was doing what she always did and hiding her true emotions behind humour. Sometimes that was the only way Liesel could deal with things, and if that was the case this time, then just for now she'd have to let her be.

'Okay, okay. Just one more question before the subject becomes officially closed . . . why on earth is your hair full of petals?'

Like Liesel's love life, business was still erratic at best. As another money-saver, Marilyn had worked out that instead of contracting out for their laundry, if they bought their own sheets and washed them all themselves they would be saving a considerable amount of money every year. And so she installed two washing machines, a tumble dryer and an ironing board in one of the unused outhouses.

The problem was that although the saving was good in theory, in practice it was yet another job for someone to do, something else to add to the endless list.

Liesel and Alex complained about this new job and grumbled and got in the way so much that Marilyn had found it was easier to send them out on a Sunday morning and do it all herself whilst they were gone.

And so it was here, on a Sunday after breakfast when the hotel was all but deserted by staff and guests alike, that Ed found her up to her armpits in washing powder, starch and steam.

She looked exhausted. To be frank, she looked like someone had put her on a hot wash then a tumble and then forgotten to hang her out so the breeze could straighten out the creases.

'Where's Liesel?'

'She's taken Alex out to get ice cream.'

'You should have gone too, you need a break.'

'I don't have time.'

'Which is precisely one of the reasons you need one.'

'Could you be any more perverse?' Marilyn snapped, although not nastily.

And that was when it happened.

He stopped and smiled, a slow, deliberate smile.

'Try me.'

An independent observer would have been hard pressed to say which of the two was more surprised, but an even bigger shock was still to come for Ed, who despite his confident demeanour still couldn't quite believe what had slipped out of his mouth.

He expected her to come back at him with a Marilyn put-down, tell him to get back to work and put his dirty thoughts in the laundry along with the linen, but instead, she dropped the bundle of sheets she was holding, put her hands on her hips, cocked her head to one side and just looked at him for a long, slow, contemplative moment.

And then she said it.

'Don't tempt me.'

His lips twitched as his uncertain smile became one of pure unadulterated pleasure.

'Could I?' he asked.

'Tempt me?' Marilyn repeated.

He nodded.

And then, after another pause, she nodded too.

And there it was, out in the open.

'But I don't want a relationship,' Marilyn said. 'I want to focus on this place, and look after my son.'

'I don't want a relationship either. Relationships tie you down or screw you up.'

'A good relationship can set you free.'

'And the right man can add to your and Alex's life together, not take away from it.'

'So we're both talking rubbish because we're scared.'

'Scared witless.' He nodded his agreement.

'Then let's agree not to have a relationship.'

'If we're not going to have a relationship, what can we have?'

'Sex,' Marilyn whispered, blinking furiously as she tried to back up the brash statement with a bold stare but failed dismally.

'I don't do casual sex.'

'Neither do I.'

'Non-casual sex then?' he asked, and she nodded and tilted her face towards him in the hope that this gesture alone would be enough to let him know that now was when he should kiss her. Before she changed her mind and ran away. Locked herself in the cold room to cool down or die slowly of embarrassment, whichever came soonest.

Thankfully Ed was an intelligent, observant man who recognised the invitation and couldn't have been more pleased to receive it.

He took her face in both hands, gently but firmly enough so that she couldn't back away, and looked at her like that for a long moment, whilst she hoped fervently that her face wasn't squashed up like a frog in a vice and tried to remember if she'd gargled with mouthwash after cleaning her teeth so hurriedly that morning.

And then he kissed her.

Soft but firm, and so much the way she liked to be kissed that she forgot about being embarrassed or worried and let her mouth part softly as she kissed him back.

Afterwards, lying together in a tangle of clean sheets, he asked her about Nick, and for once Marilyn told all without hesitation.

'I hated him when he left us, but now I think I

understand more why he did. What I can't forgive is what it's done to Alex. Leave me, fine, but leave Alex? Cut off all contact? I don't understand that. I would never have tried to stop him seeing his son. I could never abandon my child. Alex comes first. Always.'

'Alex and Liesel.' Ed finally spoke.

She nodded as if this went without saying.

'So any man in your life has had to come third.'

'There haven't been any men in my life.'

'Until now.' He smiled lazily at her, and stretching, a long, sated, satisfied stretch, reached out and stroked a finger along the curve of her body. Then he took her T-shirt, and looped it behind her neck and pulled her to him again. Kissed her forehead, then her lips and then her throat, before letting her loose and whispering a lustful, laden, 'So what do we do now?'

Marilyn looked at him for a long moment, took in the soft blue of his eyes, the colour of the sea on a cold and cloudy morning, the breadth of his body, sturdy and safe and yet soft and sensuous, and felt only the urge to lean into him, to fit herself into the landscape of him like a piece slotting into a jigsaw puzzle.

'Laundry,' she replied.

And so it went from there as promised. Not a relationship. Friends by day, lovers on a Sunday morning. Hidden alter egos, like Alex's favourite superheroes. Both working like crazy on the laundry together, starting earlier each Sunday morning so that they could steal some time.

The only change between them was the hour they spent together with the door locked, and a new kind of ease, as though their friendship had been cemented by more than just the progress of time.

'We have an understanding,' was how Marilyn liked to describe it when in the afterglow of sex came that small familiar pink flush of guilt that always seemed to lie upon her naked skin like a cover under which to hide her blushes.

'I'm glad to hear that,' Ed had replied with a smile. 'As I sometimes find it hard to understand women at all.'

Liesel was sad but not surprised to see her prediction come true. Since the kiss that had literally knocked her sideways, Tom had all but disappeared. She knew why. If he felt at all about her the way that she did about him, then he was feeling inordinately guilty about it. After all, she might be single, but he certainly wasn't. But although she understood why he had seemed to exit from her life as quickly and completely as he had come into it, she couldn't understand why she felt so truly and utterly awful about it. How she could miss someone she really hardly knew so badly that every time a footfall was heard on the Victorian tiles of the hallway, her heart would ricochet against her ribcage like Ruby's ball bouncing repeatedly against the walls of the courtyard, in case it was finally him.

And so to take her mind off Tom Spencer, Liesel threw herself into organising another social event. The wine tasting had been great, but this time she decided to opt for something a little less dangerous, and went for a fish night instead. With Ed and Eric's help, she had worked up a beautiful menu consisting solely of locally caught seafood, and then Jimmy and David had dropped flyers for her through the whole of Piran, Piran Bay and Piran Cove. As a result, although the hotel was empty, the dining room was fully booked.

'Word's spread further than we thought. Look who's here.'

Liesel followed Marilyn's gaze.

A man in a sharp suit was lounging at the bar, elbow on

wood, glass of whisky reflected amber in the firelight clutched in his hand, eyes scouting the room keenly.

'Sean Sutton.' Liesel sighed. 'What's he doing here.'

'It's probably something to do with the fact that I told him this morning that we were no longer interested in selling the hotel,' Marilyn said, trying and failing to look nonchalant.

'You did what!'

'I was going to tell you tonight when we finished, but I wanted you to hear it from me, and not him. Please tell me you're happy, Liesel. I know I should have discussed it with you first, but he phoned and was so pushy about it, and I suddenly thought, why sell, why not stay, we're happy here, aren't we? I know business is a bit tough at the moment, but we're used to tough, and this is the best kind of tough I've ever known . . .' Marilyn had to stop talking, as her mouth was suddenly muffled by Liesel's arms as she flung them around her sister and started to scream so loudly with joy that people turned to look.

'I take it this means you approve.'

Liesel nodded furiously.

'I've never been happier, and as you know I'm a bit down in the dumps at the moment.' She looked over at Sean and frowned. 'So he's probably here to try and change your mind. I thought we were serving sea bass, not shark.'

'Predatory, dangerous, but intriguing,' Marilyn mused.

'Intriguing?' Liesel, who agreed wholeheartedly with the predatory and dangerous, was surprised by the final word.

'We have to concede he is very good looking.'

'Very.' Liesel nodded her agreement. 'But that's not enough to make him intriguing.'

'To be as successful as he is, there must be more to him than meets the eye.'

'Ah.' Liesel nodded her understanding. 'The power element. It's amazing how we women can find the ugliest man attractive if he's very successful.'

'You don't have to be gorgeous to be attractive,' Marilyn pointed out. 'So what happens when you get gorgeous and successful together?'

'Intriguing,' Liesel repeated, understanding. 'Shame he's so far up himself I can see him peering out through his own lips when he opens his mouth, though, isn't it?'

Marilyn snorted with laughter.

Perhaps alerted by the laughter, or the feeling of two pairs of eyes burning a hole through his impeccable Hugo Boss suit, Sean Sutton chose this moment to turn, and caught Liesel staring at him. To her surprise he broke into a warm and rather pleasant smile.

She wanted to pretend she hadn't noticed him, but that would have been too obvious a lie, and when a smile was that friendly there was really only one thing you could do, so she smiled back. And then of course when she returned to her post behind the bar the connection was already in progress and the next step was conversation.

'How are you?' A fairly innocuous start.

'Very good, thank you.' A lie, but a stock reply was all she could really manage.

'You look it,' he said, his eyes travelling up and down the length of her.

Liesel resisted the urge to stab a cocktail stick in his eyeball, and instead showed her disapproval by folding her arms across her chest and tightening her mouth.

'Must be the Cornish air agreeing with you,' he said, seemingly unperturbed by her reaction.

'I have to confess that it does,' she said, more to goad him, aware that Marilyn's phone call to tell him they were staying on would not have been taken so well once disconnected.

'So you're staying, then?'

Liesel nodded. 'It's what we all want. We're at home here.'

'That's good to hear.'

'It is?' She blinked at him in surprise.

'Of course. It's nice to know that you're happy here.'

'But if we're staying, that means we're not selling.'

'Obviously.'

'And you're not bothered?'

'I've lived in or near Piran for the whole of my life; it's actually a really good feeling when other people appreciate a place that you yourself care about very deeply.'

This was a new side to him.

'So you're not here to try and persuade us to change our minds?'

He shook his head.

'There are enough hotels in Piran Bay begging me to buy them. I can live without the Cornucopia.'

And there it was again, that arrogance she found so offputting.

In Liesel's view, confidence was good; arrogance was attractive in a Jane Austen novel, but only when the snooty hero revealed his deeper, sensitive side.

Was there a deeper, sensitive side to Sean Sutton?

Was Liesel really bothered about finding out?

She thought as always of Tom. Pressed that bruise again. Tom Spencer. Beautiful. Funny. Kind. Unobtainable. The whole package, wrapped up in a box she wouldn't have dreamed of even rattling before, let alone prising open with eager fingers. Sean Sutton was certainly no Tom Spencer.

But at the moment, that was probably a good thing.

And then he surprised her.

He leant back on his stool, put his whisky down on the

bar as if it were hindering his view of her and said, 'Come out for dinner with me.'

To her credit she only lost it for a moment before managing a cool, 'That's probably not a good idea.'

'Why not?'

Put so bluntly, Liesel struggled to come up with an answer.

'Um . . . I don't get nights off at the moment.' She stuttered so badly it was obvious she was feeding him a line.

'That's a lie, isn't it?'

'No, not really.'

'Okay, you're busy, but you could get a night off if you wanted to.'

'Um . . .' Truth was somehow easier this time. 'Yes, I suppose.'

'So it's an excuse. Come on then, what's the real reason? Or are you going to tell me that you spend most evenings washing your hair?'

'Well, that would be true.' She managed a laugh, thinking of how the first thing she always did as soon as she'd finished work was throw herself in that big old bath and soak away the stench of bar and kitchen and other less salubrious parts of the hotel.

'But not the truth I'm seeking.'

'You want the truth?'

He nodded, and threw a slow smile her way.

Infuriated, but oddly intrigued by the come-hither brazenness of his stance and his stare, Liesel found herself matching him with frankness.

'Because I don't know if I like you very much.'

'If you don't know, then come out with me and find out for sure rather than sitting on the fence.'

Liesel couldn't help herself. She laughed. And she had always been a sucker for confident, slightly twisted men who made her laugh.

'Well, when you put it like that . . .'

'Are you saying yes?'

'I'm saying maybe.'

'I suppose that's better than an out-and-out sod off. What do I have to do to turn that maybe into a yes?'

'Don't talk to me for the rest of the evening,' she threw back at him.

'A man like me, keep my mouth shut for,' he looked at his watch, 'three hours? Especially when you're the one I need to ask for a top-up?' He picked up his glass again and waved it at her. 'I don't suppose there's an alternative?'

Liesel bit her bottom lip, unaware of how attractive he found her with her hands on her hips and her head to one side, silken hair escaping from the ponytail she always wore when she was working.

'Convince me you have a soul.' She smiled, and signalling to Ed that she was going for a break, slipped out from behind the bar and hurried across the hall into the kitchen.

She had to confess that after the initial displeasure at seeing him, she was actually enjoying the laden banter, being flirted with so openly. There was nothing more soothing to a bruised ego than the sweet sugar-coated balm of flattery.

'I've just been asked out to dinner,' she announced to Marilyn, trying to stifle the smile that was tickling the corners of her mouth.

'Really?' Marilyn frowned, trying to fathom who on earth could have made her sister smile like this after so many days of silent suffering.

'By Sean Sutton,' Liesel blurted, abandoning the idea of toying with her sister before revealing the man in question.

Marilyn's eyes widened in concern.

'And you said no, of course. Please tell me you said no . . .' she urged as Liesel didn't immediately respond with the expected resounding negative.

'Well yes, of course I did . . .'

Marilyn's relief was palpable.

'But then I kind of changed it to a maybe . . . Don't look like that. You were the one who told me to be more open to the idea of romance.'

'Sure, but not with *him*.'

'He made me laugh.'

'Oh dear.'

'I know.'

'Men like him are only after one thing, you know.'

'Yeah, the hotel.'

'Okay, two things then.'

'He's not getting either of them from me. The hotel's not mine to give, and as for my body, we both know it takes a lot more than one meal to get me out of my clothes.'

'Sure, but I don't want you to get hurt any more than you already have been, and he's the kind of guy who specialises in it.'

'He won't hurt me.'

'How so?'

'Because I don't like him enough,' she replied, shrugging matter-of-factly. 'In fact, it will be quite nice to go out with someone who fancies me more than I fancy them. It'll make a lovely change. I can be the arse who sits back in their chair, accepts the attention and enthusiasm, gives the pretence of having a good evening and then never calls afterwards. And I can have a few glasses of wine and eat dessert without worrying whether he thinks I'm a lush or a pig as well. Yeah, that's it, I'm going to do it. I'm going to go out for dinner with him, and I'm going to flirt, drink Pinot Grigio, and eat sticky toffee pudding, and then pretend he doesn't exist.' She pursed her lips and nodded determinedly.

Marilyn crossed her eyes and shook her head in despair at her sister.

'I meant to talk you out of it, not into it.'

'I need some fun, Marilyn. Just a little bit of fun.'

'And you think a night out with a man like Sean Sutton will be that?'

Liesel nodded again, more determinedly than her own convictions really allowed.

'Well, it's your choice,' Marilyn huffed unhappily. 'You're an adult, I can't tell you what to do.'

When Liesel had finished her coffee and headed back into the bar, Sean Sutton was waiting for her, holding something out to her.

'There you go,' he said, handing her a plate.

Liesel took it on autopilot, looked down, and saw two flat fish grilled to a golden-brown perfection by Eric.

'What's this?'

'You wanted me to show you that I have a sole. Well look, I have two. Is that enough for you?'

Her lips began to twitch; as much as she tried to keep them flat-lined, they kept turning skywards.

'You can pick me up at eight o'clock, Thursday night, don't be late,' she blurted hurriedly, and ran off taking his two devilishly fried soles with her.

Liesel was in their private sitting room, on the sofa, Mitten perched on her shoulder, sharp little claws delicately hooking fish from the plate Liesel still clutched without really noticing.

She wasn't quite sure what a crisis of conscience was, but it was quite possible she was having one. Why on earth had she said that to him?

'I've just agreed to go out with Sean Sutton,' she said aloud, as if doing so would make it seem more real. 'Well, that wasn't one of your finest moments, Liesel Ellis.'

Ruby, seeing Mitten devouring something with such relish, jumped up next to her mistress, sniffed the plate, pulled a face and settled down underneath it instead on Liesel's lap.

'So will you guys tell Marilyn for me?' Liesel asked as Mitten jumped down from her shoulder to get closer to the plate.

'Tell Marilyn what? What are you doing hiding out in here?'

'Taking a break.' Liesel coughed, jumping up guiltily and dislodging a disgruntled cat and dog in the process but somehow still holding on to the plate of fish.

'I thought you just had one.'

'I did, but I was suddenly overcome with . . .' Liesel was about to say fatigue, but in truth what she had really been overcome by was the rashness of agreeing to go out for dinner with someone she really wasn't that keen on, despite the sole joke.

Marilyn looked keenly at her sister for a moment, whilst Liesel fidgeted uncomfortably under the scrutiny. It was moments like this that made her swear that sometimes Marilyn could almost read her mind.

'You said yes, didn't you?'

There you go, proof.

Liesel sat back down.

'How can you tell?'

'You've got the "guilty face" on.'

'Damn that guilty face!' Liesel joked, trying her best 'you can't honestly be cross with someone as cute as me' expression complete with blinking eyelashes and toothy goofy smile.

'Don't even try me with the butter-wouldn't-melt face.'

'Damn, you know me too well. Are you mad at me?'

'It's your life.' Marilyn shrugged, feigning nonchalance. 'It's your ride. I can only guide you over the bumps and around the arseholes where possible.'

'Don't you mean potholes?'

'Nope,' she replied tight-lipped.

21

It was seven o'clock, and Liesel was dressed and waiting in the hall for Sean Sutton to show up.

Unfortunately, so was everybody else, from Eric through to Alex. Even the guests, Mr and Mrs Polbrook and the Garrity sisters, who by now on every other evening had been sitting at their tables anticipating the soup of the day with moist tongues and smacking false teeth, were gathered to see where the lovely Liesel in her pretty dress was going this evening. And more importantly, who she was going with.

'Woah! Look at that!' This was the call of Alex on his usual sentry duty, prompted by the arrival of a black limousine almost too long to turn into the steep driveway.

'You have a chauffeur.' Marilyn observed drily.

'So I see.' Liesel nodded.

Although Alex was obviously very impressed, Marilyn wasn't so sure that her sister was. In fact Liesel looked rather horrified. She didn't know what she had been expecting, but it wasn't this.

Liesel looked at Sean Sutton, resplendent in the back, smiling at her through the lowered window, and sighed heavily.

His plan was obviously to drink lots of wine and eat sticky toffee pudding as well. What a car. It was so ostentatious; to travel in something like that would be a rather embarrassing ordeal instead of the pleasure he so obviously thought it would be for her.

The realisation that they didn't know each other, and that this date had been arranged on her part because her ego needed boosting, and on his because he liked what he saw on the outside, was not such a fortuitous start to the evening.

Liesel suddenly felt unbelievably nervous . . . well, not nervous, a better word was apprehensive, the feeling you got when you just knew that what you were doing wasn't a good idea. It was too late to back out now, though. She was standing there in her posh frock, and he was getting out of the car in his smart trousers and sports jacket. She could hardly turn on her heel, run inside and lock herself in the tower, could she?

Apparently unperturbed by the not-so-welcoming committee, he took her hands and, leaning in, kissed her on the cheek.

'Liesel, you look absolutely beautiful. Your carriage awaits, my lady.'

Marilyn muffled her laughter, Alex's mouth fell open even further, Lorraine almost swooned, and Kashia, Ed and Eric were ready to kill on command; in fact Liesel was sure she heard Ed murmur, 'Tosser'. Liesel simply thanked Sean politely, threw a quavering smile over her shoulder at the throng behind her, and stepped into the limousine as if it were an everyday occurrence and not her very first time.

It took her a few minutes to find her voice.

'So where are we going?'

'I'm taking you to one of my favourite restaurants in Padstow.' He beamed his obvious pleasure at this fact. 'It normally takes months to get a table, but the owner's a personal friend of mine. I think you'll like it. The food's phenomenal, the atmosphere great. Best fish restaurant in

Cornwall. The sea bass with fennel sauce is just divine.'

'Divine,' Liesel repeated, surprised that he'd used such a word.

'Oh yes. A real experience. You'll enjoy it.'

He's patronising me, she thought crossly, assuming it's not usual for me to eat in good restaurants or ride around in chauffeur-driven limousines. Well, he's right, she told herself, it's not usual. I normally wait on people who eat in good restaurants and drive around in chauffeur-driven limousines. She pulled awkwardly at the hem of her skirt, which, respectable in the safe haven of the Cornucopia, seemed to have suddenly shrunk several inches. But this only served to make him look at her legs, which made her feel even more uncomfortable. An uncomfortable Liesel usually chattered nineteen to the dozen, but today her brain was devoid of any small talk, her lips pursed tight shut.

Sean Sutton, who could usually talk about himself for a long time if necessary, did so for a while with no reaction, then decided that the best way to avoid the silence was to give her a guided tour and tell her about every inch of the coastal road they were travelling. Pointing out Jamie Oliver's restaurant at Watergate Bay, and Bedruthan Steps, and telling her about John Betjeman's time on the Pentire headland.

For Liesel, starved of the local culture she craved, it was the best thing he could have done to garner her interest and make her relax. His enthusiasm was also infectious. By the time they had reached their destination, they had both begun to enjoy themselves a little more.

Padstow itself was beautiful, a steep, winding road that curved like a race track down into one of the most picturesque harbours Liesel had ever seen. The restaurant itself was a converted harbourmaster's house, with wide windows overlooking the harbour, dark slate floors, low-beamed ceilings, and jazz playing at just the right level.

They were greeted by a dapper little Frenchman whom Sean introduced as Evariste, which was the name of the restaurant as well.

After the initial hand-shaking, and back-clapping, Liesel was offered three kisses, one lucky cheek getting two, and then they were ushered to a table with a good view of the estuary, where Evariste sat backwards on a chair with them for a while and talked to Liesel with great passion about the history of the little harbour.

When a bottle of champagne was delivered minutes later, she had to admit that she was actually starting to enjoy herself, even more so when handed the menu. The food sounded wonderful. Unfortunately it all started going downhill a little when the first course arrived. Liesel's wonderful-sounding lobster citrus salad was simply a pretty pattern on a plate that looked like someone else's leftovers, there was so little of it.

'I think they forgot to put the lobster on there,' she joked, prodding the small tower of food with her fork. 'Oh no, there it is, at least I think it's lobster; the size of it, it could quite possibly be a small prawn masquerading as a lobster, or maybe the trend for size zero has hit the shellfish world as well as the selfish world.'

She looked up with a grin to see that Sean was smiling, but it was indulgently, like a father regarding a small child who was being faintly amusing. And then he started what she had hoped this evening wasn't about. He started talking about the Cornucopia.

He didn't actually ask outright about the hotel; he kind of skirted round the issue, asking related questions that to the less observant would not seem obvious but which gave him the answers he was seeking nonetheless, such as how had Alex seemed to settle in to his new school, had he made friends, was he missing London, was she missing London, all things that would give him an idea if they had any inclination at all to go back there, and hence sell the hotel, whilst maintaining the outward appearance of being truly solicitous about the family's welfare. He was obviously still keener to buy than his cool dismissal at the fish night would have her believe.

Well, two could play at being slippery, and she'd had plenty of practice at avoiding the issue over the last few weeks. So everything he asked she turned around. When he mentioned Alex, she asked if he had any children of his own; when he talked about jobs, she asked about his; when he mentioned London, she turned the conversation to his own visits there, what hotels he had stayed in, restaurants he had eaten at. In fact he didn't get one straight answer until the question was 'Would you like a dessert?'

To her disappointment, there was no sticky toffee pudding on the menu. Sean ordered a coffee and a whisky. Determined to have her cake and eat it, Liesel ordered something chocolate and calorific, and then, too embarrassed to stuff herself when he wasn't, took one mouthful before excusing herself and going to the loo.

A swift pee was followed by a protracted session in front of the mirror.

Her face was flushed. She splashed cold water on it and thought about reapplying her lipstick and maybe some mascara, then realised that he would probably notice and think it was for his benefit, and she really didn't want him to think that. She didn't want him to get the wrong idea and think that she found him attractive, because let's face it, she didn't, at all.

Even though he wasn't as bad as first impressions had led her to believe. Yes, he was a bit 'I am' and self-obsessed, but he wasn't unpleasant with it. And he certainly knew how to treat a girl. She had to confess she had been forced to revise her opinion of him a little. The thing was, he had probably done the same, and not for the good. She hadn't exactly been scintillating company this evening. She felt the urge to apologise for this, but what could she say: sorry I've been a miserable old cow but I've fallen head over heels with someone who isn't available and so it was a big mistake coming out with you?

Then again, she might be flattering herself. He had talked about himself a lot of the evening, and in a way Liesel had been happy to let him. But if she was being honest, he was probably talking a lot because she was so bloody quiet. He had at one point paused and looked deeply into her eyes and said, 'So tell me about yourself,' but she'd been so offput by the intensity, she'd just muttered, 'Not a lot to tell, really.' He was probably texting friends and organising rescue calls whilst she was hiding out in the loo, but to her surprise there was another glass of champagne waiting for her upon her return.

'Anyone would think you're trying to get me drunk.' She smiled nervously.

The expected lascivious look was duly given, but then he totally flummoxed her by apologising and ordering a bottle of water.

When the meal was finished, she had assumed that he would be as desperate to escape as she was, but instead when he stood and pulled out her chair for her, his next suggestion was, 'Let's go through to the bar and have another drink,' and because by this point she felt guilty about being such bad company, she nodded brightly and agreed, determined to at least give him a little bit of value for his money. Having sneaked a peek at the bill when he was distracted by Evariste, she knew she should really be offering him a comedian and a floor show, but as it was she told him one of her best bad jokes, which he dutifully laughed at, and so she hit him with another one. Four bad jokes later and he was laughing uproariously and offering one in return. When he suggested a refill, she nodded without pausing to think.

And then she spotted him, at the other end of the bar in a group of friends.

'Tom!' she said aloud without thinking.

'Sorry?' Sean Sutton looked at her quizzically.

'Tom . . . er, I mean Tommy Cooper. I used to love Tommy Cooper.'

'I wouldn't have thought you were old enough to remember him.'

'Re-runs . . .' Liesel muttered, slipping off her bar stool. 'Look, would you just excuse me for a moment? Ladies' room, nose to powder and all that . . .'

She hadn't seen him since the kiss. Surely this was too much to be a coincidence. Cornwall was one of the largest counties in the country after all. He saw her coming, detached himself from his friends a little. It just looked like two acquaintances bumping into each other in a bar.

'What are you doing here?' His question caught her off guard.

'I was about to ask you the same thing.'

'I asked first.'

'I've been having dinner,' she replied guardedly.

'With him?' He nodded over to Sean, who was thankfully once again in conversation with Evariste.

Liesel nodded.

'What on earth are you doing with Sean Sutton?'

'Like I said, having dinner,' Liesel repeated carefully, more confused than ever at why he was there.

'You know what I mean.'

'Why shouldn't I be here with him? We're both single,' she said pointedly. 'He's good looking and successful and intelligent . . .'

'He's an idiot.'

For a moment they looked daggers at each other, and then Liesel couldn't help it, her mouth quirked into a smile and she couldn't stop herself from whispering the embarrassed confession. 'I know.' Then, defensively, she turned the tables. 'What are you doing here?'

'I'm having a drink with some friends.'

'Do you come here often?'

This one made him smile and look embarrassed at the same time.

'No. I never come here, it's pretentious and the prices are a total rip-off.'

'Then what are you doing here tonight?' she said, but she almost knew the answer before it came. 'How on earth did you know I'd be here?' she added.

'Being a bit presumptuous, aren't we?' He tried to look affronted and failed dismally. 'Okay, so maybe the fact that your waiter this evening is a good friend of Lorraine's might have something to do with it . . .'

He bit his bottom lip and smiled so charmingly she would have forgiven him anything.

'He might perhaps have texted her and she might perhaps have mentioned something to Adrian . . .'

Good old Lorraine. But how absurdly pleased she felt was still tempered by confusion.

'Well, now I know the Cornish jungle drums have been on full volume, I'll try again.' The answer was suddenly so important. 'What are you doing here?'

He looked down at the floor, rubbed the side of his nose with a finger and then caught his bottom lip between his teeth, a habit of his she had noticed.

'Well, I had this mad idea of coming down here, pushing Sean Sutton into the harbour with a weight around his ankles, and then asking you to run away with me.'

Self-protection banishing the smile that was threatening, Liesel peered into his glass and sniffed suspiciously.

'What are you drinking?'

'Tonic water. Run away with me.'

'Tonic water with about three shots of gin?'

'Just tonic. I want you to run away with me,' he repeated, 'now, right now. Leave this place, that man, and run away with me.'

'I can't do that. You're practically a married man.'

'I am not—' he began, but Liesel interrupted him before he could get her hopes up.

'Besides, it would be *so* rude to Sean. You see, he may be an idiot, but he's actually been really rather nice to me this evening. I mean, if he was being an arsehole and you could come over and rescue me from him, then that would be another thing, but between you and me, he's actually been quite decent.'

'Mmm. I see what you mean.' He thought for a moment and then looked back up at her hopefully. 'But is he *boring* you?'

'Oh Lord, yes.' Liesel sighed automatically.

'Well, there you have it.'

'I do?'

'Absolutely. Boring your date is as bad as being an arsehole.'

'Quite possibly.' Liesel nodded, unable now to stop herself from smiling. 'Although if I'm being completely honest, I would imagine I'm boring him as badly . . . You know what it's like when you find someone really difficult to talk to so you just clam up? Well, I never clam up, you know that, but with him, there's nothing, just silence.'

'So you're boring him too?'

'Oh, absolutely, the poor man. He'd have had better conversation from the table decorations.'

'He's made you switch off.'

Liesel thought about it.

That was probably a good way to phrase it.

No matter how handsome and successful the man was, that was exactly what he did to her, switched her off instead of turning her on. Whereas Tom ... well, extremely unfairly, considering the circumstances, he turned her on as brightly as if he were some ridiculously famous pop star flicking a switch, and she was Oxford Street at Christmas.

'So run away with me ...'

'Tom, don't ... please ...'

'I'm being serious, leave with me now.'

'I couldn't. I'd never forgive myself for being so awful.'

He took her hand, an action that made her jump, and said so earnestly that it negated the arrogance of the statement, 'What would you regret more in the morning? Leaving with me? Or *not* leaving with me?'

'You know what you're saying, don't you?'

'Yep. I'm being an arrogant sod and assuming that you feel the same way I do.'

'You know I do. But more to the point, you're admitting that you have feelings for me.'

'You know I do.' He repeated the same words intentionally.

'And you're acting on those feelings despite ...'

She was silenced as he put a gentle finger on her lips

'Please. No words beginning with E, F or C,' he murmured softly.

Liesel looked at him in confusion.

'Engaged. Fiancée. Caroline,' he explained.

'How about G?' she said as he removed the finger.

'G?'

'For guilt.' She shrugged.

'Have we done anything to feel guilty about?'

'Not yet, I suppose.'

'I like that word.'

'Which word?'

'Yet. It leaves room for potential.'

'Are you sure you're not drunk?'

'I'm not drunk. You?'

'No.'

'So we have no one and nothing to blame but ourselves?'

She nodded her agreement.

'So will you run away with me?'

'Yes,' she whispered.

Padstow to Port Isaac, not a terribly long distance in miles, but a hell of a long car drive for someone whose mind was so torn she could surely be declared two people in the same body.

The restaurant to Tom's car: one small step for Liesel, one giant leap for unkind.

A scribbled note of apology on a table napkin citing a family emergency was not the way to thank Sean Sutton for their inordinately expensive meal.

Enter Liesel, Queen of Guilt.

He has a fiancée, she told herself repeatedly, even as her hand itched to work its way across to rest upon his thigh, which kept tensing temptingly as he drove.

A fiancée who chose to live miles away in London, who apparently didn't return his phone calls and cancelled visits all the time. One who made him look miserable when all Liesel seemed to do was make him smile.

No matter how she tried to justify to herself where she was, who she was with, it still wasn't sitting too well in her stomach; or maybe that was the prawn masquerading as lobster.

What was she doing?

How well did she actually know this man?

Not well at all, if truth be told, but a few sessions of dog training and she was ready to beg and roll over.

She looked across at Tom as he drove, that perfect profile.

'Take me home,' she thought, but she couldn't bring herself to say it. The truth was, she knew the difference between right and wrong, and at the moment she couldn't bring herself to do the right thing, because to use a cliché, the wrong thing felt so right.

At Port Isaac, he manoeuvred the Range Rover through the narrow streets, down towards the harbour, the big car getting slower as the road got steeper, and finally pulled up outside a tall terraced stone cottage.

He switched off the engine, but neither of them made a move to get out.

In the silence, Liesel could hear the sound of the waves against the harbour wall.

'So this is me,' he finally said, still clutching on to the steering wheel as if it were a lifebelt.

They both knew why they were here. Run away with me, he had said, and she had. Run away with me, forget about everything, pretend we don't have other responsibilities. Let's make our own little world for a while where nothing and nobody matters but us.

But the problem with other worlds was they were normally just fictional. Take Narnia, for instance, Liesel thought. How many of us have headed inspired and hopeful into the back of a wardrobe only to come out disappointed and smelling of musty clothes? Real life always had a habit of shoving its sharp corners through the iridescent bubble that other worlds tended to float along in, and pop, there you were, flat on your arse on the floor, sobbing into your burnt fingers.

No matter how much she wanted him, the dirty truth was, he wasn't free to be had. Why did dirty truths always struggle out just when you thought you had them under your heel?

'Maybe we should just be friends for a while.' It wasn't what she wanted to say, but it was what she thought she should say.

He glanced across at her, and then unbuckled his seat belt and turned to face her properly.

'In case you'd forgotten, that was my line a couple of weeks ago.'

'And I've just realised you were right. Do you really want to mess up your life for someone you've only known for five minutes?'

'Who says you'd mess up my life?'

'You're in a relationship and I'm not very good at relationships. Bad start.'

'True.'

'And I'm a serial monogamist,' Liesel blurted, scrambling around for a reason other than the obvious.

'Better than a serial philanderer.'

'And I know you said not to mention any words beginning with E, F or C, but you are E'd to your F, C, and I really don't think that C would exactly appreciate me being here.'

'That's very true.' His mouth twisted into a wry line.

'And there's no getting away from the fact that you are E'd to C, and as much as I wish that . . .' She trailed off, suddenly feeling very stupid and very vulnerable.

'You wish that what? Tell me, Liesel Ellis, what do you wish for?'

She looked back up at him from under thick dark lashes, and although she said nothing, her eyes were screaming the answer at him.

'You,' they shouted. 'I wish that I could have *you*.'

And Tom knew that right now, right at this exact minute, resistance was futile, as Spock so succinctly put it, and not the Spock who told you how to rear your children, the one from *Star Trek* with the Beatles haircut, pointy ears and the logical nature. And so he ignored his morals and his manners and his mother and his education and everything that had been drummed into him from childhood about how one should behave in this life, with the feelings of others always foremost, and for once simply followed his instinct, and his instinct right now was to lean towards her, tilt her chin with his finger and kiss her oh so gently on the lips, a kiss that segued smoothly from light and gentle into intense; into sinking slowly into the most pleasurable pillow of feelings, both emotional and physical. Such a difference to the collision that was their first kiss, but just as powerful, more so maybe for that first moment of contemplation.

And with that kiss they both knew that all hope of being good and honest and decent was gone.

'So are you coming in?' he asked gently, reluctantly, pulling away.

Unable to speak, Liesel simply nodded.

22

The ground floor of his three-storey house was open plan and split level, with a large kitchen-diner to the front, then three steps down into the sitting room. The whole rear wall was glass, leading out on to a wide wooden balcony, home to wooden furniture and hardy plants housed in glazed tubs, lit by low lights that were a lure to insects whose wings reflected the light like little mirrors.

Furniture was minimal and seemed to have a faint nautical theme with soft blues and off whites. It was beautiful, but he was apologetic.

'I know, it's like a show home. I'm not here that often. Work.'

Liesel's eyes immediately honed in on the one personal thing in the room.

The photograph of Caroline.

'She's really pretty,' she said enviously.

'We've hardly seen each over the past year or so,' he replied as though this mitigated her looks.

'But you call?'

'Yes, but we keep missing each other.'

'Deliberately?' It was a joke, but the question still had a ring of hope to it.

'Maybe,' he said, for the first time acknowledging the subconscious thought.

'She looks nice . . . Is she?'

She wanted to hear him talk about her; she supposed it was the same kind of pleasure as picking at a scab.

He pondered the question simply because it was something he hadn't considered before. When people described Caroline, they used words like beautiful, intelligent, driven, dynamic, but never nice. Was that, he wondered, because she wasn't?

Liesel was nice, wholeheartedly so, and not in the tedious way that nice could sometimes be misused, but nice as in good, and sweet, and funny, and caring, all of the words that had somehow over the decades moved from compliment to insult.

But was Caroline nice?

He shook his head, not as a negative response, but to shake the question from his mind, to shake Caroline from his mind. It wasn't as easy as a simple movement, though. Toby was right: he wasn't the kind of person to cheat on someone. So why was he here now? Why had he called the friends he had been out with tonight and insisted that they change the venue for the meet from Rock to Padstow? As Harry had laughingly put it, "No worries, mate, if that's what you want, but I don't really see the point when you're at Port Isaac and we're at Rock. What is it? You like the view better from that side of the water? No, don't tell me, there's some girl you're chasing. You know, whilst Caroline's away, Tom's going to play . . .' and then he had laughed uproariously, as if the idea of Tom cheating on Caroline was about as likely as him quitting his job.

And it had been.

For someone who had women throwing their coats – with them still inside – over puddles for him, he seemed on the whole oblivious to the effect that he had, a naivety that the less kind, or those who didn't know him well, would assume was ingenuous.

He had only realised Liesel liked him at the point when he had realised he liked her, and despite having an IQ that would be coveted by quite a few 'just scraped in' Mensa members, both realisations had come as a bit of a shock.

She was apparently thinking along similar lines.

'I'm not the kind of girl who usually does this sort of thing,' she said, looking at him with a mixture of hope and apology.

'I know you're not. That's one of the things I like so much about you.'

One of the things? That meant there were more. She stopped herself from asking what they were. After all, how could she still be insecure about his feelings for her after this evening? He had heard about her date with Sean and he'd come to Padstow to find her. For Liesel, that told her nearly everything she needed to know. The only question it didn't answer was where did this go after tonight. At the moment, that was a question she didn't really want to contemplate. Not whilst she was here with him now. Not whilst he was reaching out to gently take her face in his hands to draw her to him for another kiss.

He opened his eyes and realised that she was looking over his shoulder at the picture of Caroline.

He wasn't the kind of man to do something so deliberate as turn it to the wall or put it in a drawer, and so he reached behind him and simply put it on the kitchen counter, partly obscured by the toaster.

Out of sight, please get out of my mind, Liesel thought, but it was the next kiss and not the toaster that actually pushed the image of the smiling girl with the deep blue eyes out of her head. The slow closing of her own eyes, the mental drawing of a veil over the picture that still sat, staring at her, over his shoulder.

Somehow still kissing, they made it upstairs to his

room and Liesel sank back down on to the bed behind her. Not wanting to lose contact with the soft skin of her cheek, he went with her, over her, his hands unbuttoning her dress, hers pulling the shirt loose from his jeans so that they could slide indulgently inside across the taut muscles, the soft skin.

And as if on cue, the telephone began to ring.

'That's Sean Sutton, he's tracked you down,' he whispered against her neck.

Liesel laughed, and then the guilt at her behaviour this evening past and current kicked in and she swallowed the laughter and became serious.

'Should you get that?'

'Probably, but I'm not going to.'

'What if it's work? It's gone midnight, it could be an emergency.'

'They'll call Adrian instead.'

'Poor Lorraine.'

'Are they out tonight?'

'They're *in* tonight.' Liesel stressed the word, to carry the meaning. 'For the first time. She's cooking dinner and everything, and trust me, Lorraine can clean like a Dyson on steroids but she doesn't do cooking.'

This made them both smile, despite the fact that the phone was still ringing, its bell tolling through this temporary idyll like a warning alarm.

'I'm still going to let the machine get it,' Tom whispered, his breath warm and sweet against her neck.

'Thank heavens for the machine.' She smiled, reaching up to kiss him again.

'She still not back?'

Marilyn had been determined not to fall asleep, but she had obviously failed, as the sound of Ed's voice from the doorway woke her with a start.

She shook her head and looked at her watch. It was nearly three in the morning! She sat up with a start.

'Look at the bloody time! Where the hell is she!'

'I'm sure she's okay, you know.' Ed came into the room and sat down on the edge of the sofa. 'I'll go and look for her if you want me to.'

Marilyn shook her head.

'I wouldn't know where to send you.'

'In that case, want some company?'

'It seems daft for neither of us to get any sleep.'

'I wouldn't sleep now anyway, because I'll be worrying about you sat here on your own worrying about Liesel.'

He was pleased to see Marilyn smile.

'So, what do you think? Want some company? There's nothing worse than waiting for someone on your own . . .'

In answer, Marilyn lifted the duvet to give him room to sit down properly.

'Do you know, this is the first time for over three years that I've shared my duvet with a man.' She laughed drily as he settled underneath it.

The light was filtering through the partly drawn curtains, sea gulls woken by the dawn circling and crying outside. His arm was around her waist, his body against hers, cheek against her cheek. He opened his eyes seconds after her, smiled.

'Morning.'

'Morning,' she whispered back.

'Well good morning.' The third voice was so unexpected and so full of venom that they both jumped so hard they collided with each other. Liesel, not knowing where to put herself, slipped further under Tom's arm and under the duvet. She just about managed to resist the urge to hide herself completely and looked over to the source of the sound.

She was sitting on a chair in the corner of the room, knees tucked to her chest, clutching on to rather than smoking a cigarette. She was even more beautiful than the photograph, but in place of a smile was a look of pure hard hatred.

How long she had been there would have been anybody's guess.

'I didn't want to wake you, you both looked so . . . comfortable,' she said coldly as Liesel tried to pull the duvet further around her naked body. 'No wonder you didn't answer the phone last night. You know, he told me you were very pretty, and he was right. What he didn't tell me was that you were a total whore!'

'Caro!' His voice was pure anguish.

'Don't. Say. My. Name!' The words were spat at them like arrows one after the other, and then she pushed herself upright so hard the chair toppled backwards and fled.

Tom leapt from the bed and began to pull on the clothes that Liesel had helped him to remove only hours before. As he did up his belt, he stopped for a moment and looked at her watching him in rigid shock, his own eyes appealing, pleading for her to understand.

'I'm so sorry. I have to go after her.'

A beat of two seconds, and then Liesel nodded, and he was gone.

As soon as they had left, Liesel scrambled for her own clothes, ripping her dress in her haste to pull it on. Panic set in as she couldn't find her shoes, but then she spotted them kicked off into a corner, and for a moment she remembered the sheer joy of the moment before bumping back to reality as she heard the front door go again.

As she came down the stairs he was coming back in.

'She's gone,' he said simply.

'I think I'd better go too,' she replied.

And instead of begging her to stay, which was of course exactly what she wanted and needed right now, he just nodded.

'I'll get my keys.'

'I'll get a taxi.'

'It's too far, I'm taking you.'

If she had felt uncomfortable on the way to his house, it was nothing compared with the journey back to Piran, which passed in silence until he pulled up outside the hotel. Quite simply he did not know what to say, and told her so.

'I don't know what to say, because in truth I don't know what this is. I'm running on instinct here, Liesel, and that's just something I don't do.'

'You have things to sort,' she said stiffly, reaching for the door handle.

'Liesel, please . . . wait a minute.' His hand was gentle but firm on her shoulder, pulling her back into the seat. 'I'm sorry.'

'That you came looking for me last night?'

'That's not what I mean and you know it.'

'You didn't know she'd turn up like that.'

'That's not the point, is it?'

He was right. The point was that it was Liesel who wasn't supposed to be there, in his bed, in his arms.

'You're right, we made a mistake.'

'You don't mean that, do you?'

She shook her head.

He took her hands.

'This morning was horrible, but don't let that make you forget that last night was amazing. The only mistake that's been made is on my part for not being honest enough, with myself, and with Caroline, but not with you, Liesel; everything that's happened between us has been true, but it's also true that it's something I shouldn't have allowed to happen whilst I was still with Caroline. Not that it's felt like I've actually been with her, not for some time. This is going to sound so clichéd, but since she moved to London we've drifted apart. To be honest, we couldn't have been that close before she went or she wouldn't have gone, or else I'd have gone with her . . .'

'But it's not over. It's far from over.' It was a statement, not a question.

'When I'm with you I forget all of that. It's us that seems right, seems real.'

'And now she's back?'

He couldn't answer, and that was answer enough.

If there was one thing that she did know, it was that he must feel exactly as she did at the moment. And she felt sordid. There was no other word for it.

'You'd better get back.'

He nodded. 'I'll call you, okay?'

Marilyn was of course waiting for her, mother hen, head jerking backwards and forwards in angst and controlled fury, a fury that exploded the minute Liesel stepped through the door looking like she'd just fallen into an azalea bush again.

'Where have you been! I've been worried sick, we've barely slept a wink all night.'

'We?'

'Me and Ed, we were waiting up for you, Leez, we were worried. Please tell me you didn't stay the night with Sean Sutton, please tell me you didn't.'

'I'm sorry, Maz, and no, I definitely didn't stay the night with Sean Sutton.'

'Then where have you been?'

Where had she been? Liesel sighed heavily. Where did she start?

Marilyn did as she always did and listened quietly and patiently as Liesel told her from start to finish the highs and the lows of the last twelve hours. Spinning from ecstatic one minute to ashamed the next.

'I'm a cow,' was how she finished the tale. 'It doesn't matter what I feel for Tom, what I did was wrong.'

' "When one is in love, one always begins by deceiving oneself, and one always ends by deceiving others . . ." ' Marilyn murmured.

'What?' Liesel asked, puzzled.

'Oh, it's one of Ed's proverbs . . . well, not Ed's, actually. Oscar Wilde, to be precise.'

'What do you think he meant by that?'

'I'm not sure.' Marilyn shrugged. 'But I think maybe he just meant that love can be pretty complicated sometimes, that everyone has expectations and sometimes it's hard to meet them.'

'Well, I don't think Caroline was expecting to find Tom in bed with someone else,' Liesel groaned. 'I felt so awful, Maz, I didn't know what to do . . .'

'It's not all your fault. It takes two to tango, you know.'

'Yeah, but if the tango was all we were doing, then we wouldn't be in this mess! And what about Sean?' Liesel exclaimed. 'What I did to him, well, it was pretty rotten, wasn't it? He must be hating me as well.'

'Well, I don't think he's in a terribly good mood. Kashia was given notice on her room this morning.'

Liesel frowned, puzzled.

'He owns the house she lives in,' Marilyn explained. 'Big old Victorian place just the other side of Piran harbour. He's given the entire building two weeks to quit. Turning it all into luxury flats, apparently.'

'You're kidding me. You think he did that because I pissed him off?'

'Don't be silly. I'm just trying to show you what a

shithead he is, and how you shouldn't worry about him, okay?'

Liesel nodded gratefully.

'What's Kashia going to do?'

'Well, we nearly had another permanent guest. I was just about to offer her one of the attic rooms, and then Lorraine stepped in and said she could move in with her. How things change, eh?'

'And what am I going to do, Maz?' Liesel hung her head in her hands.

'Sometimes you don't have to do anything; sometimes you have to wait for others to do the doing.'

'Is that another one of Ed's proverbs?' Liesel looked up and smiled half-heartedly.

'No, it's a Marilism.'

'A Marilism?'

'Yeah, it means someone who spouts crap when they don't have any good advice to give.' Marilyn smiled apologetically and gave Liesel another hug. 'The next trick up my sleeve is to tell you to trust to fate, and start singing "Que Sera Sera".'

Liesel rested her chin on her sister's shoulder and rolled her eyes in despair.

'Well, I suppose Doris Day will make a nice change from Julie Andrews . . .'

23

They had a flurry of bookings that morning. In fact it
was so busy it was almost enough to take Liesel's
mind a little off the night before. But only a little. The
more she thought about it, the more awful she felt. And
not just for herself.

Poor, poor Caroline, a woman who would harshly
reject her sympathy and yet deserved it none the less.
How could she have been so selfish? What had happened
to her last night? Well, she knew what had happened to
her last night, something amazing, and yet this morning
the amazing had turned so sour.

When lunchtime came, she took her sandwich and an
orange juice into the garden and worked off a little guilt
by spending some time with Ruby, who had thrown
herself at her mistress when she had returned that
morning, in a yelping frenzy of ecstatic yet miserable
abandonment.

She had unearthed her favourite ball, the little yellow
one that Tom had given her, and every time Liesel threw
it for her, Ruby would chase it and bring it back. Every
time without fail. Every time she called her, Ruby, no
matter what she was doing, would trot back and sit at her
feet, tail wagging, waiting. Unfailing loyalty. A rare thing.

Suddenly the little dog paused and sniffed the air, and
then she began to yap in excitement and shot off around

the corner of the building, to return seconds later in the arms of Tom, her small pink tongue repeatedly kissing the cheek that only hours ago had lain against Liesel's whilst she slept in sated peace.

His beauty was faded at this moment. He looked grey and ashen.

'Hi.'

'Hi.' Although her body didn't move, her eyes were a giveaway; they reached out to him, touched him as she so obviously longed to do herself, and yet she held back, because he held back, the pull between them reversed and pushing them apart.

'Can we talk?' It was said in a way that made her want to say no, because she already knew from his face what he was going to say.

So instead of answering, she opted to say nothing.

Tom's face fell.

Silence from Liesel, he had already learned, was not a good sign. She was only ever truly quiet when she was really upset. He didn't want to make her unhappy, far from it; what he wanted . . . what he wanted . . . Oh Lord! He couldn't have what he wanted. Could he?

Why did things have to be so complicated? But then emotions weren't simple things, they were complex and messy and sometimes bloody hard to deal with, and when it became like that, the only thing a man like him could do was the right thing, no matter how hard.

Caroline had been waiting when he returned to the house, a sodden traffic wreck of tears and recriminations. It had been his wake-up call. No matter what his feelings for Liesel, and they were feelings that had taken him completely by surprise, he was engaged to Caroline. He had made a promise, and she made it quite clear over the three hours of shouting, fighting, clinging, rejecting, sobbing, insults, recriminations and declarations that she wanted him to stick to it. He had been with Caroline for four years, he loved her. Maybe it wasn't heart in mouth every time he saw her or spoke to her; maybe he didn't miss her as much as he thought he would when she moved away; maybe he didn't think about her all the time, fantasise about her, hell, even dream about her, the way he did about Liesel, but who knew what his feelings for Liesel were. They were new, they were quite frankly frightening, and for all he knew they could be an infatuation that would be about as lasting as high-street fashion.

What he had with Caroline was his reality. And no matter how distant they were at the moment, you didn't just give up on a person you'd made a commitment to, you worked at things. She wanted them to try. She'd begged him to try. He had never seen her so upset. But now Liesel was upset too, and it was as though someone had a hold of his vital organs and was twisting them hard. Whatever he did was going to hurt someone. Himself included.

'This is so hard,' he sighed.

Oh boy, I hope so, said her mind, as her whole body sighed with longing and a remembrance of a pleasure so intense it had been like nothing she'd ever felt before. Stop it, you moron, she chastised herself severely. Get your mind out of the gutter, out of his bed. But the way he had touched her, kissed her . . . She had never had a kiss that had spread from her lips to every single other part of her body before making her muscles shiver and her toes curl upwards in delight. Had never simply fitted into someone so well, so beautifully, so harmoniously. Even the first time they had kissed, though it had been more of a collision than a kiss . . . well, put it this way, even falling from the balustrade she hadn't felt a thing, so enveloped had she been by it. Although she still to this day had the faint traces of the bruises as a reminder.

'Liesel?'

His anxious voice pulled her out of her fantasies, where quite frankly they were already in that big old double bed, making the *Kama Sutra* look old hat. He looked so genuinely upset, it brought her to her senses.

'I'm sorry.' She was apologising for the thoughts in her own head, but of course he didn't know that.

'So am I. Don't you see that? Truly. You know I care about you, have feelings for you; it would be stupid to deny it, because you'd just know that I was lying to you, and I don't want to lie to you, I want to be as honest as I possibly can . . . with everyone.'

'You're right. You're trying to be a saint and I'm just a plain old sinner. Or at least I want to be . . .'

It was an invitation.

'I have a responsibility to Caroline . . .' he answered hesitantly.

'I know.'

'I have to do the right thing.' It was like he was telling himself this, not her.

'You do? I mean, of course you do. Of course you do.' Liesel sighed, and he was now so close he felt it feather her face like an air kiss.

'I've made promises, Liesel. I don't break promises.'

And there was the rub. The truth. The core of him. What made him what he was, what made her love him, and what made it impossible for her to have him.

Although she was biting her bottom lip so hard it was white and bloodless, she nodded, and he knew she understood.

'Okay. I know this is difficult and I don't want to make it worse, but there's just one question I have to ask you, I have to. I don't expect an answer now, but please think about it sometime . . .'

She waited for him to nod, then took a breath.

'It may sound really naive, but I think that if you really

truly love someone, there isn't any room left in your heart for someone else. I know that I wouldn't want you with me unless that was where you really wanted to be . . . so this is my question. You think that keeping your promise to Caroline is doing the right thing, but how can you truly make someone happy when you're not sure whether you actually want to be with them?'

He took a moment to answer, and she could see he was digesting the truth of her words.

'You're right, you are, completely right, but don't you see, I owe it to her to take the time to find out.'

She nodded unhappily and he had to fight the urge to reach out and hold her.

'I'm not saying never, Liesel, I'm just saying not now,' he said softly.

'Maybe it's now or never,' she threw at him, bottom lip trembling no matter how hard she tried to stop it.

He sighed then, long and heavy, obviously torn, obviously hurting himself, and at the sight of the pain and confusion on his face, Liesel's innate goodness kicked in again.

How she had loathed Nick for just giving up on Marilyn and Alex.

How she had hated Samantha for making it easy for him to do that.

Would she want to be that person herself?

Of course she wouldn't.

She reached out and put a gentle hand on his.

'I'm sorry. I didn't mean it. And I do understand.'

He looked up at her hopefully.

'You do?'

'Sure. This is what you have to do.'

'You understand that I have to try and sort things out? Do things right?'

She nodded, unable to speak and not quite sure how long she could keep up the stoicism.

'But I think you should probably go now,' she managed to whisper.

He nodded his agreement, touched her face, smiled sadly, but didn't move.

'Please.' Her voice had dropped even lower.

Tom literally had to force himself to turn and walk away, but a little like Lot's wife, when he reached the corner of the building he had to turn back and take another long and lingering look.

She had slumped back against the wall, and looked so small and vulnerable, all he wanted to do was turn back and take her in his arms and tell her everything was going to be okay. But he couldn't do that, because he didn't know that it was the truth, and she had asked him for the truth. Always. All he could manage right now was a choked, trite, 'Take care of yourself, okay?'

Liesel managed a stiff nod.

'Always have, always will,' she uttered defiantly as he turned the corner.

Her legs suddenly unable to hold the weight of her, Liesel pushed through the stiff French doors into their own sitting room and collapsed on to the sofa.

'Don't need a man, don't need nobody, don't need anything or anyone, except what I have,' she recited like a mantra.

And then Ruby came skittering in after her from the garden, full of the joys of garden and friends and little yellow balls, and all the simple things that make a dog's life delightful, and jumped on her lap and covered her face in kisses, and Liesel clutched on to the little dog as though for dear life and began to cry.

Marilyn and Alex found her twenty minutes later.

'Go and wash your hands and face and get ready for dinner.' Marilyn gently ushered a concerned Alex out of the room, then took a deep breath to halt the tears that had sprung instantly to her own eyes at the sight of her sister sobbing.

Liesel didn't cry. She just didn't. Ever. Not since she was a kid. Marilyn always remembered one particular occasion when they were on holiday in the South of France one year. Liesel must have been about the same age as Alex was now, and she had slipped and fallen on some rocks on the beach and split open her knee so badly she'd had to have stitches. She'd spent an entire afternoon sitting in a hot rural French hospital, waiting to be manhandled by an unsympathetic foreign doctor, but did she cry once? No, she didn't, just gnawed on her pretty little bottom lip until it went white through lack of blood, and then quite literally bit through it with the pressure.

She still had the scars. On both knee and lip.

Sunshine, their parents had nicknamed her. Our sunny funny girl. Our sunshine.

Today black clouds obliterated that golden glow. Marilyn simply sat down next to her and held out her arms, and Liesel fell into them. She hugged her until the crying had almost stopped before asking her, 'What is it?' even though she already knew.

The story came out in a long and convoluted way between snotty sobs and hiccups on a wave of emotions that fluctuated like the rolling tide between resignation, hope, despair and anger.

'Why am I like this?' Liesel asked in confusion, having gone from laughter to more tears in about ten seconds.

'Because you're in love.' There, Marilyn had finally said it.

'Rubbish.'

'I'm sorry, sis, but it's true.'

'If that's the case, then love stinks. It's shit. If this is love, who needs it?' Liesel took the hundredth Kleenex

Marilyn had offered and blew her nose loudly before chucking the used tissue on the fire.

'Why him, Maz? Out of all the men I've met, all the *single* men, why do I feel this way about him?'

'Because he's sweet, kind and thoughtful; he's a lovely man, Leez, a true gentleman, and seeing as you've never really met one of them before, it's kind of knocked you sideways. But it's exactly for those reasons that he's trying to do the decent thing. You must see that. He can't just dump on someone he obviously still cares about.'

'But I know he cares about me too.'

'Of course he does, any idiot can see that he's crazy about you, but he's not thinking of himself here. You must see that for him to put her first, well, that's what makes him the man he is, makes him the man you fell for.'

Liesel laughed, a dry, hollow laugh with little humour.

'But why him, Maz?' she repeated forlornly. 'My type's always been Bono, not Brad. Passionate, not pretty. Joker, not gentleman.'

'Because if you think about it, he's all of the above. He's a good person, Liesel. He has values.'

Liesel sighed heavily.

'That's a plus in my book, not a negative,' Marilyn urged.

'Sure, but if he wasn't such a good person . . .'

'He wouldn't be so worried about Caroline? He might not care about calling off a four-year engagement for someone he's only known for a few months? Or he might string you both along together? Carry on seeing you behind her back? Would you really want him on those terms?'

Liesel was about to say that she wanted him on any terms, but then she hung her head and shook it slowly. Marilyn was right. Wonderful could be soured and sullied by sordid so easily. She knew Tom had feelings for her, but now it was her turn to do the right thing and leave him be until he'd sorted out his feelings for Caroline.

'They have some very loose ends,' Marilyn continued.

'Yeah, and she's going to tie him up and tie him down with them,' Liesel muttered unhappily.

'Maybe so. But if that does happen, then it means it was never really over between them in the first place, and if it's not ended between them . . .'

'Then it can't be the beginning of us,' Liesel finished for her.

'Exactly.'

Liesel nodded: Tom was doing the right thing, being careful of Caroline's feelings. But then the indignation rose again. It was all very well and good thinking of how this was affecting Caroline, but what about her, what about how it was affecting her!

'What about my feelings?' she cried. 'Who decided her feelings are more important than mine?'

Marilyn shook her head in despair. It was one of those moments when she had to say it as she saw it. As the cliché went, sometimes you had to be cruel to be kind.

'He did, Liesel.' She sighed. '*He* did.'

The silence seemed endless as Liesel digested her sister's words. And then a kind of calm resignation fell like a blanket over the sorrow. Marilyn was right. She hated to admit it, but she was. He didn't have a choice to make. He'd already made it.

Liesel sighed and laughed at the same time, a bleak little laugh that was almost worse for Marilyn to hear than the sound of her sister crying.

'You're right. You're absolutely right. I'm being an idiot.' But although rationality had been kicked back into life, the thing that struck Liesel hardest was the overwhelming sense of disappointment she felt, so strong it made her want to just go to bed, bury her head in her pillow and yell silent, aching screams of frustration.

So why was she so disappointed?

Well, that was a simple question to answer. It was because there had been the promise of something there, something amazing. Not just your usual run-of-the-mill attraction, but something big-time, long-term, proper, for want of a better word; not just her usual stupid little flings that were destined to finish before they'd even really got started.

This little buzz that had been ticking away inside of her, a tingle of recognition, of excitement . . . a new world full of hope . . . that had suddenly imploded and disappeared into nothing.

Nothing.

The bleakness of it made her want to cry again.

'Anyway . . .' Marilyn took her sister's face in her hands and forced a huge smile at her, trying desperately to bring some lightness to the situation, 'I thought you didn't want a man. I thought this was your summer of abstinence, your man diet . . .'

'I don't . . . I mean, of course I do, but I really thought it would do me good to have a break, and look at me, I was bloody right wasn't I? If I'd stuck to what I said, then I wouldn't be like this now, would I?' Liesel scrubbed the back of her hand across her tear-stained cheeks and sniffed loudly.

'You will be okay, you know. I know it doesn't feel like it at the moment, but you'll be fine.'

Liesel looked hopefully at her. Marilyn had been through something far worse and survived. Sure, three years on and she still hadn't so much as kissed another man, but at the moment that really didn't sound too bad.

'How did you get through it? You know, when he left . . .'

'Time. And Alex, of course.'

At the mention of his name, Alex, who had been hovering outside in concern, pushed the door open slightly and peered around the edge of it.

'You okay now, Auntie Leez?' he asked anxiously.

Liesel snorted back the last of the tears and managed to smile at him as brightly as she could.

'Yes, thank you, Lex.'

'You sure?'

She nodded and opened her arms, and for the first time in weeks he ran across the room and hopped on to her lap without hesitation.

He had brought her a Mars bar, slightly warm and melting from his pocket.

'Share?' she offered.

He nodded happily, unpeeled and offered her first bite.

'Sure you're okay?'

Liesel took a mouthful of the chocolate bar, chewed, and swallowed not only the chocolate but the lump that was sticking in her throat like a marble.

'So long as we have chocolate and each other, I will always be okay,' she said, kissing his golden head and breathing in comfort from the familiar smell of sun and sand she found there.

'That's my girl.' Marilyn winked at her.

'Why were you crying, Auntie Leez?' Alex asked, relieved to see that she had all but stopped.

Liesel frowned and found that she had a headache pulling between her eyes. How could she explain to an eight year old what had made her so upset without passing on some of that upset to him?

'I lost something I really care about,' she finally answered.

'Want me to help you look for it?' he immediately offered.

Liesel couldn't help but smile, a proper smile this time. 'Thanks, kiddo, but I don't think I'm going to find it.'

'Well, I wouldn't worry too much,' he said, sounding very grown-up, then offering her another bite of chocolate. 'Things have a habit of turning up when you least expect them to.'

24

'I don't believe it.' Marilyn slammed the phone back on its receiver rather harshly, before taking the coffee Liesel was offering and slurping at it noisily. 'That's the second last-minute cancellation we've had this week.'

Liesel's face fell.

'Who's cancelled now?'

'The Merryweathers from York. You took the booking last Friday.'

Liesel remembered it well. It had been just before Tom came to see her.

'Maybe it's the weather.' Marilyn looked worried.

'Rain.' Liesel nodded. She didn't mind the rain; rain matched her mood at the moment, which since the previous week had been pretty grim. As expected, she hadn't heard from Tom. But she heard bits via Lorraine. She was still trying to work out whether this was a good thing or not, because she knew that right now Caroline was on extended leave and staying in the three-storey show home in Port Isaac. She also knew that Tom was trying to work fewer hours. Caroline in Cornwall, Tom taking time off; that only meant one thing: they were trying to work things out. Which was what he had said he was going to do, but maybe a little bit of Liesel had been hoping that he would declare his undying love for her and send Caroline packing back to

London, then return on his white charger to whisk her off into the sunset.

Some hope, but a hope it had been.

'Well, that's it, we've no guests.' Marilyn leant against the reception desk and buried her face in her hands. 'The last four have just called to say that their coach has broken down and they've got to wait two hours for a repair man to reach them. They're not going to get here until after midnight. We're empty. Again.'

'Again,' Liesel repeated, biting her bottom lip in worry. 'I don't understand why it's been like this; we've had a ton of bookings.'

'Followed by an avalanche of no-shows and cancellations.' Marilyn shook her head and sighed so hard she must have emptied her lungs completely of air.

'But we'll get through this, won't we?' Liesel asked hesitantly, surprised by how defeated the normally upbeat Marilyn looked.

'Of course we will.'

But she had hesitated for a fraction of a second too long before forcing a smile and answering. Liesel took her hands.

'Be honest with me, Maz, are things really bad?'

'Well, if we want to stay open until the end of the season—'

'We've *got* to stay open until the end of the season!' Liesel interrupted sharply. 'And beyond. For Alex, and for us too. This is home now, Marilyn . . . we've got to make it work.'

'I know that.'

'Then what do we need to do?'

'The simple answer is get some bookings.' Marilyn took a breath, reinflated and tried to look more positive. 'And we'll make sure that we do just that, even if I have to go and stand at the fork in the road between

Piran Bay and Piran Cove naked except for a sandwich board and a big sign to drag the customers down our way . . .'

Liesel tried to laugh, but only managed a hiccuping kind of half-laugh, half-sob. The thought of losing the Cornucopia made her wholeheartedly want to cry for only the second time in her entire life. Not that she was going to. Once was enough. Now wasn't a time for wallowing in self-pity; it was a time for action.

'Right, I think we should do a mail shot. I'm going to email everyone we knew in London, and get them to email everyone they know . . .' Sniffing back the unwanted tears, she began to push up her sleeves and head over to the computer, but Marilyn, who had watched her sister's big amber eyes fill like the river at full tide, held her back.

'Do you know what,' Marilyn said, forcing a bright and genuine-looking smile. 'That's a fantastic idea, and we'll get on to it first thing tomorrow, but I think seeing as we have a night off we should all go out somewhere. I don't know about you, but I could do with some time out, and the one tiny bonus of us being empty is that the place can survive without us for a few hours.'

'What if the coach gets fixed earlier than expected? Marilyn . . . Marilyn?'

Marilyn wasn't listening to her sister; she was looking over her shoulder.

'Are you listening to a word I'm saying?' It was a silly question, because she obviously wasn't.

'You look as though you've seen a ghost. Don't tell me we're haunted after all?'

And still Marilyn said nothing, simply stared towards the front door, her mouth hanging open, rigid with shock.

Hurriedly, worriedly, Liesel turned around to look in the direction her sister was staring, and had to stop her hand from automatically crossing herself. Standing in the doorway of the Cornucopia was a man, and it wasn't a mere ghost . . . it was Satan himself.

'Hi, Marilyn. How are you doing?'

He had a few more lines around the eyes, a better tan, perhaps a peppering of grey, but he looked no different really from the last time she had seen him.

Out of all of the things she had imagined him saying to her, it had never been 'Hi, Marilyn. How are you doing?' Like a neighbour who'd just popped in to borrow a cup of sugar.

'Good Lord!' It was Liesel who shrieked. Marilyn suddenly found herself speechless.

'Aren't you going to say hello, then?'

Still silence. Marilyn opened her mouth, but absolutely nothing came out. Not even a squeak. And then Alex came into the hall from the tower, Godrich on his lead. He was grinning away, and then he saw his mum's face, and he looked from her to Liesel, and then to where Liesel was still looking, and he stopped, frowned, shook his head a little, and she saw the recognition dawning.

'Alex?' Marilyn heard the question in Nick's voice, and she hated him for it. He wasn't even certain that it was his own son. But then he said it again, louder, more certain, 'Alex!' and held out his arms.

Alex looked in disbelief at the father he hadn't seen or heard from in three years.

'Come on, Alex,' Nick encouraged, his voice too hearty. 'Come and say hello to your dad.'

And then the tears began to well in Alex's eyes, and a tentative step forward turned into a jog, which turned into a sprint, and as Alex ran towards him, Nick looked up and smiled at Marilyn, a smile that to Liesel looked more self-satisfied than doting dad. But instead of Alex throwing himself into those wide-open arms, he put his head down and with a bellow of pure rage speeded up and head-butted his father full on and as hard as he could in the stomach.

Nick curled up, shrieking with shock and pain.

Alex, reeling himself a little from the impact, looked at his father, and for a moment a fleeting look of guilt flitted across his innocent young face. Then the smooth brow knitted into a furious frown again and, swinging his leg back, he kicked Nick hard on the shin.

And then he burst into tears and ran out of reception.

Godrich von Woofenhausen, having some kind of canine revelation, saw his usually happy shadow, willing shit-shoveller, and provider of the forbidden Mars bars running off in a snot-choking stream of tears, and paused only long enough to cock his leg against the crumpled figure of Nick and shower him in warm and acrid pee, before galloping away in pursuit.

Ed and Eric, who had come running at the sound of Liesel shrieking, sped straight after him. Marilyn, still in shock, walked in slow funereal disbelief over to Nick, who was by now crouching on the floor cursing, torn between holding his stomach, rubbing his shin, and mopping ineffectually at his sodden trouser leg with a handkerchief.

He looked up at her and attempted one of the charm-laden smiles he used to use every time he knew he had done something to upset her. It was probably the smile more than anything that made her snap.

'Hi, Nick. How are *you* doing?' she said, and upturned her barely touched coffee over his head.

'Jesus!' he blasphemed loudly, wiping frantically at his coffee-covered face.

'Well, what do you bloody expect?' she spat, before bursting into tears and running off after her son as well.

'What is noise? Is things okay, Liesel.' Kashia and

Lorraine had been changing sheets in one of the attic rooms when Kashia had spotted Alex running into the garden, closely followed by Ed and Eric and then Marilyn.

'Not really.' Liesel had a look on her face that Kashia and Lorraine had never seen before. It was Kashia who recognised it first, as hatred, pure and simple. It was an emotion they hadn't thought Liesel possessed.

'This man bother you?' Kashia asked, her frown and tone of voice so sharp, Liesel could have borrowed them to stab Nick with.

'Always,' Liesel replied.

She looked at the sorry state that was her loathed ex-brother-in-law, and found herself battling with the very strong urge to head-butt, kick, pee on, and cover him in lukewarm coffee herself. But she managed to restrain herself.

'I think you'd better go.'

'I want to see my son.'

'Well, I think he's made it pretty clear that he doesn't want to see you.'

'I have rights . . .'

'You haven't bothered to contact him once in three years, and you march in here and start to bleat on about rights!'

'Look, I know I was wrong. I've come to make amends.'

'Out of the blue, after three years, without even a phone call or a letter first? You didn't think how just turning up like this might upset Alex, did you? You decided that *you* wanted something, and therefore *you* had to have it! Well, you might suddenly want to be forgiven for being the biggest shit on the planet, but it doesn't mean we have to welcome you back with open arms like the bloody prodigal dad. I never got the chance to say this to you before, Nick, mainly because you disappeared in the middle of the night . . . but you're a complete and utter bastard! Okay, so you fell out of love with Marilyn; it happens, but pretending Alex doesn't exist for three years? What did he do to deserve that? Nothing, that's what. There's absolutely no excuse for that I or my sister or even your son could ever accept, so save your breath, okay, and just bugger off and leave us all alone.'

Nick pulled himself up off the floor, opened his mouth to say something, then obviously thought better of it. He closed it again, nodded, and, turning, made his way across the hallway. When he got to the door, he turned back and marched over to the desk, where he pulled the scribble pad towards him and wrote down a phone number in big bold letters.

'I'll go for now, but I have a right to see my son. If Marilyn wants to discuss this like adults, get her to call me. And I'll be back, you know.'

'Unfortunately, I have no doubt of that,' Liesel replied, folding her arms across her chest. 'And we'll have the doors locked and the boiling oil waiting,' she added as he finally strode off.

'Is big mess!' Kashia exclaimed, looking at the sodden floor.

'A bloody big mess,' Liesel replied, watching Nick retreat up the drive.

'He is bad man?'

'That was Nick.'

'Oh, I is seeing now.' Kashia nodded furiously. 'Bloody big mess. Two messes. Well, we clean mess on floor, you go find Marilyn and the boss, okay?' she urged, ushering Liesel towards the door.

The rain had stopped and Alex was sitting on a rock at the end of the garden, Eric on one side, Godrich on the other. Ed and Marilyn were talking, Marilyn in harsh whispers,

Ed's voice softer, more conciliatory, his hands on her shoulders as if to stop her taking off like a sky rocket.

When she saw Liesel, it was like a vocal explosion.

'Oh Leez, I nearly had a heart attack! What's he doing here? I just want to chop his legs off, turning up out of the blue like that, scaring us all half to death. What does he think he's playing at, typical selfish moronic Nick Hamilton, thinks of no one and nothing but himself! Poor Alex, he's in a right state, won't even talk to me now, said he wanted to be alone to think. HUH! An eight year old says he wants some time alone to think!'

Liesel looked at the hunched figure of her nephew, squatting on the rock, throwing stones rather violently into the river.

'He doesn't seem exactly thrilled about it, does he?'

'At the moment he doesn't know whether he wants to kiss him or kill him.'

'Or head-butt or kick him.' Despite the gravity of the situation, Liesel couldn't help herself from smiling wryly at the new memory.

'What do you expect, poor kid.' Marilyn wasn't smiling. 'Do you know, the first thing he asked me was had Nick come back to take the hotel away from us.'

'And what if he has, what if that's the reason he's suddenly decided to turn up after all this time?'

'Don't think that hasn't crossed my mind as well. It's a bit too much of a coincidence, isn't it?'

'And is *she* here with him?'

Marilyn shrugged and then managed a soggy kind of smile as she looked over to Alex again, to see that Ed had coaxed him into talking. She wasn't sure what was being said, but Ed's face was earnest and then smiling, and Alex from sunken and soggy began to change to giggles, reluctant giggles, but giggles none the less.

'He's great with him, isn't he?' Liesel said.

Marilyn nodded.

'So what do we do now?'

'I don't know.'

'What does he want? He said to me he was here to see Alex, but why now?'

'I don't know that either. That's the thing, Leez, there's so much we want to know and don't, and there's only one way I'm going to get any answers. I have to talk to him. No matter how much I don't want to, I've got to speak to the man.'

They met on neutral ground.

Liesel had suggested the headland. Her reasoning: it was near enough for them to be able to watch out for Marilyn from the top tower window, and it had a tall enough cliff to push Nick off. Marilyn had managed to laugh at this, until she realised that Liesel was being serious.

He was waiting for her in the car park, in a hire car. He opened the passenger door when he saw her walking towards him, obviously expecting her to get in with him, but Marilyn couldn't bring herself to be that close, that confined, and so she walked past the car over the grassy headland and sat on one of the benches that dotted the peninsula.

Most of them memorials, this one had a plaque that read, 'For my darling Edward, who loved this view. The tides may change, but my heart stays true.' Already emotional, Marilyn suppressed the sob that filled her throat; it made her think of Ed, and for a moment she found herself wishing that she'd let him come with her as he'd begged to, but then Nick, who had followed her down, came into view. Obviously sensing her need for a little distance, he sat at the other end of the bench and waited until she turned towards him before speaking.

'Hi, Marilyn.'

Ignoring the greeting, Marilyn looked sideways at him through wary eyes.

'Why now, Nick? Why after all this time?'

She could see he was taken aback by her direct-ness. The Marilyn he knew had always been more wary, would tread around in circles before moving in with the punch.

'Do I need a reason to want to see my son?'

'No, but you bloody well need one for *not* seeing him for three years! No visits. No calls, no letters, no cards, at Christmas, his birthday . . .'

He didn't answer, just nodded slowly, heavily.

'And now Alex inherits the hotel and then suddenly there you are. You must understand why I'm just a *little* bit cynical about your reasons for doing a Lazarus on us!'

For a moment he looked affronted, and then he nodded.

'It's a fair enough question. I'd be lying if I said it had nothing to do with it, but only in so far as it made me realise that life is too short . . .'

Marilyn obviously didn't look convinced, so he turned to her and said earnestly, 'I'm not here to try and take anything away from my own son, for heaven's sake. Nancy made the decision to leave everything to Alex, and I'm glad, it was the right thing to do. He's set for life now, and I'm grateful to her for that; after all, what have I done for him? Nothing, that's what, nothing except bury the guilt and tell myself that he'd be better off with a clean break, it would be better for him than the long-distance-dad thing, the brief hellos and constant good-byes. I've realised how wrong I was . . . Nancy dying, well, she was my only living relative apart from Alex. I couldn't go on kidding myself that what I was doing was the right thing.'

He looked down at his hands for a moment, then back up at Marilyn.

'It breaks my heart to think how much upset I must have caused.'

Marilyn remained stony. She was glad if he was telling the truth this time; she wanted him to hurt the way Alex had. Wanted him to feel some heartache.

'I screwed up big time, Marilyn, I know that now. I thought what I did would be best for Alex. I was wrong. I miss my son. I want him back in my life.'

'You should have thought about that when you decided to leave him and not look back. It's been three years, Nick. Three bloody years. You don't know what that boy went through when you left, you don't know what he's going through now . . .'

'Let me make it up to him, then.' He was pleading now. 'Let me be a father to him again.'

'What, let you back in, so that when you go next time you can break his heart all over again?'

'I understand you're angry with me. I understand the fact that you probably hate my guts right now, but don't do this, Marilyn. Don't make it about you and me. This is about Alex. All I'm asking is that we *keep* it about Alex, and for Alex's sake . . .'

'For Alex's sake!' Marilyn bellowed back at him, going so purple with immediate rage that Nick shuffled further away from her, as if he thought she might explode and he was in the firing line. 'When has anything you've done in the past three years been for Alex's sake!'

He was so quiet for a moment, she thought he had nothing left to say, but then he turned to face her, his voice calm, his eyes steady.

'Three days ago, I quit my job, my house and my partner, and I got on a plane and flew to England, leaving everything behind me, having been told in no uncertain terms that if I did, then I'd have none of it to go back to. But I still did it, Marilyn, and I did it for one thing and one thing only. For Alex.'

Liesel was waiting by the gates, leaning on a pillar, chewing on her nails and looking murderous.

'How did it go? What does he want?'

'Where's Alex?'

'Killing zombies with Ed and Eric. What did he want, Marilyn?'

'What do you think he wanted? He wants to see Alex.'

'And you're going to let him?'

Marilyn shrugged. 'We have to think about what's right for Alex. I could never deny him the chance to see his father if that's what he wants.'

'And is that what he wants?'

'I really don't know.'

'And what about the last three years, what did he have to say about the fact that he just abandoned his own kid, not a word, nothing? What did he say about that, eh?'

'He said all the right things.'

'Yeah, I can just imagine.' Liesel screwed up her face in disgust. 'He probably had a list, looked up platitudes on the internet and got as many into his allotted time as possible. "I'm so sorry, you don't know how much I regret it, if I could do it all again I'd do it so differently . . ." ' she sang crossly in a whiny voice meant to imitate Nick's.

Marilyn was loath to admit to Liesel how closely she had echoed what Nick had actually said.

'And what about *her*?'

'They split up because she didn't want him to come back to England to see Alex. In fact, he gave me the impression she's been a big factor in him not keeping in touch.'

'What kind of woman doesn't want a man to see his

own kids . . . Then again, what kind of man lets a woman stop him?' Liesel huffed.

Marilyn reached out and put a hand on her sister's arm. Liesel was shaking, but strangely Marilyn was oddly calm.

'Look, Leez, we both know, we both feel the same, we went through it together, and Nick . . . well, in many ways I wish he was still in Perth, swimming with the crocodiles, so I do understand how you're feeling, and I'm sorry I didn't push him off a cliff for you.' She smiled, and elicited a small smile in response. 'And I know that you're pretty raw yourself at the moment, so this is the last thing you need—'

'This is different, Maz,' Liesel interrupted, frowning. 'This is Alex; you know it makes everything else seem less important somehow, not worse . . .'

'Okay, that's good, but what I'm trying to say – and I don't think you'll like it, but I've given this a lot of thought – is that taking everything else out of the equation, you, me, Samantha, everything, Nick is here to see his son, and there's only one person who has the right to deny him that.'

Liesel nodded, understanding despite everything that what Marilyn was saying was right.

'So what are you going to do?'

'There's only one thing I can do . . . Don't pull that face, Liesel, please. I know you don't like him . . .'

'It's not that I don't like him, I mean I *don't* like him, but it's not that, it's the fact that I just don't trust him. Why has he come back now? Oh, could it be that Alex has suddenly inherited a property worth an absolute fortune? You think? Could it be that?' Her voice was edged with sarcasm.

'Don't you think I've thought that? But I have to give him the benefit of the doubt.'

'Why do you have to—' Liesel began, but Marilyn held up her hand to stop her.

'I don't want to argue with you about him.'

'Me neither.'

'Then don't.'

'But you're letting him back in, Marilyn. Just like that?'

'I have to. For Alex's sake.'

'But Alex doesn't even want him here.'

'That's what he says, but it's only because he's so cut up by everything he's bottled up over the past three years. He needs this, Liesel, he needs this chance to reconnect with his father.'

'So you're going to convince him to try?'

'I have to.'

'And what if he hurts him all over again?'

'If, heaven forbid, it does all end in tears, then we'll do what we always do: we'll pick up the pieces and get him through it . . . won't we?'

Liesel nodded miserably, and Marilyn reached out and gently pushed her hair out of her downturned face, then, putting a finger under her chin, tilted it up so that they were looking into each other's eyes.

'And *then* we'll push Nick off a cliff . . . okay?'

25

For the third time that week, Nick arrived to pick up Alex and Marilyn.

For the third time that week, Liesel wished that they kept a machine gun behind reception so that she could gun him down as he walked in the door.

Each time Alex had looked a little less reluctant, but each time it had been harder for Liesel to let them go. Especially as Marilyn still looked like she was going to the gallows. Why were people so obsessed with doing the right thing, and what was the right thing anyway? Right for who, that's what she wanted to know. If it was down to her, she'd have Alex locked in the tower where Nick couldn't reach him. Maybe she should take Nick up there too. She could push him out of the highest tower window at high tide and let the lovely sea dispose of his body for her. He might have been making Alex frown less every time he saw him, but he was growing on Liesel like fungus on damp wood. Each time he saw her, he seemed to do something deliberately to get under her skin. Yesterday he had winked at her as he walked in the door. Not a friendly wink, which would have been unwelcome as it was, but one which implied oneupmanship.

Today, as they walked out of the door to his car, he had the audacity to turn and wave at her, like they were mates. Liesel had only just managed to stop herself from throwing him the finger back, because Alex might have seen it, and the last thing she wanted to do was upset Alex.

Liesel wasn't of the disposition to hate anyone, but oh boy, how she hated Nick Hamilton.

There was nothing else for it. She needed to let off some steam. Lorraine was in the dining room helping Kashia set up for dinner, the two of them laughing like drains as Kashia tried to teach Lorraine something very rude in Polish. Lorraine hadn't been due in until seven, when she would take over on reception so that Liesel could open the bar, but the two women had taken to coming in together now that they were fledgling roommates. They had been living together for a week in Lorraine's two-up-two-down in town, and all was amazingly harmonious. They were even going out for dinner that night as a threesome with Adrian to celebrate. It was incredible how emotions could swing so. From enemies to the best of friends. Could Liesel learn to love Nick again? She had loved him once, when he and Marilyn were first together and he was sweet to her and made Marilyn happy. More importantly, would Alex learn to like his father again? He didn't need to start loving him again, because the love had never stopped. That was the funny thing about family: you could hate their guts, but deep down there were ties that never broke. Always a little bit of you still yearned, no matter how much the rest of you disclaimed.

'You opening the bar early?' Lorraine asked, coming over as soon as Liesel called.

'Something like that.' Liesel smiled.

'You okay?'

'Yeah.' Liesel nodded, her usually smiling mouth in a tight line.

'I know it sounds trite, but things have a habit of working themselves out, you know.'

'Alex needs the chance to get to know his dad again,' Liesel said, trying to be reasonable about things.

'Actually, I wasn't talking about Alex.' Lorraine looked apologetic, and then lowered her voice as if she didn't want anyone to hear what she was going to say next, despite the fact that it was just her, Liesel and Kashia. 'Tom's back at work again.'

'Oh really?' Fake reason gave way to fake nonchalance.

'Adrian said that he doesn't seem very happy.'

'That make two then, does it not?' Kashia pursed her lips. 'He no deserve to be happy, he make Liesel sad.'

'I appreciate the loyalty, Kash, but he's just trying to do the right thing.'

'And who say that right thing is what he do now? Right thing to do in life is to be with person you love. He love Liesel. I see that if other peoples do not. My mama tell me when I come to England, in England things different, people more polite, people talk proper, act proper, so I must to behave like an English lady. Well, I say horse's shit! You want this man, you fight for this man. Is good Polish proverb. I teach you, Liesel Ellis: "If you love him, don't lend him"!'

'What is it with everyone and proverbs at the moment?'

'Ed.' Lorraine smiled. 'He's got us hooked.'

'Ed say key to full life is open mind.' Kashia nodded. 'Open mind always want to learn new things. We learn new thing every day now. Lorraine teach me English saying, I teach her Polish.'

'You teach me bad Polish!' Lorraine exclaimed, eyes wide with pleasurable embarrassment.

'I teach you *good* Polish!' Kashia exclaimed.

'She meant bad as in rude.'

'Ah, I see now.' Kashia nodded sagely. 'That is big cause of problem in life; when things get translated wrong way, people have argument for no reason. You must to make sure that things are clearly said so that they are clearly understood. You are in love with vet Tom Spencer.' She held up her hand to silence Liesel as she began rather predictably to protest. 'Why you deny? What good that do if it not truth? If he know one hundred per cent that you love him, then maybe he no have such trouble sorting out what he do now.'

'He knows how I feel,' Liesel said weakly.

'Ah, so you already tell him that you are being in love with him?' Kashia demanded, knowing full well that Liesel had not.

Liesel couldn't answer.

'There, I have my say.' Kashia took an open bottle of Pinot Grigio from the bar fridge and handed it to Liesel along with a glass. 'Now you take bottle of wine and go think about what you need to do to make happy again, okay?'

Liesel went outside clutching her wine and her glass and her confusion. Marilyn had said to wait; Kashia had told her to get out there and do something. Tom himself had asked for time, but he hadn't specified how much. And time for what? 'To do the right thing' had really been all he'd said. What did this mean to him? Fix things, or finish things? She didn't know. She just knew that she had done as he'd asked: let life carry on around her and tried not to think too much about it. But thinking about it, she realised that at the moment she felt as if her whole life was suspended, not particularly comfortably, in mid-air, pinched between the thumb and forefinger of her own and someone else's indecision.

'I'm going to be decisive,' she said out loud. 'I'm going to make a decision right now and stick to it.'

But all she could manage was the decision that she was

not just going to have one glass of wine, she was going to sit on the rocks at the end of the lawn and watch the incoming tide swell the river full to bursting, whilst she swelled herself full to bursting with Pinot.

Someone else had already beaten her to it. When she reached the end of the garden, Ed was sitting there, his face set, his usually smiling mouth a thin line.

'You look how I feel,' Liesel said, selecting a smooth stone and sitting down next to him.

Ed shrugged and held up the bottle of wine he was holding.

'If you feel like shit, then you're spot on. Fancy joining me? As you can imagine, I'm not a big advocate of drinking alone.'

'Neither am I, but today would have been an exception.' Liesel smiled wryly as she showed him her own acquisition. 'What's driven you to drink, then?'

'What do you think?'

'The return of the prodigal dad?'

Ed nodded.

'Penny for them? Or should I offer you a tenner, due to inflation?'

This elicited a smile, but it wasn't a happy smile.

'Actually, I was thinking that maybe it's time I moved on.'

'You serious?' Liesel gasped in horror.

He nodded glumly.

'Because of Nick!'

'Because of and in spite of, I suppose. I don't trust him, Liesel.'

'I don't think any of us do, really.'

'And every time I see that smug face, I just want to thump him.'

'I can relate to that one as well.' Liesel nodded.

'The boy is his son after all; I can't argue with that. But

the major problem is that I really want to argue with it. I can understand why Marilyn's doing what she's doing, and right now they need to be left alone to sort things out. If I stay, I'm going to end up sticking my oar in, and I just want to fold him painfully into a very small suitcase and send him back where he came from. Which isn't exactly constructive or helpful . . . so I was thinking that maybe it would be better if I left.'

'Oh God, no!' Liesel exclaimed, horrified by the mere suggestion of Ed leaving the Cornucopia. 'You can't go. We need you here, Ed. This is your home now as much as it's ours. You're not going to go, are you? Promise me you won't leave us. We need you. Eric needs you. And as for Alex . . .'

The words were garbled, but the panic in Liesel's voice at the thought of him going was strangely enough exactly what Ed needed to hear.

'Are you saying you'd miss me?'

'Are you kidding? We all would. You're part of the family now. If I had a brother, I'd want him to be just like you.'

'Thanks, Liesel, I really appreciate that, but you know what, I'm worried that that is exactly what your sister thinks.'

Liesel raised her eyebrows at him in question and for a moment he looked coy, but then he frowned and said, 'I have to confess that things are a little more complicated than you might realise. I . . . I have – and despite my love of clichés, I really hate this word – *feelings* for your sister. I know she doesn't want a relationship at the moment, and to be honest, although I know she likes me well enough, I don't know if she likes me *well* enough, if you understand what I'm saying . . .'

'Don't be daft. Marilyn loves you to bits, and definitely not in a brotherly love kind of way. Her feelings for you are far too carnal to be even remotely connected with a brotherly kind of love.'

'You think so?' he asked, looking more cheerful.

'I know so,' she said so resolutely she surprised him.

'How do you know?' he asked in concern, suddenly wondering if their Sunday mornings hadn't been so private after all.

'Because Marilyn may love fish, but she hates eating it, that's how. Hasn't eaten a single fillet since a dodgy bit of cod on Brighton seafront turned her fourteenth birthday into a scene from *The Exorcist*. But now, well, you catch them, she eats them.'

'That could be for Alex.'

'Alex knows that the only sea-scavenged thing his mum will ever eat is the occasional prawn cocktail.'

'He's never said.'

'He's not daft; thought that if you knew Maz didn't like fish, then you wouldn't be quite so keen to go and catch them for her any more, and he likes spending time with you, Ed.'

'Same here.'

'Oh, and there's one other thing that makes me absolutely certain,' Liesel said, looking at him sideways and suppressing a smile.

'What's that?'

'The laundry room.' she said, and winked broadly.

His eyes grew wide with horror.

'You know about the laundry room?'

'Do I know about the laundry room?' Liesel guffawed. 'Doing laundry, my arse. Doing my sister more like.'

'Liesel, please.' Ed hid his face in his hands, peering out at her through splayed fingers, a picture of embarrassment.

'Well, it's true. And what's more, I'm glad it is. You're

good for her, Ed. And Nick Hamilton is very, *very* bad. Please hang in there. It may not be obvious to either of you at the moment, but she needs you, even more so now that he's hanging around again like a rotten fish stinking out the back of the larder. Don't let him push you out.'

'But don't you see, Leez, he has every right to push me out. I'm not Alex's father, and Marilyn and I, well, we're not exactly in a relationship, are we?'

'Of course you are. Just because you're not running round declaring to everyone that you're together – or even to each other, for that matter – doesn't mean that what you have isn't a relationship. Same with Alex. No, he's not your son, but I know that right now he values your friendship far more than the relationship he has with his father.'

'You think so? Even now?'

'A McDonald's the first night, Pizza Hut the second, and KFC today? He might be appealing to Alex's stomach, but that's as far as it goes. Trust me, three nights of junk food don't make up for three years of disappointment. Nick didn't just miss birthdays and Christmas, he missed Alex learning to ride a bike for the first time without stabilisers, he missed sitting up all night with him when he had chicken pox, he missed swimming certificates, gold stars, school reports good and bad, bad days, happy days, holidays, school plays and sports days . . .'

'It's his sports day next week.'

'See, you know that. Nick doesn't.' Liesel tucked an arm through Ed's, and looked at him earnestly. 'Credibility is like virginity . . .' she prompted him.

'You can only lose it once,' he finished.

'Well, Nick lost it a long time ago. And you, well, you've been so good to Alex, to all of us. Do you really want to go? Do you actually want to leave?'

Ed shook his head.

'No, but I don't want to ruin things for Alex.'

'Don't you see?' she pleaded. 'The only way you could do that is by leaving him.'

Ed was silent for a moment, and then he exhaled, a short, derisive snort at his own stupidity.

'You're right. Totally right. Me leaving now would only hurt Alex. Why couldn't I see that?'

Liesel laughed drily. 'It's so much easier to find clarity when you're dealing with other people's problems rather than your own.'

Ed looked at her. There was something about Liesel that normally shone, like a bright little star. She'd lost her glow.

'You okay?'

'Lorraine asked me that ten minutes ago.'

'And what did you say?'

'I said yes . . .' She blinked up at him. 'I was lying.'

Her arm still tucked through his, Ed took her hand in his own and found it to be cold and slight.

'Can I give *you* some advice?'

'Please.'

'You don't know what to do about Tom because you're worried that he's going to hurt you. Well, the way I see it is, if you do nothing, then you're hurting yourself.'

She nodded.

'What do you want from him, Liesel?'

Liesel thought for a moment.

'Truly? I want him to finish things with Caroline, and come and find me, rescue me from the tower, throw himself at my feet and declare his never-ending undying love.' The smile as she said this was embarrassed, but the truth of it was in her voice.

'And you expect him to do all of this on his own whilst you just sit and wait for it to happen? Why does the man always have to be the hero, Liesel? Maybe this time it's the man that needs some rescuing . . .'

*

The sun was sinking lower over the hills as Nick drove the big hire car back down the drive of the Cornucopia.

To Marilyn, in the passenger seat, it felt good to be getting back to what was at the moment her reality. The last three evenings had been difficult on so many levels, both practical and emotional.

The decision to let Nick see his son had never been hers to make, but persuading Alex to see Nick had been by far the hardest task. After a while he had listened to his mother's reasoning that he was being given a chance to get to know Nick again and that he might end up regretting it if he didn't take it.

On the first night he had hidden himself in his cape for the first half an hour, until Marilyn had managed to coax him out with a large strawberry milkshake. He had then stared at Nick for the entire night, but refused to actually speak to him.

When they had got back to the Cornucopia, his only comment had been that he thought he looked nothing like his father, and was Marilyn sure that Nick was his real dad. Marilyn didn't know whether to laugh or cry until Liesel saved the situation by saying that she thought Alex looked more like Godrich, and was Godrich perhaps his brother?

The second night, Alex had amazed Marilyn by having a tantrum in the middle of Pizza Hut in Truro. The last time he had had a tantrum he had been four. She watched in amazement as he threw his pizza on the floor, and then ran and locked himself in a toilet cubicle. But Nick had been textbook perfect. 'He's just testing me,' he'd said gently, before going in to coax the boy out, and then ordering him another pizza.

Tonight Alex had been more like his normal self. He had even spoken to Nick, asking him questions about what it was like in Australia, being particularly interested to know if Nick had ever run over a kangaroo, because Ed had told him that kangaroos caused lots of traffic accidents. Nick had replied that maybe Alex could see a kangaroo for himself sometime, and Marilyn's heart had lurched like a drunk falling in the street as the reality of Nick being back in the boy's life hit home. He would be going back to Australia, he had said as much; he had no plans to stay in England, and that meant that at some point he would expect Alex to go and visit. Endless summers stretched before her without him, visions of waving him off at the airport. It had been all she could do to stop herself from having her own tantrum in KFC, throwing her fries on the floor and jamming a chicken drumstick in Nick's ear.

Alex was out of the car before it had even stopped rolling. Godrich was waiting in the doorway, and the two of them had a joyful reunion, as if they had been separated for months rather than hours. Godrich then peed profusely up the wheel of Nick's car before they both galloped into the garden.

Thankful for the light relief, Marilyn laughed quietly to herself while she gathered her bag to go, but as she reached for the door handle, Nick caught her elbow.

'Wait a minute.'

'What?'

'I saw your face when I said about Alex coming to Oz sometime.'

'I'd miss him,' Marilyn said, her voice catching. 'But that's not on the agenda yet,' she said determinedly.

'Sure, but it will be, won't it, if this works out, and I think I know how you feel about that.'

'Like I said, I'd miss him.'

'I know you would . . . and I don't think you should have to.'

'What are you saying? That you'll come back to England?'

Nick shook his head.

'I'm saying sell this place and come back to Australia with me.'

Marilyn blinked at him in surprise.

'You are kidding me, aren't you?'

'I'm being serious, Marilyn. It makes perfect sense.'

'To you maybe; to me it sounds ridiculous.'

'We were good together once . . .'

'So were Bogart and Bacall, but that doesn't mean you want to dig them up and start rattling the bones.'

If she'd said that to Ed he would have laughed, but Nick . . . well, he frowned at her.

'You always were too bloody obscure.'

'That's funny. Liesel says I'm the most straightforward person you could meet.'

'Oh, it always comes back to Liesel, doesn't it?'

'And don't you hate that! How could you have resented her? She's my sister.'

'And you were my wife.'

'It's a shame you didn't remember that fact when you met Samantha.'

To her surprise, he didn't bite back; in fact he hung his head in what looked suspiciously like shame.

'I'm sorry I hurt you.'

'That's an easy thing to say, isn't it.'

'I mean it.'

'I don't believe you. You come hear saying that you want to make amends, and then after you've seen your son three times, you're already picturing a big family reunion. You say you've changed, but you haven't changed at all if that's what you think could happen. You seriously expect that after six hours in your company, me and Alex are going to abandon our lives and travel halfway across the world to be with you?'

'No, that's not what I expect.' He let go of her arm, and then, hanging his head, looked up at her through thick lashes. 'But is it so wrong of me to hope for it? I may only have been here for three days, but I've been missing you both for far longer. There's not a day that goes past when I don't regret the choices I made. They were the wrong choices, Marilyn. The wrong ones.' His face was a picture of regret. 'Okay, maybe seeing you again, spending time with you, has made me a little nostalgic, a little too hopeful, and we're dead and buried like you say, but why not bring Alex to Australia? It was always a dream of yours to go there, remember?'

Marilyn nodded.

'You're slogging your guts out at a hotel that's got about as many occupied rooms as the *Mary Celeste*, and you're doing this because you're looking for a better life for Alex. Well, imagine what kind of life he could have in Australia. He'd love it. You think this place is great, it's nothing compared with what it's like over there: the sun, the sea, the beaches, the sealife. The cost of living is much lower, and the schools are great too. You could even finish your own degree if you wanted. And you know the best bit, he'd have his mum *and* his dad. What kid doesn't want that, eh? I know you find it hard to picture at the moment, and I understand, truly I do – if I were you I'd hate me too – but I know I've done wrong and I so want the chance to make amends, to give Alex everything he's missed out on by not having me around. You never know, maybe one day we could be friends again; maybe one day we could be more . . . maybe we could give it another go.'

'Us? Together?'

The idea both appalled and intrigued her. Her and Nick together again? But before she could even contemplate such a bizarre idea, he was talking again.

'You're an amazing mum, Maz. You've put Alex first his

entire life. Don't stop doing that now. Think of him, think of what would make him happy. What kind of life is this for him, with you working all the hours God sends? Sell this place, get his money; you'd live like kings over there on what the Cornucopia would sell for, and you could devote all of your time and energy to him instead of running this crappy heap of responsibilities. You could be an even better mum than you already are, and me, well, you'd be giving me the chance to be a dad. Let me be a dad to my son, Marilyn. Please. Don't answer me, just promise me you'll think about it.'

26

'**O**ne bottle of celebrating red wine,' Kashia announced, returning to their table from the busy bar of the Three Horseshoes public house and restaurant. 'To toast whole week of sharing house and no argument.'

'Cheers, roomie. Who would have thought it, eh? You and me sharing.'

'Is good, yes?' Kashia asked anxiously.

'Very good.' Lorraine nodded.

'I to say very big thank you and big apologise also for being ignorant pig for past three years.'

Lorraine shrugged to show she knew her own shortcomings.

'I'm not exactly the easiest person to get along with.'

'I no give you chance.'

'It's all in the past.' Lorraine smiled at Kashia, and the older woman beamed back.

'What time your Adrian coming here to join us for the dinner?'

'He'll be here in about three quarters of an hour. He should have been here sooner but he had a late call out to an injured dog or something.'

'Is not Godrich?' Kashia sighed, crossing her eyes.

'No, I think he would have mentioned if it was Godrich again. He said to go ahead and order, though; it can get so busy here it will take that long for the food to come through.'

'Is nice to have person waiting on me for change,' Kashia said, handing Lorraine a menu.

'And the food sounds good too. I think I might have the lamb shank, what do you think, Kash?' Lorraine lowered her menu to look at her friend only to see that Kashia wasn't looking at her own menu, but staring over the top of it at a man seated in a booth on the other side of the busy restaurant.

'Who is that man?' Kashia asked, frowning.

'Who is who?'

'That man over there. I am knowing him, I think?'

Lorraine followed Kashia's frowning gaze, her own brow knitting as she dragged her memory cells for some points of recognition.

'Oh, it's him.' She pouted crossly. 'That horrible Sutton man, the one who's turning your building into posh flats, and who wanted to buy the hotel . . .'

Before she had finished, Kashia was standing up and pushing up her sleeves as if preparing to fight.

'What are you doing?' Lorraine hissed, eyes darting about the room in embarrassment. Honestly, Kashia was almost steaming at the ears with indignation and people were starting to look over.

'I know second chef who work in kitchen here. I think I go spit in horrible man's food.'

'Oh Lord, you don't do that at the Cornucopia, do you?'

Lorraine put a hand on Kashia's shoulder and pulled her back on to the velvet padded bench seat they were sharing.

Kashia's eyebrows flared in indignation.

'I tell you before, I never base myself to do that, but now I happy to make exceptional!' Kashia folded her arms across her ample chest and shot eyeball daggers at Sean Sutton's broad back.

'Horrible man,' she grumbled again, but Lorraine wasn't listening. She had just spotted another familiar face crossing the room, and unless she was very much mistaken, Sean Sutton was standing up to greet him.

'Oh my word.' Lorraine clapped a hand over her mouth. Kashia followed her gaze and stopped cursing in Polish, and the two girls instinctively slid lower into their seats. 'What on earth are those two doing together?'

'Very bad things, I'm sure.'

'You know, I think you're probably right. Should we call Marilyn?'

'And tell her what? That her ex-husband is having the dinner with man who could be just old friend from when he stay here as small child?'

'You think that's all that's going on?'

'I think Sean Sutton is nasty weasel man who want hotel, that is what I think. He no have friends to eat with, he have partner criminals to plot with. But I think you tell Marilyn old husband is here and he find some excuse to blow her up with.'

'Blow her off, Kash, blow her off.'

'Whatever. He weasel too, he talk his way out of it.'

'True. Which means it's up to us to find out what's going on.'

'I is agreeing.'

'I need to hear what they're saying. Would your friend in the kitchen help us, do you think? If I can go wait on their table, I can listen in to their conversation.'

'But what if they remember who you is?'

'Nobody ever remembers me.' Lorraine shrugged. 'I have one of those faces that people forget five minutes after we've been introduced.'

'That is not true.'

'Well, you called me Elaine or Loretta or Louise for the first six months that we worked together.'

'My English not so good then.'

'Liar.'

The two women smiled at each other.

'We take long time to get to know each other properly, that is all,' Kashia said, putting an unexpected hand over Lorraine's.

Lorraine took the hand.

'Things have been different since they came, haven't they?'

'Is much better.' Kashia nodded, knowing immediately that Lorraine was talking about Marilyn, Alex and Liesel.

'They don't forget who I am.'

'Adrian does not so either, I think.'

Lorraine paused and smiled softly.

'No, he doesn't, does he. And that's all thanks to Liesel too. I'd never have dared if she hadn't . . .' Lorraine's smile set into a determined line. 'Come on, Kash, introduce me to your guy in the kitchen.'

'Why, you go spit?'

'No, I go spy.'

Kashia shook her head. 'No. I is having much better idea.' And she waved for the maître d'.

Minutes later, they were in the next-door booth, Kashia's right ear and Lorraine's left pushed tight up against the flimsy partition wall.

A waiter was there getting their order. The first few minutes were spent listening to Sean Sutton order medium rare fillet steak and Nick prevaricate between steak and duck, before plumping for the same as his friend.

Then there was some chat about a mutual friend who was getting a divorce, and some leg-pulling about Nick's tan fading, by which point Lorraine's ear had begun to ache. She had just pulled away to rub some life back into it when Kashia's eyes shot wide and she pulled Lorraine back against the wood again in time to hear Nick say, 'It'll be great to get some proper food. I've spent every bloody night this week eating junk.'

Kashia and Lorraine exchanged a frown.

'Worth it, though.'

'Oh, absolutely worth it. What's a little high cholesterol compared to the chance to get to talk to Alex one on one?'

The frown eased a little.

'How are you getting on with the boy?'

'Well, he was difficult at first, but I expected that. I'll bring him round.'

'He's a good-looking kid.'

'Yeah.'

'Must get his looks from his mother. If he took after you, he'd be an ugly son of a bitch . . .'

They both laughed.

'Yeah, he lucked out on that one,' Nick said graciously. 'He's really clever too,' he added, and the girls' frowns turned to smiles.

'Yeah? Maybe I'll give you a little genetic credit on that one. So apart from the junk food, your little family reunion's going great guns, then?'

'Oh yeah, it's been great spending time with them both. I'm having a blast.'

Kashia saw the relief at this last on her friend's face and began to nod her approval, but then Sean Sutton started to laugh.

'You know, you said that so convincingly, I almost believed you myself!'

'Well, I've had to practise my sincere face rather a lot this week, haven't I, to convince the stupid cow that I'm for real, but it's working. I think she's really starting to trust me again.'

'You think so?'

'Oh yeah. Leave it with me, Sean. I'll have her ready to sell that place to you in no time . . .'

'And I'll have your share of the profits ready to wire to Perth. You must have been gutted when you found out your aunt had left the lot to the kid.'

'I should have guessed the mad old boot would do something like this.'

'Still, we're redressing the balance, eh?'

'It's a dirty job . . .'

'. . . but somebody's got to do it.'

The two men clashed glasses.

Lorraine's soft face crumpled like a used tissue, whilst Kashia's did the opposite, going as hard and set as quick-dry concrete.

'So tell me, how is the delicious Samantha?'

'Still mad as hell at me for not bringing her over here with me, but I'll talk her round when I get back to Australia. I'll pick her up something nice from duty free. You know what women are like: a bit of jewellery and some perfume and I'll be back in her good books in no time. And don't forget you're sending me back first class, Sutton, you tight-arse. It's a long old trip in economy; you're lucky I agreed to come all this bloody way considering.'

'If I get my hands on the Cornucopia, it'll be first class all the way, my old friend. That's almost a four-acre site; do you know how many units I can get on there once I've torn the old monstrosity down? And we're talking over a half a mill each for a two-bed with sea views . . .'

Lorraine and Kashia had heard enough.

All further conversation was halted as Kashia's furious face appeared above the barrier of plants and fretwork that separated the two tables.

'*Moja dupa i twoja twarz to bliźniarcy!*' she spat

ferociously before up-ending her red wine over Sean Sutton's head.

'That goes the same for me, double!' Lorraine appeared next to her, then disappeared, then reappeared with the first weapon that had come to hand, which just happened to be a ceramic pepper pot. She looked at it for a moment, as if uncertain what to do, and then launched it squarely between Nick's eyes. She could hear the thud as it hit home, but it was the look of sheer surprise that was the pleasure.

'Maybe you should have had DUCK after all!' she yelled before disappearing again.

Whilst shock rendered the two men temporarily immobile, Lorraine and Kashia grabbed their bags and scarpered hand in hand.

'Maybe you should have had duck after all!' Kashia repeated in awe. 'Lol, I is so proud of you! His face when you throw pot. Priceless. I hope he bruise big time!'

'I hope I knocked some sense into that stupid bloody head of his. How could he! What an arsehole!' It was the first time in her entire life that Lorraine had ever sworn.

'By the way, what did you say to him?' she gasped as they pelted out to the car park.

'I tell him that my arse and his face are twins!' Kashia announced with satisfaction.

'Oh, you shouldn't have said that.'

'I should not?' Kashia exclaimed in disbelief.

'Absolutely not.' Lorraine grinned wickedly. 'Your arse is far nicer than his bloody stupid face!'

As they sprinted out of the restaurant car park and down the road, too high on adrenalin and too scared of being followed to stop in the foyer and call a cab, they were relieved to see Adrian's Volvo coming down the road towards them.

Lorraine flagged him down, and they sped straight to the Cornucopia, filling him in on the details as they went. Falling out of the car as frantically as they had fallen in, they staggered breathlessly and thankfully into the cavernous hall of the Cornucopia like refugees claiming sanctuary, and collapsed against the empty reception, where Kashia began to furiously ring the little brass bell.

Seconds later, Marilyn and Liesel came running, faces aghast at the commotion, the worry turning to puzzlement when they discovered the source.

'What on earth's going on!' Marilyn cried. 'Are you okay, what's happened?'

Kashia was the first to get her breath back.

'Please, Marilyn, you have brandy?'

'Of course!' She rushed to get a glass of cognac, but when she offered it to Kashia, Kashia pushed it back to her.

'No, is not for me, is for you. I am thinking you might have need of it.'

Marilyn listened to the whole story without saying a single word, and then to Liesel's surprise she simply nodded quite calmly, hugged them each in turn, including a surprised Adrian, gave the brandy to a shocked Liesel, and then sent the others into the bar to get one for themselves.

Liesel, who hated brandy, put the glass down on reception and turned to her sister in open-mouthed wonderment.

'Did you hear what they just told us? Has it actually sunk in?'

Marilyn nodded.

'Of course.'

'Then how can you be so calm? How come you're not screaming and shouting and calling him every name under the sun? You don't even look surprised.'

'Maybe that's because I'm not. Honestly, Liesel, Alex inherits a fortune, suddenly his father decides he's worth a visit . . .'

'But I thought . . .'

'That I was being suckered into Nick-world again?' She sighed heavily. 'Well, maybe I was for a second. I wanted to believe that he meant it all, for Alex's sake, but in truth . . . oh Lord, Leez!' Marilyn looked down at the floor, and for a moment Liesel thought she was crying, but when she looked up again, her sister realised that she was actually laughing.

'Marilyn?' Now Liesel was worried. The laughter was pretty manic: Marilyn must be in shock. And then she began to laugh even harder at the sight of Liesel's puzzled face.

'Oh Lord, Leez,' she repeated. 'For my own sake . . .' She paused again, and then, raising her hands high as if praising God, she literally sang three little words: 'Oh, the relief!'

'The relief? Kashia and Lorraine have just told you that he's plotting behind our backs to steal from his own son, and you're relieved?'

Marilyn nodded happily.

'You mean you're actually happy Nick's still a lying, cheating bastard?'

Marilyn nodded again, so hard she almost gave herself a headache.

'Yes. I am. You don't know what a dilemma I've been through, Liesel. Giving Nick the benefit of the doubt. Trusting that he was being honest in saying he wanted to be with his son, to make amends. That he wanted us with him. You know, he asked me if we'd think about going back to Australia with him earlier. And I've actually spent the last few hours doing just that! Should I give the boy a chance to be with his father? He's missed out for the last three years; it would be so unfair of me not to give him the chance to have a dad. They're blood, after all, aren't they, and as the saying goes, blood is thicker than water. As far as we're concerned, family is what it's all about, but the actual truth of the matter is that blood is just genetics. Family doesn't have to be by birth or marriage; family is about being there for each other the way we are, through the good and the bad, the way you were there when Eric needed you, Kashia and Lorraine tonight, Ed . . . well, Ed's been more of a father to Alex in the past few months than his own ever has. In fact, Alex doesn't even *like* Nick. But Alex *loves* Ed, really loves him . . .'

She paused, and frowned for a moment, and then a smile as bright as the sunshine flooded her face

'I love Ed too.'

'I know. We all do. He's great.'

'No, I mean, I LOVE ED, Liesel. I love Ed.' This second time she was saying it to herself, just to see if it had sunk in properly.

'You do?' Liesel asked, unable to disguise the hope in her voice.

Marilyn nodded frantically.

'Jeez, Leez, how could I have been so stupid . . . in so many different ways!'

'You're not stupid, Maz, you just want to see the good in people, that's all.'

'Yeah, and I've been looking so hard for it in someone who hasn't got any that I've kind of missed it in the ones who have. How could it have taken this to show me what's been slapping me round the face with a cold fish. I told you that I was over Nick, but I was lying to myself. Everything I've done since he left has had this big Nick-shaped shadow hanging over it . . . everything, but not any more! Not any more,' she repeated in wonderment, and then she looked up at her sister, her face earnest. 'Liesel, you asked me for some advice and I couldn't give it to you before, because, let's face it, I didn't have a clue myself. But I know now that what I had with Nick wasn't love, it was a broken fragment of it, and we all know that broken things are sharp and dangerous. Real love, Liesel, *real* love is whole and wholesome, it's open and honest and happy; it doesn't make you want to sit in corners and weep, it gives you strength, it doesn't sap it from you.'

'Two hours ago you were contemplating emigrating,' Liesel said, her voice choking.

Marilyn reached out and took her sister's hands.

'I'd never have gone anywhere without you, you know that, don't you?'

'Sure, but it's not just the three of us any more, is it? One more on board and Team Alex could field its own football squad.'

For a moment the two of them contemplated the truth of this.

'They always say it takes a tragedy to make you count your blessings.'

'This isn't a tragedy, Liesel.'

'It will be for Nick if I get my hands on him. Do you think he'll dare to show his face?'

'Oh yes, definitely. He'll be here soon with some excuse or other. The problem with Nick is he likes to think he's far cleverer than he actually is. He's always thought he's got the gift of the gab; he'll have thought of something to try and explain it away, I'm sure.'

'Well, I don't know what. He was pretty much caught bang to rights, or caught "red-bottomed", as Kashia so charmingly put it.'

'True.'

'And what about Alex? What are you going to tell him?'

Marilyn sighed, and Liesel saw the only real sadness

still in her, the weight of telling her son something so sordid. So hurtful.

'We do what we always do.' She shrugged. 'We tell him the truth, and then we help him deal with it.'

None of them went to bed until the small hours of the morning. It wasn't just Alex who needed an explanation; there was Ed and Eric too, and when Marilyn said to Alex that she had something a bit awful to tell him, he immediately asked for them, so Marilyn decided to call everyone together.

Ed simply wrapped his arms around them both and stood silent and strong until Marilyn stopped shaking and Alex's wrestle grip on his leg had loosened a touch, and then he helped Marilyn carry Alex upstairs and tuck him into bed.

At Marilyn's door he stopped and gently touched her face.

'You know where I am; just let me know if you need me,' he said, but Marilyn caught his hand as he turned away.

'I need you,' she whispered. 'Stay with me.'

'I'd like nothing more, Maz. But you're tired, and you're upset, and you're not thinking straight, so for me to stay the night . . . As much as I want to, it's probably not a good idea.'

But she reached out and took his other hand as well, and smiled softly at him.

'I don't just mean for tonight, Ed.'

She could see the hope flicker in his eyes.

'Do you know what you're saying?'

'I don't think I've ever been thinking quite so clearly in my entire life as I am right now. Stay with me, Ed. For always, stay with me.'

*

Nick arrived so early the following morning, the only people up were Marilyn and Liesel, both of whom for very different reasons had hardly had any sleep at all. It didn't look as if he had either. He slid into reception unshaven, eyes shadowed, bruise on his forehead, sob story written all over him.

As she looked at him, so obviously mentally preparing his piece, Marilyn thought of everything she had ever wanted to say to him, and hadn't had a chance to. Suddenly she found she didn't want to say a word of it, because to do so would imply that she still cared. And it was really only now that she knew absolutely that she didn't.

This man standing in front of her might have looked familiar, but he was a stranger, a total stranger. She didn't know him; she didn't want to know him.

He was looking at her now with puppy-dog eyes.

'Marilyn . . .'

'Uh-uh.' She shook her head.

'Please . . . give me a chance to explain.'

'No.' Marilyn reached out and gently but firmly put her finger over his mouth. 'Don't say a word, Nick. Not one word. You've done enough talking this week to last a lifetime. Now it's my turn. I want you to leave. I want you to go away and never come back. You had your second chance. You blew it. Simple as that. When Alex is old enough, well, then if you're lucky he might come looking for you, and you can save the explanation for him, because you'll bloody well need the best excuse you can give him.'

And then without even a goodbye, she turned and walked away through the door marked Private, and closed it very firmly behind her.

Upstairs, Marilyn looked at Alex.

He was sitting on the window seat in his pyjamas, his

back to her. Godrich was next to him, great hairy body pressed tight up against him, chin resting on the boy's shoulder.

Marilyn tried to scrutinise what she could see of that adorable little face, trying to make out if he'd been crying. If he had, she was going to go after Nick and smash his head in with Liesel's wrench.

'You okay, kiddo?'

Alex didn't look round; instead he leant his head against Godrich and asked, 'I saw Nick come in. Has he gone now?'

'Yeah.' Marilyn sighed. 'He's gone. How do you feel about that? Do you feel really sad?'

To her surprise, he turned to face her and shrugged.

'Not really.'

'Do you mean that?'

'Well, I think we're probably better off without him.'

He must have heard her or Liesel say that and was repeating it.

'But he's your dad, Alex . . .'

'He may be my dad, Mum, but it's like Auntie Leez says: it's a sad fact of life that not everyone is a nice person, and he wasn't a very nice person, was he?'

'Does it make you sad that your dad is one of the people in life who isn't very nice?'

Alex thought for a moment.

'I s'pose it should. And if he was all I had, then I s'pose it would.'

'What do you mean?'

'Well, I thought I missed him . . . I mean, I did miss him, but, well, what I'm saying is that I don't think I will any more 'cause now I know that what I was missing wasn't him, Nick, I mean; what I was missing was having a dad and doing stuff like you do with a dad, and I think if it's okay with you and with him, not Nick, Ed, if it's okay with Ed, I'd rather do dad stuff with him, 'cause Ed does dad stuff with me 'cause he wants to, not 'cause he wants something, and that's what dads do, isn't it, they do stuff with you 'cause they want to, 'cause they like being with you, so I'm not missing anything really if Nick goes . . . Do you understand, Mum . . . Mum?'

But Marilyn couldn't answer, because this time *she* was crying.

Alex frowned in concern.

'Don't cry, Mum. Don't you see, we don't need to be sad any more 'cause we've got our family, haven't we? We've got us and we've got Ed, and Eric and Lol and Kash. You don't need to be related to be family, do you? I mean, we're not actually related to Godrich and Mitten and Ruby 'cause that just couldn't happen, could it, but they're still our family . . . Don't cry, Mum!'

'Don't worry, darling.' Marilyn sniffed, clutching on to him. 'I'm crying 'cause I'm happy.'

'What is it with girls!' Alex said, rolling his eyeballs, but he hugged her back and pulled faces at her until she began to smile again.

Nick looked over at Liesel, who had protectively followed Marilyn from behind reception. His face was outwardly calm, but the way his left nostril kept flaring gave away exactly how much control he was having to exercise to appear so.

'I suppose you want to get yours in as well,' he said, his voice low and restrained. 'Go on, then. Hit me with it. Or actually hit me, you know, whichever you prefer. I'm sure everyone here will agree I deserve it. Big fat bastard Nick . . .'

'Actually, I just wanted to say thank you.'

He blinked at her in disbelief.

'You what? Yeah, nice one, Liesel. The high-handed

approach. You're a bigger, better person than me and all that crap . . .'

He stopped as Liesel held up her hand and said, 'No, Nick, I mean it. You coming back here was for all the wrong reasons, and you've been an absolute shit, but you *must* realise that yourself. You don't need me to tell you what an arsehole you've been; that's something you've got to live with for the rest of your naturals. But whatever your reasons, and however you've behaved whilst you've been here, I'll always be grateful that you *did* come back.

'You see, they needed to see you again, if only to say goodbye, because the last time you went, you just . . . well . . . *went*, no goodbyes, nothing . . . and what you did this time, well, it makes this goodbye far easier than the last one. The last goodbye left a big hole in that kid's life, in Marilyn's too if we're being honest, but this one . . . well, it's closed the gaps, because let's face it, not having you in their life . . . well, you've made them realise that it's no big loss, that they're both so much better off without you. So thanks, Nick. From the very bottom of my heart and truly meant. Truly,' she repeated, nodding her sincerity. 'Thank you.'

She reached out and took his very limp hand and shook it.

'God speed and safe journey back to Oz . . . shithead.'

L iesel had turned to walk away and so she didn't see him come up behind her. She only turned back when Ruby started barking, and by then it was too late, he was right up next to her, but as his arm swung back, Liesel did what he should have done the night before when faced with a vengeful Lorraine: she ducked.

The crunch of breaking bones and the resulting scream of agony were therefore his as his hand hit the wall, and Liesel would have remained unscathed if her instinct hadn't then been to try and catch him as the momentum of the swing and the pain of his hand sent him falling to the floor.

His good hand reaching out blindly, he seized upon Liesel's outstretched arm, pulling her down with him, twisting as they went, so that she ended up pinned beneath him, his face, inches from hers, itself a twist of pain and loathing.

'Oh my God, my hand, my bloody hand, you bloody little . . .' But the rest of the words were yanked from his throat as a pair of hands grabbed him by the scruff of the neck and pulled him off her.

For a moment Liesel thought that Ed had come to her rescue, but the angry voice that followed wasn't his. Nor were the conker-coloured hair and the perfect face that at this moment was livid with anger.

'What the hell do you think you're playing at!'

Strong hands pinned Nick against the wall as Liesel scrambled upright into a sitting position.

'Tom?'

His eyes turned to her, black with concern, with barely controlled fury.

'Are you okay?'

She nodded.

'Is this Nick?'

She nodded again, puzzled at how he could know, what he was doing here.

'For God's sake get off me!' Nick spat, wriggling like a fish on a hook, then wincing as his hand started to hurt again.

Mercy came from an unexpected source.

'Let him go, Tom.'

'Liesel?'

Liesel nodded. 'Please, let him go. The only person he's hurt is himself.'

'Are you sure?'

'Yes, please, I just want him to leave.'

'If that's what you want.' Still holding on to the scruff of Nick's neck, Tom frogmarched him across the hall and out of the door to his car, where he opened the door, and shoved him none too gently into the driver's seat.

'I take it you don't need me to tell you not to come back.'

For a moment Nick looked like he was about to protest, but then Tom leaned in closer so that only he could hear.

'You're still in one piece because of Liesel, but trust me, if our paths ever cross again . . .'

'Then you'll what?' Nick spat back at him contemptuously. 'You'll offer to try and take me out?'

'Not exactly, but shall I tell you how many castrations I've carried out since I became a vet? It's a simple operation, you know, I could almost do it in my sleep . . . or yours . . .'

Nick closed his mouth as abruptly as he had opened it, slammed the door of his car so violently Tom had to jump out of the way, and floored off up the drive, engine and tyres screaming his protests for him.

Somewhat in shock, although not sure whether it was from Nick's unexpected attack or the appearance of Tom, Liesel was still sitting on the floor, gathering herself, as Marilyn called it, although she didn't feel particularly gathered. In fact, she felt rather unravelled.

Taking advantage of the fact that Liesel was down at her level, Ruby came and sat on her lap, which was good as it gave her another excuse not to get up. Tom squatted down next to her.

'Are you okay?'

'You could say I'm a bit floored.' Liesel attempted a smile, but it came out kind of wobbly. 'Not that I'm not grateful or anything, but what are you doing here, Tom?'

'Adrian called me an hour ago, and told me what happened yesterday. I had to come and see you, and it looks like it was a good job that I did. The man's an idiot. Promise me he didn't hit you, Liesel.'

'I think he tried, but he wouldn't have touched me if I hadn't got in the way of him falling,' Liesel said ruefully.

'And you're okay?' he repeated.

'Does Caroline know you're here?' she asked, ignoring his question.

He nodded.

'You told her you were coming?'

'She was listening in on the extension when Adrian rang . . . Liesel, can you get up?'

'I can, but I'm not sure I want to . . . And she didn't try and stop you?'

Tom sighed. 'I don't know about that. She told me that

if I left to come and see you, we were over.' He offered her a hand, which she also ignored.

'But you still came?'

'I had to come. I had to know that you were okay.'

'Do you think she meant it?' she pressed, anxious for clarity.

'It doesn't matter if she did or not.' He sighed again, then, giving up, sat down on his heels next to her. 'I told her that we were over anyway.'

'You finished things?' Her voice was a whisper, not quite sure that she could believe what she was hearing.

He nodded slowly. 'It's over.'

'You and Caroline? Done? She's gone?'

'Done. Finished. And I'm pretty certain that she won't be there by the time I get back. You see, I told her how I felt about you, Liesel, everything. I told her that the last thing I wanted to do was hurt her, but that if I stayed with her I'd end up hurting her more because all I really wanted was to be with you. And like you said, how can you truly make someone happy when you don't really want to be with them?'

'You told her all of that?' Liesel repeated, struggling to get it to sink in.

Tom looked away, looked at the floor.

'I had to. Adrian told me what shit you'd been going through with Marilyn's ex, and I suddenly realised that I'd been bleating on to you about being honest, and that all the time I was trying to work things out with Caroline, I was lying to her and most of all lying to myself.'

And then his eyes flicked back up to her, steady, composed.

'All I've been able to think about is you, Liesel. I've missed you, I've missed our time together, the way you make me laugh, the way when you smile it makes the whole room fill with sunshine . . . I've even missed Ruby.'

He reached out and stroked the little dog's head, and was rewarded with a curling kiss to his wrist. 'I told her that, and I asked her to leave, to go home, back to London . . .'

'And what did she say?'

To Liesel's surprise, he laughed, a dry laugh.

'She said okay, I'll pack my bags . . .' He paused and closed his eyes, and the smile that creased his face was one of disbelief, of brittle humour. 'And then she told me she'd been sleeping with her boss.'

'You're kidding me?' This one brought Liesel to her feet.

He rose to meet her, shaking his head, catching her hand as she stumbled slightly.

'Are you okay?' he asked again, concerned, but still she didn't reply, anxious only for the details he was giving her that were somehow slowly making his words form a reality.

'How long?' she asked.

'For the past two months or so, she says. It was only when I first told her that I'd met you that she apparently came to her senses, finished it and came home to try and work things out with me . . .'

'So she'd cheated on you before you and me ever . . . and she didn't say until today, not even after she caught us?'

'Yeah. Ironic, isn't it?'

'Oh my God, are you okay?'

'Am *I* okay?'

He started to laugh again, this time in disbelief, and then, reaching out, he pulled her to him, wrapped his arms tight around her, breathing in the scent of her hair, pressing his forehead against hers just so he could feel her flesh.

'After everything that's happened in the past few days, and you ask if *I'm* okay? Oh, how I love you, Liesel Ellis.'

When he realised what he'd said, he pulled away a little and looked at her face, into her eyes, anxious for her to know that he meant it.

'I love you, Liesel,' he repeated, and then again more softly, 'I love you.'

And Liesel, finding her smile again, looked deep into his eyes, and decided that they were green, a deep green like the leaves on the cedar tree in the garden.

'Then I'm okay . . .' she replied, reaching up to do what she had longed to do for weeks, to kiss him, deep and slow, like they had all the time and the right in the world to do so.

'Although . . .' she continued when they finally drew apart for breath, their fingers automatically interlacing to lock them together still in some way, 'I'm not so sure Nick will be.'

'Nick?'

'Yeah.' Liesel nodded, her smile turning wicked. 'Marilyn's definitely going to push him off a cliff now.'

His eyes narrowed.

'For trying to hit you, I'm not surprised. I should have pushed him off myself.'

But Liesel shook her head to show that wasn't what she had meant.

'No.' She pointed behind them to the wall where Nick's hand had connected with so much force a large hole had formed, a chunk of greying plaster on the floor below it. 'Because he's totally *ruined* her William Morris.'

Epilogue

'What do you call a hotel with no guests?' Liesel asked her sister.

'Is this a joke?' Marilyn frowned.

'Do you see me laughing?'

'I don't understand it. We've worked so hard to get the place full, I've been turning away bookings . . .'

'And the ones we've taken have been cancelling.'

Marilyn's frown deepened, and then her eyes slid sideways as though something had just occurred to her. 'Can you print me out a list of the names and phone numbers of the people who have cancelled on us in the last couple of weeks?'

Half an hour later she was back, looking like thunder.

'None of these numbers are real,' she said, throwing the sheaf of paper down on the desk.

'What do you mean?'

'Exactly what I said. Something wasn't right, Leez, so I rang round. Every booking we've taken that's cancelled, you can't get through on the contact number, so I called all of our other bookings and about seventy per cent of them are the same, right up to the beginning of September.'

'They're all fake?' Liesel's eyes popped wide in disbelief.

Marilyn nodded. 'And it doesn't take Brain of Britain to work out who was behind it all. You know, I wish Nick hadn't gone.'

'You do?' Liesel asked, perturbed.

'Yeah, so I could bloody kill him! Him and that Sean Sutton. Fill us up with people who don't exist, so we can't take proper bookings. Clever way to put us out of business. I bet he thought that by the end of the season we'd be begging him to buy us out! Talk about hedging their bets. If Nick couldn't charm us out, then Sutton was going to screw us out . . .'

'I'm so sorry.'

'Why? It's not your fault.'

'I'm sure I didn't help. What I did to the guy wasn't exactly nice, was it?'

'Leez, trust me, this isn't your fault. He had an agenda before he even met us.'

'So what do we do now?'

Marilyn shrugged helplessly.

'I was thinking you could ask Tom to move in properly, seeing as he's practically been living here full time since last week anyway. I'll rent another pair of rooms to Kashia and Lorraine; they pay a fortune for Lorraine's place in town . . .'

'You can send Ed out as a kiss-a-gram, Eric as a grandad-gram, we'll both get other jobs on the side that fit in with this place – you can stack shelves overnight in the local supermarket, and I'll get a milk round – and we can set the dogs and Alex to work delivering papers,' Liesel cut in with an inappropriate burst of humour.

Although she truly didn't feel like it, Marilyn laughed.

'We might just manage to keep the hotel going if we all chip in like that, yes . . . Joking aside, Leez, we're in trouble. Nancy's insurance is nearly gone. If we want to keep this place . . . hell, if we want to get through to the end of the season, even . . .'

'And we need to get through to the end of the season.' Liesel nodded, serious again.

'We'll need a bloody miracle,' Marilyn finished with a heavy sigh.

'What's the matter, Mum?' Alex, coming from the kitchen bearing cakes for them to try, had overheard his mother's last sentence and was looking worried.

Marilyn's eyes darted to Liesel. She didn't know what it was, but Liesel had a knack of explaining things in a way that Alex would understand without him getting too involved.

'Someone mean has phoned up and booked lots of rooms that they're not going to use, so that we can't let them to other people.'

'Why would they do that?'

Marilyn looked once again at Liesel. She didn't want to have to explain that after everything his father and Sean Sutton had already done, there was now more trouble to bear.

'Well, I'm afraid it's a sad fact of life that not everyone is a nice person,' Liesel said gently.

'That's true.' Alex nodded, and then he asked something completely unexpected. 'Do you think Great-Aunt Nancy was a good person?'

'We didn't really know her well enough to say for sure,' frowned Marilyn, 'but we know she did some good things, like leaving you the Cornucopia, that was good.'

'And Godrich.' Alex nodded solemnly. 'She left me Godrich too.'

'Why do you ask, Lex?' Liesel asked curiously.

'Well, school says that good people go to heaven, and school says that heaven's where miracles come from, so we don't have to worry, 'cause if we need one, and Great-Aunt Nancy's there, then she can send us one . . .'

'That's a nice thought, kiddo.' Marilyn hugged her son and smiled sadly at Liesel over the top of his golden head. 'But I'm not sure that ordinary people get to give out miracles. I think that might just be down to the people in charge up there.'

'What, like angels?'

'Maybe.' Marilyn nodded, sending a 'help me' face to Liesel.

But Alex was satisfied.

'That's okay, then, 'cause I looked up benefactor on the net 'cause you said that Great-Aunt Nancy was mine, and it said a benefactor was like a guardian angel, so now we know that, we don't have to worry . . . she'll make sure that everything's okay.'

Oh, the certainty and innocence of youth. If only it were that easy to solve their problems.

'Not interrupting anything, are we?'

The little group looked up to see Jimmy and David coming in from outside.

'Why aren't you at school, young man?'

'Mum said I could have some time off 'cause my real dad's a shithead,' Alex replied, nodding gravely.

'What an excellent excuse to give your teacher.' Jimmy grinned. 'Wish I'd thought of that one when I was a kid.'

'And where's Superman today?' David frowned, noticing the shorts and T-shirt Alex was dressed in.

'He flew away.' Liesel smiled, regaining her bounce and heading over to welcome them both with a kiss. 'At roughly the same time as Nick. Do you think they caught the same flight, by any chance? What are you doing here, guys?'

'Well, we wondered if we could have a word with you both.'

It sounded remarkably formal for them, so Marilyn nodded and, sending Alex into the kitchen to see Eric, led them through into their private sitting room.

'Would you like a cup of tea?'

'Or something stronger?' Liesel added, knowing their preferences.

'Not right now, ta, darling.' David smiled. 'We need a chat.'

'We need to ask a favour, actually.' Jimmy nodded.

'Of course. Anything you need.'

'Well, I'll try and get straight to the point.'

'If he does, that will be a first,' David mocked him gently.

'Like I said, straight to the point.' Jimmy continued as if he hadn't head David. 'For the past two years the winter seasons have been a real struggle on pre-booked and pick-ups only; we're not turning over enough to survive.'

Marilyn, having spent most of last night poring over the books in despair, nodded sympathetically.

'And so our Dave here has decided to fall into bed with Tourista Britannia.'

'Tourista Britannia?' Liesel queried.

'UK coach company,' Marilyn said knowledgeably.

'The Piran Bay Hotel is going to be their new "Tourista Britannia Cornish Haven",' he quoted sadly, as though their beautiful hotel had been demoted to the status of holiday camp. 'Complete with nightly bingo, old-time dancing, and canteen food. Now, the naughty man has committed us to not one, not two, but three coaches, which means when they run in full, which they're bound to do in the summer—'

'If we don't accommodate them in summer, they won't use us in winter when we're empty!' David insisted. 'And I know they pay less than our pick-up rate, but if you work it out over the year, we still make more than if we book our own in summer and twiddle our thumbs in winter . . .'

Jimmy silenced him with a look.

'Now, if the coaches run in full, and they will run in full because the sun is set to shine for a long time this summer, according to the lovely Sian Lloyd, then we will be over-subscribed every week to the tune of at least five rooms.'

'Which means we simply ship out a few people to another hotel,' David insisted.

Jimmy rolled his eyes and shook his head; it was obviously a point David had tried to press home previously.

'And so . . .' he said loudly, 'we came up with a remarkably cunning plan . . .' He paused for dramatic effect. 'We thought to ourselves, now if we were being sent away from our beautiful Piran Bay, where would we want to go, and of course only one place came to mind: the lovely Cornucopia and its even lovelier management! What do you think? We'd give you some of the lovely old ducks who didn't pay the supplement for a sea view, they get river view instead, à la carte in the restaurant, and your fabulous personal service, and they'll think they've had a free upgrade! We'll pay you what they're giving us, of course. If we were sending them somewhere else, then we might try and stiff them by ten per cent, but we wouldn't do that to you, my darlings . . . so what do you think?'

'At least five rooms a week, every week?'

'For the rest of the year, including winter.' David nodded, looking pointedly at Jimmy.

'Five rooms a week and we're over half full . . . every week,' Marilyn said hopefully.

'For the rest of the year,' added David again, obviously still keen to drive home his point about winter numbers.

'What do you say?' Jimmy beamed at them both.

Liesel didn't say anything; she simply squealed in a rather undignified fashion and then ran at them, arms outstretched, and threw herself upon them in a frenzy of hugs and kisses.

'You didn't get a message from Nancy, did you?'

'We haven't been to any seances recently if that's what you mean,' Jimmy replied, looking puzzled.

'This isn't a charity do, is it?' Marilyn asked cautiously, watching their obvious affection for her sister and suddenly wary that their motives were a touch too altruistic.

'Of course not. You'd be helping us out enormously. But even if it was, which it isn't,' he stressed as he saw Marilyn about to object, 'I couldn't think of a nicer one to donate to.' Jimmy pinched Liesel's already pink cheeks affectionately, and in return she planted a big kiss on his wrinkled forehead.

'So what do you say?' Jimmy repeated.

Liesel looked at her sister pleadingly, silently willing her to say the obvious yes but aware that misplaced pride might make her think twice.

The more sensitive David, aware of this, put a hand on Marilyn's and, adopting just the right amount of desperation, urged her, 'Please say you'll do it. You'll be getting us out of an enormous hole. Purlease . . .' he persisted, giving her puppy-dog eyes as Marilyn hesitated.

'Well, if it's helping you out . . .'

'Oh, it is, it definitely is.'

'Then yes, of course we'll do it, and thank you, thank you so much.'

'Thank you, thank you, thank you,' Liesel echoed, and then she turned to her sister and took her hands, grinning like an idiot.

'You know what this means, don't you?'

Marilyn nodded. 'It means . . .'

She paused and bit her bottom lip, almost bursting at the fact that she could finally say it. Now that the time had come, however, she found she couldn't get it out just yet, and so she nodded furiously whilst the words welled up in her throat and eventually exploded in a bellow so loud that the others heard and came running from their various corners of the hotel.

'We don't have to sell!'

You can buy any of these other
Little Black Dress titles from your
bookshop or *direct from the publisher*.

FREE P&P AND UK DELIVERY
(Overseas and Ireland £3.50 per book)

TO ORDER SIMPLY CALL THIS NUMBER

01235 400 414

or visit our website: www.headline.co.uk

Prices and availability subject to change without notice.